This book may be returned to any Wiltshire library.
To renew this book, phone your library or visit the
website : www.wiltshire.gov.uk

Wiltshire Council
Where everybody matters

KILL ME AGAIN

Rachel Abbott

black dot
publishing

Published in 2016 by Black Dot Publishing Ltd

Copyright © Rachel Abbott 2016

The right of Rachel Abbott to be identified as the author of this work
has been asserted in accordance with the Copyright, Designs
and Patents Act 1988 Sections 77 and 78.

ISBN 978-0-9576522-7-9

British Library Cataloguing in Publication Data
A CIP catalogue record for this book is available from
the British Library

Page design and typesetting by SilverWood Books
Printed in the UK by Latimer Trend & Company Ltd
on responsibly sourced paper

Prologue

It was raining when they came for me. I was staring out of my window watching fat raindrops flow down the glass, streaking across the reflection of my pale face. I was regretting the impetuous decisions I had made – even though at the time they had seemed right – and wondering what was going to happen next in my life.

When the knock came at the door, I didn't even check who it was. I thought I knew. I thought I had been forgiven. I hurried to the door, pulling it wide, smiling to show my visitor how pleased I was to see him.

I knew instantly it wasn't the person I had been expecting. I felt a surge of fear travel through my body as I tried to close the door, but it was too late. A second face appeared around the door – a face that matched the first in every detail. Two sets of identical features, their shiny cheeks almost cherubic as they reflected back the light from my hall.

I looked at the matching Chinese masks, and my legs nearly gave way beneath me. The plastic a smooth yellowish flesh tone, the eye sockets diamond-shaped, empty, revealing the glare of human pupils beneath.

I didn't have time to scream. A gloved hand shot out and grabbed me around the throat, squeezing tighter and tighter until I was sure I would pass out. *Why were they here? What could they want with me?*

They spoke quietly, without the rough accent of local thugs that I was expecting. Somehow that made it worse. They were here for a purpose, and I had no idea what that was. They didn't speak to me; they spoke to each other, as if I wasn't even there. The urgency in their tone was at odds with the smiling faces of the masks, and every inch of my skin rose in prickles of terror.

I could see the first man's teeth between the red lips of the mask. They were pressed together, the pale shape of his mouth wide and straight, as if the effort of choking me one-handed was too much for him. The two sets of lips – a human flesh pair within a solid plastic pair – made my blood freeze, but still I couldn't take my eyes from the mask and the glimpse of the person I could see beneath.

The second man grabbed my arms and fixed them tightly behind me with something hard and cold that bit into my skin. And then came the gag – between my teeth, tearing into the corners of my mouth, the rough material chafing my flesh.

The two men spoke again, but their words blurred in my head and became little more than a buzzing sound.

I watched as the first man went into the hall. He was leaving us, pulling off his mask as he reached the front door. He didn't know I'd seen him, reflected in the hall mirror. I realised that seeing his face, knowing I would recognise him again anywhere, could be the end for me. I looked down quickly, hoping neither man had caught my eyes, watching, recording the chiselled features and the slightly hooked nose, knowing my fear had imprinted every detail into my memory. It was a face I would never forget.

The second man turned to look at me, his mask firmly in place.

'And now we wait,' he said.

1

Wednesday

The foyer of the eight-storey office block was flooded with bright light, which only served to emphasise the impenetrable blackness of the car park beyond. The receptionist had left for the night and Maggie Taylor waited inside the glass doors, peering out into the night. She glanced over her shoulder, watching in vain to see if the red light above the lift would change and begin to count down. Maybe the doors would slide open to reveal another late worker, someone who would be happy to walk with Maggie through the deserted car park – a vast empty stretch of dark tarmac leading into the distance, her lone car sitting waiting for her somewhere out of sight.

The weather warnings had provided the perfect excuse for people to leave early, though, and she was sure nobody would be coming to her rescue. She could kick herself for staying so late, knowing there was nothing that made her more anxious than a large empty building that seemed to echo with silence.

A sound behind her sent tiny spikes of fear up Maggie's arms, and before she could turn she felt a hand low on her back. She spun round and let out a huge breath.

'Jesus, Frank, don't creep up on people like that. You scared the life out of me.'

The slight form of Frank Denman stood half a metre behind her, a guilty smile on his thin face.

'Sorry, Maggie,' he said, looking down at his feet. 'It's these brothel creepers. I bought them for comfort, and of course they do make me look a couple of inches taller, but they barely make a sound on a solid floor.'

She couldn't help but smile back at him. He had saved her skin once today, and it wasn't his fault she was as jumpy as hell. He was a quiet, easy man who never seemed at all fazed by the terrible people he sometimes had to come into contact with.

'Why are you standing here?' he asked. 'Dreading the thought of the cold night air? I would have thought you would have been keen to get back to that man of yours you're always going on about.'

'Oh God, do I really talk about him that much?' she said, pulling a face. 'Sorry. How boring of me.'

Frank was one of the few people Maggie had got to know reasonably well since she had moved to Manchester seven weeks ago. As a defence lawyer, she had needed a psychologist on more than one occasion to help her understand the likely success of a plea of mental incompetence for one or other of her clients, and she and Frank had shared a few sandwich lunches. He was a great listener – no doubt an asset for a psychologist.

'Let's make a move, shall we? Or has our charming client today given you the heebie-jeebies?'

She didn't want to admit even to Frank how their mutual client had unnerved her. It was her job to deal with people like him, for goodness' sake. She just wasn't used to criminals who stooped as low as this one had.

'Come on,' Frank said. 'I'll walk you to your car.'

He leaned forward and pulled the door open, and they stepped out into the silent car park.

'*Out of the night that covers me / Black as the pit from pole to pole...*' he said quietly as they inhaled the frigid air.

Maggie glanced at him as the door swung to behind them. She heard a soft click then a clunk as the locks dropped into place.

'Sorry,' Frank said with an embarrassed smile. 'Just a line from a poem that sprang to mind.'

'A cheery little number, if you don't mind me saying so,' Maggie said, nudging him gently with her elbow. 'Anyway, I'm off now. You don't need to walk me to my car, really you don't. I'm being a bit pathetic. But it's good to know you've got my back.'

Frank gave her a small bow. 'That I have, my dear.'

Maggie laughed. She loved his occasional formality. 'See you soon, no doubt,' she added and with a small wave set off in the general direction of where she thought her car might be.

She turned up the collar of her coat, but once away from the shelter of the building it offered little protection from the sleet-like rain that assaulted the skin of her cheeks with hundreds of tiny, icy arrows. Turning her head to left and to right and with a quick glance over her shoulder to check there was nobody else about, she hurried towards her car, following the same path she had taken a dozen times without a moment's concern. Tonight was different. Tonight she sensed the threat of the shadows, which seemed to circle her, growing ever closer. Even with Frank within shouting distance, she felt uncomfortable.

Her new Audi was parked about as far away as it could be from the bright lights of the office building, and as her eyes sought out its dark shape she remembered how she had smiled when told that the colour of her much-loved car was Phantom Black. Now it seemed more like an omen as it merged seamlessly into the moonless night.

Maggie pressed the remote, and the double yellow flashes of her indicator lights gave brief warmth to the monochrome scene. With relief she grabbed the door handle and pulled on it sharply. She jumped into the car, pressed down the central locking switch and leaned back hard against the headrest, breathing again, only to jolt forward and spin round, nervously scanning the rear seat.

'*Jesus*,' she muttered, turning back and thrusting the key into the ignition. Glancing in her rear-view mirror she could just make out the silhouette of Frank, still standing where she had left him. *Bless him*, she thought.

She knew her fears were irrational. But today she had met the devil himself and he had warned her – warned her of something but she had no idea what. She was an experienced defence lawyer, but the firm she had worked for in Suffolk, where they had lived until recently, dealt with the tamer end of the criminal spectrum and the villains had seemed so normal. She had longed to work on more complex cases, but with the exception of one or two infamous cases for which nobody had as yet been charged, serious crimes there were few and far between. This man today, though – Alf Horton – was the worst she had ever met.

'I'm so pleased to meet you, Maggie,' he had said, holding out his hand to shake hers. She had looked at the dry skin on his face and had known exactly how his hand was going to feel.

As she briefly touched his paper-like flesh in the obligatory handshake, thinking of the dead cells that would have been transferred to her own clammy fingers, Horton continued to speak.

'I've heard all about you, and I'm so looking forward to getting to know you better.'

What could he know about her? She had fought to keep all expression from her face as she went through the process of asking the standard questions to begin to formulate his defence. Ten minutes into the interview, she was relieved to receive a call from the custody sergeant to say that Frank had arrived to begin his psychological assessment. He would be watching and listening from the adjoining room. As Maggie replaced the receiver, Alf leaned across the table towards her, discoloured teeth showing between dried, split lips, and she felt herself backing away as far as she could, so not even his breath could touch her.

'Watch yourself out there, Maggie. Nowhere's safe.'

Some days she wished with all her heart that she was a prosecutor and not a defence solicitor, because this man – this sadistic monster who had hurt so many people – had finally been caught red-handed, and was as guilty as sin. She wanted to see him locked up, preferably for life. That was not the way she was supposed to think, though.

Manoeuvring out of the car park and onto the busy wet streets of central Manchester, she kept seeing the eyes of her client, as flat and dark as twin disused railway tunnels, daring her to explore their chilling depths. She had calmly gone through the details of the numerous violent assaults he was charged with committing, every one against a frail, elderly lady, and she had seen his tongue whip out of his smiling mouth to wet his lips. He was reliving the torture and abuse, and his eyes momentarily glazed over before returning to their flat stare. Maggie had felt an almost unstoppable urge to jump out of her chair, pick it up and smash it over his head.

Perhaps she should have refused to take the case, but she had been so lucky to get this job with a top firm of solicitors. They were offering her the chance to become a partner, so against her better judgement she had smiled and agreed to represent Horton. She had had her share of clients who sickened her with lack of remorse for their crimes, but there was something about this man that made her flesh crawl.

And what had he meant when he said, 'Nowhere's safe'? The memory of his expression as he spoke those words was fixed in her mind, and as she drove through the city centre each passing pair of headlights appeared to project a holographic image of his face floating just beyond her windscreen.

Maggie pulled quickly off the road and into a bus bay, leaning forward to rest her head on the steering wheel.

'Get a bloody grip,' she said to herself. She reached up and pulled her long dark hair free from the doughnut holding it in place at the back of her head. Opening her bag, she threw the grips and bands in, hoping that the switch in appearance from criminal lawyer to wife and mother would restore some rational thought. She twisted the rear-view mirror and groped around in the bottom of her bag to find a lipstick.

Better, she thought as she looked at her full red lips.

There was a bang on her rear window. Maggie spun round, suddenly anxious about whether she had locked the doors. There was a laugh. A group of teenage boys stood on the pavement, preening themselves, pretending to put lipstick on and shake their hair, one making obscene gestures with his right hand. They weren't even worth a look of disgust.

Maggie wrenched the mirror back into place and pulled back out into the road, focusing on nothing more than what Duncan might have cooked for their dinner that night.

2

The roads were terrible. The sleet had quickly turned to snow, and as usual Manchester was ill-prepared. Maggie had seen a couple of cars slide into the kerb already, so knew she had to take it slowly, much as she was anxious to be home. Desperate for some normality in her day she spoke to the car's Bluetooth connector.

'Call home.'

She waited. Nobody picked up. Funny that. The children should have had their tea by now and be getting ready for bed. At least Lily should. Maybe it had snowed a lot more at home, and it would be just like Duncan to wrap them up warmly and go outside for a snowball fight. She decided to leave it five minutes and then try again.

In the nearly two months since they had moved to Manchester the children had settled into their new school, but Maggie was concerned about Duncan. As a couple they had decided long ago that Maggie should be the principal earner and Duncan the main carer for the children. It made sense. Duncan accepted that Maggie could bring in much more than he could earn as a plumber, and so now he only took jobs that he could finish in time to do the school run. Both he and the children had seemed to be thriving under this arrangement, and Maggie had to admit that it was wonderful to come home to a meal cooked for her. She made a point of taking over the cooking at the weekend to give Duncan a rest, and it worked.

Duncan had been surprisingly unenthusiastic about their move to Manchester, though. In her view there had been nothing much keeping them down south – except perhaps the weather, which without a doubt was better than the cold and wet of Manchester – and Duncan had seemed to finally recognise the sense of it. Maggie's huge pay rise had probably helped, but still Duncan had seemed resigned rather than excited about the move, and maybe it was time they had another chat about it. She wanted them to be as happy here as they had always been, and for the last couple of weeks Duncan had definitely been quiet.

It was time to try calling them again. She waited and listened, and was about to end the call again when the phone was answered. *Thank God.*

'Hello. Josh Taylor speaking.' Josh sounded as timid as he always did on the phone. Lily, aged five, had far more confidence than her older brother.

'Hey, Joshy. I thought you'd all be outside having a snowball fight or something.'

'No.' That was her son. Monosyllabic.

'I'm going to be a bit late, I'm afraid. The roads are awful because of the weather. Can you put Daddy on the phone, sweetheart?'

'He's gone out.'

'What's he doing? Clearing the drive?'

'No. He's gone out.'

Maggie took a deep breath. Sometimes her son's lack of words could be frustrating.

'Okay, love. Where is he exactly?'

'I don't know. He started to make the tea, but then he went out. In his van.'

Maggie screwed up her face in puzzlement.

'So who's there with you and Lily?' Josh didn't answer immediately. 'Josh?'

'Nobody. There's just me and Lily.'

A jolt of shock fired through Maggie's body. What did Josh mean?

Her limbs suddenly felt leaden, as if everything she was doing was in slow motion. 'Daddy has gone out in his van? Are you sure, Josh?'

She heard a sigh from the other end of the phone and then, as if a dam had burst, her son started to speak. 'Yes, Mum. I told you. He was making our tea, and then he stopped. Me and Lily are starving. He's been gone ages. He came into the sitting room to say goodbye.'

'And what did he *say*?' There was a loud blare of a car horn and Maggie realised that the traffic lights had changed to green.

'He said he was sorry.'

Maggie's head was spinning. She needed to get home. Her kids were in the house alone – an eight-year-old and a five-year-old in a dark old vicarage at the end of an unmade cul-de-sac. She didn't know the neighbours – didn't know their numbers – hadn't bothered to invite people round yet. She had been so keen to get them all settled.

'Josh, listen to me, sweetheart. Take the phone and go into the kitchen.' She listened to her son's faint footsteps. 'Okay. Now pull a chair over to the door and stand on it. I want you to fasten the bolt at the top of the door. Do you know what I mean, baby?'

Logically, she knew there was nothing to panic about. She would be home in less than half an hour, and Josh was nothing if not sensible. But after today's meeting and Alf Horton's warning, all she could see was the black outline of her house against the night sky and a stranger approaching the door.

Striving to keep the tension from her voice, she spoke to Josh again.

'How are you doing?'

She heard some grunts as he struggled with the door.

'Okay. Done it.'

'Right, Joshy, I need you to go to the front door and do a double turn on the lock there. Do you know what I mean?'

'Course I do. Then you won't be able to get in, Mum.'

'That's right, love, but when I get home you can look through the window and check it's me, and you can undo the lock. Okay?'

She listened while he did as she had asked.

'Now listen to me, Joshy. Whatever you do, don't let anybody and I mean *anybody* – even if somebody says he's a policeman – through that front door. Only me or Daddy when he comes back. Do you understand, darling?'

'It's not hard, Mum. Just you or Dad. Nobody else.'

'I'll be home as soon as I can, but I'm going to phone Auntie Suzy and ask her to talk to you until I get home – then you won't feel so alone. Is Lily okay?'

'Yes.'

Maggie breathed in and let it out slowly, keeping her tone level for her son. 'Can you be a bit more specific, love? What's she doing?'

'Lying about two inches from the TV screen watching that stupid film. Again.'

It would take a bomb going off to dislodge Lily from the TV if she was watching *Frozen*. Trying desperately to stop the panic from spilling over and passing her fear to Josh she told him she was going to be as quick as she possibly could, but to wait for the call from Auntie Suzy.

Hurriedly disconnecting she called her sister.

'Don't ask me any questions, Suze. Please call Josh and keep him on the phone until I get home. Dunc's not there for some reason. The kids are on their own. I know I'm being moronic, but until I'm back can you keep him talking? Please? I'd do it myself, but the signal drops in a few places on the way home.' She knew Suzy would hear the panic she was no longer able to control and would do what she asked without question.

All Maggie wanted to do now was call Duncan. To ask him what the hell was going on. How could he leave his children alone in the house? What was he *thinking*? She didn't know whether to be livid or terrified. Her worry about Duncan had to come second, though. In her mind all she could see was two heads – one a mop of dark curls, the other covered in wispy white-blonde waves. Two young children alone in that house, and she thought of all the things that could happen, that could go wrong.

Her voice trembling, she whispered, 'Call Duncan,' into her phone, almost afraid of what he would say. She heard the dialling tone. She heard the staccato tune made by the numbers. And then a long continuous tone.

Duncan's phone had been disconnected.

3

It had to have been the longest half-hour of Maggie's entire life. She desperately wanted to slam her foot down hard on the accelerator, but knew that would be a mistake. The snow had settled on the main roads, and as she drove further north it was coming down more heavily with every minute that passed.

Her fear was tearing her in two. She focused on her worry about the children, but thoughts of Duncan kept slamming in, knocking her sideways. What on earth could have happened that would force him to leave the kids at home on their own? Where had he gone? As far as she knew, he hadn't had much chance to get to know anybody locally. To be honest, he hadn't seemed inclined to make the effort, so she had decided to give it a while before inviting people round. If he wanted time to get used to the idea of living here, she would give it to him.

Despite his initial reluctance, when Duncan realised how excited Maggie was by the challenge of defending criminals who had done more than the odd bit of burglary, he had smiled and said it would be fine. And then they had found the house and he had started to get excited. A Victorian vicarage, it needed a lot of work, and he had said he was looking forward to it.

It was dark down the end of the cul-de-sac, and one of Duncan's first jobs in the spring was going to be to cut back some of the overgrown trees to let light in. The silence of the property that she loved so much when she was curled up with her husband and children in front of their wood burner didn't have the same appeal when she thought of Josh and Lily alone there. The tall windows were single-glazed – another job on the soon-as-possible list – so easily broken; so easy for a grown man to climb through.

She was getting closer now, and she remembered the first time they had travelled along these roads with the children a few short weeks ago.

'We're nearly there, kids,' Duncan had said, grinning at them in the rear-view mirror as Lily squirmed with excitement and Josh gazed out of the window taking in every detail. They had arrived at their rather decrepit home, but the children saw nothing of that as they raced across the bare wooden floors trying to decide who was having which bedroom. Duncan had even picked Maggie up and carried her over the threshold, as if they were newlyweds. She had loved it. But that was Duncan. From the day they met he had been attentive and romantic, and even after ten years of marriage every now and again he still surprised her. That day she had appreciated how lucky she was.

At last Maggie turned into their road and bumped her way along, unable to see the potholes in the unmade surface for the deep snow. She didn't care. She could see the house ahead, every light blazing from the huge windows, and was glad. Maybe Suzy had told Josh to switch them all on.

The car skidded to a halt at an angle on the drive and she jumped out. She had already kicked off her stupid power heels for fear of falling flat on her face on the slippery ground, and she ran barefoot through the snow to the front door. She opened the letter box and called through.

'Josh, it's Mummy. It's okay now, darling. You can open the door.'

She waited, transferring her weight from frozen foot to frozen foot. Where was he? Why wasn't he watching out for her?

'Come on, Josh,' she whispered, the cold now forgotten as she longed for some sign of life from within the house.

After what seemed like ten minutes she saw the sitting room

curtain move slightly and Josh's face, pale against his mop of dark curly hair, appeared in the gap, the phone pressed against his ear. He gave her a little wave. *Thank God.* It looked like he was okay, which meant they were both okay.

She saw him speak and nod, and then the curtain fell back into place. A minute later she heard the double lock turning. Finally the door opened.

More than anything, she had to keep calm. She had to try her best not to convey her confusion and panic to her son. She sometimes forgot how young he was because of his serious attitude to life – a total contrast to his fidgety, perpetually cheerful sister.

'Hey, Joshy. Well done, looking after Lily. She's okay, is she?'

Josh nodded, staring at her feet. 'Where are your shoes?'

She almost wanted to laugh. Trust Josh to notice that.

'Is Auntie Suzy still on the phone?' she asked.

Josh nodded, handed her the phone and sauntered off into the sitting room as if nothing unusual had happened.

'Hi, Suzy. Thank you so much for keeping him talking.'

'What's going on, Mags? Where's Duncan?'

'I can't talk now. I'm sorry. I need to see to the kids, and I need to keep this line free in case Duncan tries to call. You know my mobile's a bit flaky here. Look, I'll call you later, or tomorrow. I don't know what's going on, Suze. I'm bloody furious with him. I know he wants to bring in some money, but if he's left the kids to go and deal with a faulty boiler…'

She quickly thanked her sister and said goodbye before she could give in to the desire to list all the things she might do to Duncan. The lack of any response from Duncan's phone was nagging away at the back of Maggie's mind, but in this weather that could be down to a poor signal from the local tower.

For now, her priority had to be her children. She pushed open the door to the sitting room. Josh was on the sofa, staring at the screen of his iPad Mini. Lily was lying on her stomach far too close

20

to the television, swinging her legs and banging her feet together in time to the music.

'Mum, can we have something to eat, please? I'm starving, and Lily's been moaning for ages.'

'I have not, Joshy,' Lily said without turning round. 'That's a fib.'

'I'll make you something in a minute, but first can you tell me what happened when Daddy went out?'

She could see that Josh was worried, and she felt bad for not doing a better job of protecting him. Lily ignored the question.

'He was making our tea. Then he came in to say that he had to go. He went into the garage, probably to get some tools. I expect somebody's got a burst pipe or something.'

That would have made perfect sense if it hadn't meant he would be leaving the children alone in the house. Surely he wouldn't do that for some stranger's burst pipe?

Maggie sat down next to Josh and stared into thin air, trying to calm down. Duncan wouldn't have done this without good reason. She was going to have to wait until he got home and stay calm.

As she pushed herself off the sofa to go and see what she could make for the children's tea, Josh muttered something.

'Sorry, Josh. What did you say?' she asked.

'I just wondered why he needed a posh bag to go out on a job.'

Maggie sat down again.

'What do you mean?'

'When I went to wave to him from the window he was carrying the bag you use when you go away for work.' Josh shrugged.

Maggie felt her chest tighten and pushed down the fear that was rising through her chest. She knew which one Josh meant. And she knew Duncan would never use that to carry his tools. It was a weekend bag – brown leather.

Maggie leaned forward and gave her son a hug, which for once

21

he reciprocated. She was struggling to hide the fact that something was terribly wrong, but he was a perceptive child.

'Thanks, Josh. I'll make you some food in a moment, but keep an eye on Lily for me, would you?'

Maggie left the room and raced upstairs to their bedroom, pulling open drawers at random. A few clothes were missing; his toothbrush and razor had gone from their en-suite bathroom too. She stood still and stared at the empty space where Duncan's toiletries should be. She felt her throat tighten and her eyes flooded with tears.

Garage, she thought. Josh said he went to the garage.

She ran downstairs and out through the connecting door into the garage. Standing to one side against a breezeblock wall was a dark green metal cupboard, a cupboard that had been padlocked since she the day she had met Duncan. Now both doors stood open, the padlock hanging loose. The cupboard was empty.

Duncan had gone.

4

The evening briefing session for DI Becky Robinson's team had been a miserable affair. She was glad they had caught the bastard who for the last few years had been terrorising elderly women, but she wished she could think of some way to protect such poor old souls so no one had to suffer horrors like these again. What if it were to happen to her own gran? Next chance she had, Becky was going to get herself back down to London for a few days and sort out how best to keep her safe. Not that her gran would take any notice. She believed everybody was inherently good, while Becky was increasingly of the opinion that people were inherently bad; it was just a matter of how well they controlled their badness.

Cynical bugger, she thought as she made her way back to the incident room. There was still work to be done on the case, of course. Alf Horton might be locked up now, but they had to make sure they had enough irrefutable evidence to put him well and truly away. One of her sergeants was managing the interviews with Horton and his solicitor, who was apparently a woman. How could she bring herself to represent a rat like him?

Passing her boss's office as she made her way along the corridor, Becky glanced in through the open door. He seemed deep in thought and didn't even look up as she walked by. Detective Chief Inspector Tom Douglas was her ideal boss in so many ways, although for a while last year – immediately after the Natasha Joseph case – Becky had been worried about him. He had seemed a lot chirpier for the last few months, though, and appeared almost back to his normal self. Anyway, whatever had ailed him was none of her business, although she wished he would realise that she was always there for him. Whatever he needed.

'Becky!'

Tom may not have looked up as she passed his door, but obviously he had recognised her footsteps. She turned and peered around the door jamb.

'Yes, boss?'

'Come in a minute and sit down.'

Tom closed a thick buff folder and stuck it on top of a pile of about twenty similar files that looked perilously close to falling over. He sat back in his chair and smiled at Becky, giving her his full attention. She noticed that his dark blond hair had grown a little longer recently, and was touching the collar of his white shirt, the top button of which was undone. Becky picked up Tom's discarded tie from the back of one of the visitors' chairs, reached over and laid it gently on top of his black suit jacket, which was hanging over the only other chair.

'Well done today,' Tom said. 'I know you got your man, but just give me the edited highlights of the evidence we've got against him.'

Becky pulled a face. 'You really don't want to know about this guy, Tom. Alf Horton is the lowest form of human life. To have committed the crimes he has I can only assume that he's a true psychopath. There's no sign of guilt at all, and his victims were probably all so trusting. Mind you, how anybody would trust him, I don't know. He looks as if he's never seen sunlight – you know, one of those pasty almost grey faces with lips that are too thin with spittle in the corners of his mouth.'

Tom seemed amused by her distaste. 'Bloody hell, Becky – you've met worse than him before. Why's he creeping you out?'

'I can't believe everything he's done. The man lives with his elderly mother, for God's sake, but she won't hear a word against him. Says he's an angel from heaven. He reminds me of Hannibal

24

Lecter when he smiles at Clarice. I get the feeling he would like to jump over the desk and rip me apart with his teeth.'

Tom was still laughing at her expression when his phone rang. He gave her a smile of apology and picked it up.

'Tom Douglas.'

There was a pause of several seconds and Tom frowned.

'Sorry, Max, but I genuinely have no idea. I haven't seen Leo for months. Why are you worried about her?'

Becky pretended to read the file she was holding, but couldn't help listening when she heard Leo's name mentioned. Becky had always thought Leo – or Leonora as she was more accurately called – would eventually move in with Tom, but in a rare moment of familiarity when Becky was waxing lyrical about her own love life Tom had mentioned that his relationship with Leo was over. He had never said why, but he had announced it with an air of such determination that Becky was certain Tom had been the one making the decision.

Becky could hear a deep voice at the other end of the phone, but couldn't catch the words.

'Do you want me to go round to her apartment?' Tom asked. He paused again to listen to the caller. 'Okay. Well if you change your mind, let me know. The neighbours know me and I'd be happy to go. But don't you think it more likely she's gone away and forgotten to tell anybody? You know how independent she is – she probably thinks nobody will miss her.'

After that the call was brought swiftly to an end and Tom raised his eyes briefly to the ceiling. 'Bloody women.'

'Problem?' Becky asked.

Tom leaned back and rotated his pen between his fingers, a habit he had when thinking, or possibly when not wanting to look the other person in the eye.

'That was Max Saunders. He's married to Leo's sister Ellie and was my neighbour in Cheshire until I sold the cottage a few months ago. According to Max, Leo didn't turn up for their new baby's christening last Sunday. Ellie was just angry with her to start with, but they've tried calling and she isn't answering her mobile. Ellie's worried now. Max will go round to her apartment if they can't track her down in the next couple of days. If it was anything else, I would guess she'd gone off somewhere, not thinking anybody would care about her enough to wonder where she was. But surely she wouldn't miss the christening?'

Becky saw a flash of irritation on Tom's face and was desperate to ask him more questions, but her hopes of him confiding in her were dashed as he pointed to the file on her lap.

'Where were we, Becky? You were going to tell me about your arrest, I think.'

❖

Tom's session with Becky lasted no more than fifteen minutes as the Alf Horton case appeared to be cut and dried. Horton had refused to sign a confession, but he hadn't denied anything either, and as a minimum they had the most recent crime, where he had been caught red-handed. It seemed Horton was likely to plead guilty, and that made everybody's life easier. There was still work to be done to give the CPS rock-solid evidence of the earlier crimes, though – the more cases, the longer the sentence. And this needed to be a long one.

Much as Tom preferred discussing an active enquiry rather than ploughing through the mountain of paperwork piled on his desk, he could see that Becky was itching to get on with pulling the case together. Either that or quizzing him about Leo.

Talking about his ex-girlfriend was difficult. He had cared deeply about her, but her fundamental lack of trust in men and the fact that she had constantly backed away from him whenever she had thought he was getting too serious had eventually become too much. He thought back to their last few weeks together. In so many ways they had appeared to be closer than ever, but the flashes of suspicion on her face whenever he had received an unexpected text or call, and her momentary silence whenever he said he was working late had started to rile him and put him permanently on edge. He had never given her any reason to distrust him, but he was a policeman, and that meant that sometimes he couldn't tell her about every call, every case, every unexpected meeting.

She was beautiful. He loved her style, her obsession with only wearing black and white and the way she wore clothes that skimmed her figure, their ultra-soft fabrics moving with her, just giving a hint of the body that lay beneath – a body that had never failed to thrill him.

The crunch had finally come nearly a year ago. The kidnap case he had been working on was complex enough, but it had been so much more than that for him.

Tom fought to push the memories of that intense twenty-four-hour period from his mind – the revelations about the death of his brother, Jack, all those years ago and the ongoing consequences were something he rarely allowed himself to think about, at least during working hours. When the case was finally over Tom had needed somebody to talk to and he had wanted that person to be Leo, but mistaking Tom's twenty-four-hour silence for an act of betrayal, Leo had taken herself away on holiday, out of touch, as if to punish Tom for a sin he didn't know he had committed.

He had known then that there was no way back. He needed a woman who trusted him, and experience told him that, whatever their best intentions, people rarely change.

Tom realised that he had been staring at the same piece of paper for ten minutes while his mind wandered to Leo. Where the hell was she this time? Who had rattled her enough to cause her to rush off without telling anybody where she was going? Or had something happened to her – an accident in her apartment and nobody knew she was hurt?

He sighed and pushed the papers away. Visions of Leo

sprawled on the floor, in pain, wouldn't leave his mind.

'Bugger,' he said quietly as he grabbed his car keys from the desk. Max might have told him not to check up on Leo, but he knew he wasn't going to be able to focus until he was sure she was okay.

5

The snow was getting thicker now and starting to drift in the wind. As Maggie looked out of the bedroom window she could see the thick flakes swirling in the amber glow of the streetlights lining the deserted cul-de-sac. The room behind her was in darkness. She felt as if she had been standing there for hours – waiting, hoping, *praying* to see Duncan return in his pristine white van. It was only three hours since she had arrived home, but it felt like days.

She ached to hear his voice – hear him tell her that he was on his way home and whatever had happened was a mistake; hear him say that he loved her. Had he left her? Really? Without a word of explanation? She racked her brain trying to think of a single reason why he would do that.

His phone still appeared to be dead, although she had called it every ten minutes, and she was trying hard not to let the children realise that something was wrong. Lily was oblivious to it all, but Josh knew that his daddy shouldn't have left him alone in the house to look after his young sister. He was a sensitive child, and Maggie knew he would be going over everything in his head. He had looked at her as if she held the answer, but she was no nearer to understanding what was happening than Josh.

Suzy had sent her a text asking for an update, and Maggie was ashamed of the fact that she had lied to her sister. Or avoided the truth. She had just put 'All okay now. Speak tomorrow.' She hadn't wanted to get involved in a long discussion. She didn't have any answers.

Maggie had been through Duncan's wardrobe to see what

was missing, but she wasn't capable of working out if her husband taken enough for a night, for a week, or maybe for good. She stifled a sob at the thought.

A sharp gust of wind outside blew snow across the road and against the wall of the house. Whether Duncan was here or not, it seemed unlikely Maggie would be able to get the car out of the drive first thing in the morning, and for a moment she was relieved. The sick bastard she had been asked to defend would have to be passed on to somebody else. She could stay at home with the children, and wait for her husband to return.

Where are you, Duncan? I miss you.

Maggie's limbs were tight with cold and lack of movement. She backed stiffly up to the bed, sitting down and wrapping the duvet round her shoulders. Her whole body started shaking, and she didn't know if it was fear or the frigid air of her bedroom that was causing it. She didn't want to leave her vigil at the window, though. She bit her bottom lip, trying to stop it from trembling. Crying wasn't going to help. She had to think.

The cupboard in the garage was niggling her. What had he needed to take out of that cupboard, and why? It wasn't his work tools. She knew that.

Ever since they moved in together, Duncan had kept the green cupboard locked. Initially Maggie had decided not to make an issue of it. He was entitled to his own space, and if she was honest there were things in her past she would rather he knew nothing about – such as her appalling choice of partner before Duncan. A married man with three children. She shuddered at the thought. She hadn't lied about that terrible period in her life, but she hadn't volunteered the information either.

After she and Duncan had been together for a while she had asked him for the key to the cupboard – she was clearing away some clutter – but he had refused to give it to her, saying he would do it himself. She hadn't pushed it. She had always thought the cupboard might contain something to do with his mother because he had nothing of hers around the house – no photos or mementos – and yet she knew how much Duncan's mother had meant to him. He had given up his studies at Leeds University to look after her when she was ill with cancer, and had nursed her while simultaneously training to be a plumber, a job he thought he might be able to combine with being her carer. Sadly she had died a couple of years before Maggie met him.

Maggie heard a noise and turned her head.

Josh was standing at the door in his pyjamas.

'Are you okay, sweetheart?' she asked. Grasping the duvet in her hand, she held out her arm so that her son could snuggle in under it against her.

'Why are you sitting in the dark, Mum?'

'Just thinking.' She tried to smile at him.

'About Dad?'

Maggie didn't want to lie to her son. 'I'm wondering when he's going to be home, Josh. That's all. But don't worry. I'm sure he'll be back by the time you wake up in the morning.'

'Is it my fault?' Josh's voice was as quiet as a whisper, as if he was afraid to say the words. Maggie pulled him tightly against her.

'Of course not, sweetheart. Why on earth should it be your fault?'

'Because of the message.'

'*What* message? You never mentioned a message before.' Maggie could hear the desperation in her voice and tried hard to soften it. Josh looked up at her, his little face a picture of confusion.

'I'm sorry if I did something wrong, Mummy.'

'I'm sure you've done nothing wrong, Josh, but you need to tell me properly what you mean.'

'Dad's phone was in the sitting room. I heard it beep, so I knew it was a message. I took the phone to him in the kitchen.'

'Joshy,' Maggie began, trying to choose her words carefully,

'I know we've said it's rude to read other people's messages, but did you by any chance catch a glimpse of what it said?'

Josh looked at the floor for a moment, and when he looked up his cheeks were pink.

'I didn't read the words, Mummy. Honestly.'

Maggie knew there was a 'but' in there, and that she was going to have to wait for it. She smiled her encouragement.

'When Daddy opened it, I was standing right next to him. There was a picture. I only looked at it because I thought it was you.'

A picture? Of me? Josh couldn't mean that. He must have got it wrong.

'It's okay, sweetheart. I'm not cross with you. Tell me what you saw when you looked at the screen.' She relaxed her hold slightly, certain that Josh would be able to feel the thumping of her heart, and turned to look at him.

'A photo of a lady with red lipstick and long dark hair – spread out like yours sometimes is on the pillow.'

It sounded as if the woman, whoever she was, had to have been lying down. *Why would Duncan get a picture of a woman lying down – a woman that looks like me? Is he having an affair? Has he left me for this woman?* She felt a solid ball of despair settle deep inside her.

'I thought you'd sent a selfie to dad,' Josh said, 'but I kind of knew it wasn't you.'

'What made you change your mind?' she said, stroking his hair gently in an attempt to calm his anxiety.

'They weren't your eyes. The lady in the picture had eyes like that doll of Lily's – the one Auntie Ceecee bought her.'

Maggie felt a chill. He didn't need to say any more. Her aunt had bought a Victorian doll for Lily when she was three – a strange choice because Ceecee said the doll was too expensive to play with. So the doll, named Maud by Lily, had sat on a shelf in her bedroom, to be looked at but never touched. Then Lily had started to have nightmares.

'What were you dreaming about, baby?' Maggie had asked after she had brought a terrified Lily into bed with her and Duncan.

'It's Maud. She watches me.'

'What do you mean, Lil?' Duncan had asked. 'She's just a doll.'

'Does that mean she's dead, Daddy?'

'No, sweetheart. Somebody made her, like we sometimes make things out of Play-Doh. She's never been alive.'

'Is that what people's eyes look like if they've never been alive?'

The doll now lived in a cupboard, but Maggie knew exactly what Josh meant about the eyes.

6

12 years ago – May 7th

Sonia Beecham almost didn't recognise the eyes staring back at her in the mirror. They were still pale blue, of course, but the pupils were slightly dilated with excitement, and the eyelashes were tinted with grey mascara – an unusual indulgence, but she wanted to look her best because today was special. In fact Sonia thought it was her best day since starting at Manchester University six months previously. She had always found it difficult to make friends, and the eagerness on her parents' faces when she came home each night was painful to watch as they waited to hear whether she had met new people. She knew it was out of love for her, but they didn't understand the pressure it put her under.

She was shy. Painfully, embarrassingly shy. If anybody spoke to her, she blushed bright red. It was an instant reaction, and one that made her turn away. Never in her wildest dreams could she imagine starting a conversation with anybody. She would rather stick her head in a vat of boiling oil, if the truth were known.

She had heard her parents talking once, a few years ago. They wanted to know what they had done wrong – why their daughter had grown up the way she had. So now she had that guilt to bear as well. If only she could make some friends so they would know they had done nothing – nothing, that is, except love her and shelter her from anything and everything that would be considered by most people to be a normal experience.

Now, though, things were changing. Her mum had been so con-cerned that she'd persuaded Sonia's father to stump up for some counselling. Sonia had been horrified. The idea of sitting in a chair telling a complete stranger how embarrassed she was to open her mouth in company made her legs go weak. She had resisted for months, but after Christmas not only had her mum arranged the counselling sessions, she had insisted on going with Sonia for the first few meetings to be sure that Sonia was over her initial embarrassment and was happy to carry on alone.

Sonia had hated it to start with, but gradually her counsellor had given her some tools to help build her confidence. The best of these was the name of a website designed for people like her. She had heard of chat rooms but never been in one. Within a month she had realised that she had plenty to say as long as she could keep it anonymous and nobody could see her face. The best of it was, people wanted to listen. She didn't have her own computer to access the site, but there were plenty she could use at the university, and that was better because nobody would know what she was doing. If she had had a personal computer at home her mother would forever have been looking over her shoulder.

What she hadn't told a soul – because he had asked her not to – was that she had met somebody online who was as crippled with shyness as she was. He had told her he was surprised he could even type without stuttering, and that had made her laugh. That was his issue, the burden he had to bear. He couldn't get a whole sentence out without this dreadful stammer halting him in his tracks. They had been talking online now for a couple of weeks, and he said that he thought he might possibly be able to speak to her. They had agreed that if she went red, or if he stuttered, it wouldn't matter. They were both in the same boat. And tonight she was meeting him for the first time.

She had lied to her parents. She had never done that before, but Sonia had known what her mum would say: 'Bring him home, first, love. Let me and your dad meet him – do it properly.' Her mother didn't seem to have any concept of how things were done now. Not that Sonia wanted to behave like some of the girls on campus, but having to be vetted before he could even go for a drink with her was a sure way to frighten a man off – especially one as shy as Sam.

Sam was a good name. Solid-sounding, reassuring. He had said it wasn't a good idea to meet anywhere too public. Having other people around was sure to make them clam up and not be natural with each other. So she was going to meet him in a little park just off the Bridgewater Canal towpath. He said it would be okay there, because there would be people on the other side of the canal at the cafés and bars, but nobody would be able to hear if they made complete fools of themselves.

Sam had even told her which tram to get and where to get off. She had followed his instructions to the letter. The walk along the canal was fine to start with. It was quite pretty, and she thought it was wonderful the way places like this were being brought back to life. But as she walked further on it all changed. There was a lot of redevelopment of old mills, their blank windows facing onto the canal. There were no cafés and bars. And no people.

Sonia hurried along the towpath, ducking to walk through a long, low tunnel. She was nearly at the meeting place. As she neared the end of the tunnel, a tall figure stepped out onto the path and for a moment Sonia felt a jolt of fear, but he gave her a little wave so she carried on walking. She knew who he was. He was taller than she expected, and as she got closer, she could see him smiling at her.

'Hi, Sonia,' he said. 'I'm Sam.'

He didn't stutter once.

7

Tom usually enjoyed the experience of going back to somewhere he was once familiar with. The streets, the houses, the places that had once been important to him evoked distant memories that rushed at him, jumbled and incomplete but soothing in their ordinariness.

Driving to Leo's didn't give him the pleasurable buzz of a flashback to another time, though. Perhaps it was too soon. All he could remember now was his final visit this time last year – when he had told Leo that they had no future. He hadn't been sure he could go through with it, and had hoped that somehow he would see a gentler side of her.

'You must do what you must do, Tom,' was all she had said, even though he could see how hurt she was. He had started towards her, wanting to pull her to him, but she had held her arms out in front of her, palms facing him.

'No, we don't need to touch. It was always going to end this way. I told you at the start.'

He had been so exasperated with her that he had turned on his heel and left. It shouldn't have had to end that way. All she'd had to do was trust him.

Now here he was, pulling into the all-too-familiar visitors' parking space of her apartment building and looking around. Nothing had changed. Not that he could see much. The heavy clouds that had been threatening snow all day were obscuring both moon and stars, and the white lights that lit the pathways around the old warehouse in which Leo's apartment was situated didn't shed much light above knee height.

Tom hadn't meant it to be this late when he arrived, but no sooner had he picked up his car keys to drive here than he had received a summons to brief his boss on a current case. Still, even if Leo had been out during the day, she should be back by now.

He pushed open the car door against a gust of icy wind and pulled his jacket across his chest. There was still no snow here in the urban heat island of central Manchester, but he was well aware that in the outer reaches of his patch the roads would be treacherous.

Head down, Tom walked to the main entrance and pushed Leo's buzzer.

Nothing.

He could try again, but it was bloody freezing, so he pressed the buzzer of one of Leo's neighbours, an Italian girl called Daniela whom Tom had met on a few occasions.

'Si. Chi è?'

Tom had forgotten that her spoken English was so poor, although she appeared to understand everything that was said. He hoped her boyfriend was with her to interpret if he wanted to ask her any questions.

'Hi, Daniela. It's Tom – a friend of Leo's. She's not answering. Can you let me in, please?'

He heard some muttering in the background, none of which he understood, but then the door buzzed and clicked, and he was in. He decided to walk up the three floors to Leo's door.

Daniela and her boyfriend were standing on the landing waiting for him.

'Buona sera,' Daniela said. That much Tom could understand. He nodded to the girl and her boyfriend, whose name he couldn't remember for the life of him.

'Buona sera. I'm so sorry to disturb your evening, but can I ask if you've seen Leo at all? Her sister's worried about her because she didn't turn up to a party on Sunday.'

Daniela frowned and turned to the boyfriend. Her voice rose, and she gabbled away in her own language, complete with hand signals that made no more sense to Tom than her words.

'Daniela says she hasn't seen Leo since Saturday, but her car's still in its space,' the boyfriend said.

It seemed to Tom that Daniela had said much more than that, and he couldn't decide whether the fact that her car was in the underground garage was good news or bad. Was she ill in bed? Or had she gone away for a few days and maybe taken a taxi?

'Do you mean her car hasn't moved?'

Daniela clearly understood that and nodded. She started speaking again, and Tom waited for the interpretation.

'Dani has knocked on the door a couple of times, but Leo hasn't answered. We didn't want to pester her. Leo's a very private person.'

Tom kept his thoughts on that subject to himself. 'Have you got a key, by any chance?' he asked, still not sure what he should do.

Daniela nodded and rushed into her apartment, returning seconds later holding a key.

Tom felt uneasy. Going back into Leo's apartment would have been difficult at the best of times, and he felt uncomfortable. What if she was ill and was simply nursing her sickness by herself? What if she had a man in there, and they had simply holed up for a week, switching their phones off?

'Would you mind coming in with me, Daniela?' Tom asked. Even though he couldn't see Leo making a formal complaint about his visit, he wanted to cover himself. He turned the key and pushed the door open.

'Leo? It's Tom,' he shouted. But he knew instantly that the apartment was empty. It had a dead feeling to it that only comes with houses that have been left vacant for a few days. There were no smells of food – not that cooking was Leo's forte, but she had to eat – or coffee or even perfume. Tom was assailed by memories: walking into the apartment at the end of a long day, Leo coming to greet him, smiling; cooking her dinner while she sat on a counter stool and told him about her day; listening to music; lying entwined together on the sofa.

He took a deep breath and signalled Daniela to follow him. The boyfriend, who he now remembered was called Luca, waited at the door.

The apartment consisted of one huge combined sitting room, dining room and kitchen. It was neat and tidy with no sign of recent occupation. There were also a bedroom and bathroom. Certain now that the apartment was empty, Tom nevertheless knocked on the bedroom door and shouted Leo's name. As expected, there was no answer. He turned the handle and stopped short in the doorway.

The room was a mess. Clothes were all over the bed; cupboard doors stood ajar, and underwear was spilling out of open drawers. Leo was meticulous about her clothes. She loved silk and soft jersey, and everything had to be steamed to remove each and every crease. The steamer stood at the ready next to her wardrobe, yet all her beautiful clothes were heaped in piles on the bed, some even on the floor.

He moved over to the dressing table. Leo hadn't worn much jewellery and only had a few simple silver pieces. They all appeared to be there, so this wasn't a burglary. *What the hell had happened?* He felt a tightness in his chest. Had there been a fight here, and if so, where was she now?

Tom glanced into the bathroom, which was as orderly as ever. Only the bedroom was a tip. He walked over to the window and looked out at a view he had seen on so many occasions at this time of night. The lights of Manchester lit the sky. Was Leo out there somewhere close by? Or was she far away? He had no idea, but he couldn't help feeling that something dark had happened within these four walls.

He turned back to the main room and walked over to the fridge. There was no milk, no vegetables – nothing fresh that would deteriorate in her absence. Did this mean she had left by choice, or that she had given up any pretence of looking after herself and decided to rely on black coffee and takeaway food?

He stood and stared at the empty shelves, thinking but coming up with nothing. He looked at the worktop, and something caught his eye. It looked like a rose petal, shrivelled and browning at the edges. He checked the bins to see if any flowers had recently been thrown away, but although there were empty packets and some coffee grounds, there were no flowers.

He turned back to the neighbour.

'Thanks, Daniela,' he said. 'I think we're done here. I'm going to phone Leo's sister and let her know what we've found.'

With a frown and a typically expressive Italian shrug, she wished him a buona notte and went back to Luca, who was still hovering in the doorway. Tom could hear what he assumed was Daniela's explanation of what they had found, and he gently closed the door. He pulled his phone out of his pocket to call Max. He didn't know what he would say, but his gut was telling him that Leo had not gone away. She was missing.

8

12 years ago – May 8th

If there was one thing that Tom hated, it was a missing persons case. The devastating thought that it was bound to end badly seemed to be uppermost in everybody's mind. The family or friends who had reported their loved ones missing were inevitably terrified, and Tom never knew how to offer them comfort. In the early stages of an investigation he probably had no more information than they did, and for a policeman that wasn't a good place to be.

Although it was only late afternoon he knew that unless the missing girl turned up in the next couple of hours – and he hoped for everybody's sake that she did – tonight was likely to be a late one and he would have to cancel his plans. It was supposed to be one of his Jack nights – the occasional evenings when Tom and his brother Jack had a few hours to themselves, drinking beer, listening to and arguing about music.

He needed his evenings with Jack. He needed to think and talk about something other than the job, something other than his wife, Kate. An evening with Jack would take his mind off the struggle he was having with his current boss and the doubts about his marriage. Things were up and down between him and Kate all the time, and Tom never knew where he was. She hated Tom's job, and he could understand that. Just like tonight, he couldn't always be relied on to be home at a set time, and he knew she wanted him to change careers to something more lucrative with better hours.

But Tom loved being a detective – except at this precise moment, when he wished he could be somewhere else, doing a different job.

A middle-aged couple had reported their nineteen-year-old daughter missing, and somehow Tom had to penetrate the wall of fear they were trapped behind to uncover details of their missing child. He wasn't looking forward to it.

Sonia Beecham was a student at Manchester University and apparently she was the perfect daughter, still living happily with her parents. Last night she hadn't come home. She'd said she had a late lecture, and when she wasn't back by the time her parents went to bed they assumed she had gone for a drink with some of the other students; unusual for Sonia, but they had been pleased she was making more of an effort to make friends.

According to the PC who had been dispatched to talk to them, the parents always left the landing light on when their daughter was out late, and she always turned it off when she got in, so if they woke up, they would know she was home. The light wasn't turned off last night.

'I don't think this is a case of a kid forgetting to let her parents know she was staying out, or meeting some guy and going home with him, sir,' the PC had said when Tom had spoken to him. 'It doesn't fit with everything they say about her. They may be delusional, but I think we need to take it seriously.'

As Tom pulled up outside the family home, his radio buzzed.

'You're not in the house yet, are you, Douglas?' It was the brash, abrasive voice of Tom's boss, Detective Chief Inspector Victor Elliott.

'No. I was about to get out of the car.'

'Well don't. Get your arse down to Pomona Island. We've got a body, and it's a girl.'

The warm spring sunshine gave Pomona Island the feeling of a lost slice of paradise. It was hard to believe that this slice of land bordered by the Bridgewater Canal and the River Irwell was just a few minutes' walk from the centre of Manchester. Wild and uncared for as it was, the late spring flowers were bursting through the scrubland, and even last year's dead buddleia plumes had their own beauty when backlit by the sun's dying rays. The air was buzzing with the sounds and sights of insects: crickets and grasshoppers, bees and butterflies, all somehow indifferent to the proximity of the busy city.

But there was nothing beautiful about the crime that had brought Tom to this wasteland. DCI Elliott had told him the body of a young woman – little more than a girl – had been discovered by a dog walker that afternoon, and as Tom made his way along the path he felt a wave of sadness for the Beecham family. It was no use hoping this wasn't Sonia. If the victim wasn't the Beechams' child, she was certainly somebody's.

In the distance Tom could just make out the top of the tent that would be protecting the body and preserving evidence, but before approaching the scene of crime team who were waiting for him, Tom stopped and looked around. He had lived his whole life in Manchester and had never been aware of this sliver of wasteland. Pomona Docks had once been part of the thriving port of Manchester, and old tyres still hung down the quaysides to protect the ships as they pulled into the wharves. But now there wasn't a boat in sight.

Tom started off again, walking slowly along a well-made path between the scrubland and the water. A strong metal fence along the water's edge looked to be in good condition, and large lamps stood tall at regular intervals. Tom wondered if these were still in working order, but he somehow doubted it.

He looked back the way he had come. He had already been told that, based on the lack of blood in the vicinity of the body, it seemed unlikely the victim had been killed here; it was probable that she had been brought here after death.

Why walk so far in, probably the best part of half a mile, and yet still make no attempt to hide the body? Why not tip her over the fence and into the water, or carry her to the back wall where the arches were? But she had been left right by the path, as if waiting to be found.

Tom made his way towards the tent, following the designated

44

route to the crime scene. Donning protective clothing, he lifted the flap of the tent and went inside, muttering a subdued greeting to the SOCO team.

The girl was facing him. Dressed in blue cut-off jeans, flip-flops and a T-shirt, her blonde shoulder-length hair looked newly washed and shiny, and she was wearing hardly any make-up. Sitting propped against the stump of an old tree, she looked like an innocent child hoping to catch a few rays of sunshine.

There was one thing marring the picture. The girl's neck had been slashed from ear to ear, and her eyes were open and glassy, staring at nothing.

Leaving the tent to give the newly arrived forensic pathologist a bit more room, Tom walked outside the perimeter of the crime scene and took a good look around. Across the wide stretch of water where the River Irwell and the Manchester Ship Canal became one he could see buildings, but they seemed mainly to be warehouses with their backs towards the water and not a window in sight. There was evidence of some new building further along – probably apartments or offices overlooking the water – but they were too far away for anybody to have seen anything, particularly given the dense undergrowth.

He turned to look the other way, back towards Manchester. In the distance he could see tall buildings and a skyline punctuated by cranes as the last of the redevelopment following the 1996 IRA bombing was completed. The new Metrolink tram line was barely visible through the trees, but Tom remembered reading that in the three years that the line had been open Pomona station had been the least used on the whole of the tram system so he didn't hold out much hope there. A smaller canal and a railway line separated Pomona from a number of old mill buildings, but although some seemed to be in the process of being renovated, there was little sign of activity at this time of day. At night he imagined the area would be deserted.

Tom pushed his hands into his trouser pockets and allowed ideas and impressions of the area to flow freely though his mind, hoping for some insight into how or why the girl had been brought here. He was in no doubt who the victim was. She fitted the description of the missing girl perfectly, although of course there would have to be a formal identification. Somebody was going to have to inform the parents, and he was sure his boss would nominate him for that task.

'You're good at it, Douglas,' he would say. 'You've got the kind of face that people trust.'

It was just about the only compliment he ever got from Victor Elliott, and only then because the DCI knew it was an awful thing to have to do.

There was no doubt at all what had killed the girl – her slit throat said it all – and yet there was no blood at the scene. Only her blood-soaked clothes bore witness to the violence with which she had been murdered. So the victim had to have been carried or transported by some means or another, exactly as the SOCOs first thought.

'You can't get a car onto Pomona Island unless you have a key to the double gates at the end,' Carl, the head of the team, said. 'They could have been left open, I suppose, but it's unlikely. It's a long way to walk with a body over your shoulder – I wouldn't want to try it – so we're wondering about a wheelbarrow or something like that. We're checking it out.' He nodded towards two of his team, on their hands and knees in their white suits, fingertip-searching the area for traces of footprints or tyre tracks. 'It's been dry for a while now, so we're not holding out too much hope.'

A shout came from inside the tent.

'Inspector Douglas, you might want to see this.'

Tom made his way back into the tent and crouched down next to the forensic pathologist.

'I noticed that there was a flap cut in her jeans at the top of the left leg. I wasn't going to remove her clothing of course until we got her onto my table, but I saw this and decided to take a look. Come here – lean over to your right, her left.'

46

The pathologist reached out and pulled back a flap of fabric about ten centimetres square. Etched into the top of the girl's thigh were three straight horizontal lines.

9

Thursday

As yet another train rumbled out of Manchester Victoria station, Becky buried her head deep beneath the duvet.

'Hmm, this is interesting,' Mark mumbled, stirring from sleep and turning on his side towards her. 'Feel free to continue.' He reached an arm towards her to stroke her hair.

Becky pulled the duvet back so that her face was visible.

'Very funny – and no such luck, mate. I'm trying to block out the incessant racket of trains. It's not even six in the morning yet. Why can't they wait until some sensible time? And why the hell did you have to buy the closest flat to the station, Mark? Nobody in their right mind would do that.' She pulled a pillow dramatically over her head, but it didn't cut out much sound.

'It may come as a surprise to you, given that I'm a British Transport Policeman and all that, but I actually *like* trains. I love to be able to hear them. For some people it's the sea swooshing up on a pebble beach, for me it's trains leaving the station, wondering where all those people are going.'

'Don't they make timetables to solve that little conundrum?'

'Ha ha. It's more than the destination. I look at people waiting for trains, and I think about *why* they're going. Are they going towards something or away from something?'

'That's a very romantic notion for a big burly policeman.' Becky giggled at the understatement of her description. With his massive shoulders and broken nose, Mark looked like a rugby player who had been involved in a few too many collapsed scrums.

48

'What?' Mark feigned puzzlement. 'Oh, I get it. You think I mean people, relationships, that sort of crap. Don't be daft, Bex. I'm talking about the shady characters who are probably off to commit some evil crime, or escape from one. Romance doesn't come into it.'

Becky pushed a cold hand under the covers and wrapped it around his warm back. 'No? Not keen on romance then?' she murmured innocently as she pulled him closer.

'Ouch – your hands are like blocks of ice. Give them to me and I'll warm them up for you.'

Becky laughed and pulled one arm back out from under the covers, waving it around in the air. 'Just getting it nice and cold for you.' She pushed him onto his back and rolled on top of him, pinning his arms above him on the pillow. 'I like to torture you.'

She was no match for Mark of course, and in the ensuing tussle and laughter she nearly missed the buzzing of her phone.

'Bollocks,' she said softly as she reached out to pull it from the bedside table. She loved her job, but right now she didn't want to leave this bed.

'Becky Robinson.' Becky listened as she heard the voice of the duty sergeant rumbling down the line.

'Becky, sorry to wake you, love, but we've got a body, and as you're duty SIO it's all yours. Discovered under a bridge down by the canal – an adult female, that's all we know for now. Sounds like you'll be wanting to call DCI Douglas in. There's not much to go on yet, cos other than checking life extinct the uniform has just cordoned off the scene to wait for you. But my guess is that this one's going to be above your pay grade.'

She suspected the sergeant was right. If it was murder, she would have to call Tom in, but she would go and check it out first.

'Jumbo and his team are on their way, so you've got the best.'

Becky grabbed a pen and paper to jot down the details of the location, ended the call and swung her legs out of the bed.

'No good me trying to persuade you to come back to bed for ten minutes, I don't suppose? From what I could hear, your man's dead already so a few minutes wouldn't matter.' Mark was crawling across the bed towards her.

'It's not a man. It's a woman, and if I thought for even a moment that was a serious comment, Mark Heywood, you wouldn't see me for dust.' She leaned back against his warm chest for a moment. 'Make me a coffee to take with me while I have a quick shower – there's a love.'

Becky knew that joking was one way of dealing with what they had to do. Most people thought that Mark's job for BTP was an easy one – patrolling railways stations and controlling the rabble. But who did they think dealt with the hideousness of the bodies of people who threw themselves in front of trains? That had only happened once since she had been with Mark, but she could remember now his almost manic humour for two or three days after the event. He would understand more than anybody the adrenaline that would flow through her as she raced to get to the scene. It sounded as if it was a suspicious death, and the sooner she got there, the sooner she could help catch whichever bastard had caused somebody else to die.

She turned the water up as hot as she could stand it, and scrubbed the pleasure of the past few hours from her body.

❖

A chill wind was causing ripples on the oily surface of the murky water as Becky picked her way along the canal towpath towards the uninviting black entrance to the tunnel ahead. The full force of the cold air struck her face, whistling past her ears, and she breathed in a smell unique to canals, a smell that suggested decaying matter of God knows what origin in its depths.

She stared at the dark mouth of the long tunnel. Even with a uniformed officer standing guard at its entrance she had no wish to enter with little more than a torch to light her way, but just as she was mentally preparing herself to step into the void, a bright light came on ahead, deep in the shadowy depths. The forensic guys must have beaten her to it, and Becky breathed again.

Silently admonishing herself for being such a wimp, she gave her name to the policeman, whose face was mottled pink with the cold, pulled on a protective suit and stepped carefully onto the metal plates of the approach path laid to preserve any evidence close to the body. A train thundered overhead as it sped out of Piccadilly station, drowning out the sound of the water gently lapping against the canal bank. Becky shuddered; she'd had her fill of train sound effects for one day.

The bulk of Jumoke Osoba, head of the crime scene team and better known as Jumbo, was always reassuring, and Becky could see him ahead, his wide silhouette backlit by the pale light of the distant exit of the tunnel. Jumbo loved a crime scene but was the first to admit that he preferred those that didn't contain dead bodies. As Becky got closer, he glanced towards her, and she caught a glimpse of pearly teeth in a jet-black face – a face that would have blended into the background were it not for his wide smile – albeit less exuberant than usual – and the creamy white of his eyes.

'Tom not with you today, Becky?' Jumbo asked.

'Not yet. Technically he's not on duty for another couple of hours, but if it's a murder I'm going to have to call him. Let's see first, though. If it's a suicide, I can leave him in peace for a bit longer.'

Becky switched her attention from Jumbo to the scene in the tunnel, illuminated by dazzling arc lights as if they were about to shoot a movie. She took in the damp walls covered in some kind of green slime that could have been moss or algae – she didn't know which – but her eyes were drawn like magnets to the young woman sitting upright, her back pressed against the cold damp brickwork, her head lolling forward, long dark hair obscuring her features. Her legs were spread wide and straight, holding her in place, but she was fully dressed right down to a pair of ankle boots with chunky three-inch heels poking out from under her black jeans. She had no coat on, though, just a black and white patterned shirt.

Why did this girl have to die? On the face of it, it wasn't a sexually motivated crime, although it was a mistake to make assumptions. *Why kill her here and not tip the body into the water?* Becky knew that this stretch of canal had turned up more than its fair share of bodies in the recent past, so why hadn't this one been pushed in too? The chances of her being found would have been much lower. Perhaps the killer *wanted* her to be discovered.

Becky crouched down and inspected the area immediately around the body. There was no sign of a handbag or purse of any kind.

'Did you check her pockets for any ID, Jumbo?'

'As far as I could without disturbing her. I couldn't find anything, but there may be something in the back pocket of her jeans; we'll check as soon as we can move her.'

'I know it's not your job, but any idea how long she's been dead?'

'From experience I would guess at least ten to twelve hours, but don't quote me on that until the doc's done his stuff. She was found at five this morning by a jogger, poor bugger.'

Becky crouched down in front of the dead woman. She couldn't see her face, but she could see from the long slender legs that she was tall with a slim build. Her geometrically patterned shirt was buttoned to the top, and her clothing didn't appear to have been disturbed.

'She couldn't have been here all that time, though, could she? While I don't see why anybody in their right mind would walk through this tunnel in the dark, we know people do. So I don't see how she can have been here since six o'clock last night without being found before now, do you?'

'No. I think she was brought here and dumped. The ground's quite soft along here, and I've had a preliminary look. There's lots more work to be done, but at first glance I can't see any sign that those heels have been anywhere near the mud.'

'I'd better phone Tom, I suppose. Not much chance this is a suicide, is there?'

Jumbo knelt on one of the plates and Becky heard his knees creak. He was a heavy man to be doing all this crawling around, but she wouldn't be without him now.

'None at all,' he said as he lifted the hair slightly from the side of the girl's face.

Becky saw it straight away. A dark red line around her neck. She'd been strangled.

As Jumbo dropped her hair, a gust of wind lifted some strands from around the girl's mouth, and Becky got a glimpse of dark red lipstick. Suddenly her stomach felt as if it had been hollowed out and she thought she was going to vomit.

'Becky? What is it, kid? You've seen worse than this.'

Becky swallowed hard. 'Do you think you could lift her hair off her face for me? I need to see her properly.'

'Do you *know* her?'

'I don't know. I hope not.' She silently offered up a prayer.

Jumbo put one massive arm around Becky and signalled one of his team to help, quietly giving instructions. The technician knelt down on the other side of Jumbo and with one hand lifted the hair away from her face, raising the chin slightly with his other hand so the girl's features could be seen.

Becky stared at a face she had never seen in the flesh before, but one she hadn't been able to resist checking out on social media. She could feel Jumbo's eyes on her but couldn't speak. The seconds ticked by, and still she felt unable to move or respond to Jumbo's unspoken question. All she could think about was Tom.

Finally Jumbo nodded to the technician, who settled the girl back in position and let her hair drop forward. 'Come on, Becky – let's get you out of here.'

Dazed, Becky allowed herself to be led carefully to the mouth of the tunnel, not letting go of Jumbo for a moment until they emerged into the cold harsh light of the winter morning.

'Who is it, Becky?'

She didn't want to say the words out loud. That would make it real, and she felt a sudden urge to rush back into the tunnel and shine her torch into the young woman's face again and see a different set of features. Maybe she had imagined it because of the phone call yesterday.

But she hadn't.

'I'm pretty sure it's Leonora Harris.'

She heard an intake of breath from Jumbo. 'What, Tom's ex?'

Becky stared into the distance at nothing in particular, wishing she was anywhere else but here.

'Tom had a call last night from Leo's brother-in-law to say she was missing,' Becky said quietly. She raised her eyes to Jumbo's and saw the sympathy in his gaze. He knew what she was thinking. *How the hell am I going to tell Tom?*

10

What am I going to tell the children? The thought hit Maggie as the sky outside the open bedroom curtains lightened. Morning was here – a morning without Duncan. How could she know what to say when she didn't know what to think? She felt sick with the fear that she had lost him.

On any other Thursday Maggie would have been up by now, showered and dressed in a smart suit with every hair in place, mentally preparing for the day ahead as Duncan saw to the children's breakfasts and smiled at her over his second cup of coffee. This morning, as she lay in bed, Josh snuggled against her side, it felt more like a Saturday, and she could almost believe that any minute now Duncan would appear with a cup of tea for her, telling Josh to budge over as he climbed back into bed, pretending to squash the boy against his mummy, waiting until Lily – who had always been such a brilliant sleeper – heard them. She would come racing in, full of early-morning giggles.

But Josh hadn't crept in first thing in the morning while his daddy was downstairs; he had crept in hours ago in the middle of the night, and she had quietly held him tight while he trembled and tried not to cry, her own tears falling silently onto the pillow above his head. Josh knew something was wrong, and whatever she said, he still seemed convinced that it was his fault.

Until her son appeared, Maggie hadn't even considered going to bed; the sheets would feel cold and empty without Duncan by her side. But Josh needed some sense of normality, so she had climbed under the duvet with him and had lain awake all night, the curtains open, hoping and praying that beams from a pair of headlights bouncing off the walls of her room would signal the return of her husband.

Who was the girl in the picture? Duncan had to be having an affair. The thought pierced Maggie, and she bit her lip to stop herself from sobbing out loud. The only thing that made any sense was that the woman in the photo must have sent it to him – to entice him away. Perhaps she had begged him to go to her.

Who *was* she? Duncan had been quiet for a couple of weeks, but Maggie hadn't pushed him. She knew how he hated to be analysed, so she had let him be, trying to be extra loving towards him.

She glanced at the clock. It was after eight now, and still no word. She had stopped trying his mobile. It was a waste of time.

Maggie decided to let Josh sleep as long as possible and use the time to try to pull her thoughts together, to think through every small thing she knew about Duncan and try to work out what could have made him leave without a word of goodbye to her.

They had met at a friend's party. Duncan had been twenty-two and Maggie almost two years older, but she had instantly felt a strong attraction to him physically, and he was so charming and thoughtful.

He wasn't especially tall at about five foot ten, nor was he ripped with muscles. But he had shoulders that she felt she could rest her head on, regular features and an air of vulnerability that intrigued her. He treated her with respect, and after her previous relationship that alone was a bonus. The fact that he had nursed his mother through the last years of cancer spoke volumes about his character, and Maggie had always wondered if he regretted giving up his degree course.

'I don't mind being a plumber,' he had said. 'I'm my own boss. I can work or not work, as I please.'

She had no argument with that, and in those early days when

he had bombarded her with gifts of flowers, chocolates and bottles of her favourite wine she thought she was the luckiest girl alive. Sadly, Suzy hadn't seen it in the same way. The two sisters had always been close, but after the death of their father and their mother's second marriage and relocation to New Zealand, they had depended on each other for support. Suzy had initially been unsure of Duncan.

'Why is he love-bombing you?' she had asked. 'It's not normal.'

Suzy's doubts about Duncan had made Maggie less inclined to confide in her during the occasional periods when Duncan was more withdrawn. But those times never lasted long, and Maggie had learned to be patient and wait for him to get back to normal. She was certain he was thinking of his mother and how much he missed her.

As Maggie shifted a pillow into a more comfortable position she felt Josh move against her. He was starting to wake up, and she gently stroked his hair, knowing this would settle him just as it had always settled his daddy. There was no need for him to wake up to his unhappiness. She hoped he would sleep for a little longer. He wouldn't be going to school today; the snow had settled thickly and driving was impossible.

But lying here going round and round in circles wasn't doing Maggie any good. Her stomach was knotted with stress, and she had to move – to do something, anything, to release the tension gripping her.

Gently extracting her hand from underneath Josh's head, she slid from the bed. She grabbed a fleece from a drawer, pulled it on over her pyjamas and made her way quietly downstairs.

Why? she wanted to scream. They had been a happy couple – or at least that's what she had believed – until yesterday. Where was he? What had she done wrong? Why had he stopped loving her? What had happened between her leaving the house that morning and Duncan walking out? He had actually been in the process of making the children's tea so surely that meant it couldn't have been planned? Had he just snapped?

Whatever questions she asked herself, she had no answers.

She tried to think through everything Josh had told her, to see if there was a clue. Duncan had read the message and seen the photo that Josh thought was his mummy. Then he had gone out to the garage, and it seemed he had emptied his private cupboard.

Maggie dashed into the garage, desperate to see if she had missed anything. It all looked exactly as it had the night before. The only difference this morning was the bright white light of a snowy landscape creeping in through the side windows, lighting up the empty shelves of the cupboard. It would have been dark when Duncan left the night before, with only the overhead bulb of the garage to reveal the contents. Perhaps he had missed something.

Maggie crouched down and peered inside.

Nothing.

The green metal cupboard was worktop high, and she could see one empty shelf. She bent low and pushed her hands to the back of the space below the shelf, a place even the pale light from the window couldn't illuminate. But there was nothing. The cupboard was well and truly empty.

As she withdrew her hand she felt a sharp pain. Pulling her arm free, she saw a thin trickle of blood on the back of her hand and felt inside the cupboard to see what had scratched her. If it was rusty, she might need a tetanus jab. All she could feel was some jagged metal where the shelf had been damaged underneath. But something was attached to the metal, and she gently drew it off.

It was a piece of paper, and Maggie nearly cried with disappointment when she saw it. Clearly the header of a page from some newspaper or other, all it gave was the date; there was no other indication of why he might have kept it. She couldn't even see which newspaper it was as only some black marks – the tips of a few letters from the masthead – were showing. They meant nothing.

16th November, 2003.

It was the only thing she could read. There was nothing else at all. It was no use to her. It might not even be Duncan's, or it might have been wrapped around something. She would probably never know.

One thing she did know, though. She was going to have to call the office and let them know she wasn't going to be in today. She wouldn't be popular. Some other poor devil would have to take over the interviews with Alf Horton. But it couldn't be helped. She couldn't get the car out of the drive for the snow, and she needed to be here in case Duncan came home. No. *When* Duncan came home.

11

The phone was answered on the second ring. Becky had been hoping for more time to gear herself up for what lay ahead, but she should have known Philippa Stanley would pick up immediately. She probably had a rule that no phone should ring more than three times.

'Detective Superintendent Stanley speaking.'

'Ma'am, it's Becky Robinson here. I'm sorry to disturb you, but we've got a situation and I need your guidance.'

'Can DCI Douglas not help?'

'Sorry, ma'am, but he's part of the problem.'

She shouldn't have said it like that. Why did this woman always make Becky talk gibberish?

'I mean, I don't know whether I should be talking to him about this or not.' Becky heard her own voice wobble slightly.

'I suggest you tell me, and then we'll work it out together, shall we?' Philippa's brisk tones made it sound more like a threat than a promise of assistance.

'I was called out this morning to attend a suspicious death. Jumbo – I mean Dr Osoba – is here with me. The body is that of a young woman in her mid-thirties.' Becky could almost hear Philippa tapping her fingers on the desk, wondering when she was going to get to the point, but to give her credit she remained silent, waiting for Becky to finish.

'The thing is, ma'am, I think the girl is somebody DCI Douglas knows. So I don't think he should come here, and I don't know if I should tell him who I believe it is.'

'Well, we should definitely prevent him from attending the scene, and he'll understand that. I'll have a word with him and apprise him of the situation. He'll probably call you to ask for more details – is that okay with you?'

Becky held her breath for a second before letting it out slowly, shakily.

'The thing is, I think it's his ex-girlfriend. They were close once, and I don't know how he'll take it.'

There was a moment's silence at the other end of the phone.

'Ah. That's not going to be easy, is it? Have you met this woman, DI Robinson?'

'No, ma'am. But I was in DCI Douglas's office yesterday when the woman's brother-in-law called to say she was missing.'

'Just because you know somebody's missing and a dead woman of the right age turns up, you shouldn't jump to conclusions. Why have you made this assumption if you never met his ex-girlfriend?'

'I've seen a photo of her. I've seen several, in fact.'

There was a moment's hesitation on the other end of the line.

'Okay. I suggest you leave it with me, Becky. I'll tell Tom.' Sometimes the uber-efficient Superintendent Stanley surprised Becky. Tom always said there was a pussycat lurking beneath the tiger stripes, and Becky was relieved not to have to be the one to break the terrible news.

'Thank you, ma'am.'

'Give me her name so I can be straight with him, and we'll take it from there. I'm assuming this is murder?'

'We think so. Her name is Leonora Harris.'

'In that case, I'll come out myself as acting SIO. Would you rather be removed from the case if I assign it to a different team?'

'No, not at all. If it *is* Leo I'd want to help arrest whoever did this to her.'

'I'll be with you shortly. You know what to do.' Philippa Stanley was back to business again and Becky was glad of it. She felt herself stand up straight, ready to do what had to be done.

'Yes, ma'am.'

The line went dead, and Becky began to breathe again.

❖

The shower felt good, and Tom stayed under the pounding torrent for a good five minutes longer than usual. He tipped his head forward, enjoying the pummelling of the pulsating jet on his head and shoulders, clearing his mind of everything but the pleasurable sensation of hot water hitting his body. He had just grabbed the soap and started to rub it up his arms and across his chest when through the open door of his en-suite bathroom he heard the telephone ringing in his bedroom. For once he decided to ignore it. By the time he got there the answerphone would have picked up, so whoever was calling could leave a message. He would get back to them as soon as he was dry.

Tom had had a restless night, wondering where Leo could be. He had spoken to Max to let him know he had been to the apartment, but there was nothing he could say to put Max and Ellie's minds at rest. He hadn't known whether to mention the fact that Leo's clothes were scattered around the bedroom, but he couldn't see what would be gained. It would only add an extra layer of worry, and he didn't have any rational explanation at the moment, so he kept it to himself. Nevertheless, he was cross with Leo. Sometimes he could kill her for her lack of consideration.

He had finally got out of bed at about 5.30, knowing he wasn't going back to sleep, and made himself a proper breakfast for once – bacon, scrambled eggs, grilled tomatoes and mushrooms – and he had felt better for it. He was still going to be early for work, but he should miss the morning rush hour, and that would save him about twenty minutes of sitting in traffic.

He switched off the shower and shook the water from his body.

'Bugger,' he muttered as he heard the phone ring again. He

grabbed a towel and dripped his way from the bathroom to his bedside table, leaving wet footprints in the pale cream carpet.

'Tom Douglas.'

'Tom, it's Philippa.'

Tom perched on the edge of the bed, clutching his towel around him with one hand, his phone in the other, as he listened to Philippa explaining that Becky had been called out that morning to a suspicious death. Never one to mince her words, Philippa got straight to the point.

'I'm sorry, Tom, but I'm afraid it's Becky's opinion that the body is that of Leonora Harris.'

Tom drew in a lung full of air as he heard Leo's name. It couldn't be true, surely? He closed his eyes and saw her face, her hair, her body. He heard her laugh, felt her arms reach towards him. Not Leo. Please, not Leo.

'Tom?'

'Sorry, Philippa. Is she *certain*?' Tom let go of the towel and held the phone in both hands, for a moment scared he would drop it.

'She says this woman is missing. Is that right?'

'Nobody's heard from her in a while, but I think *missing's* a bit strong.' That was exactly what he had thought himself the night before, but now more than anything, he wanted to rationalise this – to convince himself she wasn't missing at all. 'Leo's very independent – she could be anywhere. Why does Becky think it's her?'

'She says she's seen photos.'

'Well I don't know where. I never had one in the office.'

'Don't be naïve, Tom. Becky's a resourceful girl.'

Christ, not Leo. She couldn't be dead. Tom felt a rush of guilt, as if he should have kept her safe. Maybe if he hadn't ended things all those months ago she wouldn't have been vulnerable to something like this. He would have known where she was – would have been able to protect her. Maybe having nobody in her life had put her at risk. *No. It can't be right. Surely Becky's wrong?*

'Was there any identification on the body?' Tom could hear the unsteadiness in his own voice and coughed quietly.

'None that they've found up to now. When I've seen the body we'll get her moved and search through all her clothes, but as yet there's nothing.'

'I need to see her, Philippa, before you do anything. I don't want to alert her sister until we're sure it's her, and I want to say goodbye.'

He should have known better. Philippa played by the book.

'You know that's not possible, Tom. You know we can't risk your DNA getting onto her body. I'm in the car now on my way to the scene. My driver says we're two minutes away, then we'll get her shifted to the mortuary. A forensic pathologist is on his way so we'll be as quick as we can with the PM. Then, if you still want to, you can make a preliminary identification. Are you okay?'

'Fine,' Tom said. 'I'm fine.' He hung up without saying anything more.

Placing the phone gently back on the bedside table, he rested his hands, arms straight, on the bed by his side, clutching the now-damp duvet cover tightly in clenched fists. He glanced over his shoulder at the pillows and for a moment saw Leo's face there, smiling at him as he dressed in the morning or gazing at him as he undressed to join her in bed. He remembered the way her feet always poked out from under the covers because she couldn't stand to be too hot, and how she had wrapped her long limbs around him each morning. At that moment he wanted nothing more than to stretch his naked body along the length of hers and hold her, safe and secure.

She couldn't be dead. There was too much *of* her, somehow, to have been wiped out – so many complex layers, some of which had ultimately resulted in the end of their relationship, but others so sweet and vulnerable that he had never lost the desire to keep her safe. And he had failed.

The fact that he no longer loved her didn't for a second reduce the pain. If anything it intensified it because his sense of loss was merged with the ache of regret and with pangs of conscience for the hurt he had caused her.

He dropped his head and took several deep breaths. He was no good to anybody if he couldn't get some control back. His whole body was prickling, and he realised that he was covered from head to toe in goosebumps – whether from the shock or the cold he had no idea. He pushed himself off the bed and pulled open a drawer. The best thing he could do for Leo now was ignore the ache inside and find out who had killed her. It was time to get dressed and face whatever the day was going to bring.

12

Concentration was out of the question, and Tom stared blindly at the pile of papers in front of him. There was no point even pretending to work – the numbers on the spreadsheet just blurred into one incomprehensible mass. He wanted to speak to Becky and Jumbo, but he knew he had to wait for them to come to him.

He had asked to be kept up to date and had been told that the body was being moved. They had collected what evidence they could, but would of course continue to search once the body had gone from the scene. He shuddered at the thought of Leo being referred to as 'the body' and hated even more the concept of her being bundled into a body bag. Most of the time bodies were treated with respect, but there was the odd guy who thought that as the person was dead, there was no need to consider their dignity. Tom didn't agree. At the end of their lives, more than ever, people should be treated with consideration and thoughtfulness.

He wasn't going to be allowed near Leo's body in case he contaminated her with his own DNA – which would cause catastrophic complications for the case. Normally the PM was completed before identification for that very reason – any traces on the body from the smallest fragment of skin to a stray hair could convict a murderer. If people other than the investigating team came into contact with the body, it brought into question the validity of the findings. He wanted to see her though – he needed to be sure.

The wait seemed interminable, and there was nobody he could talk to. He hoped and prayed that Max wouldn't call him for an update.

Over an hour later there was a knock on his door, which for once he had closed. Becky poked her head into the room.

'Is it okay if I come in, Tom, or would you rather I left you on your own?' Her voice was shaking.

'No, no. Please, Becky, tell me what happened, or what you think happened, and why you're sure it's Leo. Come in. Sit down.'

Becky was biting her lip. Much as he wanted to fire questions at her, he needed to give her a moment. If she lost control, it would take him longer to get the facts.

'I'm so sorry, Tom. But I couldn't risk you turning up and seeing her like that.'

Her words made the weight in his chest feel even heavier.

'How bad was it? I need to know.' He stared at Becky and forced the words out. 'Had she been raped?'

Becky spoke softly, her words echoing in Tom's head as he visualised the scene that Becky described.

'We don't know. She was propped against the tunnel wall, fully clothed, but Jumbo is certain she wasn't killed there. She was wearing boots with heels and there was no mud on them – no sign that she had walked through that tunnel at all. Until they remove her clothes they're not going to know for sure if she was sexually assaulted. My guess is that it's unlikely. If she had been stripped and dressed again when he'd finished, he did a good job of it. Too good, really. Everything was buttoned correctly. She looked too tidy, if you know what I mean.'

Tom knew exactly what she meant. He had seen several bodies that had been redressed after a sexual assault, and they all looked wrong somehow, as if their clothes belonged to somebody else. He felt himself shudder. The only thing he could do was focus as if this were just another body.

'Did we manage to get a forensic pathologist quickly enough?' For a murder, they couldn't bring in any old pathologist. He or she had to be accredited by the Home Office, and sometimes that meant quite a wait, occasionally with the body remaining in situ.

'Yes, it's James Adams, and we know he's good and incredibly thorough. He'll work out what happened to her, Tom – and we'll catch him, whoever did this to her.'

'How do you think she died?'

Step by step, Becky ran through the morning's events, going over each point as often as Tom wanted her to. Philippa had opted to go to the post-mortem, and one of Becky's sergeants was setting up the incident room. Tom knew Becky could justify spending this much time with him because he knew Leo better than anybody, and he might well be the best person to provide a starting point for their investigation.

They were interrupted by the telephone, and Tom signalled Becky to answer it for him. He didn't want to speak to anybody right now. She listened for a second and handed the phone to Tom, mouthing, 'Philippa.'

'Tom, there's been a change of plan,' Philippa said. 'Can you get over to the mortuary right now, do you think?'

'Are you going to let me see her?' A mixture of hope and dread hit him in equal measure.

'I've spoken to the pathologist, and we're confident that when he's finished all the external examination and the body can no longer be compromised it would be safe for you to come and take a look.' Philippa's voice softened. 'I don't like the thought of you sitting there wondering and hoping, if I'm honest.' Sometimes Philippa surprised Tom, but he wasn't about to argue.

'I'm on my way,' he said, pushing back his chair. For the first time since his shower that morning Tom felt a sense of purpose.

❖

With all her heart Becky was hoping that she was wrong about Leo. But there was a small, unwelcome part of her brain that almost wanted to be right simply because she didn't want to discover she had put Tom through all this grief for nothing. That would be truly terrible. She quashed the thought the minute it sneaked into her consciousness.

She insisted on accompanying Tom to the mortuary. She couldn't let him go alone. He had started to stalk off across the car park to his old BMW, but Becky grabbed his arm.

'There's no way you're driving. Come on – I'll take you.'

For a moment she thought he was going to refuse. She knew he hated the way she drove, but surely for once he could forget that? And he wanted to get there quickly, didn't he?

They jumped into Becky's black Golf. She slammed it into reverse to get out of her parking spot, then pulled out onto the busy main road. It wasn't far to the mortuary, but the traffic in Manchester could be hell, and she wasn't sure which would be the best route. She turned her head to ask Tom, but closed her mouth and looked back at the road. If ever there was a face that said 'Please don't talk to me' it was Tom's. The tension was causing deep creases between his nose and the outer corners of his mouth, and the fine lines around his eyes were accentuated. She could see that every muscle in his face was rigid, and she glanced at his thighs to see one leg tap, tapping. She had never seen Tom like this, and more than ever she wished she hadn't been the first person on the scene.

They completed the journey in silence, and on arrival at the mortuary Tom was out of the car and walking at speed into the building almost before Becky had the key out of the ignition.

Philippa was waiting for them in reception and reached out a hand to clasp Tom's arm. He nodded his thanks and followed her down a long corridor, Becky keeping a few metres behind.

When they reached the final door, Philippa stopped.

'We've put her in the chapel, Tom. We haven't opened her up yet, but there are some marks on her neck that tell their own tale. We would obviously cover these for family, but I thought you could cope. If it's Leo, and you're certain, we'll crack on with the

PM and send someone straight off to break the news to her sister and brother-in-law.'

'I'll do that,' Tom said.

'Are you sure?'

'Absolutely. Nothing can reduce the pain, but at least when you get this kind of news from somebody you know it feels slightly less intrusive.'

'Okay. We need you suited up even though we've done the external examination.'

Tom reached down to a pile of plastic bags, each containing a clean white suit. He slipped one over his clothes. Becky and Philippa did the same.

'Are you ready?' Philippa asked, her voice quiet.

Tom nodded, and Becky felt a lurch in her gut. In a way she felt she had no right to witness Tom's grief, because she knew better than most how much he had suffered – silently, but without a doubt deeply – when he and Leo had split up. She didn't look at him. She focused on the room in front of her.

A woman lay on a table, her body covered in a white sheet. The contusions around her neck were obvious, but even in death this woman was beautiful. Her dark hair had been neatened and pulled back from her face.

As they entered the room, Becky heard a small gasp from Tom. He stood at the doorway staring, and she drew her eyes away from the body to look at him. After a second, his eyes narrowed and he started towards the body. He stood looking down at the lovely face, and for a moment it seemed as if he was going to reach out and touch her. Philippa made a move to get closer, clearly prepared to stop him before he did, but his arm dropped to his side and he just stared.

His head dropped, and Becky swallowed a sob but couldn't stop the tears streaming from her eyes. So intent was she on controlling herself that she almost missed his words.

'It's not her,' he said quietly.

'Sorry, Tom. Can you repeat that?' Philippa said.

'This woman looks very like Leonora Harris, but it's not her.'

Tom turned to face them both, his mouth smiling, but his eyes frowning, as if he didn't know what to feel.

'Oh God, Tom, I'm so sorry,' Becky burst out, tears now flowing freely down her cheeks. 'I was so certain. I even found her picture online and showed it to Jumbo, and he agreed. I don't know what to say to you.'

Tom closed his eyes for a moment and then turned to Becky.

'It's okay, Becky. You did the right thing. If I'd turned up at the scene, I'd probably have thought this girl was Leo too for a moment. It's an uncanny likeness, but there are lots of differences. The nose isn't right, and this girl's a bit broader in the shoulders than Leo. To me, now I'm looking properly, they look nothing like one another. But that's because I know Leo's face so well.'

'Is there anything more specific, Tom?' Philippa asked. 'It would be useful to have something more tangible than "not right".'

'Leo has a small scar on her chin from a childhood accident. I'd completely forgotten about it. I only noticed it now because it's not there – if that makes sense. I knew the moment I saw her, but if I'd had any doubts, the lack of the scar would have confirmed it.'

For a moment, the room was almost silent, the only sound an occasional sniff from Becky.

Then Philippa straightened her spine and turned to Tom. 'Right,' she said briskly. 'Let's get on then, shall we? She's all yours now, DCI Douglas. Let's find out who the poor woman is and discover what happened to her. Get an artist to do a picture wearing the shirt she was found in. It's very striking. I'd like a report by the end of the day, please.'

With that, she turned and marched purposefully out of the door, leaving behind her a room rocked by emotion. Tom looked dazed, and Becky could only imagine how he must have geared himself up for the pain of seeing somebody he cared about on that table. She felt an immense weight of guilt – she had caused this man so much distress and didn't know how to put it right. She stared at him, waiting to see his reaction.

Tom held out an arm. 'Come here, Becky,' he said. 'I think we both need a hug.'

He gently pulled her towards him and held her close. She buried her head in his shoulder, slowly putting her arms around his waist, gradually tightening them to try to stop the shaking.

13

The snow provided Maggie with a perfectly valid reason for not going to work, and she was relieved that it hadn't been necessary to invent some lame excuse. She certainly didn't want to tell her colleagues what had *really* happened.

She almost fooled herself into believing that Duncan's absence was down to the weather too – that he had gone out to deal with some emergency or other and hadn't been able to get back. Perhaps his phone was dead so he couldn't call her.

Telling herself this was realistic and an obvious answer, she had used the time before the children woke up to phone around the hospitals and check if there had been any accidents. There had been plenty of bumps because of the snow, but Duncan hadn't been involved in any of them. She had asked a friend in the police to break a few rules and see whether Duncan had perhaps been arrested for driving without due care and attention, or maybe he had been drinking and tried to drive home. But there was nothing.

Maggie knew there was no point in reporting him missing. She could recite the questions she would be asked verbatim, and she would have to admit that he had left of his own volition, that he wasn't a vulnerable adult and that he had been carrying a bag of clothes – so he might not be at home, but he could never be defined as a missing person.

The certainty that he had left her for another woman punched her once more in the gut. How long had it been going on? Did he love this woman, or was it a fling? Why choose somebody who looked just like her – wasn't she enough for him? Once again hot tears stung her eyes and she fought off the ache of loss, trying to convince herself that he would be back, that he would have a perfectly valid excuse. Try as she might, though, it was a hard sell even to herself.

She had nothing to tell the children – no answers to give them. She didn't like lying to them, but she didn't want them to be upset so she said she had had a call from Daddy while they were asleep. If he had left them for good, she would have to find a way of explaining that to them, but for now she needed them – particularly Josh – to stop worrying.

'Daddy said he was fine, but he'd had to rush out to help an old friend – where we used to live. He said to give you both a big kiss from him.'

'He left us on our own. He's not supposed to do that, is he?' Josh wasn't going to be diverted so easily, now he'd had time to think about it.

She ruffled his dark curls as if everything was all perfectly normal. 'He was worried about the weather, sweetheart. He knew if he didn't go straight away, he would be stuck in the snow.' Her story seemed to calm the children down, and the snow provided another useful distraction. Both of them were now outside in the back garden building a snowman.

She had time to think.

She had nothing to go on, though, no starting point. All she had was Josh's story of a photo on Duncan's phone and a scrap of newspaper. She had tried to work out what the tops of the letters told her, but they were just black marks. She pulled her laptop towards her and typed 'British newspaper masthead' into a search engine and selected 'Images'.

Even if she found the paper and the date, what would it tell her? It could be any story. And he might just have had some tool or other wrapped up in the paper. It was hopeless. She pushed the laptop away from her, sick of clutching at straws. He had left her.

That's all there was to it. But more than anything in the world, she wanted to know *why*.

Maggie had never had the slightest inkling that Duncan was interested in anybody else, and she knew all the signs – she remembered them from when Suzy's partner, Ian, had been having an affair that ultimately resulted in him leaving her sister and their children. When you knew what to look for, it was obvious: the name introduced into the conversation with unnecessary frequency; the phone calls taken in the locked bathroom; the trips to the gym to 'tone up'; the nights he was 'out with the boys' wearing his best clothes and aftershave; the fact that he would never leave his mobile unattended in the room.

Duncan hadn't behaved like that. But then he had always said that his job as a plumber gave him freedom. She didn't know what he did all day and she never questioned his earnings. He had always put whatever he could afford into the joint account.

Fighting hard to keep control, Maggie got up from the table. She needed to make some lunch for the children, although raising the necessary enthusiasm was going to be difficult. Her mind miles away, she grabbed a pan and was filling it with water when the phone rang, jolting her back to reality.

'Oh crap!' she shouted as she dropped the full pan on the floor, soaking the bottom of her jeans and her bare feet. Scared of slipping on the wet tiles, but equally terrified of missing the call, she slid across the floor to the phone.

'*Duncan?*' she said. 'Oh, thank God. Are you okay?'

'Maggie? I thought you were going to phone me back. What the hell's going on?'

'Oh shit, it's you. Sorry, Suze. I should have called you, but I've got a bit of a situation here, and I need to keep the line free.'

'What's the matter? What's happened to Duncan?'

For some reason, she couldn't tell Suzy. Not yet. It would make it real; she would cry again; the children would see her. She made every excuse she could to herself, but deep down she knew that she couldn't at this minute tell anybody – even Suzy – that her husband had left her without saying goodbye.

'I'm sorry, Suzy, but I can't talk now. We've got thick snow, and both the children are at home, so now isn't a good time.'

'But what about last night? Why were the kids alone?'

'Please, sis, don't ask me to explain right now. I promise I'll call you tonight when the children are in bed. If you don't hear from me, everything's okay. I've got to go – Lily's shouting.'

Lily was in fact about to open the back door. She didn't know how to enter a room quietly, and Maggie knew she would notice the tears running down her mummy's face, and shout it out for Suzy to hear.

Maggie disconnected before her sister could say another word, and quickly scraped the sleeve of her jumper across her eyes.

'Was that Daddy?' Lily said, skipping across the kitchen floor in her socks, having discarded her wellies at the door. Maggie was excused the need to reply as Lily shouted, 'Ooh, the floor's all wet. Oh yuk, Mummy. I've got soggy feet.'

The phone rang again. It was bound to be her sister with some more questions. Maggie was about to ignore it, but Lily was heading towards it with great glee. She loved answering the phone, but Maggie didn't want Suzy questioning her niece so she grabbed the phone.

'Look, Suze, I promise I'll call you back if I need you. Please, can we keep the line free?'

There was a silence at the other end, and for a moment it felt as if ice was blowing down the wire. Maggie shivered.

'Hello, Maggie,' a voice said. It was a voice that she didn't recognise, but the tone was oily, slick. 'I'd like to speak to your husband. Get him for me, would you?'

'May I ask who's speaking?' she answered, hearing a slight tremor in her voice.

'No, you may not. Is he there?'

'I'm sorry, he isn't. Can I take a message?'

'He's not answering his mobile, and that's not good enough,' the man said, his words clipped. There was an undercurrent to the voice that she had heard so many times in the voices of her clients. It was the sound of threat.

'Well, maybe I can ask him to call you,' she said, trying to pretend that this was all perfectly normal.

'He's not coming home, though, is he, Maggie? He's run – run from his obligations. Again.'

Maggie didn't respond. She didn't know what the man was talking about, and she stared down at Lily, her gaze fixed, her heart pounding. She was waiting. For what, she didn't know, but she knew it wasn't good.

'I'm glad I've found you, Maggie. It makes it all so much more worthwhile. Your husband has had his first warning. If he calls, remind him of that, and be sure to tell him we know where you live. Do you understand? We know where you live. Tell him.'

The phone went dead.

14

It was minutes since the call had ended, but Maggie was still holding the phone, looking at it as if the answer lay there. What did the man mean?

He had said, 'I'm glad I found you.' Did that mean he had found *her*? Or found *them*? Or did he mean he had found *Duncan*?

'If he calls...' he had said.

What did he mean about running away from his obligations – again? Did the man mean Duncan had run away from her? Was she – or his family – an obligation?

Finally, Maggie slowly replaced the receiver, and without conscious thought made her way across to a chair and sat down heavily, her eyes unfocused.

She was vaguely aware that Lily had been saying something, but the little girl had obviously given up on her mummy and gone back outside because the kitchen was now quiet. Quiet enough for her to think.

She grabbed a piece of paper and a pencil and wrote down what she remembered of his words. The words themselves seemed fairly innocuous. They could almost have been the words of a disgruntled customer. But it wasn't the words that had made the hairs on the back of her neck stand on end; it had been the tone of his voice.

There was no doubt at all in Maggie's head that this was a threat, and she sprang to her feet, rushed to the back door and called the children into the house. She didn't want them out of her sight for a moment.

The children didn't understand why they couldn't stay in the garden, but she silenced them by saying Josh could download a new game for his console and plug it into the TV in the study and Lily could watch *Frozen* for about the fiftieth time in the sitting room after lunch. Bolting all the doors, including the one from the garage into the house, her mind spun through all the different options.

What had Duncan done?

From nowhere, an answer hit her. If Duncan had run off with another woman, it must have been the woman's husband on the phone. And he was after Duncan. It was the only thing that made sense.

And yet somehow it didn't.

What else could it be? A debt that he hadn't paid, maybe? She had known of some dreadful crimes committed against people who owed money. But surely he would have told her? They had some savings – money for the renovation of their house – they could have used.

She could develop any theory she wanted, but the truth was she didn't *know*, and the uncertainty was unbearable. She could face the truth, she was sure – if only she knew what the truth *was*.

Maggie picked up the phone and dialled.

'Suzy,' she said when her sister answered, 'I need to talk to you. I'm sorry about earlier, but I didn't think I could speak right then – not even to you. I've come unstuck, though, and—' Maggie's voice broke '—I don't know what to do.'

'Hey, don't cry, Mags. Tell me. Let's see if there's something I can do to help.'

'It's Duncan. I think something might have happened to him.'

'What sort of thing? Is it something to do with last night?'

Maggie took some deep breaths and tried to control herself. 'I don't know where he is.'

Somehow Maggie managed to stumble through most of the story of the last few hours.

'He's having an affair. I know he is.'

'That's a bit of a leap, Mags,' Suzy said.

Maggie was about to tell her sister about the photo on Duncan's phone and the threatening call, but the sound of her mobile ringing in the next room set her pulse racing.

Duncan. It had to be.

She quickly ended the call with Suzy, promising to call her over the weekend and dashed into the hall. As she got there, the ringing stopped.

'*Shit!*'

She grabbed the phone and stared at it as if by some magic it would ring again. The screen said number withheld. She wanted to throw the phone at the wall. It had to have been Duncan, and she had missed him.

She sat down heavily on the bottom step of the stairs, rested her folded arms on her knees and dropped her head.

15

12 years ago – May 15th

The television news was showing photos of dark-haired beauty Penelope Cruz arriving at the Cannes Film Festival, and Tamsin Grainger stared at the screen hoping to catch a glimpse of the actress's current boyfriend, Tom Cruise. She was out of luck.

With one eye on the television and one on the mirror, she continued to apply her make-up, going a bit heavier on the eyes than usual.

Tonight was going to be the party of the year. Tamsin could feel it, and she wanted to look her best. Especially now she had rid herself of that wanker who seemed to think he was the love of her life. What a prick he had turned out to be. A good-looking prick, though, she had to admit.

She had never said they had an exclusive thing going – she was having fun, and nothing was going to interfere with that. Maybe messing about with that lecturer had been a bit stupid, but at least it might get her some good marks in her next exam.

Tamsin giggled. Of course, the word had got out that she was up for a good time, and she was getting more than her fair share of offers now. Some crazy guy was leaving her email messages saying what he wanted to do to her. She liked his inventiveness and hadn't discouraged him.

She didn't know how he knew her webmail account – hardly anybody did, but somehow he had found it. She didn't understand technology that well, but she knew enough to realise she wouldn't want some of her more juicy messages to come back to haunt her in a few years' time when she was a respectable woman married to some rich man who knew nothing about her past. So she deleted every single one of his messages from the university terminals she was forced to use because her dad was too tight to buy her a laptop.

Tonight the email guy said he was going to reveal himself to her. She didn't know exactly what he meant, but it sounded good. All she knew about him was that – in his words – he was a big man. She wasn't sure what that related to either – tall, fat, or something else entirely. She giggled again.

She was dressed for the occasion in a crop top and some tight white jeans. The trouble was, how was she going to know it was him?

The party was in full swing when she arrived, so she headed straight for the centre of the room where she could be easily spotted and started to dance. She didn't want him to leave because he couldn't find her.

Tamsin looked around to see who was watching. The truth was, a lot of guys were looking at her. Girls too, but not in the same way. She didn't care. She didn't much like girls anyway.

As the night wore on, she began to think he wasn't coming. She didn't even know his name. Her dancing grew increasingly frenzied as she became more and more desperate.

And then she saw him. It had to be him. Tall, blond, and way too refined for this party in his smart white shirt with a button-down collar. Gorgeous, though.

She threw him a smile and then spun round to dance with her back to him. Make him work for his treat. She felt a hand on her hip. She didn't turn but backed up slightly so she could feel the warmth of his body through her thin top.

She felt his breath on the side of her neck and shuddered. He smelled good.

'Tamsin,' the man said, 'there's somebody waiting for you. He's outside.'

She turned then and looked at the man in front of her.

'It's not you?' she said, disappointment clear in her voice.

'No, no,' he said. 'He's outside, waiting for you. Hurry now. He won't wait forever. His name's Sam.'

16

Tom was grateful that the pathologist had agreed to wait ten minutes to give him time to knock back two cups of strong black coffee, although whisky would have been better. He wasn't looking forward to the next hour or so, but finally he was ready to go and watch this woman who looked so like Leo being cut open, all of her internal organs removed, weighed and examined. It wasn't going to be easy. He knew it wasn't Leo – and he kept saying that over and over to himself – but she was so much like her that he had to cast his gaze back repeatedly to where that tiny scar should have been and focus on the differences between the two faces.

There was little doubt about the manner of this woman's death. They still had no idea who she was, though, and the artist was waiting to draw her so an appeal could be launched on the TV and in the press. Somebody, somewhere, was bound to be missing this young woman.

The pathologist turned to Tom and spoke through his mask.

'We cleaned the body externally before you were allowed to see her, as you know. I would say it's unlikely that she's been raped. There's no external bruising, but of course I'll need to do a full internal examination to be sure. Before we do any more work on her, there's something I'd like to show you.' He beckoned Tom closer. 'I don't know if it's significant, but these marks were made after she was killed.'

The pathologist asked one of his assistants to move to one side, and Tom saw the long, lean, naked legs of the woman. She was obviously fairly fit, and from the colour of the skin of her thighs it would appear she had recently had some winter sun. But it wasn't the skin or muscle the pathologist was keen for Tom to see. Carved into the top of the woman's left thigh were three straight horizontal lines about four inches long. They were deep, and yet there was no blood.

'I've no idea what they mean, Tom, but it would seem that her jeans were pulled down after her death solely for the purpose of carving these lines. Her jeans were then refastened. As I say, there's no sign of sexual trauma up to now, but these marks were definitely made after she was killed. It's as if they're a message of some kind. Do they mean anything to you?'

Tom was only half listening. He was in a different time, a different place, looking at the same three lines carved into a young girl's thigh, and not for the first time.

12 years ago – May 17th

The nine days since the discovery of Sonia Beecham's body at Pomona Island had been both intense and frustrating. Progress was negligible, and Tom couldn't help feeling they were missing something. But Victor Elliott had his way of doing things, and he was not impressed by anyone in his team using their initiative if it in any way reflected badly on him.

Tom had been hoping that tonight might be the first night since Sonia's murder that he would be able to get away on time, and if the call had come in fifteen minutes later, this latest shout would have been somebody else's responsibility. He was torn between the familiar buzz of a new job and the realisation that it was going to be another late night. Once again he was going to have to phone his wife and make his apologies.

Right now, though, there was nothing he could do about it, so he parked his car and headed towards a uniformed policeman standing in front of a temporary-looking corrugated iron fence. The young PC nodded at Tom and slid back a section of the fence to let him through

85

into one of the hidden parts of Manchester that few people knew existed.

The disused section of Piccadilly railway station known as Mayfield station was a favourite location for television crews. Where else could companies find a ready made set for post-war dramas? Tom climbed the wide staircase that rose from street level to the platforms. He glanced at the massive Edwardian buffer stops terminating tracks that had long since been removed, leaving deep pits full of weeds and detritus. The original glass sections of the roof were mostly gone, lying in pieces that had either fallen or been kicked onto the sunken track beds, and Tom and the rookie detective constable who had been waiting for him to arrive picked their way carefully along the abandoned platform, trying to avoid the broken glass and the worst of the drips coming from what was left of the roof. A pigeon flapped its wings suddenly, making the young female detective nearly jump out of her skin.

'Bloody horrible place,' she whispered as if scared of waking the living dead. 'Why's it still here? It's the obvious place for every down and out in Manchester to hang out.'

'I think you'll find there are better places once you get to know the area,' Tom said. 'Watch out for the rats, though.'

'What?' The young detective looked momentarily embarrassed, as if it was inappropriate for her to be scared of anything. She was one of the chosen few on the fast-track scheme and was working for a brief period in CID.

He smiled sympathetically at her. He wasn't a big fan of rats himself, but the only time he had been here before today something had spooked the rat population, and thousands of them had come pouring out of holes everywhere in the station, leaping up from the sunken track beds and charging towards the staircase and escape. The rats hadn't bothered the humans in their midst; they had swarmed around them like a dark grey sea flowing past a rocky outcrop. He shuddered as he remembered.

'They'll keep out of our way. Don't wander off on your own if you don't like them.'

Tom knew little about this case as yet – just that they had a body, it was female and it was almost certainly murder. His second in ten days. First Sonia Beecham and now this. They hadn't been able to find one piece of evidence that pointed to Sonia's killer. She had, so it seemed, been a quiet, unassuming girl who took her studies seriously. She hadn't been in a relationship either at the time of her death or for at least six months previously, and nobody could think of a single reason why anybody would want her dead.

Tom's boss, DCI Victor Elliott, would be on his way to Mayfield station by now and would technically be the senior investigating officer on this case. He wouldn't do any of the hard work, of course. He spent too much time trying to impress the powers that be, striving towards his goal of becoming chief constable before he was fifty.

Tom pulled on a protective suit and mask, lifted the flap of the tent erected by the SOCO crew to protect the body and crouched low to step into the confined space. The victim was propped against the red-brick wall, her arms folded across her chest. A SOCO was kneeling to one side, bending over her. The victim appeared to be fully dressed, although that wasn't saying much. It was still only May, but she was in tight white jeans and a crop top. Had she been out in Manchester dressed like this, or had she been plucked from her home and brought here after she was killed? Tom felt certain that the body had been positioned after death.

As he bent closer, he noticed something on her left leg, the leg that was further away from him. Tom asked the man in his white Tyvek suit if he would move to one side so he could get a better angle, and he bent over the girl's thigh. Her jeans had been cut, and Tom pulled back the flap. Etched into the skin were three horizontal parallel lines.

'Carl,' Tom said to the head of the SOCO team, 'have you seen the leg?'

Tom couldn't see the man's expression because of his mask, but he saw him nod. His voice was muffled.

'Just like the last one. The first one had her throat slit, though, and this one's been strangled. No blood anywhere.'

Tom knew they hadn't released any information about the three cuts to the press, so it couldn't be a copycat killing, but to go from a slit throat to strangulation didn't fit either. Could these be some kind of cult killings?

Carl pulled his torch away slightly so that it illuminated the girl's head, rather than the area he had been inspecting.

'The three cuts aren't the only odd thing, Tom. Have you looked at her face?'

Tom shuffled round to where the technician had been kneeling a few moments before. He stared at the face, brightly lit by the white torchlight, then glanced up at Carl's worried eyes, then back at the face. He didn't say a word.

He left the tent and walked about ten metres away, pulling the mask from his face. He stared away from the station into the city of Manchester beyond, seeing nothing. He heard steps behind him and a rustle of Tyvek.

'What do you think?' Carl said.

Tom shook his head slowly from side to side.

'If I didn't know it was impossible, I would say the same girl had been killed twice.'

17

The rest of the day had dragged for Maggie. She knew she should be doing something, but she didn't know what. She felt helpless, and alone. In the end she sat with Lily for a while mindlessly watching her daughter's favourite film, her silent phone on the sofa beside her. She had left the room for just a moment to get the charger from her bedroom when she heard the unmistakable ringtone of her mobile.

She turned and flew down the stairs, but she hadn't allowed for Lily.

'Hello. Lily speaking,' she heard a high-pitched voice say. 'Yes, she's here. I'll get her for you, if you want,' Lily added, turning to beam at her mummy, whom she clearly expected to be overjoyed by her daughter's grown-up telephone manner. Maggie tried her best to smile at her as she took the phone.

'Who is it?' she mouthed to Lily.

'A man,' Lily answered loudly, turning back to the television.

Maggie swallowed. Not Duncan, then. She took the phone out into the hall and sat down on the second stair. The phone said the number had been withheld, just like last time.

'Hello,' she said softly.

'Cute kid, Maggie. You've got her well trained. You just need to get her to ask who it is next time, so you don't have to whisper to her so obviously.'

Maggie felt her muscles relax.

'Frank, it's you,' she said unnecessarily, recognising the voice of the psychologist. 'Did you call earlier?'

'Yes, but there was no answer. Are you okay? You sound a bit croaky.'

Maggie tried to clear her throat of tears. It hadn't been Duncan before, and the thought was unbearable.

'I'm fine. It's such a crappy mobile signal here. Do you want me to call you back on the landline?'

'No, I can hear you. As long as you really are okay.'

'I'm fine, thanks. What can I do for you?'

'I wanted to talk to you about your number-one weasel client.'

Maggie should have been seeing Alf Horton, the old-lady batterer, before he had to go in front of the magistrates, but she hadn't been able to make it.

'Sorry I couldn't be there, but I can't get out of our road. We're snowed in here.' Maggie glanced out of the window. In truth the road was still covered with snow, but it had turned slushy and several people had managed to escape from their cul-de-sac – as, under normal circumstances, she would have done.

'Your bosses sent one of your colleagues. I watched the interview. The guy's not as good as you, and Alf's backtracking like mad. He's now saying he had nothing to do with the attacks on any of those women.'

Maggie sighed. She could really do without this.

'We all know he did it, so when he didn't deny it yesterday I thought it was only a matter of time before he confessed,' said Maggie. 'If he's going for a not-guilty plea, though, it means we've got hours of his delightful company to look forward to while we work on his defence.'

Frank laughed and tried to engage Maggie in a discussion on the case for a few more minutes, but her mind was far away from Alf Horton.

'Are you sure you're okay, Maggie? You don't sound yourself at all.'

Maggie took a deep breath. 'It's just Horton. I wish to God I didn't have to defend him.'

'You can refuse. You would be within your rights, you know.'

It was tempting, but she couldn't do it. It would definitely set back her promotion hopes – not that they seemed relevant at this moment.

She tried to draw the conversation to an end, but Frank seemed in a talkative mood.

'The police are going to apply for a forty-eight-hour extension before they formally charge him,' he said, interrupting her thoughts, 'which means you'll have the joy of talking to him again. Will I see you tomorrow?'

She had to say yes. She had no idea whether she would make it to the office the following day but couldn't think of an excuse. Ending the call, she ran her fingers through her hair, pushing it back off her face. She felt she was drowning. Elbows on knees, she rested her chin on her cupped hands, unable to get her thoughts and fears under control.

Sitting there was achieving nothing though, so pulling herself together she pushed herself up off the stair and opened the sitting room door. 'Lily, five minutes, sweetheart, and you'll have to turn that off.'

'Can I see what happens, Mummy?'

Maggie was tempted to remind her daughter that she knew *exactly* what happened next and could recite almost the whole film verbatim. But why bother if her daughter was happy. She had the feeling that unhappiness was waiting around the corner, ready to bite, so she would let her have any happy moment she could.

'When I call you, tea's ready, and you need to come. But you can pause it, if you want,' she said.

She went towards the study, surprised it was silent in there. She pushed open the door.

Josh was kneeling on the floor, staring at the television,

but there was no sign of a game on the screen, only the face of a woman. Josh was holding the remote.

'Josh? What are you watching?'

Her son spun round, a look of something like guilt on his face. What did he have to feel guilty about?

'Look, Mummy,' he said, his voice tight with emotion. 'She does look like you, doesn't she? I was right.'

Maggie turned her attention to the screen. Staring back at her was a drawing – a realistic one – of a woman with long dark hair and red lipstick, wearing a shirt with a black and white geometric pattern. She had to admit the woman did look strangely like her.

'Yes, she does a bit. Who is she?'

'She's the woman who was on Daddy's phone yesterday. She's on the news.'

Maggie felt a thud of fear deep in her chest.

'Are you sure, Josh? It's just a drawing.'

Josh nodded, his eyes round with alarm. 'Yes, but it's her shirt. That's what the woman on Daddy's phone was wearing.'

There was something about the face – something that made Maggie want to rush over to the television and turn it off right now. But she couldn't let her son know how she was feeling.

'There's nothing to worry about, darling. Perhaps that's why she was on Daddy's phone. Maybe he'd seen something on the news about her, or perhaps somebody sent him the picture thinking it was me.'

Josh shook his head with determination.

'No. That's not right. She wasn't in the news yesterday. They said the picture has just been released. And anyway this is a drawing. On Daddy's phone it looked like a photo.'

Soft fingers of dread were crawling up Maggie's spine.

'So what's she on the news for? What's she done?'

'She hasn't done anything, Mummy. She's dead.'

18

The girl in the drawing looked very real – a bit too real to Tom, who had so recently been looking at the same face on the autopsy table. The artist had done a good job, and now they could only wait and see if the picture's publication in the papers and on the local news would bring any results.

Tom had already phoned Leo's family to let them know the woman in the picture wasn't her, and he had also made a quick call to his daughter, Lucy. She had come to know Leo well during the time Tom had been seeing her, and the drawing was so lifelike he didn't want Lucy to see it on the television and think, even for a moment, that it might be Leo. He also had to prepare his daughter for the fact that he might not be able to see her that weekend. She was used to him having to change arrangements whenever some serious crime or other took over his life, but he hated it.

'I'm sorry, Luce,' he said. 'As soon as this is over, though, I'll have a word with your mum and see what we can sort out.'

Lucy had been quiet, and for a moment he had thought she was upset. When she spoke, though, he could sense reluctance to tell him something.

'Actually, Dad, I was going to call you. I asked Mum to, but she said it was up to me to tell you.'

'That's okay, sweetheart. Just say it, whatever it is.'

'You won't be cross, will you?'

Tom laughed. 'I seriously doubt it, Lucy. Try me.'

'Well, the thing is that I've been picked for the school swimming team, and we have practice on a Saturday morning. I haven't said yes yet, because I know it means I wouldn't be able to see you for the whole weekend.'

Given the number of times he had had to let her down, Tom didn't think he deserved this level of consideration.

'Of course you've got to be in the team! I'm proud of you. Would it be okay if I came to watch when I'm not working? Maybe I could pick you up afterwards. Do you think that would work?'

'Oh Dad, that would be brilliant,' she said, and he could hear how pleased she was.

They talked for a few more minutes and, promising to call her again over the weekend, Tom hung up and went in search of Becky.

'Becky, can you get someone to pull some old files out for me, please?' he asked.

Tom saw Becky's puzzled frown. She still didn't seem to have entirely recovered from the morning's upset, and her face had remained slightly flushed ever since, in spite of Tom making it clear that he fully understood the conclusion she had leaped to.

'What old files?' she asked.

'We had two murders twelve years ago. Two girls were killed in fairly quick succession, both from Manchester University.'

'Do you think they're connected to this case?'

'It's a possibility.'

In all honesty, Tom didn't know what to think. He remembered his shock when he had seen the second of the two dead girls all those years ago – girls whose murders he had been tasked with solving. The second girl had looked so similar to the first that it had knocked him for six. It almost felt like some kind of sick joke, but when later he saw pictures of the two girls alive and animated they actually weren't that alike. The same blonde shoulder-length hair and the same blue eyes had seemed enough, though, when their faces were expressionless in death. There was something particularly sinister about the murders, as if it was the girls' physical appearance that had got them killed, and the two abandoned locations – Mayfield station and Pomona docks – had somehow made the crimes feel even more disturbing.

The woman found this morning had no physical resemblance to those girls, but the three lines cut deep into the flesh of her thigh couldn't be a coincidence. They had suspected twelve years ago that it might be the start of a serial killing spree, but the murders – as far as they were aware – had stopped. So did the three cuts signify that this was the same killer, and if so, why start again now?

In the original enquiry they had interviewed vast numbers of people, but there wasn't a single tangible clue worth following up. The two murdered girls appeared to be totally unconnected, other than by their physical appearance. They were both students at Manchester University, but then so were thirty-odd thousand other kids.

He explained the background to Becky.

'The first girl was called Sonia – I can't remember her surname. The other was Tamsin Grainger. The reports are thorough – most of them were written by a trainee detective, a young lady by the name of Philippa Stanley.'

Becky looked up from where she was scribbling notes, her eyebrows raised. 'You are kidding me?'

'Nope. She was originally on the fast-track programme, heading for the heights of assistant chief constable or something like that. But her stint working with me gave her a taste for being a detective. She got no end of stick from our DCI at the time, who was a misogynist tosser, but she stuck with it and opted to stay in CID.'

Tom knew that Becky was aware of Philippa's period as his inspector when he first became a DCI, but she hadn't known the full history before. It gave him a certain edge when it came to dealing with Philippa, although he never forgot that she was now his boss and he respected her.

'What do you want me to look for in particular in the files?' Becky asked.

'To be honest, I don't know. Until we know who our latest victim is, it's going to be difficult to find any links, but at least if we've dug out the information we're ready to go as soon as we've got an ID.'

'Okay,' Becky said, pushing her chair back as if ready to leave.

'Are you all right now?' Becky flushed. 'Look, it's been a shit day. Why don't you get one of your team to call you if we get any info on our victim and get off home. You've been at it since the early hours. They can hold the fort for now. Go and see Mark and get some rest.'

'No chance,' Becky said, standing up to leave the room. 'I've still got bloody Alf Horton to sort out.'

'We didn't get the expected confession, then?'

'No, sadly not. DS Blake conducted the interview yesterday, and apparently Horton gave every indication that he was ready to admit to his sins. Blake said Horton's solicitor looked as if she was going to be sick as the crimes were listed. It would have saved a stack of work and money if he had said, "Yes, I did it."'

'Who's his solicitor?' Tom asked.

'A new woman. She's supposed to be a very good defender. I suppose she's going to come up with something clever to get him off.'

Tom smiled. 'That's her job.'

'Yeah, I know.' Becky gave a slight shrug of her shoulders as she opened the door, knowing this was par for the course. 'I don't envy her, though. Fancy knowing you might be putting a bastard like that back on the streets.'

19

The picture on the TV in the study was still paused. Maggie had sent Josh to wash his hands before going to the table, but she hadn't been able to take her eyes off the screen. She rewound the news article. The woman had been found dead that morning, several hours after Duncan had apparently received a photo of her. Josh might have been wrong about the photo, but the drawing was life-like and Maggie could see her own likeness to the victim. If Josh had caught a glimpse and seen the dark hair and the red lipstick it made sense that he had thought it was her. The dead woman's geometric top was distinctive and unusual too. Josh was such an observant child she didn't think he would have made a mistake. This was the woman in the photo sent to Duncan's phone.

Maggie switched the television off and collapsed onto a chair. She didn't think her legs would hold her. Why in God's name had a photo of this woman been sent to Duncan's phone? She was *dead*. The woman had been *killed*. For a moment she felt relieved that if this was a photo of Duncan's lover, she was no longer a threat, then dismissed the thought with a degree of self-disgust. If she had been Duncan's lover, maybe the woman's husband had killed her. He might even have been the man who called earlier.

She thought about the call for a minute. How did it all tie together? She hated the thought that somebody she didn't know could phone her any time. Did that mean he knew her address too?

Maggie couldn't control her thoughts or even keep pace with them. Fragments of ideas intruded and escaped before she could catch them. Had the woman already been dead in the photo that

Duncan received? She thought again about the words Josh had used – about Maud's eyes – and she knew without a doubt that the woman had already been killed when the picture was taken.

She now had a genuine reason to call the police about her husband's disappearance. But if she told them about the photograph, Duncan would become the number-one suspect in a murder. Was she ready to expose her husband to the inevitable manhunt without knowing more?

Not yet.

What's going on, Dunc? Call me, call me, call me. She repeated the thought over and over in her head, hoping that some sort of telepathy would get the message through to him.

She didn't think she could move. She didn't want to move. But she had no choice and so made her way unsteadily into the kitchen. She was going to sit the children down with their tea and then hunt online for every single piece of information she could find about this dead woman.

When the children were settled at the table, Maggie took her laptop over to the kitchen counter, away from Josh's eyes. She had to distance herself from the smell of food too. As it hit the back of her throat she thought she was going to retch.

There were a few articles saying a body had been found, but they were all sketchy. The woman hadn't been named, but it was understood she had been killed some time the evening before. Maggie closed the screen with unnecessary force and pushed the computer away.

'Mummy,' Lily shouted even though Maggie was only a few feet away, 'can I have some milk, please?'

'Of course. Do you want some, Josh?' Even to her own ears her voice sounded brittle, and she was speaking too quickly. She had to quell the rising panic.

What was Duncan involved in? Why did that man want to speak to him? Who was the woman?

'Yes, please.'

On autopilot Maggie walked over to the fridge and opened the door. *Damn it.* There was no milk. She usually did an online order on a Wednesday night, and Duncan picked up the groceries on his way to get the children on a Thursday. But of course none of that had happened.

'Right, kids, grab your coats. We're going to walk up to the shop for a few bits and pieces. Come on. It will do us good to get a bit of fresh air.'

Suddenly getting out of the house seemed like the best idea she had had all day. The walls were crowding in on her and the cold air might clear her mind. She quickly helped Lily into her coat and her wellies, and grabbed a thick poncho and a scarf for herself.

The snow had nearly gone now; just slush remained on the streets, white in their quiet cul-de-sac, dirty dark grey on the main roads. Josh kicked it with the toes of his wellies, clearly less than pleased to be out. Maggie knew she should be trying to talk to the children, but what energy she had left seemed to be used up by the simple process of putting one foot in front of the other.

When they reached the shop, she bent down to the children and forced herself to speak normally. 'Go and have a look at the sweets. Don't touch, but decide if there is something you'd like. Josh, keep an eye on Lily for me, please.'

Josh gave her a look that said 'What's going on?' and Maggie did her best to give him a reassuring smile.

She picked up some milk and headed to the newspapers. Copies of the *Manchester Evening News* were piled up as if they had only just arrived, and eagerly she pulled one towards her. The front page was full of news of a fire in Chadderton, and Maggie quickly flicked to the next page. Nothing.

'Are you looking for something, love?' the man behind the counter asked. Maggie looked up, a guilty expression on her face. Her frantic search had creased the paper badly.

'I'm so sorry, but I am going to buy this,' she said hurriedly. 'There was something on the TV earlier – on the news – and I wondered if it was in the paper.'

'Not if it only happened today. Probably be in tomorrow's.'

'The article was about a woman found murdered in Manchester. Did you hear about that?'

The man shrugged. 'Yeah, but I expect the police are being tight-lipped. Means they don't know anything.'

She knew it had been an outside chance. 'I'll take the paper and the milk, please, and the children want some chocolate.'

She turned to Lily, who was pointing at some chocolate buttons. Josh didn't look very interested.

They made their way home slowly, Maggie having to resort to carrying a tired and unusually whingey Lily for the last five minutes. It was still cold outside, and Maggie was disappointed that there had been nothing more to be learned from the paper. As she turned the corner into their road, she felt a rush of hope that Duncan's white van would be sitting lined up in front of the garage.

It wasn't.

She bundled the children back into the warm house and went through to the kitchen, where she hastily made them bowls of bananas and warm custard to finish their meal.

'Why isn't Daddy here to make our tea?' Lily asked.

'He's working, sweetheart,' Maggie said, drawing another look from Josh. What was she supposed to say?

Maggie still couldn't face the thought of food, but sat with the children while they finished theirs. Normally full of chatter, they were both quiet and withdrawn. Shifting her laptop, Maggie placed it on top of the discarded copy of the *Manchester Evening News*, and glanced at the paper's masthead. Only the corner was visible. She inched the laptop a bit higher up the paper and a bit further to the right so that everything except the top left corner was hidden.

That's it, she thought, feeling a faint leap of hope in her chest swiftly followed by the inevitable crushing dose of common sense. It would probably tell her nothing.

'Back in a sec,' she said to the children, who barely raised their eyes to hers as she pushed her chair back. She went to the shelf where she had placed the scrap of newspaper from Duncan's cupboard. She stared at it for a moment, certain she was right, and took it to the table to compare with the exposed section of the front cover of that evening's edition. The piece of paper she had found in the cupboard dated 16th November 2003 was from the *Manchester Evening News*.

But how could that be? Duncan had never been to Manchester until they moved there seven weeks ago.

Convinced she was making far more of this than was absolutely necessary – after all, the newspaper could have come from anywhere – she put the scrap away, opened the laptop and found Google. She knew she was clutching at straws, but maybe there was something significant in the news on 16th November 2003. She typed 'Manchester Evening News archive' and got a hit immediately. But it was no use. There was nothing more recent than 1903.

She stared at the screen, drumming her fingers as she considered what else she could do. But her thoughts were interrupted by the ringing of the telephone.

Lily leaped off her chair.

'Lily, come back to the table please,' Maggie said automatically. 'You know you don't just leave like that. I'll answer it.'

Hoping beyond anything she would have believed possible that this would be Duncan, she lifted the phone to her ear but said nothing.

'Hello, Maggie.' It was the voice from earlier in the day – the voice that made her shiver. This time she noticed that it was a voice with no obvious accent, and it wasn't the voice of either

101

a very young or a very old man. She took the phone through to the hall and closed the door.

'What do you want? Where's my husband?' She fought to keep the tremor out of her voice. She didn't want this bastard to know how much he was scaring her.

'I hadn't realised he was such a coward. He's running out of time, and you need to tell him.'

'What are you *talking* about? How do you know Duncan?' She was shouting and saw the kitchen door start to open. Josh must have heard her.

'Have you seen the news this evening, Maggie?'

She stayed silent. She didn't need to ask which story he was referring to. His voice was slow and measured, almost refined.

'Your husband knows what he has to do. He has one more chance. Tell him, if he calls. It's his last chance.'

The line went dead.

20

Maggie kept her back to Josh for a moment or two longer, breathing deeply to steady herself before she faced her son. She couldn't let him see the fear in her eyes.

How was she going to keep them safe when she didn't even know what the threat was? Had she double-locked the front door when they came in? Worse still, they had all been out to the shop with only the Yale lock securing the door. She knew that a Yale wasn't enough to deter any burglar worth his salt. What if somebody had broken in? Somebody looking for Duncan – or maybe looking for her?

She was certain she had left the other doors bolted. They hadn't been unlocked since she had called the children in earlier. Without turning to look at her son, she moved quickly to the front door and twisted the double lock.

Maggie breathed out. She had to know. She had to be sure that they were alone in the house. What if the man had broken in while they were out? What if right now he was upstairs, phoning her from his mobile, waiting for her? She had to check – she couldn't let the children go upstairs to bed if there was the slightest chance that somebody was up there, waiting.

'Josh, I'm going to pop upstairs. Will you stay with Lily while she finishes her banana, darling? I'll only be a minute.'

'Why were you shouting?'

'Oh…it was some silly salesman on the phone. Nothing to worry about.'

Her heart was pounding, but she managed a thin smile before

she turned to face the bottom of the stairs. She took the first two steps, then there was a pop and the house was plunged into darkness.

'*Shit!*' she cried, her voice breaking. That was all they needed – a power cut. Her mind spinning, she couldn't quash the thought that maybe it wasn't a power cut at all. Maybe somebody had switched off their electricity. And the fuse box was in the garage – the one part of the house that any burglar could get into with ease.

'Mum?' Josh was still in the hall. His voice echoed her fear. There was nothing more than a trace of light from distant street lamps coming through the stained-glass fanlight above the front door – just enough to see his shape.

'It's okay, baby,' she said. 'Are you all right in there, Lily?' she shouted.

'Yes, but it's gone dark,' came the response.

'I know, darling. Stay where you are. I'm going to find the torch and come and get you. Don't move, Lily.'

All Maggie could think was that there might be somebody in her house, in the kitchen with Lily or waiting behind a door.

Where the fuck was that torch?

She could see Josh moving. He was walking away from her. What was he doing?

'Josh! Where are you going?' He had gone into the study.

The door swung to behind him and seconds later she saw a flash of light.

There was somebody in there with him! Somebody with a torch. She stumbled down the stairs, missing the bottom one in the dark, catching herself on the newel post. She recovered quickly and flung the study door open. A bright white light flashed into her eyes, and she couldn't see a thing. Just as quickly it moved away.

'Sorry, Mum. Didn't mean to blind you.'

Josh was standing there with his iPad Mini. 'I thought this might help.'

Maggie leaned back against the door and took two deep breaths. 'Let's get Lily, and we can all search together.' The idea of leaving Lily on her own while they looked for the torch was frightening her, and she put her arm round Josh's shoulder. 'You're a star, Josh Taylor. Do you know that?'

Instead of shrugging her off as he might do normally, he pressed against her, and she knew how frightened he was. She opened the door to the hall, and heard a footstep. She squeezed Josh tighter and he spun the light round.

Lily.

'Hey, Tiddles, you were supposed to stay at the table,' Maggie said, her voice cracking at the edges.

'I know, but then the moon came out and I could see the man. I was scared.'

Maggie's body turned to ice.

'Where was the man, Lily?' she asked, trying to keep her tone level.

'In the garden. I didn't like him looking at me.'

Maggie realised that she was still holding the telephone.

'Okay, don't be scared. I want you to stay close to me.'

The children nodded mutely.

'I'm going to open the kitchen door so the man will see me and know I'm calling the police. That will make him go away.'

Lily started to cry noisily. Clutching his iPad in one hand, Josh reached out his other to Lily.

Maggie didn't want to see the man in the garden. She didn't want his face to bring her fear into focus. But she had to do it – he had to know that she was calling for help.

She pushed open the kitchen door with her shoulder and stood there, looking out into the garden. At first she saw nothing, but then the moon shot out like a bullet from behind a fast-moving cloud and illuminated the garden. She jumped.

There he was.

She peered out for a moment to be sure, then let the door slam shut and hurried back along the hall to the children.

'Lily, the man you saw in the garden. What did he look like?'

Lily's eyes were like saucers as she turned a serious face up towards her.

'He was white, with black eyes and an orange nose.'

Josh dropped Lily's hand and let out a bark of nervous laughter. 'Lily, you idiot, that's the snowman.'

Lily gave Josh a fierce look.

Maggie sagged with relief and bent to hug both children to her. One fear may have evaporated, but it didn't do anything to help the greater worry that there might already be somebody in her house or the garage.

'Let's find as many candles as we can, light them all, and then get that torch.'

By the time they had located candles, matches and a not very impressive torch, Maggie's heart rate had dropped a little, but she wasn't looking forward to what was ahead. One thing was certain: she was not going out into the garage to check the fuse box without full-on illumination. A feeble torch or Josh's iPad wasn't enough. If it was a fuse, it could wait until morning and they could all barricade themselves in the sitting room with candles until it was light.

Maggie didn't want to leave the children alone while she searched the rest of the house, but she had checked all the downstairs rooms and anybody hiding upstairs would have to pass her to get to them. A part of her knew she was being neurotic, but another part of her was screaming that twenty-four hours ago she wouldn't have believed any of this was possible – and if the man on the phone had been watching the house he would have seen them go to the shops.

The rest didn't bear thinking about. Neurotic or not, she had to know they were safe.

'Okay you two. Just sit quietly at the bottom of the stairs

while I see if there's anything stopping the lights from coming on upstairs.' She couldn't think of any other way of explaining why she was searching the entire house.

'Can I watch the television, Mummy?'

'No, Lil. It won't work, darling. Sit with Josh, okay?'

Slowly, not knowing if she should be stealthy or should stamp her feet, Maggie made her way up the stairs to the first floor.

She went into Josh's room and flashed the feeble torch around. Nothing. She walked across to his wardrobe and paused. She had to look inside. She waited, counted to ten, reached out and wrenched the door open then jumped back, shining her light directly into the cupboard. Standing leaning against the wall was a toy sword. She picked it up and used it to push the clothes to one side, but there was nobody there.

With relief she turned, knowing there was one last place to look. She dreaded getting down on her hands and knees. The door was open behind her. She was a perfect target for anybody who wanted to jump her. But she had to check under the bed. She could only do it by counting. She knew when she got to ten she was going to have to get down on the floor and prod under the bed with the sword.

'Eight, nine, TEN,' she said and fell to her knees, immediately lifting the covers and poking underneath. The sword didn't go far. It met resistance – something that gave slightly when touched. Maggie nearly screamed. She shone the light under the bed and fell onto her hip. '*Jesus*,' she muttered as she looked at the giant panda they had bought Josh when he was little. She had forgotten it. There wasn't space for anything else under there.

She stood up slowly. There was a flash of light and she almost jumped out of her skin. But it was the power coming back on. *Thank God.* It really had only been a power cut. Or had somebody switched the power back on in the garage? No. She had to believe it was a power cut.

After the terror of the last thirty minutes, the rest of the search felt relatively easy. It wasn't until she was coming downstairs that she remembered the loft. And with that thought came a memory of a television drama that had frightened her half to death. A woman was walking unafraid towards her bedroom, pulling off her blouse, getting ready to take a shower. Behind her head, two legs appeared, dangling from the loft hatch. A man had been up there, hiding, waiting for his moment.

Maggie stopped on the stairs and gazed at the hatch. What should she do?

Nothing. She was being ridiculous. There was no reason at all to suspect anybody was in her house. She had to hold fast to that belief. Feeling more than desperate for a glass of wine and cursing Duncan for his rule that no alcohol was kept in their home, she almost collapsed from fear-induced exhaustion on her way downstairs. She had never known her husband to drink anything alcoholic, and if she had more than two glasses of wine he could be distant with her for days. Tonight she would have drunk a whole bottle if it wasn't for the responsibility of looking after the children. But one glass would have been good.

She let Josh and Lily stay up for longer than usual that evening, and in the end she settled them both in her bed. She climbed in with them and softly sang a few of the silly songs they always sang in the car on long journeys. Lily joined in for a while, but gradually her voice faded and Maggie knew she was asleep. Josh was silent, but his body was too rigid for him to be sleeping. She lowered her voice a little and carried on singing, stroking his curly mop of hair gently. Finally she felt his body relax.

She had to decide what to do next. Even though her earlier fear had gone, it had been replaced by a fear that her husband was involved in something – something bad – and terror of what the caller was planning to do. What was he expecting Duncan to do? Why did her husband only have one more chance? What was happening to her life? How long was she prepared to let this go on before she took control – whatever the consequences?

Every curtain in the house was tightly closed, but somehow that didn't make her feel safe. Gently extracting herself from her position between the children, she tiptoed over to the bedroom window and pulled back a corner of the curtain to peer out into the night. She could see footprints in the rapidly melting snow, but they could have been theirs from the shopping trip. She couldn't see anything on the lawn at the front of the house, and the cul-de-sac seemed empty. There was something about a deserted street after snow. It always seemed eerily and unnaturally silent to Maggie.

Realising that she couldn't get out of bed every five minutes to check if anybody was about, she decided to pull the curtains wide open. If she sat up in bed, she could see the road and watch for anybody walking towards the house. Making as little noise as possible, she pushed a chest of drawers across the door. Nobody was getting in.

As she climbed back into bed to take up her vigil, it felt to Maggie as if the air around her was charged, and she could no longer ignore the fact that something was terribly wrong.

She had no choice. She had to do something. Maybe she could report the threatening phone calls but leave Duncan out of it? But they would ask what the man had said, and it was all about Duncan. If she told them everything, she could see the headlines now: LOCAL PLUMBER, DUNCAN TAYLOR, WANTED IN CONNECTION WITH MURDERED WOMAN. What would that do to her children? Duncan couldn't possibly have anything to do with it, but nobody would ever trust him again. And what if Duncan was in trouble and she made it worse?

What should she *do*?

Resolving to tell the police only that her husband had left her, but that since he had gone she had received threatening phone calls from somebody, Maggie picked up the house phone, dreading the conversation ahead. At that moment her mobile buzzed. A message. No number shown, so it had to have come via a website.

With a shaking hand she lifted her phone. If the man had somehow got hold of her mobile number, it could be him. But at least she would have some evidence for the police.

It wasn't him.

Mags, please, I beg you, don't go to the police. I can and will explain everything. I've done nothing wrong, I promise, but it might be difficult to prove. Please, Mags, trust me. Dunc xx

21

The words of Duncan's text had been spinning in Maggie's head all night. At least she knew he was alive. She missed him so much, but why had he hidden his number? Why wouldn't he speak to her? He wanted her to trust him, to keep away from the police. But how could she trust him when he had disconnected his phone, left her without a word and been sent a photo of a dead woman? And somebody was making threatening phone calls, somebody who clearly knew Duncan. How *could* she trust him?

But he was her husband – the father of her children. How could she *not* trust him? She wanted to scream.

At least it was daylight now, and the fear of last night had retreated to a dark, distant place in her mind. What she was left with was confusion and a low ache of dread – a combination of alarm at the phone calls, the horror of believing that her husband had left her forever and shuddering unease that he was somehow mixed up in the murder of a young woman.

There was something she felt compelled to do. Yesterday, before the horrors of the evening, she had gently quizzed Josh. What time did Daddy pick you up? Did you come straight home? What time was it when he went out again? That wasn't the only thing she had done. She'd gone into Duncan's work diary on their shared calendar on her laptop. On Wednesday he had been fixing a boiler for a Mr Jackson. Maggie had jotted down the man's number and decided to call him before he left for work. He sounded groggy with sleep.

111

'I'm sorry to disturb you so early, Mr Jackson,' she said. 'My name's Maggie Taylor, and I believe my husband fixed your boiler on Wednesday – is that correct?' The man grunted a confirmation. 'He's misplaced one of his tools, so I'm going through his diary trying to work out where it might be. Have you found a pipe cutter, by any chance?'

She waited for him to say no before asking the critical question. 'Do you know what time he left?'

She knew this last question was a complete non sequitur, but Mr Jackson didn't comment. He muttered that he thought Duncan had left at about three o'clock in the afternoon and hung up.

According to Josh, Duncan had picked him and Lily up from school at four. Josh said they had been in the after-school club for about half an hour. He could have been wrong, but since getting his first watch he was fairly keen on checking it regularly. That meant it had taken Duncan an hour to get from Mr Jackson's house to the school. She quickly opened Google Maps and checked the journey. It should only take twenty minutes. That left forty minutes unaccounted for.

He had brought the children home and left again at around 6.30 after receiving the image on his phone.

Although the woman's body was found in the morning the police believed she had been killed the evening before and the body moved to its final location during the night. They estimated the time of death to be before six pm, but depending on where the body had been kept in the intervening hours – inside or outside – it could have been earlier.

What had Duncan been doing in those missing forty minutes?

The ringing phone made Maggie jump.

'Maggie? Are you there?' It was Suzy. 'Is Duncan back?'

Maggie's heart slowed to its normal speed. But the relief at it not being her anonymous caller coupled with disappointment that it wasn't Duncan reduced her to tears.

'He's not back. I don't know what to do. I feel so lost.'

'Have you tried calling him?'

Maggie choked out a mirthless laugh. 'What do *you* think? But his phone's been disconnected. I just get a long tone. He sent me a text, though – at least, I think it was from him.'

'How did he do that if his phone's cut off?'

'I don't know, Suze – there was no number, so perhaps he sent it from his laptop. Too much has happened since I spoke to you. I don't know where to start.'

Slowly, over the course of the next ten minutes, Maggie told her sister the whole tale. She left out nothing but felt like a traitor when she mentioned the photo of the woman on Duncan's phone. To her credit, Suzy didn't make it sound any more dramatic than it already was.

'There's bound to be an explanation, Maggie. Don't panic – it won't help. Look, I'll catch the first train north tomorrow. I can be with you by the afternoon. We'll sort it out. Have you called the hospitals?'

Maggie recited everything she had done, but much as she loved Suzy, she didn't want her here. It would make it so much more difficult for Duncan to come home if he knew he had to face her too.

'Suzy, please don't come. I'm sure it will all blow over, whatever *it* is, and what about the kids?'

'Ian can have them. He's been a complete twat recently. He's cancelled so many times. Let's see how Rampant Ruthie copes with that, shall we?'

Maggie knew her sister was still struggling to deal with her ex-partner's betrayal. The hurt shone through each time she mentioned his name.

'Look, I'll call you if I need you to come. Okay?'

'If you're sure. Just a thought, though. Did Duncan take his passport or any of his other papers?'

Maggie's breath caught. *Why didn't I think of that?*

'I've not checked. Sorry, Suze, but I need to go. I've got to get the kids to school and go to work. I can't take another day off – you're expected to turn up even if you're dying. I'll call you tomorrow.'

She ran up the stairs, glad to have a sense of purpose. All of their papers were kept in the bottom of their wardrobe in a locked tin box. She retrieved the key from the top drawer of her bedside cabinet, knelt down and pulled it out from under a pile of shoe boxes. Opening the lid, the top item in the pile was Duncan's passport, and she breathed again. *Thank God.*

Slowly she went through the papers. Everything seemed to be there, but there was no birth certificate for Duncan. Then she remembered – he had used his passport as evidence of his name and date of birth when they got married. He said his birth certificate had been lost.

She stared at the information page in his passport, which had been renewed a couple of years ago. It occurred to her that this was all she knew of his past – his date of birth and where he was born. She realised she didn't even know what his mother had been called, and Duncan said his father had never been part of his life.

Slapping the passport against her open palm, she started to wonder whether everything that was happening was somehow related to Duncan's past – to the part of his life that seemed to be in the shadows, the dark recesses that he had been unwilling to shine too much light into. He had talked in general terms about growing up, but without the detail that would have allowed Maggie to picture him as a child. He was a bit like Josh sometimes – a man of few words when there was something he wasn't keen to talk about.

It suddenly seemed crucial to Maggie that she uncovered every facet of her husband's life – as if only by knowing all there was to know would she be able to understand what was happening now. It might be a wild-goose chase, but it would provide a focus. The starting point was his birth certificate. Then at least she would know who his parents were.

Back in the kitchen she pulled her laptop towards her. She had done this job many times for work and knew the websites that provided access to birth certificate details. She typed in his name then entered his birth date, expecting there to be a long list of Duncan Taylors born in 1982. A handful of names appeared, but only two had birth dates in the last quarter of the year. She requested the details of these, paid for the privilege and quickly scanned the results.

She looked again, not believing what she was seeing.

Not one of the entries matched Duncan's details as shown on his passport. There was no Duncan Taylor with her husband's date of birth.

It didn't make sense. To have a passport he would have had to provide evidence of his date and place of birth. So how could it be that there was no Duncan Taylor born on the day listed on his passport?

She triple-checked all the details.

Duncan Taylor did not exist.

22

In the absence of any ID found on or near the dead woman, Tom had hoped the artist's drawing would tell them who she was, but the results were even better than expected. From the moment the television news had broadcast the drawing of the dead girl, the phones hadn't stopped ringing in the incident room, and one name was coming through loud and clear.

Hayley Walker.

Initial investigations had gone on through the night, and had already revealed that Hayley worked at the Manchester Royal Infirmary as a staff nurse in the cardiology department. Every loss of life felt appalling to Tom, but when it was somebody who had dedicated themselves to helping others it seemed particularly unfair.

Hayley was originally from Australia and had no relatives in the UK. Her parents had been informed there was a possibility that the victim was their daughter and had tried repeatedly to contact her, but on getting no response had decided to catch the first flight from Melbourne. Tom could only imagine what a journey that would be as the agony of uncertainty stretched for twenty-four hours.

Becky had gone to the hospital to interview colleagues of Hayley Walker to get as much background as she could, so Tom was surprised when he received a call from one of the team manning the incident room.

'Sir, a doctor from Manchester Royal has come in. She saw the news this morning and came straight here, not realising that we were interviewing at the hospital. She said she'd like to talk to somebody. DI Robinson says she's not going to be back for hours yet, and wondered if you'd be happy to talk to her.'

Tom asked the sergeant to show her to an interview room, and wait with her. He would be down shortly. He pulled the sparse file towards him and made his way downstairs.

When he pushed open the door to one of their more pleasant interview rooms, an attractive young woman with mid-length wavy auburn hair was pacing up and down the room, still wearing a dark grey raincoat over jeans and flat-heeled boots. She stopped when Tom entered and turned towards him.

'Hello,' she said. 'I'm Louisa Knight. Can you tell me what's happened? Is it really Hayley's body you've found?'

She looked up at Tom, her brown eyes pleading for a denial.

'Please, Miss Knight, do sit down and I'll tell you what we know.'

She reversed up to the seat, never taking her eyes off Tom. 'It's Doctor, actually, but call me Louisa.'

'Okay, Louisa, I'm Detective Chief Inspector Tom Douglas.' He held out his hand and she gave it a brief, firm shake.

Tom pulled out a chair facing her and sat down. He took out a copy of the drawing of the victim from the file and placed it face down on the table.

'We don't know for sure if this is Hayley Walker,' Tom said, 'but the body of a young woman was found yesterday morning very early, and it's my opinion that the drawing is accurate.'

Tom turned over the picture.

'Oh my God.' Louisa's hand shot to her mouth and her horrified eyes turned to Tom. 'That's Hayley.'

Tom could see the genuine distress in the young woman's eyes; she was clearly fighting to retain some control.

'How do you know Hayley?' he asked.

'I expect you already know she's a nurse on the cardiology

117

ward. I'm an anaesthetist, and I spend a lot of time with patients in that department, so I'm on and off the ward several times a day.'

'It would be helpful if you could tell me a bit about Hayley – who her friends were, whether she had a boyfriend. Basically anything and everything you can think of. The top she's wearing, for example. Is that something she would have only chosen to wear for an important occasion?'

Louisa nodded, looking down briefly at her hands before raising her eyes to Tom's.

'It's her one and only designer item – Issey Miyake, I think. She bought it on eBay and couldn't stop talking about it at work. She said it was the bargain of the century. She wouldn't have worn it to go to the shops, that's for sure. She must have been going somewhere special.'

Speaking quietly, Louisa Knight provided Tom with as many details as she could. She and Hayley had been friends but weren't particularly close. They worked on the same ward and had done now for over a year. It was a small team, and they were quite sociable when they were off-duty.

'Did she have a boyfriend, do you know?' Tom asked.

Louisa frowned. 'I'm not sure of the answer to that. I've been on nights, and Hayley was on the early shift, so I saw her to say hi to as she arrived and I left, but not much more than that. There was something, though. Recently she had a bit of a glow about her – a kind of secret smile. In the one brief conversation we had a couple of days ago I jokingly asked her if she had a new man and she blushed. She said she hadn't, but she did think somebody was interested – somebody who she'd known a while but who had never seemed keen until recently. She said she'd felt his eyes watching her.'

Tom felt his pulse quicken a fraction.

'Did you get any indication of who this person was?'

'No. Nothing. She wouldn't tell me any more because she

thought it might influence the way I behaved towards him. I said, "Do you mean it's one of the team?" and she clammed up completely, saying she was probably imagining things.'

Tom waited, wondering if Louisa would have anything to add.

'If we hadn't been chatting in the corridor I would have asked for more details, but it didn't seem appropriate with other people walking past all the time. I should have pushed her, shouldn't I? If she was wearing that top I bet she was on a date, and I might at least have been able to tell you who with.'

Tom couldn't deny it because whoever Hayley had been planning to meet he or she hadn't come forward. And that wasn't a good sign.

❖

Louisa Knight had seemed like the perfect person to ask to give a preliminary confirmation that the dead girl was Hayley Walker. A formal identification would also be necessary, but for now Louisa's word would be enough to use as the basis of their investigation, and as a doctor she wasn't going to be fazed by seeing a body. The faster they had some focus, the better their chances of catching the killer, and after the debacle with Leo it was important they got this right. Tom asked Louisa to take as long as she needed.

'Yes, it's her,' she said to Tom, her voice quiet and even. 'That's definitely Hayley Walker.' She held her hand against the pane of glass, as if wishing her friend goodbye. Her eyes looked huge, swimming as they were with unshed tears, but she was composed. 'What can I do to help you catch the person who killed her?'

Tom looked down at her slight figure and felt an urge to reach out to her. Having been through a similar experience that morning, he knew how she must feel, and seeing the body again had reminded him of Leo. He wished to God he knew where she was so that he could stop worrying about her on top of searching for this killer.

'It would be helpful if you could try to remember everything Hayley said to you about the person who suddenly seemed interested in her. Was there anybody she was especially close to? Did she have a particular friend who might know more about this man?'

'Not that I know of. As I said, we're a friendly bunch and socialise quite a bit. But not in a best-friend sort of way, if that makes sense.'

It made perfect sense to Tom. Work colleagues were great to spend time with, but perhaps not always the people you chose to share your happiness or fears with.

'Could you give me any suggestions as to who it might be, do you think? It doesn't matter if you're wrong. I'll get my team to interview everybody at the hospital to see if she mentioned who she was meeting or where she was going.'

'As far as I can tell, they're a harmless bunch, and I've honestly no idea who she was talking about. I'll go home and make a list of everybody that Hayley came into contact with, if you like. What shall I do when I've finished?'

Tom fished in his pocket for his wallet and drew out a card. 'Give me a call. We'll get a list from the hospital too, but it would be great to look at the two side by side to see who she's most likely to have had some sort of relationship with.'

Tom's phone rang. It was Becky.

'Excuse me,' he said and walked a few feet away so that Becky's voice couldn't be heard.

'Tom, we've been through everything here at the hospital and nothing is standing out at the moment. We've been to Hayley's flat – it's only about ten minutes away. We've found nothing to indicate where she went on Wednesday afternoon or evening. We know she left work early. She said she had a blinding headache and thought she was getting a migraine. It was nearly the end of the shift, so they said she could go.'

'Did anybody speak to her later, to check how she was?'

'We haven't been able to find her mobile. It's probably at the bottom of the canal, so we're waiting to find out which phone company she was with to get her call records. But we checked her home phone, and only one call was received between her leaving the hospital and the time we assume she met her killer. It was from the cardiology ward.'

'I assume you've asked everybody if they spoke to her?'

'Of course, and nobody's admitting to it.'

Tom ended the call with Becky and turned back to Louisa, explaining that Hayley had left early but had received a call from the ward.

'Who would have been around on the ward? We need to concentrate on those who had the opportunity to phone her.'

Louisa frowned and shook her head.

'I'm sorry, but if the call came at around the handover time between the early and late shifts, everybody except the night staff would have been there. The phone's in use a lot, so even if we made a list of people who were seen making a call, it probably wouldn't help.'

'And of course,' Tom said, 'the call from the ward may have had nothing to do with it at all.'

23

Josh had been a complete pain that morning, and Maggie could have done without him playing up. He wouldn't get out of bed, and then he got dressed so slowly she thought they were going to be late for school.

'Josh, come here,' she said as she sat on his bed watching him laboriously put his socks on. He shuffled across the floor and leaned against her legs. 'I know you're worried about Daddy. We all are. I'm not going to lie to you. I don't know why he had to go when he did, but there will be a good reason. I promise you.'

Maggie stroked his hair gently.

'Why do you have to go to work? Why can't you stay with us?'

The last thing she wanted to do was leave her children. But yesterday she had used the weather as a barely plausible excuse and if she called in sick today she knew the partners would start to think she was a skiver. She was on a three-month probationary period and right now the last thing she needed was to lose her job.

'I'm going to take you to school and book you into the after-school club. I will be coming for you, I promise – just a bit later than Daddy picks you up. Okay?'

She couldn't see her son's face, but his head nodded.

'Come on then, and perhaps we can grab a pizza for tea tonight. How does that sound?'

This time the nod was marginally more enthusiastic.

The drive into work had passed without Maggie noticing it – all she could think of was Duncan: where he was, *who* he was. Even the thought of the interview she had to conduct with

Alf Horton that morning didn't succeed in pushing her thoughts away from her own problems. The colleague who had taken over from her yesterday had already called to say he was only too glad to hand her client back to her. Now she was at Manchester's divisional police HQ waiting to see Horton, and every muscle in her body was taut. She had to will herself to enter the room.

The new custody suite was better than most, but an interview room was an interview room. The smell of fear hadn't yet permeated the walls, but if anybody was frightened right now, it was Maggie, not her client. Her job was to find a way to get this dreadful man off – to have him found innocent of crimes she was certain he had committed. Before facing him, though, she had asked Frank Denman to attend for the final time to assess whether Horton might be considered mentally disordered, bringing into question his fitness to plead.

'How have you been, Maggie?' Frank asked as he walked into the featureless room, removing his overcoat. For a man who she guessed was in his mid-fifties, Frank's clothes had always struck her as belonging to somebody older. Maybe it was the shades of beige that he favoured and the chunky knitted sweaters, which seemed to accentuate, rather than disguise, his slender form.

'Fine, thanks. Let's make a start, shall we?'

'Fine? Really? Why don't I believe that?' he asked, his eyebrows raised. 'You don't look fine. Do you want to talk about it?'

Maggie took a breath and let it out slowly. 'Thanks for asking, but honestly I'm okay. Just stressed by bloody Alf Horton. I'm sorry I was snowed-in yesterday, but I'm here now so let's get on with it, shall we?'

'Okay. You know where I am if you need me. Any time.' Frank pulled some papers out of his briefcase and stuck a pair of frameless glasses onto his slightly beakish nose. 'What do you know about personality disorders?'

'Not much. Why? Do you think that's what Horton has?'

Frank shrugged. 'At one time psychopathic disorder was classified as a mental disorder. But not all psychopaths are violent, and not all violent people are psychopaths. Whether we can still play that card or not, I don't know. I suggest you look at the most up-to-date thinking on personality disorders. You might find it useful. I'll email you some links.'

'Thanks.'

Frank made his way into the adjoining room so that he could listen to the interview, and Maggie put on a headpiece so he could prompt her with any specific questions. Frank had opted to be absent from the interviews, convinced that Horton would respond better to a one-on-one situation, particularly if that one was female, but she was relieved that he was close by.

She looked up and saw the custody sergeant at the glass window in the door. He nodded to her – the signal that he had brought her client.

She shuddered at the thought of having to talk to this man. But the police were right outside the door, and Frank in the next room. Nothing could happen to her.

By the time her interview with Horton concluded, it was almost lunchtime. Maggie normally grabbed a sandwich at her desk, but today she was going to take her full hour and drive into town to visit the newly refurbished Central Library, the home of the more recent *Manchester Evening News* archive. She wasn't holding out much hope that the scrap of newspaper would prove significant, but she would try anything at this point. She was desperate.

The impressive Central Library building made little impact on Maggie as she entered, although she was struck by how the atmosphere of libraries had changed. There was no sense of a hush and whispered voices; people were talking at their normal volume. The smell of fresh paint mingled with a whiff of burnt toast coming from the café on the right, and she felt her stomach rumble.

She had barely eaten for the last two days, and had no idea what would happen if she tried. Her throat felt permanently closed with fear and stress.

She looked around at the banks of computers and microfilm machines, unsure where to go until a helpful volunteer pointed Maggie in the direction of a small, insignificant-looking desk at the back of the room. It was unmanned. Maggie looked at her watch and scanned the room right and left, unable to sit or stand still.

'Come with me. We need to go to the microfilm section,' the librarian said when she finally turned up. 'Can you give me the year, dear?'

Maggie gave her the full date, and the woman selected a drawer and pulled out a white cardboard box marked 'November 10th–16th, 2003'. She took Maggie over to a microfilm machine and threaded up the reel.

'There are fast and slow buttons in both directions – it's really easy to use,' she said with a smile.

Maggie knew she should respond positively, but said nothing. Her hands had gone damp. She didn't know if she should look or not. Would it be worse to find something that related to Duncan, or to find nothing and discover her only lead – if that's what it was – was worthless? She didn't know.

Finally she leaned forward and stared at the screen. She pressed a button and heard the machine whirr into life. It was easy to find the date she wanted. One story dominated the front page.

It was a report of a hit-and-run accident in central Manchester. A boy, Stephen Latimer, had been on his way home from a club in town at two in the morning. He had stepped out into the road to avoid some people walking in the opposite direction. A car had hit him from behind, but the driver hadn't stopped. He was now critically injured in hospital. There was a description of the car – a dark blue Renault – but no registration number. Stephen had been with two other people, Carl Boardman and Adya Kamala.

The driver of the car was described as young – no more than early twenties – with dark hair.

Maggie leaned back in her chair and looked up, hoping for inspiration.

The librarian walked across. 'Are you okay?'

Maggie sat up straight. 'Yes, I'm sorry. Is it possible to get a printout of this page?'

Five minutes later Maggie was handed the page, paid and put it into her bag. A glance at her watch told her she still had about fifteen minutes before she needed to get back to the office. She had noticed the signs advertising free Wi-Fi so pulled her laptop out of her bag and found a desk. She started to work her way through the names she had found in the newspaper article and found plenty on Stephen Latimer and his accident but nothing on either of his friends. It appeared that the driver of the car had never been traced – or at least if he had, it was never reported.

She was running out of time, and at the last minute thought about Frank Denman's suggestion that she look up personality disorders. If she could find something that would get Alf Horton off her hands, that would be one less thing to worry about.

She loaded up the first of the reference pages he had suggested.

The psychopaths around you

Given the estimate that as many as 1 per cent of the population could be psychopathic, it follows that we must all know somebody who fits that category. But can we recognise him or her?

Psychopaths learn to mimic emotions, despite their inability to actually feel them, and will appear normal to unsuspecting people.

The mother of famous serial killer Ted Bundy said he was 'the best son any mother could have' and many psychopaths hold down important jobs. Key characteristics of psychopathy include pathological lying, a lack of remorse and a high degree of superficial charm, and it is these traits that enable a psychopath to hide in plain sight. He (or she) might adopt a persona and play the role so well that those associated with him (or her) have no concept of the true lack of emotion that exists beneath the well-thought-out personality that has been adopted.

Maggie read on about how psychopaths were meticulous planners and how this distinguished them from sociopaths. She wasn't sure how this related to Alf Horton. Had people around him thought of him as an average bloke? What did his mother, with whom apparently he had always lived, think of him? Was he, in fact, a psychopath at all, or was he a sociopath?

She didn't have the energy to worry about Alf Horton's mental state right now. She was far more concerned about what was going on in her husband's mind.

24

12 years ago – May 31st

Serial killers were nowhere near as common as television and film would have you believe, and definitions varied. But most authorities agreed that two or more murders committed by one or more offenders constituted serial murder. Tom knew that if this was what was happening here, it was unlikely that the perpetrator would stop at two.

Another myth was that serial killers are all dysfunctional loners. Most appear to be normal members of the community. But without any link between the girls, where were they supposed to look?

Two dead girls, and not a single tangible lead they could follow up with any degree of enthusiasm. Other than the fact that they were both students, there didn't appear to be any connection between the two victims at all, although they were a similar age with the same body type and hair colour and in death they had looked practically identical. But in life they appeared very different – their make-up, their smiles, their clothes, their attitudes.

It hadn't taken long to identify the girl found at Mayfield station as Tamsin Grainger – a party girl, by all accounts. In photographs provided by family and friends she was clearly posing for each picture, head tilted slightly back and showing a full set of teeth. Sonia's pictures, on the other hand, showed a girl smiling shyly, as if caught unawares. Although their features were similar, in every other way they were chalk and cheese. They moved in different circles – or in Sonia's case no circle at all to speak of – and they were studying different subjects with lectures at opposite ends of the campus.

The truth was, Victor Elliott's crack team of detectives couldn't

128

find one point of contact between the two girls, and it was getting Tom down. He knew he wasn't the only one who was frustrated, but the dispirited air in the incident room was preventing him from thinking straight.

He moved away from his desk, mentally shutting out the background noise of the room – the ringing phones, the quiet voices of detectives engaged in endless telephone interviews with anybody and everybody who might know something – and looked out of the window at the darkening skies, brooding and threatening. It had been hot for May, and the pressure had been building to its current oppressive state for days. A storm was needed, but until it broke the muggy atmosphere settled around everybody like a heavy overcoat.

Something had been nagging at the back of Tom's mind but he couldn't grasp the thought; it kept slipping away. He had to escape the stifling atmosphere and get some air.

Almost without a conscious decision, Tom found himself back at the scene of Sonia's murder, absorbing the tranquillity of Pomona Island. It felt like a place apart, removed from the real world. While the rest of Manchester carried on its day-to-day business with trains, cars and trams buzzing noisily around the city streets, here there was a sense of being cut off from reality. Manchester was reduced to no more than a background noise, and by focusing on the sounds in close proximity – the lapping of the water, the birdsong and the hum of insects – it was possible to believe the city was miles away. Tom sought the same peace in his mind, thrusting his myriad confusing thoughts into the background to focus solely on what had happened here.

He struggled to suppress an irrational sense of guilt about these murders: he had been desperate for an interesting case, anything to take his mind off his own worries. It hadn't worked, though. He managed to focus on the case for most of the time, but his concern about his marriage kept sneaking up on him. Throughout the second half of last year Tom had been sure he was heading for a divorce. Kate had seemed to be permanently irritated by him and by his choice of career. Then suddenly she had changed – smiling more, singing around the house. A couple of months later she announced she was pregnant. Excited as he was about the baby, Tom still didn't know what had changed, and he didn't want to think about it too much. That was why he had silently prayed for a case that would occupy his mind – to make sure it had no time to wander into uncharted territory.

Now, as he walked along the overgrown path that ran through the middle of Pomona Island and back towards the crime scene, it felt as if his desire for something more intriguing had been granted – and in spades. He had not one but two cases, and they were going to need all of his brainpower.

It was over three weeks since Sonia had died, and now the only thing marking the spot was a piece of crime scene tape that had caught on a woody shrub and was fluttering in the warm, humid breeze. He pictured Sonia Beecham as she would have looked before the tent was erected around her – the way she would have been found by the dog walker. She had been sitting up.

That was another reason Tamsin's body at Mayfield station had spooked him. Not only did she have similar colouring and hair to Sonia Beecham, she too had been sitting up, propped against the wall. Why was sitting up important? Or was it? Maybe it was convenient to leave the bodies like that, but it seemed like something more. The similarity between them and the way in which they seemed to have been positioned suggested that they were on display. But to whom? And why?

The dark skies were suddenly split apart by a bright shard of sunlight, illuminating the exact spot where Sonia had been found, which reminded Tom of an idea he'd had, an idea his boss seemed to think was irrelevant. Sonia wasn't a big girl, but she wasn't tiny either. She looked to Tom's untutored eye to be a healthy size twelve. Transporting her here would have been no easy matter, as the SOCO team had said.

He looked about him. The general view was that she had been

brought by car to the Pomona Strand entrance to the island because it was the most accessible by vehicle. But it wasn't the only possibility. There were other ways onto the island that were less accessible by car, but what if she had been killed somewhere nearby, and a car hadn't been necessary at all?

There was still the issue of having to carry a dead weight for some distance, and Tom couldn't help wondering if this was the work of more than one person. But his boss wouldn't have it. 'This isn't bloody America, Douglas. Our serial killers come in singles.' And that was the end of it – no further discussion allowed – but it didn't stop Tom thinking, and he fought the temptation to mention Brady and Hindley or Fred and Rosemary West to Victor Elliott. It would only have made him more entrenched in his opinion.

Mayfield station presented even more difficulties for transporting a body. They had considered the use of a wheelbarrow at Pomona, but at Mayfield that would have been impossible. Tamsin Grainger must have been carried upstairs from the level of the road to the level of the platform, and she was a similar size. There were a lot of stairs, and it wasn't something Tom would have liked to attempt on his own.

As his mind spun through the options, a call came through on his radio. It was his young DC, Philippa Stanley.

'Sir, I think you'd better get back here sharpish. The boss is ranting and raving that you're never here when you're needed, and some girl has come in to say she's been attacked.'

Shit. He knew he shouldn't have risked coming here when the DCI was in the office. It was sod's law that something would come up.

Tom jogged back along the gravel path, his calm and fresh perspective shot to pieces.

By the time Tom got back to the office, Victor Elliott had wound himself up into a ball of red-hot anger. His already florid face was almost purple with totally unnecessary rage. Tom was aware that behind his back Victor always referred to him as 'smart-arse Douglas' simply because

Tom had a degree, and his dismissal of every word that Philippa Stanley uttered simply because of her fast-track status – and the fact that she was a woman – was embarrassing.

Tom listened to Elliott's rant without showing the slightest expression – something else guaranteed to rile his boss.

'And that stupid cow you've got working for you at the moment should have known where you were. I thought she was supposed to be clever.'

'Clever, sir, not psychic,' Tom answered.

Before Victor had the opportunity to respond, Philippa knocked gently on the door.

'What?' the DCI shouted.

'The young lady would like to give her report and leave, sir. She has a training session this evening, so hasn't got time to hang around.'

'Bloody hell! Does she want us to catch the guy who attacked her or not? Go, you two, and don't come back until you've got some answers.'

Tom didn't need telling twice, and on the way to the interview room Philippa filled him in. The girl had come in to report that she had been attacked the night before in her room at the university. She had called in the attack immediately, but it was only after she had gone through the standard interview process that anybody realised the incident might be related to the two murders.

'How's she coping?' Tom asked.

'She seems more angry than frightened by the fact that, in her words, "Some bastard tried to kill me,"' Philippa said. 'She's also annoyed that although she went through it all in the early hours of this morning, she's now having to do it again.'

They pushed open the door to the interview room, and Tom tried not to let the surprise show on his face. Sitting in a chair was a girl who looked remarkable similar to their first two victims. Pretty, blonde, hair in a bob, but the similarity ended when she jumped up from her chair, clearly glad to see that finally something was happening.

'Hello,' she said, extending a hand and shaking Tom's vigorously. 'My name is Freja Blom. I'm Swedish. You are going to catch this nasty bastard, yes?'

Tom was impressed by her anger. Her mouth was set in a hard line, and he couldn't decide how much of it was her way of dealing with the fear that she must have experienced. But there was no sign of that – just determination to catch the man who had tried to kill her.

Once they had convinced her that unfortunately she was going to have to repeat her version of events to them, she needed little prompting to tell her tale as quickly as she could. She started to speak before Tom and Philippa had the chance to ask her a question.

'I sleep on the ground floor of the halls of residence, but it was a warm night and I left the window open a little. Nobody would steal from me – I don't have much. I don't know what woke me, but there was a change in the feeling of the room. I don't remember a noise. More like any sound was being absorbed by another body and the air had become more dense.'

Tom remained silent and signalled the enthusiastic Philippa to say nothing either. Freja was staring into thin air, her whole body concentrating on the memory.

'When I opened my eyes, he was standing there – a man with a stocking over his face. His features were squashed, but I can tell you now that I would know him again. I am used to people's faces looking distorted, but still I know who they are.'

Tom made a note. They would need to come back to that one.

'He was holding my spare pillow. Before I could scream he pushed it down over my face and held it there. I fought him, but I couldn't get to any flesh to get his skin under my nails. So I held my breath and let my body go limp.'

She took a long drink from a bottle of water she had been clasping since she arrived, then continued her story.

'He held on for longer than I thought, and I felt myself begin to drift – to become semi-conscious. I felt the pillow lift, but I just lay

133

there. By then I had kicked off all the covers, and I was only wearing a T-shirt. I thought he was going to rape me.'

She leaned forward, her folded arms resting on the table, her face inches from Tom's. 'The sick bastard thought I was dead! He lifted the bottom of my nightie and he cut me with a knife. I show you.'

'It's fine, Freja – we can get the doctor to look,' Tom said.

She shrugged. 'It's no problem for me.'

Freja pushed her chair back, stood up and without hesitation lifted her short skirt to reveal the edge of a pair of white cotton knickers and the evidence of what had been done to her. There was one long deep cut high on her left thigh. 'I screamed, and he leaped back from the bed. He seemed more frightened than me, because he thought he had killed me. So I screamed and screamed some more, called him a dirty fucking pervert and a stream of other Swedish words, and he bolted.'

Christ – how does a girl of this age learn to be so self-possessed? Tom thought.

'Freja,' Tom said, 'you've had a lucky escape and you've been incredibly brave. Do you think you can you tell me anything about the man at all?'

'He was more a boy than a man, I would say,' she replied. 'He was tall, but not heavy or muscly.'

'And you said you are used to seeing people's faces distorted. Why's that?'

'Oh, I'm a swimmer. I see people underwater. Nobody looks normal when they're swimming.'

Tom realised that her ability to hold her breath for so long had saved her life, and was about to tell her so when she said something that made him freeze.

'Sorry, Freja. Can you say that again, please?'

'I said I thought I would recognise him, but I am not so sure about the man standing outside the window, watching.'

25

Three lines carved into a leg. Three original victims, even if one did escape. Unless, of course, there had been more victims, ones they had never found.

The more Tom thought about the victim found yesterday – Hayley Walker – the more convinced he was that she had to be linked to the murders of Sonia Beecham and Tamsin Grainger. While Hayley bore not the slightest resemblance to the previous victims, the placing of the three lines on the leg had to be significant. Did that mean that Hayley was going to be the first of three?

He stood up from his desk, grabbed his Barbour jacket from behind the door and checked he had his phone and car keys. There had to be a common factor, surely, between those victims and this one, but it had all happened so long ago, and even though he had read and reread the files, the words conveyed only the facts. He needed images – pictures that might spark off something, a little nugget deeply entrenched in his memory, and for that he needed to go back to where it all began. He remembered making the same trip then but hoped this time it would be more productive.

Tom headed west on the Mancunian Way, around the city and onto the main road leading to Old Trafford, turning off to the right towards the strip of wasteland that he hadn't visited for nearly twelve years. He pulled the car up behind a couple of other vehicles parked in the dead-end street. No doubt a few dog walkers would be around – whatever the weather, some things just had to be done.

The double gates that allowed vehicles through to the island were closed and padlocked, but a pedestrian gate to one side was open, and Tom walked through it barely aware of his surroundings. There were so many thoughts running through his head. Where was Leo? Had she gone away without telling anybody, or had something happened to her? Images of her in the best of their times together, memories of her warm laughter or her gentle hands, hit him whenever he allowed his mind to stray from the murder of Hayley Walker.

Right now, though, he wanted to know why they hadn't been able to solve those crimes twelve years ago. What had they missed? Was any of it his fault, because his head had been full of his worries about Kate and the future of their marriage? Had he failed to give the murders the attention they deserved? What could the past tell them that would help them find the killer this time? One thing was certain: he wasn't going to fail in this investigation. He had never stopped believing that they had let Sonia and Tamsin down badly, and had been relieved when there were no other victims. At least, not that they knew of.

He walked across the island to where Sonia had been found. He stared at the spot for a few minutes, remembering the warm day and the pretty girl sitting upright against a tree stump, looking for all the world as if she were taking some sun. At least, she would have had it not been for the eyes, staring sightlessly ahead of her, and the thick line of dark red blood around her neck. That day the earth was baked and wild flowers were blooming. Today, the ground was soggy underfoot and the island didn't look so beautiful.

He turned to look across the river. It was wide here and the water was choppy. Pivoting on his heel to look in the opposite direction, the previously derelict mills beyond the narrow Bridgewater Canal that bordered the other side of the island were now mainly renovated and converted into apartments, and only this sliver of land remained unclaimed by modernisation.

Tom remembered the mills. Twelve years ago he had wanted

to search those most accessible to the island by bridge. He had found a narrow footpath from this tiny scrap of wilderness that led back over the canal towards the deserted buildings. It was closer to where they had found Sonia's body than the main footpath. On Tom's insistence, the DCI had asked uniforms to check if entry to the old mills was possible, and they had returned to report that the buildings were secured, with all doors padlocked. So Victor had declared it a dead end not worthy of further investigation. Any traces of those murders – any blood or DNA from the girls – would by now have been eradicated during the renovation work, and Tom was angry with himself for not persisting with that line of enquiry.

He searched his memory for a kernel of an idea that might make everything start to make sense. It was there. He knew it was. And he was going to find it.

He thrust his hands into his pockets and walked determinedly back towards where he had left his car. Coming here hadn't given him the answer he craved, but it had reminded him that the past held secrets the previous investigation hadn't uncovered. And he was damned if he was going to be beaten this time.

As he drove back to the office, Tom's mind was only partly on the road – enough to avoid him hitting the car in front – but mostly he was in another time, another place, rifling through every fact, every impression that he'd had. He was only vaguely aware of the woman standing alone on the side of the road opposite police headquarters.

Indicating right to turn across the busy road and into the car park, a flash of colour caught his eye. It was an emerald-green scarf that had attracted his attention, and it was worn around the neck of a woman with long, dark hair and bright red lipstick wearing a black raincoat.

'*Leo!*' Tom almost gasped out her name.

He glanced back to where the woman stood, staring at the

offices from across the road as if unsure whether to cross or not. Unable to stop in the middle of the road, Tom drove as quickly as he could into the car park. Typically there were no spaces close to the entrance. He muttered an expletive and pulled into the first available slot, jumped out of the car and ran back towards the road.

As he reached the visitors' area of the car park, a door opened and he heard his name. 'Tom? Do you have a moment, please?'

He didn't stop to see who it was. 'Just a minute,' he called over his shoulder.

He couldn't see her. Where had she gone?

'Come on, Leo. Where are you?' he muttered, scanning up and down the road. But she wasn't there. There was no black coat, no tall, slender woman with hair below her shoulders. The scarf was unusual, though. He had never seen Leo wear any colour at all.

He stood where he was for a few minutes, knowing she had gone and he wasn't going to find her.

'Bugger,' he muttered.

'Tom?' The same voice spoke from behind him and he turned round. He recognised the face of a young man with dark, curly hair and a slightly sallow complexion, but couldn't place it.

'I'm Luca Molino – Daniela's boyfriend from next door to Leo.'

'Luca, of course. I'm sorry – my mind was elsewhere. What can I do for you?'

'I wanted to speak to you about Leo.' He looked down at the ground and back up again. 'I'm afraid Daniela didn't tell you everything.'

Tom felt a moment of anger at Luca's girlfriend. When somebody was missing, every scrap of information could help. He forced himself not to show his irritation. 'Come into the office out of the cold,' he said. 'We'll grab a meeting room and you can tell me.'

Tom ushered Luca inside, organised a cup of coffee and waited for him to find the words.

'When you came to visit, Daniela thought you were worried

about Leo because she's your ex-girlfriend, and perhaps you wanted to get back together with her.'

Tom said nothing. He didn't want to influence Luca's story one way or another, but this did explain why he had wondered about the brevity of Luca's translation of Daniela's long burst of Italian.

'She told me just to tell you when she had last seen her – Saturday – and that was the truth. Then I saw the picture of the girl who's been killed. She looks so much like Leo that I thought I should come to see you. Daniela didn't want me to, because she thought you would be angry with her for not telling you everything. She doesn't know I'm here now.'

'I'm glad you are, Luca. I'm very concerned for Leo.'

'The thing is, Leo has a new man in her life, and Daniela wasn't sure how you would take that. She's been seeing him for about two months. He's quite a high flyer – corporate finance, I believe. I think she went to Cheltenham with him, to the racing earlier this month. She had to buy a hat. I remember that because she came round to ask Dani if it suited her.'

Tom felt for a moment that it should have been *him* she had modelled the hat for. Maybe *he* should have taken her to the races. He couldn't help wondering why Ellie or Max hadn't told him about this man. As if reading Tom's mind, Luca answered the unasked question.

'She didn't tell anybody about him apart from Dani. She knew we would see him coming and going so it was better if she told Dani so she wouldn't gossip.' The look on Luca's face suggested that would be a tall order. 'She asked Dani not to say anything because she wanted to see how it went before she told her family.'

That sounded like Leo. She wouldn't want to expose herself in case it didn't work out.

'Do you know his name, who he works for, where he lives – anything that might help me track him down?'

Luca nodded. 'She said he was a partner in his firm, and we knew his name was Julian. But no surname. He drives a big Merc.'

Tom couldn't think of anything else to ask. He was fairly sure that there wouldn't be too many Julians who were partners in a corporate finance firm, so it was likely they could track him down.

He stood up. 'Thanks for coming in, Luca. You've been a great help. Leo's obviously keeping this relationship close to her chest and is waiting to see how it goes.'

'I'm not so sure if it's still going or not. Dani thought they'd had a row, because the last time he was with her – Friday, I think – he left before midnight. We were coming back from a bar in town and he came out of the front door quickly. He didn't look happy. We stood back out of his way. He didn't know us, and we only knew who he was because Dani's nosy. That was the night before we saw Leo for the last time.'

'Did he usually stay the night, then?' Tom asked, realising that this might sound intrusive, although he was actually trying to decide if this man had somebody to go home to, which could make a difference. At least, that's what he told himself as he ignored the stab of jealousy at the thought.

'Yes, I think so. Dani's not so nosy that she kept a watch on him, but we did see him leave at about six in the morning more than once. We heard Leo's door close, and of course Dani leaped out of bed to see who came out.' Luca's eyes didn't quite meet Tom's, and Tom realised that they had probably done exactly the same each time he had gone to Leo's. Six had been his normal time to leave too.

Luca headed towards the door.

'Well, I expect they made it up, and she's gone away with him somewhere for a week or so,' Tom said, holding out his hand to Luca.

'Oh, I don't think so. He turned up a couple of days after we realised she wasn't at home. That would have been Monday. He knocked on our door to ask if we'd seen her.'

Tom felt a stab of concern. He would have felt much happier if Leo had been away with her new man.

'Clearly the flowers didn't work,' Luca said, a small frown furrowing the skin between his eyes.

'Flowers?' Tom said.

'The day after the row. Late Saturday morning. A delivery guy arrived carrying a huge bunch of flowers. It was the biggest arrangement I had ever seen, so we guessed it was an apology.'

Tom remembered the drying petal he had found. But no flowers – neither in a vase, nor in the bin.

26

Tom was still struggling with the idea that Leo had been standing outside police HQ, maybe looking for him, and he hadn't been able to get to her in time. If it really *was* Leo, of course. Everything about the woman looked so similar from the far side of the road, but the green scarf was an unlikely choice. Since then he had called Leo, left messages, tried to contact her on every form of social media that he knew she used, but he had heard nothing. He had also asked one of his team to check out all corporate finance firms in Manchester with a partner called Julian, but Tom's main focus had to be on the murder of Hayley Walker.

He was in the incident room when Becky returned from several long hours at the hospital. She flopped into a chair, rested her elbows on her desk and cupped her hands under her chin. It was a pose he had seen many times. He always thought of it as her thinking-but-not-getting-anywhere-fast look.

'What's up, Becky?' he asked.

'Oh, nothing.' She blew out a puff of air through pursed lips. 'Except that all I seem to have for my day's labour is a lot of paper, several lists and not a clue who would have wanted to hurt Hayley Walker.' She picked up a pile of files and let them drop again on the desk.

Tom leaned against the wall, one leg crossed over the other. 'Well, the doctor who came in this morning – Louisa Knight – has gone away to come up with a list of people Hayley might have had an interest in, or vice versa. She's called and offered to come and talk it through with us. You bring your list, and we'll see what we've got.'

'I can do that, boss,' Becky said. 'There's no need for both of us, just because I'm in a grump.'

'No, it's okay, Becky. I want to hear what she has to say. Anyway, something might ring a bell with the crimes from twelve years ago.'

He was relieved that Becky seemed to have recovered a little from her fluster the day before, even if it had been replaced with a cantankerous attitude. He always thought Becky was at the top of her game when she was at her most stroppy, and he smiled to himself.

❖

Louisa was waiting for them in a meeting room, and she stood up when Tom and Becky entered. She had removed her coat and was wearing an apricot silk shirt that complemented the colour of her hair. She smiled at Tom and held her hand out to Becky as Tom introduced them.

'I've made the list you asked for.' She briefly waved a sheet of A4 paper in the air. 'I've named anybody who might have shown an interest in Hayley and I'm happy to run through it and give you my impressions of each of them, but I do hope none of these guys will ever know what I've said.'

'They won't hear anything from us, Louisa, and please call me Tom.' Tom couldn't miss Becky's slight raising of her eyebrows but he chose to pay no attention. 'What have we got?'

'The fact is, we're a large team. Most of our patients have a dedicated nurse assigned to them – one per shift. There are a lot of consultants, but it's the anaesthetists who tend to be around and maybe a surgical registrar or two. Given that Hayley thought somebody was interested in her, I thought I'd concentrate on the men. She's never given me any indication that she prefers women, and I'm sure it was a man she thought was watching her.'

'Okay. Any suggestions you can give us would be useful.'

Louisa opened a soft brown leather document case and

pulled out a photograph. 'I thought this might be helpful. It's the departmental photo taken at Christmas. There are a couple of new people since then, but Hayley spoke as if this person – if he's in any way implicated in her death – was somebody she'd known for a while.'

Tom couldn't be sure that the person who killed Hayley and the person who had suddenly seemed attracted to her were one and the same, but they had to start somewhere.

'I'll start from the top and work down,' Louisa said in her slightly husky voice.

She pushed one side of her hair behind her ear, as if getting down to business. As she spoke about each person, Louisa pointed to him on the photo.

'There were two male surgical registrars that Hayley knew well, Charlie Dixon and Ben Coleman.' She lifted the photo and pointed first to a man who looked to be in his early thirties with prominent cheekbones and a mop of dark curly hair. 'This is Ben.' She moved her finger to the far end of the picture. 'And this is Charlie.' The second man was much shorter with a lopsided happy grin that suggested he was rather too full of the party spirit.

'Ben is charming and popular, extremely bright and young for his level of seniority. Personally I find him a bit overconfident and slightly cynical, but that probably goes with his ability. He was friendly with Hayley, but as far as I'm aware never showed her any special attention. Charlie is friends with everybody. He's a bit of a joker. They're both attractive men, and if either of them had started to be more attentive, Hayley would definitely have noticed. It would also explain why she didn't want to tell me who it was. To some of the nurses, these guys are demi-gods, and Hayley would have needed concrete evidence of any interest before she spoke out. She wasn't desperately confident about herself, for reasons nobody could understand.'

There was one man in the picture that Tom couldn't take his

144

eyes off. Although he was with the others, he seemed somehow apart, as if he – rather than his colleagues – was making himself something of an outcast. His attempt at a smile was failing, and there was slightly more space around him than there was around anybody else.

'Who's this?' Tom said, pointing to the man and momentarily interrupting Louisa's flow.

'Ah,' she said. Louisa was silent for a moment. 'That's Malcolm Doyle. He's a fellow anaesthetist and regularly on the ward.' She tapped the photo with her short, unpolished nail. 'Malcolm finds it difficult to associate with people. But he's exceptionally good at his job when he's in theatre. It's just his interpersonal skills that aren't that great. Hayley felt sorry for him, and we do try to include him in things, but he's like a rabbit caught in headlights if anybody ever speaks to him at a party. I'm not sure how she would have responded to interest from him.'

She continued, identifying two male charge nurses as possibles, and they ended up with a list of seven men who were the most likely to have paid Hayley attention and had it reciprocated.

'Please don't take my word alone for any of this,' Louisa said, looking from Tom to Becky and then back to Tom. 'I could be miles from the right person and I'm terrified I'm wasting your time.'

'You're not. We have to start somewhere and this is as good a place as any.' Tom turned to Becky. 'I think we should get the team on checking these people out. We need to know their backgrounds: where they were brought up, went to university, worked before coming here and how old they are.'

And most specifically, Tom thought, he needed to know where they were in May 2003.

27

Maggie's ten-minute vigil outside police headquarters had left her feeling like a traitor. She still didn't know what she'd been thinking. Duncan had specifically asked her not to go to the police, and yet once she had discovered who was leading the team in the investigation, she wanted to see him – to talk to him.

Her colleagues in the office had been talking about little else but the murder since she had arrived that morning.

'That drawing gave a few people a shock, I can tell you,' one of the clerks had informed her as she walked through the door. 'When you didn't turn up to work yesterday it was mad here for a while. There were some who genuinely thought you were dead. I don't think the woman looks like you at all, really. It's just the hair and the lipstick.'

'I hope whoever's leading the investigation catches the guy who did this,' she'd said, subtly fishing for information.

'It's bound to be Tom Douglas,' the clerk said. 'He's a sound bloke, and I've got a lot of time for him.'

The suggestion that Tom Douglas was 'sound' had made her feel a little better, and without knowing how she had got there, she had found herself standing outside police headquarters, gazing at the offices. She should go in and talk to him, but what would she say? *My husband had a photo of a dead girl on his phone before you found the body? Somebody sent it to him, but I don't know who?*

She would be implicating her husband in *murder*. Did she really want to do that? But what if he knew something – something that would help the police to find the person who had killed that poor woman? Duncan hadn't killed her, Maggie was sure. He *wouldn't*.

If I found out that he had *killed her, what would I do?*

She should know the answer, but she didn't. He was the father of her children, and a *good* father. At least, she had always thought so. Wouldn't it be easier to run away together – as a family – and pretend none of this had ever happened? Wouldn't that be better for the children?

What was she *thinking*? She shouldn't be here, standing looking at an office block. She hadn't worked out what was going on with Duncan in her own head yet. What if he was in danger? What if he had been forced to send her that message telling her not to contact the police? She wasn't ready to talk. Duncan didn't want her to, and she didn't know enough. She had to give him the benefit of the doubt.

Without a backward glance she had run back to the safety of her car, where she was still sitting thirty minutes later, staring out at the miserable day, no closer to knowing what to do.

It was hopeless.

Maggie would soon need to be at the magistrates' court for Alf Horton's remand hearing, but for the moment she couldn't face him and she was putting it off until the last possible minute. She needed a distraction, so she grabbed her laptop from the back seat and the mobile Wi-Fi router from her bag and switched them on. She had absolutely no idea if her research that morning had turned up anything useful, but she wasn't going to give up until she knew for sure. She unfolded the printout of the newspaper page.

Did Duncan have something to do with the boy who had been knocked over? Surely not? She remembered Duncan's driving licence. It was only issued in 2004 so legally he couldn't have been driving *any* car, although her own experience told her that a small thing like no licence didn't necessarily prevent people from driving. She had always wondered why Duncan had left it until he was nearly twenty-two to learn, but he said he loved his mountain bike and wherever possible preferred to use that.

Her search for the people involved in the accident got her nowhere until she decided to check if either of them had a Facebook account. She got an immediate hit for a Carl Boardman who seemed to fit the age profile – a big beefy guy with a ruddy face and thinning sandy hair. There could have been more than one person with that name of course, but he lived in Manchester so it was plausible that he was the same guy. There was nothing on Adya Kamala.

She gave up and closed her computer, folding the printout again to put it in her bag. Realising both sides of the page had been printed, she glanced at the article on the reverse. There was a picture of a lady in late middle age, dressed in a smart black jacket with white edging over a black and white dress. Her black hat was at a slightly strange angle, but she had a happy smile on her face. Glad to come across something that wasn't depressing, Maggie read how the lady – a Patricia Rowe – had been awarded an MBE in the Queen's birthday honours list for services to children and families. To celebrate, Mrs Rowe had had a party. It appeared she and her late husband had fostered over a hundred children, and since becoming a widow she had continued to foster.

'I loved all my children,' the report quoted. 'It didn't matter to me what each child's background was, and their parentage was the last thing I considered. Children deserve to be loved, and so many of those who came to me had been deprived of that basic human need. I consider that I have been privileged to be able to offer them the gift of unconditional love – the same as any other parent would.'

At the bottom of the page was a message from Mrs Rowe to her foster children who hadn't attended the party, saying how much she missed them and what a shame it was that they hadn't been able to make it. She hoped they would get in touch soon.

How sad, Maggie thought, to have done so much for so many children only to find that some had moved on without a backward glance. She knew of parents whose own children never bothered to contact them, so it must be doubly hard to keep in contact with foster children. But just as heart-breaking to lose them.

She thought of her own children, and how everything that was happening with Duncan was affecting them. She was still no closer to finding out who he really was, and for just a moment her love and trust felt less secure, less solid.

28

By the time Maggie arrived home that night she felt mentally and physically drained. She hadn't heard from Duncan again. Her phone had been fully charged, and even in court she had kept it in her hand so she would feel it vibrate.

Alf Horton had been remanded that afternoon and sent to Strangeways. Fortunately she hadn't had to spend any time alone with him and had only had to go through the motions for the sake of the hearing. She hoped she wouldn't have to see him again for a while – not until they were ready to begin the preparation for his inevitable trial.

It was Friday evening, and her mind flipped back to so many other Fridays: looking forward to getting home and spending the weekend with her family, planning trips or surprises, taking over the cooking so Duncan could have a break. Tonight there was no Duncan to welcome her. No warm home, fire lit and the smell of dinner cooking.

The longest she had gone without thinking about Duncan all day was about thirty seconds. He had now been gone for forty-eight hours and Maggie was no clearer in her thinking. She had discounted most of her early theories – none of them made sense any longer. She was left with three options: an affair that had somehow gone wrong; somebody was threatening Duncan; he was somehow involved in the death of this young woman.

She had discounted the third option as soon as she considered it. How could she even *think* that about her husband? But then did she really know who her husband was?

If it was an affair, the only thing that made sense was that the dead woman was Duncan's lover; her husband or boyfriend had found out and killed her, and he was now after Duncan. If that were the case, surely she would be helping Duncan by telling the police? Or was he being framed for the woman's death?

In his text, Duncan had been adamant that she mustn't call the police, but on her drive home from work she had decided that if she didn't hear from him within the next twelve hours, she was going to ignore his plea. She would seek out this policeman – Tom Douglas – and tell him everything.

Feeling slightly better for having a plan – of sorts – she had stopped to pick the children up and been pleased to see that a day at school seemed to have settled them a bit; nothing like a bit of normality to help them get back on track. But when she glanced in the mirror as she turned into their cul-de-sac, she was sad to see Josh's look of disappointment that his dad's van wasn't parked in front of the house. She had promised them pizza, but Josh had asked if they could go home first so he could get changed. His excuse was that he didn't want to go out in his school uniform, but she knew it wasn't that at all.

Maggie was worried that Josh would say he didn't want to go out now and she would have to deal with Lily, who had been so looking forward to the treat, but she was wrong. He came downstairs ready in his jeans and a sweatshirt and headed towards the door.

'What's this, Mum?' he asked, picking up an envelope from behind the front door. He passed it to Maggie.

'I've no idea,' she said, noticing that there was no address on the envelope. It must have been hand-delivered.

For a second she thought Duncan might have returned during the day and left her a note. But it wasn't his writing.

She slit the envelope open with her finger. Inside was a single sheet of paper folded in two. Instinctively she knew that she didn't want Josh to see what was on the page.

'It's nothing,' she said. 'Only a circular. Go and find Lily for me would you, sweetheart? See if she's ready and preferably not wearing her *Frozen* costume.'

Josh trundled off, clearly not thrilled with his mission.

Maggie unfolded the piece of paper. It was a photograph printed on plain paper – a photograph of a woman with black hair and red lips. It wasn't the murdered woman who had been all over the news that day, but there was a superficial resemblance. This woman also had long dark hair, and her lips appeared to have been inexpertly painted with bright red lipstick. The woman's lifeless eyes seemed to look into Maggie's, and she felt an explosion of pain in her chest.

But the face and the hair meant nothing in comparison with the piece of cardboard propped against the woman's legs. The writing was rough, as if scribbled with a biro and gone over and over until the pen had almost pierced the card. Just two words.

You're next.

29

Saturday

It had been fairly late in the day on Friday by the time Tom discovered who Leo's new boyfriend was most likely to be: Julian Richmond, a partner in Manchester's biggest corporate finance firm. Divorced with two teenage children, he lived in Bramhall. Tom had tried to call, but there was no answer and it didn't seem appropriate to leave a message, so he had decided that today – Saturday – he would go round to Mr Richmond's house and hope to find the man at home. In theory it was Tom's day off, but in the middle of a murder investigation he rarely considered shift patterns. Nor was checking up on Leo part of his job, but he couldn't rest until he knew she was okay. Memories of the similarity of the two victims twelve years ago were haunting him. If this were a repeat performance, surely Leo's resemblance to Hayley suggested she was at risk. Was he too late?

Julian Richmond lived in a big house on a smart street, and yet to Tom's mind his home, protected from the road by a curved wall, was by far the ugliest. Tom pushed open one of a pair of cast-iron gates and walked up the paved drive towards a porticoed front door. He gazed up at the white-painted edifice and wondered what had made somebody choose to build a Mediterranean-style villa in the midst of the Edwardian elegance of its neighbours. There was no doubting the opulence of the place, though.

He pushed the doorbell and waited. It was 8.30 in the morning. Early to come calling on a Saturday perhaps, but better than arriving at ten to find Richmond had gone off to play golf.

He heard a door open inside and a brief burst of music before the door closed again. Tom could hear somebody whistling the song that had been on the radio, something Tom vaguely recognised as a Phil Collins tune from his youth.

The door opened, and a tall man with dark hair greying around the temples smiled pleasantly at Tom. He looked to be in his late forties. 'Hello. Can I help you?'

'My name's Tom Douglas. I'm a detective with the Greater Manchester Police, but I'm not here on police business right now. I wondered if I could have a word with you, please? It's about Leonora Harris.'

The man's expression changed. The smile stayed on his lips, but his eyes lost some of their sparkle.

'Ah Leo. Yes, do come in, Tom. I've heard a lot about you.'

Julian Richmond showed him into an ultra-modern kitchen that Tom loved. The shiny dark red units gave the room a warmth in stark contrast to the view outside the windows of gloomy clouds hovering above a large back garden. Julian turned off the radio and pressed a button on a coffee machine. Tom perched on a bar stool set beside a dark grey granite central island and Julian waited for the beans to stop grinding before he spoke.

'I hope you don't mind coming into the kitchen. It's the only part of the house I can stand. I made the mistake of letting my ex-wife choose our home, and then she upped and left me with a house that's not going to be easy to sell. But I'm trying. Milk?'

'Kitchens work fine for me, and no, thanks,' Tom said.

'How is Leo?' Julian Richmond asked.

Tom watched the man closely as he spoke.

'I had a call from Leo's brother-in-law a couple of days ago. His wife, Ellie, hadn't heard from Leo for a week or so, and when I called at her apartment there was no sign of her. I gather she's not been there for some days and I was wondering if you knew where she was.'

Julian Richmond handed Tom an espresso and placed a sugar bowl within reach. He leaned against the Aga rail, holding his coffee in both hands.

'Please call me Julian. I'm not sure I can help you, though. I haven't seen Leo for a few days.'

'Have you spoken to her?' Tom asked.

'No.' Julian wasn't looking at Tom; he was staring into his coffee cup. Tom said nothing and waited for the other man to break the silence.

After about thirty seconds, Julian gave a small sigh as if the recollection pained him and said, 'I asked Leo to come with me to Haydock Park last Saturday – we had invited some of our top clients. Leo had been with me to Cheltenham so I thought she would enjoy it. That time it was just the two of us. Well, it was supposed to be, although we bumped into a few of my younger colleagues, which didn't please her. Leo said she wasn't ready to go public, so a corporate day at Haydock was a non-starter.'

'So what happened?'

Julian looked at Tom and appeared to be weighing him up. He then nodded, as if Tom had passed some test or other and deserved the truth.

'I'm afraid I made the mistake of asking if she was taking me to her niece's christening last Sunday, and it didn't go down well. We had a bit of a row. I was cross and disappointed, but it didn't last long. Two days later, I'd calmed down. I tried to call her, but she didn't answer her phone or her mobile, so in the end I went round to her apartment but I didn't get any answer.'

Tom had interviewed many people in his time, and he hadn't the slightest doubt that Julian Richmond was telling the truth.

'I called round and asked the neighbours to let me in,' Tom said. 'Leo's clothes were all over the bedroom. It was a tip, and that's not like the Leo I know. Does that mean anything to you?'

Richmond looked shocked. 'Absolutely not.'

'And she never mentioned going away?' Tom asked.

'Not a word. It wasn't much of an argument. I may have rushed things, but I never thought it would mean our relationship was over.'

'What about the flowers? Didn't she respond when you sent those?' Tom asked, remembering what Luca had told him.

Julian Richmond looked confused. 'Flowers? I didn't send any; I went in person. If somebody sent her flowers, it certainly wasn't me.'

Tom's phone rang, interrupting the momentary silence.

The caller was Becky. 'Tom, you need to get back into town. Where are you?'

'Bramhall. Why, what's up?' Into his head flashed an image of Leo. *Please, no*, he thought.

'You're not going to like this, Tom, but we've got another body.'

30

The young woman's body had been squeezed into a narrow space between two arches of an old brick railway viaduct in the Castlefield area of the city and was held upright by the cramped space. The victim's sightless eyes gazed at nothing, the blood from her gashed throat staining her clothes. It had taken a while for her to be found because it was Saturday morning and the route under the viaduct led to office buildings that were deserted at the weekend. If it hadn't been for one keen young woman who had decided to put in some extra hours in her new job, the body could have gone undiscovered until Monday morning. As it was, the girl who had found the body was almost hysterical and a pair of paramedics were dealing with her.

Tom stood quietly for a moment, taking in the scene, visualising the moment when the woman's body had been so callously left for some unfortunate passer-by to discover. Becky stood silently by his side, waiting for him to give some sign that she should speak. He turned towards her and gave a brief nod.

'All we know up to now,' Becky said, her voice low, 'is that the girl who found her was on her way into work at about eight this morning. She said she hated walking under this bridge because she was always a bit spooked by that gap.'

Becky pointed to the place where the victim's body had been displayed – the only word to describe how she had been positioned – a space between two huge brick arches. The woman's body had been pushed in, facing out towards the path, her back against an old supermarket trolley, her throat slit from ear to ear.

A train sped overhead, the vibration seeming to run down the walls and into the earth below. Tom could only imagine what a shock it must have been to see a woman, sitting, staring out onto the road.

Tom crouched down in front of the body. The woman was perhaps in her early thirties. It was difficult to tell because it was clear she had had a hard life. Her skin was pitted with old acne scars, and her top lip was puckered in the way of a heavy smoker. It wasn't easy to imagine how she normally looked because of the hair and the make-up. A long dark wig had been roughly stuck on her head, and it had slipped sideways. Her lips had been painted with bright red lipstick, smudged around the edges.

'He's making a statement,' said Tom. 'He's tried to make her look the same as the first one, so the looks have to be significant. He obviously couldn't find anybody to fit the bill so he's used props – the wig, the lipstick. Do we know who she is?'

Becky shook her head slowly. 'No. We couldn't find any identification on her. I hate to generalise, but the micro skirt and high-heeled boots suggest she may have been a prostitute, although I know half the girls in Manchester go out looking like this now. But she had a few packets of condoms in her bag – different flavours, et cetera, so she could give men what they wanted, I suppose. If she was simply a woman on a night out with friends, she would have had some money on her, and she didn't have a penny, so if she was a prostitute she could only just have started work.'

'Her money could have been stolen,' Tom suggested, although he knew that wasn't the case. He knew exactly what this was. 'Has anybody checked her leg?'

He looked over at Jumbo, who had been keeping unusually quiet. He nodded his large head, his huge creamy eyes sorrowful.

'She's not wearing tights. Her legs look like she's been slapping fake tan on – they're a bit orange at the ankles. But at the top of her left leg there are three parallel cuts, deeper than the last one. And

I think the doc will confirm that they were made before death this time – there's a lot more blood.'

Tom felt the woman's pain for a moment and left the tent, walking away from the scene. He needed to think. A few metres away a narrow track led down from the path to the canal. He wasn't sure if it was still the Rochdale Canal or the Bridgewater – he would need to get a map to clarify that. The area was crawling with canals. He wondered why the woman hadn't been disposed of where she was unlikely to be discovered. It had to be because the victims – both of them – were intended to be found. They were a message to somebody. Last time there was a third victim, although fortunately she had managed to save herself. Was this one going to be the second of three?

12 years ago – early June

The incident room was filling up. It was time to admit that the team was floundering. They had two murders and an attempted murder, but they still hadn't made any progress. To Tom's surprise his boss suggested they employ a profiler.

'We need someone to tell us who we're looking for – what his motives are, and where the fuck he's hiding – because we're making bugger-all progress.' DCI Victor Elliot glared at Tom as if it was solely his fault.

Tom ignored the look. A profiler was a good idea, although he still couldn't quite reconcile himself entirely to these murders being the work of one man. The modus operandi was different for each crime – the first a slit throat, the second a strangling and the third – failed attempt – a suffocation. And then there was the Swedish girl's comment that her attacker was being watched.

The incident room was crowded with standing room only at the back when the profiler arrived. A young American woman with cropped white hair and startling green eyes, she had everybody's attention within seconds.

'There are a significant number of irregularities in this case, and if this is one man he's behaved in an inconsistent manner, which concerns me. I've looked at the victimology, and that in itself is unusual. Their backgrounds would be less relevant if these had been opportunistic attacks, but that clearly isn't the case. These were carefully planned killings of strategically selected victims. They were chosen for their looks. The three lines on the victims' legs are important. Have any of you heard of the "power of three"?' she asked. She cast her eyes around the room and everybody stared back, but nobody spoke.

'It's a concept that some people believe in: that the number three stands for that which is solid, real, substantial, complete – for example the three dimensions of length, breadth and height which are necessary to form a solid. There are three great divisions that complete time: the past, the present and the future. Thought, word and deed complete the sum of human capability: animal, vegetable, mineral – the three kingdoms of the natural world. I could go on. For some people, three is such a powerful number that everything has to be finished in threes for them to feel safe. A famous physicist, Nikola Tesla, was so obsessed with the number that he used to walk around the block three times before he would enter a building.'

She paused and again looked around the room, taking them all in, but her gaze settled on Tom, who instantly felt guilty about his scepticism.

'If this is his driver, he will try to kill one more girl to replace the failed attempt. She will look like the other three, but this time he will be sure to finish the job. I'm using "he" throughout this presentation because, as we know, the chances are that the killer is a man. However, "he" could just as easily be more than one man.'

She paused, and every eye was on her.

'But there's another theory that fits the profile. I would like to suggest to you that there was only one victim that mattered to the killer. Only one person who had to die. The others were decoys, added to confuse us. Three may have been chosen as the best number to ensure the police were chasing their tails trying to find a link between the victims when there isn't one. And if only one of them had to die, the most important job is to work out which of them it was.'

❖

Tom continued along the canal bank. Twelve years ago he had waited to see whether another victim would be found, and it had never happened. Did that mean that nobody else had died, or simply that the other body or bodies had not been discovered? And were there going to be three this time too – three women, but potentially only one for whom there was a motive for murder? And if so, which?

The problem with motives was always the same. What seemed clear and right to the killer could be meaningless to anybody else, and guessing motive was like guessing the outcome of the National Lottery.

He couldn't forget the misidentification of the first victim this week, and he couldn't drive Leo's face from his mind. Was she going to be the next victim, and if so was she the *real* target? *Leo, where are you?* He was no nearer finding her. Had the woman standing opposite police headquarters been Leo, and had he missed the chance of helping her? The only thing he knew for certain was that somebody had sent flowers to her, and that somebody was not Julian Richmond, whom Tom believed when he said he had no idea where Leo was. And what had happened to the flowers?

Tom tried to convince himself that Leo's similarity to the other women was purely coincidental, and that of course she wasn't going to be the next victim. But he didn't believe in coincidence. Years of experience had taught him that to dismiss anything as coincidence was a sure way of missing something vital. It was a lazy excuse for not investigating things properly, and he wasn't going to put Leo's life at risk.

As if to jerk him back to the present, Tom heard Becky shouting to him, and he turned and climbed back up the hill towards the crime scene, more certain than ever that Leo was in serious danger but not knowing from whom, or why. He needed to talk to Ellie. Maybe Leo's sister would have some idea.

31

When Maggie woke up on Saturday morning after a pitiful couple of hours of restless sleep, she turned onto her side and reached out for Duncan, expecting to find his warm naked back waiting for her to cuddle up to. But the other side of the bed was empty, and the memory of the last two days hit her like a stone. Her eyes swam with hot tears and she buried her face in the pillow.

Her resolve to call the police had wavered during the night. While she and the children had been eating their pizzas the evening before, she had admitted to Josh that she was a bit worried about his daddy, and Josh had seemed relieved that finally she was telling him the truth.

'So am I, Mummy, but he'll be back. He loves us,' Josh had said.

'I know he does, Joshy. I suppose we need to trust him right now.'

The words she had spoken to Josh kept piercing her thoughts. She *did* need to trust him. But was that the right decision?

'I don't know, I don't know,' she sobbed. She wanted life back the way it had been, and she knew that the moment the police were involved, any chance of that was gone forever.

She pushed her tired limbs up and out of the bed and shuffled into the bathroom with barely the energy to lift her feet. After five minutes standing under a blast of hot spray from the shower she began to feel alive again. The dull ache of loss was still there, but it was starting to feel like an old friend. She was getting used to it.

Leaving the children to sleep on, she went downstairs and

made a strong cup of coffee and sat down at the kitchen table, her chin resting on one upturned palm. Was there anything else she could do that she hadn't thought of that might help her unravel the mystery of who Duncan was? She had one idea, but only one.

She pulled her laptop across the table towards her and found the picture she was looking for – a rare photo of Duncan taken when he wasn't looking. He was convinced he wasn't very photogenic, but Maggie had always thought that was nonsense. She grabbed her handbag and pulled out the article from the *Manchester Evening News*. Carl Boardman was a friend of the lad who had been knocked over and killed. Were they friends of Duncan's?

Maggie logged onto Facebook, found Carl Boardman's page and sent him a message, asking if he knew the man in the attached photo. She gave a rather weak excuse that she was trying to track this man down, and she had remembered he had a friend called Carl Boardman. Carl seemed fairly active on Facebook, so she was hopeful of a quick response. She knew how unlikely a positive response was, but she couldn't sit here and do nothing.

She looked at the printout and read again about the amazing woman who had fostered all those children. If – and it was a big if – Duncan had kept a page from a newspaper, in theory the article of interest could be on either side of the sheet, so Maggie decided to check if Patricia Rowe had a Facebook page. She was probably well into her seventies by now, but it was worth a try.

As she trawled through the inevitably long list of Patricia Rowe entries she spotted the letters MBE next to a photo of an elderly lady surrounded by children. She had found her. Mrs Rowe didn't seem to post much herself but shared posts from other, much younger people, and Maggie guessed the lady was keeping tabs on the children she had looked after. There were no posts shared for the past two months, though.

One old post made Maggie's eyes fill with tears.

To my lost children: if you are reading this, please get in touch. I loved every one of you when you lived with me, and I need to know if you are all right now. You're all equally special to me, so I will continue to post this message on Facebook in the hope that you will call me. My number hasn't changed, nor has my address. Here are some pictures to remind you of the happy times. With love always, Pat.

Linked to the post were a number of albums, and Maggie could see they focused on children of various ages. She was sure Patricia Rowe would have been a great person to know. She decided to send her a message with a picture of Duncan too, but again she didn't hold out much hope of a positive response.

By late morning, Maggie had heard back from Carl Boardman. He said he didn't recognise the face she had posted – he didn't know the guy. So that avenue was closed for now. And there was nothing from Patricia Rowe. It wasn't a surprise, but it was frustrating.

She was about to close her computer and go and find the children when she heard a crash. It had come from the garage.

Her heart thumped.

She leaped up from her chair, ran to the garage door and stopped. Who was in there?

She was about to turn back into the house and make sure the children were safe when she heard a noise. It sounded like a sob.

Josh.

Maggie flung the door open. Josh was lying on the floor, Duncan's bike on top of him.

'Josh,' she shouted. 'Are you okay?'

Maggie rushed forward and lifted the mountain bike off him.

'What happened?' she asked as she pulled him to his feet. He was clearly not hurt – just upset with himself.

'I was trying to get the bikes down off the wall. I was going to ask if we could go for a ride. But yours was caught around Daddy's, and when I tried to get it down, it pulled Daddy's off and it fell on top of me.'

Maggie pulled Josh towards her and gave him a cuddle. She looked at Duncan's bike and had a sudden flash of memory. On his thirtieth birthday she had told Duncan to go into the garage, and there was his present – a beautiful new bike, the one he had wanted for ages. She remembered the surprise and pleasure on his face, and the happiness of that day.

Duncan's old bike had been quite a sight. The main frame was yellow, but the bit at the front, which he told her was called the suspension fork, was red, and the back bit – the seat stay, Dunc said – was bright green. He had built it from spare parts.

There was just one thing that clouded the perfection of the memory. She had told the children that Daddy had won races on his old bike, and Josh – ever fascinated by detail – had quizzed Duncan about where, when and were there photos? Perhaps they were online. Josh wouldn't shut up, and Duncan had lost his temper.

At the time, Maggie had been cross with Duncan, but it was soon over and they had all gone out for a birthday tea. Now, though, Maggie realised that like everything in Duncan's past, she only had very sketchy details about his cycling success, and the races had never been mentioned again.

32

By late Saturday morning the incident room was buzzing. Becky had been right about the body they had found that morning: the victim's name was Michelle Morgan, and she was known to the police. According to the vice team, she had been around for years, and they considered her to be smarter than most of the girls. She had always been fairly astute at judging which cars to get into and which to avoid.

She had obviously got it wrong this time, but this suggested that whoever's car she had got into, she hadn't considered him to be a threat.

She was found well away from her own patch, which was apparently the eastern part of central Manchester around Piccadilly station, on the roads that ran under the railway lines. Tom couldn't help thinking it was strange that the body had been moved to Castlefield when the first body had been found so close to Michelle's preferred working area.

According to Jumbo, the woman hadn't been killed *in situ*. There was no blood in the vicinity of her body, although there was plenty on her clothes. She had to have been transported to the position under the railway arches after death, most probably some time during the early hours of the morning. The body had now been taken to the mortuary, and the team had begun the examination of the shopping trolley against which her body had been displayed.

Tom hadn't expected to get any update until the forensic investigation of the site was complete, so he was surprised when a clearly excited Jumbo called. 'Tom, I think we might have something here. There's something I'd like to show you, if you can spare the time.'

Castlefield was only a ten-minute drive for Tom and Becky, and if Jumbo thought it was significant, Tom was only too happy to return to the scene.

Crime scene investigators were crawling all over the place, but one item was centre stage, and Jumbo was standing guard by its side.

'Take a look at the shopping trolley,' he said, his wide smile back in place now the body had gone. 'Look at its position in relation to where the body was situated. I think it was supposed to look as if it had been abandoned, but it's not been here long.'

'How do you know?' Becky asked.

'Look down here.' Jumbo pointed to where two wheels were missing. 'The body of the trolley is made of zinc-coated steel. Zinc corrodes over time, but it doesn't rust like steel. Now look at where the wheels have been broken off. You can see the bare steel, and it's not rusty. I think the wheels were broken off on purpose and very recently. We're supposed to think this is just an old abandoned trolley, but what if they wheeled the body here in it and then broke the wheels off, thinking we would disregard it as junk? We'll check it for blood, but if it is related, it's good news.'

Tom knew exactly what Jumbo meant. If the trolley had been used to transport the victim's body, the killer couldn't have brought her far. It gave them a different search area than if, for example, she had been brought here by car. They knew she hadn't been killed *in situ*, so if she had then been put into the trolley and pushed, they could start searching likely places in the vicinity. And if they checked out where the trolley had originated, it might give a geographic profiler something to start with.

Tom looked around for likely places for the murder to have been committed. There were too many, that was the problem. The arches under the railway lines were largely occupied by car repair companies and the like, and any one of the premises could be the site of the murder. They would all have to be searched.

'There's something else, Tom,' Jumbo said. 'When we were checking out the first victim, there were some wheel marks in the mud in the tunnel that could easily have come from a trolley like this. The marks were unclear because there were puddles and stony areas on the path, but we managed to get a couple of good sections. You were concerned about one man carrying a deadweight, but what if he didn't? What if he wheeled her there?'

Tom remembered them thinking the same thing twelve years ago when Sonia Beecham's body was found on Pomona Island.

'That would take some nerve, wouldn't it?' Becky said, her face displaying her incredulity.

'No more than carrying the victim over your shoulder. Either way, if somebody sees you, you've got a dead body with you. If she was in a shopping trolley you could at least cover her up with a bit of carpet or something – make it look as if you're moving some stuff around.'

If the two victims had been murdered in the same location, though, the killer would have needed more than a shopping trolley to transport them. There was about a mile and a half between the locations at which the bodies had been found. Somehow Tom couldn't see anybody trundling through the streets of Manchester with a dead body in a shopping trolley, even with an old rug covering it. If it turned out that the trolley had been used in both crimes, that suggested the killer had a van of some kind – something that you could fit a trolley into. Then he could get close to his chosen place, stick the body in the trolley and push it the last few metres.

It was one more thing to add to their list – the suspicion that this man had a van.

'Becky, let's get somebody on to tracing the supermarket trolley. I don't know how many stores from this chain there are around Manchester. Let's get them all on a map and see if it helps. Then contact them and see if they have any video of trolleys being nicked by somebody in a van.'

'I don't suppose he's left a pound coin in the trolley with a nice fat fingerprint, has he?' Becky said with a grin.

Tom laughed. He wished life was so easy.

❖

Fortunately for Tom, he and Becky had arrived at the murder scene in different cars so he didn't have her driving to contend with on the way back to the incident room. This meant he was able to spend the time thinking, rather than clinging for dear life to the grab handle as Becky swung her car between lorries, buses and trams.

He tried to focus on the two dead women, but the resemblance of the first to Leo, and then the rather pathetic attempt to make the second look similar was unnerving him. The message was clear. If the profiler had been right all those years ago, three was the key number. She had offered an alternative perspective, though – that two of the three were merely to confuse the police and were effectively motiveless murders. So in searching for motive with the two women who were already dead, were they wasting their time? Was one of these two the 'real' victim, or was that going to be the third woman?

If the second theory was right, Tom's every instinct said the crucial murder had not yet taken place. Hayley Walker didn't appear to have any enemies, and the latest victim didn't even look like Hayley – she had been made up to resemble her. So why go to all that trouble with the second one unless it was a warning to somebody else? It would also explain why the bodies had been put on show. Twelve years ago Sonia Beecham and Tamsin Grainger had been left sitting upright, but in less public places where they were unlikely to be discovered immediately. This time, the killer wanted both girls to be found quickly.

The thought that the third victim could be Leo was tormenting him. He couldn't think of a reason why anybody would want to kill her, but that meant nothing. She was out there somewhere. He could feel it. He knew it with every bone in his body. He just didn't know where, and he didn't know where to start looking.

12 years ago – June

'Douglas! My office,' the boss shouted from his open door.

Tom had a feeling this wasn't going to be a happy meeting. He picked up his files and made his way into DCI Victor Elliott's office, closing the door behind him.

'What have we got on the dead girls?' the DCI asked before Tom had a chance to sit down.

Tom pulled up a chair to the visitor's side of the desk.

'Plenty of background, that's for sure. Particularly Tamsin Grainger. She was a popular girl, although from what I can tell she was more popular with the lads than with other girls.'

The DCI's mouth turned up at the corner in a lecherous sneer. 'Bit of a tart, was she? No need to be shy, Douglas. Tell it like it is.'

Tom wasn't being shy; he just wasn't inclined to make an assumption without the evidence to back it up.

It irritated him that his boss called everybody by their surname. Perhaps he thought it made him sound as if he had been to some posh school where surnames were the accepted form of address, but he had been to the local comprehensive like everybody else in the office.

'Why are you so keen on this guy Alexander?' the boss said, pointing to a picture clipped to the file on his desk.

'He was Tamsin Grainger's boyfriend. Well, that's what he believed, but according to her friends she had a different idea. From what we can gather, he thought it was an exclusive relationship, but she had only seen him twice and he had totally misinterpreted the situation. After he found her in a car with one of his lecturers – not one of hers, as it happens – he had a massive row with her, overheard by some lads returning from the pub. She laughed in Alexander's face, told him to grow up and refused to see him again. According to the lads, he was about to punch her, but they intervened. She told her friends to steer clear of him, that he was a weirdo, but he wouldn't leave her alone – kept following her around, apparently. According to one girl, she stuck a picture of him on the wall in the halls of residence and wrote *knob* underneath it.'

'Yeah, I heard about that. The boyfriend's got a cast-iron alibi, though, so rule him out and don't waste any more time on him. It's more than likely another ex who hasn't got over her. Check them all out, and the lecturer too – dirty bugger, screwing his students.' Victor grinned.

Tom looked at his boss. He knew he wanted a result – they all did – but a result had to be the right result, not just another tick in a box. Victor wanted them to find one of the ex-boyfriends who didn't have an alibi and then pin it on him, but Tom hadn't given up on Alexander, alibi or no alibi.

He had to admit, it was an impossible alibi to break. Alexander had been in the company of about thirty other students at the time of both murders. For the first he had been in North Wales, and for the second he had been in the Lake District with a university sports club. But Tom couldn't help feeling that he knew something, although he had no motive at all for Sonia Beecham's murder as far as they had been able to tell. She was such a quiet girl, and they couldn't find any evidence that her path had crossed with Alexander's. But if the profiler was right, she could have been a decoy and her murder without motive.

There was something not right about this lad Alexander. When Tom had interviewed him he had talked too much.

'I wasn't even here,' he kept repeating. 'I was away with my team. I won my race – it's all recorded. You can check, you know.'

Tom had pointed out more than once that they already had.

'And Tamsin – I know things ended badly. What did you think of her?' Tom had asked.

There was a pause, as if the lad was trying to work out what to say.

'She was a slapper,' Alexander said, his mouth forming a tight line.

33

The cycle track was slushy and Lily loved riding through the puddles to make the biggest splash she could. Josh wasn't having a good day, though, and Maggie felt helpless. She was distracted with worries about Duncan and that awful picture that had been pushed through her door the day before, and she was only giving her children a small percentage of her attention. Try as she might, she couldn't force away the desperate fear that Duncan was in danger and needed her help, and yet she didn't even know where he was.

Lily's sturdy little legs were pedalling furiously, and Maggie increased her speed slightly to keep up with her daughter as they rounded the bends in the path that ran along the outer edge of the woodland. It was a couple of minutes before she realised that Josh was no longer right behind her.

'Lily, stop,' she shouted, applying her brakes. 'We've lost Josh.'

But Lily ignored her, or didn't hear her, her wispy blonde curls blowing in the wind as she pedalled. She often sang as she rode her bike, and she was probably lost in her own little world. Maggie looked over her shoulder again. What should she do?

Josh was probably a bit further back, round the corner, hidden by the trees. But they couldn't cycle off and leave him, and now Lily was getting away from her.

Maggie only had one choice. She raised herself off her saddle and pedalled hard until she caught up with and passed Lily. She swivelled to face Lily, coming towards her.

'Stop,' she said. Lily laughed, thinking it was a game. 'We've lost Josh.'

Lily put her feet on the ground and turned her upper body to look back along the track. There was no sign of Josh.

'Come on, Tiddles. We need to go back and find him.'

Lily heaved her bike round and started back along the track. They rounded the bend. But the path ahead of them was clear. No Josh. Where *was* he?

'There, Mummy – look,' Lily shouted, her finger pointing to the side of the track.

Lying on its side was Josh's bike, but there was no sign of her son. Maggie's heart began to hammer in her chest.

'Josh!' she shouted as loudly as she could. 'Josh, where are you?' Lily joined in.

They were right at the edge of the woods, next to a small parking area, but it was empty – or about to be. A white van was pulling out of the car park. Maggie stared open-mouthed at its retreating rear doors. 'Duncan?' she whispered, too quietly for Lily to hear her. She knew it was wishful thinking. The van wasn't as new as Duncan's. Or as clean. And there was no sign of Josh.

She jumped off her bike and threw it down on the side of the lane, screaming Josh's name as loudly as she could. She turned to Lily, who was staring at her, her mouth turning down at the corners. *Oh God, I'm scaring Lily.*

'It's okay, sweetheart. I'm sure he's hiding from us – playing a game.' She plucked her daughter off her saddle with one hand and steered the bike off the track with the other, leaving it propped against a tree. With her daughter under one arm, she climbed the bank into the wood where it bordered the small car park.

'Josh,' she shouted, trying to keep the fear from her voice.

Up ahead she saw a flash of red. His cycle helmet.

Still carrying Lily she ran the fifty metres to where she could see the helmet. It was Josh, lying face down in the grass.

'*Josh!*'

She fell to her knees at his side, put Lily onto the damp grass and reached out to her son. With relief, she saw his back moving but in seconds she knew he was crying.

'Joshy, are you hurt, darling?' she asked.

He didn't lift his head, but a weak 'No' emerged from above his folded arms.

'What happened? What are you doing here?' She stroked his back gently.

Slowly he lifted his head. 'I thought it was Daddy,' was all he said, before the tears came again. Maggie stroked his back gently. Lily stroked his leg.

'I don't think it was, sweetheart. That van was a bit old for Daddy's.'

He raised himself up on his elbows.

'I know. But I saw it this morning too – at the top of our road. I thought it might be Daddy then, but there were two men in it, so I thought I was wrong. Then it drove off.'

Maggie put her arm around her son.

'Then when we set off on the bikes, it was there again but parked round the corner outside Oscar's, so I thought it must be some men working on Oscar's house or something.'

Oscar was Josh's friend and lived just round the corner.

'That sounds right, Josh. There are always workmen there.'

'I know, but when we turned to go onto the cycle path, I put my hand out like Daddy taught me, and I looked in my mirror to check if there was anything behind. That's when I saw the van. It was following us. When we got to the car park, it was already there, and the men were watching. One of them had a camera.'

Maggie's hand flew to her mouth to cover her gasp. Why were these men following them? Why did they have a camera? But she had to calm Josh down. She rolled from her knees and sat down next to her son.

'Okay, Joshy. Not to worry. I can understand why you thought it was Daddy's van.'

'I know it wasn't, because the number was different. I checked. Wrong place, wrong year, and Bad Smelly Man.'

Josh and his friend Oscar had become obsessed with car number plates since on a long car journey Oscar's dad had challenged him to spot cars with every initial letter of the alphabet. The boys had taken it a stage further, and now made the last three letters stand for something relating to the driver – hence Bad Smelly Man – BSM. Maggie knew that Josh would have at least that part of the number plate correct.

'And then,' Josh continued, 'one of the men got out of the car and waved to me. He shouted, "Hey Josh."'

'He knew your name?' Maggie tried to keep the panic from her voice.

'He asked if I was missing Daddy. And if I see him, I have to say hi from Sam.'

'Maybe Oscar's said something about your dad being away, sweetheart. That'll be it.'

'I haven't told Oscar. I haven't told *anybody*. I just want Daddy back.'

Maggie puller him closer and grabbed Lily too. 'I know, love. We all do.'

'Then he said something weird. I think he said, "Tell Mummy she's next," but I might have got that wrong. Then they got back in the van and drove off. I ran after them. I wanted to ask if they knew where Daddy is, but I slipped and fell.' Josh started to sob again and Maggie squeezed him to her, whispering reassurances to her small son.

The damp was seeping through Maggie's jeans where she was sitting on the wet grass, but she barely noticed. She was cold. So cold.

❖

It was with a sense of relief that Maggie and the children turned the corner into the cul-de-sac to see a black cab drawing up at the end of their drive and Suzy getting out with a suitcase. She had told her not to come, but now Maggie desperately needed somebody to talk all this through with, and her sister could entertain the children while she spoke to the police. This had gone on for long enough.

'What a sorry-looking troupe you all are,' was her sister's greeting. 'Did all of you fall off your bikes? You're covered in mud, the lot of you.'

'Hi, Suzy,' Maggie said, her voice flat. 'It's good to see you, but you shouldn't have come.' Her sister looked at her silently for a beat, and her eyes narrowed as she registered the weariness in Maggie's voice.

'Nonsense. You needed me, and I needed an excuse to make Ian take some responsibility for his children for a change. So let's get my case in the door, and then you can go and get yourself showered, Maggie, while I bath these two.'

If things had been any less tense, Maggie would have giggled at Josh's expression.

'I can bath myself, Auntie Suzy,' he said, his eyebrows coming together in a look of worry. He had always been a private little boy, and had made it clear when he was about five that he wasn't sharing his bath with Lily because she was a girl. Maggie had no idea where he had got the notion from, but she hid her amusement and let him get on with it.

The shower was hot, and the pressure strong. For the second time today it was exactly what Maggie needed, and she stood under the steaming jet for as long as she reasonably could, letting the water thaw her frozen body. But there was a level of ice in her that no water was going to melt.

The problem was now much more severe. When Duncan was missing she had been genuinely frightened that he had done something stupid. Now there were men out there who were not only threatening her, but who knew her children by name.

Maggie knew she was going to have to talk to the police. Whatever Duncan had told her.

34

'Suzy, it's good of you to come. But we're fine. Confused, unhappy, terrified but fine.'

'Of course you're not fine. Josh looks lost, poor little man, and you look as if you haven't slept for a week. Have you been to the police?' Suzy asked, keeping her voice low. Maggie had put some of Lily's favourite music on to try to lighten the atmosphere, so she didn't think the children could hear.

'No.'

'Jesus, Mags! Why not?' Suzy asked.

Maggie bit her bottom lip to stop it shaking. 'Because up to now I've been trying to make excuses, and now I've run out of them. If Duncan's in trouble, I want to *help* him, not turn him in. But now I don't think I've got any choice.'

'Thank God. Common sense has prevailed at last.'

Maggie felt something burst inside her. 'It all sounds so bloody obvious to somebody who isn't involved. But forget the logic for a moment. This is my *husband* we're talking about. I love him. I trust him. He's asked me not to go to the police, so I haven't. Ask yourself, in all honesty, what you would do. Go on, stop and think. Would you trust your husband, or would you run to the police because somebody might be threatening you?'

Suzy stared at Maggie for a moment or two then turned and went to the fridge.

'Why is there never any bloody wine in this house?' she muttered, knowing the answer. 'Shall I go and get some? Duncan can hardly complain if he comes home and finds us both pissed.'

Maggie sighed and leaned back against the worktop. She was going to call the police but she would defy any happily married woman to believe this was a straightforward choice.

She could have done with a drink herself, but until this was over it didn't seem smart to let her guard down. There was one thing she wanted more than any alcohol.

'Actually, Suzy, would you mind looking after the kids for an hour or two? Then I promise I'll go and get you some wine. I'd like to disappear upstairs for a while and get my thoughts together because if I'm going to the police I have to make it good, and I have to try as hard as I can to keep Josh out of it. I don't want him questioned on top of everything else.'

Suzy walked across the kitchen and gave her sister a tight hug.

'Take as much time as you like. We'll be fine. And try and get a bit of sleep. Everything will seem clearer then.'

Maggie made her way slowly up the stairs, using the bannister for support and pulling herself up, step by weary step. She climbed onto the bed fully dressed, pulled the duvet over her legs and closed her eyes. But sleep wouldn't come. The dull ache in her chest grew and the first sob was loud – loud enough to be heard downstairs. She quickly clicked the TV remote and turned up the volume – she didn't care what was on – because the storm of unhappiness that had been building inside her was about to erupt. Her last defences had gone, and she lay on her side, her arms wrapped tightly around a pillow and wept for everything she had lost. No matter what happened now, she didn't know how they would ever recover from this and be the family they had been.

Finally the tears subsided into gulps, and she lay exhausted on top of the bed, her body shuddering from time to time. Memories of the years with Duncan flooded her senses. With her eyes closed she could hear him, smell him, taste him. She wished with all her heart that she had insisted on more photographs, but there were none of the two of them together. She tried to conjure his face in her mind, but it wouldn't come.

It was the word Manchester that penetrated her brain, and Maggie rubbed her eyes to clear them. The television was tuned to a news channel, and on the screen there was a white tent under what appeared to be railway arches. Several people in white suits were milling about.

She listened to a report of a body being found that morning. This time the police knew the name of the victim. Maggie couldn't help feeling relieved when she saw a picture of the dead woman. For a moment she had feared it would match the one that had been pushed through her door the evening before. But this woman looked nothing like her, and anyway her body had only been found that morning.

As the newsreader's face faded, the camera homed in on a full-screen image of the victim and Maggie grabbed the remote, hitting the pause button. She leaped off the bed and ran downstairs, startling her sister in the kitchen.

'What is it, Maggie? What's happened?'

Maggie ignored her and grabbed her handbag, groping around under the accumulated rubbish. Finally she walked over to the worktop and upended it. Out spilled coins, lipsticks, her purse, a pair of sunglasses, car keys, comb, tissues and several assorted bits of paper. She rummaged through these and plucked out the folded sheet she was looking for.

She pushed past her sister, barely hearing her protest, and raced back to the bedroom, flattening the paper as she went.

She looked from the paper to the screen. She was right. The woman had a mole near the bottom left corner of her mouth. As did the woman in the photo that had been sent to Maggie. It was the same woman – the garish make-up and black wig in the image sent to Maggie had obscured her natural features. But Maggie had received this photograph more than twelve hours before the body had been discovered. There was only one person who could have taken this photo – the killer.

There was no longer a choice to be made. The children's safety was everything, and this couldn't be ignored.

She picked up the telephone.

In spite of knowing how devastating the outcome was going to be, it felt like a huge relief to be doing something. Maggie didn't want to talk to just any policeman. She knew that if she told them everything, the case would end up with the detective running the murder enquiry, Tom Douglas. But she hadn't made her mind up what she was going to say yet, so decided to talk to one of the desk sergeants at divisional headquarters. She had met Bill Shaw several times, and he seemed to like her. She would play it by ear and ask him to recommend somebody who would take the threat to her and the children seriously.

To her disappointment, he wasn't on duty.

'Shall I put you through to somebody else, madam?' a polite female voice asked.

'I don't know.' Maggie couldn't decide what to do. 'When's he back on duty?'

Having asked for Maggie's name, the woman agreed to check the duty rota, and she was put on hold. If she spoke to somebody who didn't know her, it would waste so much time. 'Madam, I've had a look, and Sergeant Shaw is due in on first shift tomorrow morning. Does that help?'

Maggie sighed with relief. That would be fine. She would get Suzy to look after the children and go in to talk to him in person. She could show him the note with the picture.

She had only just put the phone down when it rang again. Assuming it was the police calling back, she picked up the phone.

'Maggie Taylor,' she answered.

'Hello, Maggie.' She froze. 'Good to see you out and about with the children this afternoon.'

Maggie wanted to scream at him – ask him what he thought he was playing at – but her mouth had gone dry. This man had somehow been involved in the murder discovered today, and probably the previous one too. Maggie had dealt with murderers before, but only in the safety of a police station. She didn't have time to plan what to say.

'Have you seen the news?' he asked. 'Did you recognise our latest offering? Sadly they showed a picture of her on the television without the special hair and make-up we gave her. But I bet you knew who it was, didn't you? That could have been you.'

The silky voice made her skin crawl. She wanted to lash out at him and suddenly she found her voice.

'Was it you in that van today? You need to know I've called the police. So don't phone again, don't leave me any more disgusting photos and *don't* speak to my children.'

When he spoke again his voice had a harder edge. 'That's a real pity, Maggie. You don't know where Duncan is, do you?'

Maggie didn't answer.

'But I do. If you show that picture to the police your husband will feel the pain. Pain you can't imagine. Duncan owes me, Maggie. He owes me.'

She could feel the man's rage now that the smooth tones had been scrubbed away by something brittle, dangerous.

'Tell me how much and I'll pay you. We've got savings.' She could hear the pleading in her own voice and hated herself for appearing weak.

A line had been crossed. She knew it. They had been playing with her before – scaring her for some reason she didn't understand. As a means of getting to Duncan certainly, but now it felt as if the game had changed.

'Money won't solve the problem, Maggie. There's only one way back for your husband. If you talk to the police, his life is over.'

The line went dead.

35

Sunday

Any ideas Becky Robinson may have nurtured of having a lazy Sunday had been blown out of the water by the discovery of the body of Michelle Morgan. Not that she would have been taking the time off anyway with so little progress on Hayley Walker's murder, but the added workload created by the second victim had made it even easier for Becky to avoid going to Mark's mum's for Sunday lunch. It wasn't that she didn't like her, but if she mentioned grandchildren one more time, Becky was going to throttle her.

Mark thought it was funny. He always put on his serious face and nodded, knowing he was winding Becky up. Last time his mother had asked if they had named the date yet, and Becky hadn't known what to say. They hadn't talked about getting married, and she wasn't sure she was ready. They had only been seeing each other for a year, and she had made so many mistakes in the past that she wanted to be sure. Becky had been certain that she loved him, but now she had a nagging doubt. If she truly loved him, why did she get all hot and flustered around other people?

Mark hadn't been annoyed that she couldn't make it; he had just teased her about missing out on the planning of their future for the next twenty years. He knew she wasn't ready to commit, and he was happy with things as they were. But that was Mark. Generally happy with life.

Becky pushed open the door to the staff restaurant. She needed food, preferably something loaded with carbs, to get her through the next few hours. As she waited in line, she turned her head and saw one of the desk sergeants standing next to her. Bill Shaw had been in the force for years and in Becky's opinion was as solid as a rock.

'How are you doing, Becky?' he asked. 'I bet you've got your hands full now. Any further on with the first murder?'

Becky shook her head slowly. 'I wish we were, but for the moment it's not coming together. It will, though.'

Becky reached out to take the cheeseburger and chips she was being handed and put them on her tray, feeling slightly embarrassed that the duty sergeant had selected a chicken salad and she'd got a burger *and* a doughnut. She walked over to an empty table and sat down.

'Mind if I join you?' he said, not waiting for an answer. 'You found out who the first murdered girl is, didn't you?' he asked as he pulled out a chair.

'Yep, she was a nurse. Hayley Walker. We've got some leads, but they're all a bit tenuous at the moment.'

'I nearly had a heart attack when I saw the drawing in the paper on Thursday. I thought, *I know that girl*, but then realised it couldn't be who I thought – I'd seen her alive and kicking when the victim would already have been dead.'

'Who did you think it was?' Becky asked.

'The drawing was the spit of Alf Horton's solicitor. I nearly picked up the phone to Tom. I would have, if I hadn't known it couldn't be her. I'm glad it's not, though. Nice woman.'

'Poor cow, getting Alf Horton as a client,' Becky said.

The sergeant laughed. 'Funnily enough, Maggie Taylor – that's her name – tried to phone me last night, but I was off duty. She said she wanted to talk to me about something but she didn't call or come in this morning.'

Becky bit on a chip. 'What did you do?'

'I decided to give her a quick call before I came over here to check she was okay. It's a bit odd, really. She tried to brush it off, but I could hear the stress in her voice.'

'Did she say what was worrying her?'

'She said she thought it might be nothing, but she'd noticed a white van parked at the top of their road a couple of times, and when she went for a bike ride with the children yesterday, it followed her.'

Becky waited. That wasn't enough to make anybody suspicious, surely?

'She's had a couple of odd phone calls too. No number came up on the screen, and I guess it'll turn out to be an untraceable mobile. She said there was no explicit threat – just a man saying he knew where she was, or something. The thing is, it was as if she wanted to get rid of me – as if she wished she'd never called. I actually wondered if she was a bit spooked because she looks so much like your first murder victim – the nurse. Maybe it's made her feel vulnerable.' Bill shrugged and stuck his fork in a cherry tomato.

Becky had never claimed to have the same level of gut instinct that Tom had, but she felt a prickle at the back of her neck. A woman that looked like the first victim – and like the second victim was supposed to look – and she thought she was being followed? Becky couldn't imagine that this woman was the hysterical type if she was used to handling scumbags like Alf Horton.

'Who's dealing with it?'

'Dan Pierce. Do you know him?'

Becky thought she recognised the name but couldn't place the guy. Tom would probably know him; he seemed to know everybody.

'Thanks for telling me. I'll mention it to Tom, if that's okay with you. I'm sure it's not relevant to our enquiry, but you never know. Have they got anything to follow up on? If it's a ubiquitous unmarked white van and the calls were from a disposable mobile it doesn't sound like there's much they can do.'

'Well, it seems we have all – or part of – a registration number. So they'll be running a PNC check to see what they come up with.' The sergeant ate his last forkful of a small salad, and stood up. 'I'll leave you to your lunch.'

Becky looked down at her plate and suddenly the burger didn't look so appetising. Tom always said he hated coincidences, and maybe it was catching. But if a woman who looked like the other victims believed she was being stalked, it wasn't something Becky should ignore.

❖

Much to her frustration, Becky had to wait to get some time with Tom. He was tied up with Philippa Stanley, who had asked for an update. That should have taken about two minutes as there was so little to report, but for some reason he was gone for an hour. She kept her eye on the door and finally saw him walk into the incident room and make his way towards her desk.

'You wanted to see me, Becky?' he asked.

'Yes. It may be something or nothing, but I thought I should run it by you.'

He signalled her with his head to follow him into his office, and once they were settled she explained what she had heard about Maggie Taylor.

Tom sat back in his chair and gazed at the ceiling in what Becky always thought of as his thinking pose. It didn't last long.

'I don't like it,' he said, leaning forward again. 'We thought the first woman was Leo. Don't look like that, Becky. We're over that, aren't we?' Without waiting for her response, he continued. 'As far as we know, Leo's missing. I accept, knowing her the way I do, that she could easily have decided to take herself off because the new boyfriend pissed her off. But failing to turn up to her niece's christening is a step too far even for Leo.'

Becky saw Tom take a big breath. 'I've suggested to Ellie that she officially reports Leo missing. She's resisted up to now for the same reason – Leo is as unpredictable as hell – but we need to take this seriously.'

Becky said nothing. There was no appropriate response, and she knew Tom was right.

'So now we've got both Maggie Taylor and Leo, who look similar to the first victim and to how the second victim was supposed to look. The thing that's puzzling me, though, is that this makes *four* potential victims, and all those years ago we were pretty certain that the magic number was three.'

'Maybe Leo has nothing to do with it. It's an unfortunate coincidence, and as you say she's gone off on one.'

Tom gave her a look that suggested he didn't believe that for one second.

'Let's make a quick call to Dan Pierce and see if he has any updates on the supposed stalker,' he said, and put the call through.

It was frustrating only being able to hear one half of the conversation, but Becky got the gist.

'What did the PNC check throw up?' Tom asked. He listened to the answer. 'And what do we know about this Adam Mellor?' There was a pause. 'You're certain about that, are you?' Tom said, looking at Becky, his eyes opening wide. 'I'll get back to you, Dan. I need to speak to my inspector, Becky Robinson. One of us will talk to you in a few minutes.'

Tom hung up and looked at Becky with raised eyebrows.

'What's up?' Becky asked.

'The PNC check. The number turned up one white van registered to an address in the Manchester area with sufficient matching digits to make it a strong possibility. It's owned by a guy called Adam Mellor. They sent somebody round to have a word with him, but apparently he's away and has been since last Saturday. Nobody knows where he is.'

Becky watched Tom's face. His eyes were focused somewhere behind her as if he was trying to match up bits of the puzzle.

'The other thing they found out is that Adam Mellor works for Maxwell Jenkins, Manchester's biggest corporate finance firm.

'And that's significant because…?' Becky said.

'You remember I tracked down Leo's new boyfriend, Julian Richmond? He's also in corporate finance. And guess which firm he works for?'

Tom's eyes met Becky's. They were both silent for a moment, and then Tom pushed back his chair.

'Get your coat, Becky. Ask one of your team to track down Maggie Taylor's address. Mrs Taylor needs to know that we're on our way to see her and she needs to be in, but we have one other call to make first.'

36

When Maggie woke up on Sunday morning she hadn't been sure what she was going to do. She had no doubt at all that the threat to Duncan was real so now she was torn. What if her children were in danger? But yesterday the two men in the van could easily have taken Josh, and they hadn't. But if they couldn't get Duncan to do whatever it was that they wanted, would they be back for her, for Lily, for Josh?

The decision felt as if it had been taken out of her hands when she received a call from Bill Shaw, the desk sergeant she had been trying to contact. A note had been left for him to say she had called, so he was calling to check she was okay.

Maggie hadn't had time to think of an excuse, so she had told him the minimum that made any sense. She had focused on the phone calls and the van – maybe enough for the police to take an interest but not enough for her to have endangered Duncan. And if the two men were watching, they would know she hadn't left the house. She couldn't tell Bill Shaw about the note and the photo – it would be impossible to keep a breakthrough like that out of the press, and she might be signing her husband's death warrant.

After the call ended, Maggie walked into the kitchen and sat down, unsure if her legs would hold her up for much longer. Without a word, Suzy walked across to the kettle and clicked it on, giving Maggie time as she stared out of the window to where her children were playing outside. At least they seemed a little more relaxed this morning.

Maggie came out of her daze as Suzy put a mug of tea in front of her. 'Thanks,' she said. 'Sorry for leaving you to deal with the kids.'

'It's okay, Mags. You don't have to apologise for anything. What did you say to the police? Did you tell them Duncan was missing?'

Maggie shook her head. How could she have told them that without explaining the rest? And if she had, how much danger would she have put him in?

'What's going to happen now?' Suzy asked.

'I don't know. I don't know *anything* any more, Suze. What's happening to Duncan? All I can think is that he's got mixed up in something by mistake, and he doesn't know how to get out of it. Maybe he saw something he shouldn't – you know, when he was out doing a job. Perhaps he saw the girl being killed but didn't know what it was at the time. What if they're threatening him, and because he's not here, they're threatening me? Maybe they're after him because he knows too much – a gang or something. So he's gone into hiding to keep them away from me. Maybe he's scared, Suzy, with nobody to help him.' Maggie's voice cracked.

The phone rang. She ignored it.

'Shall I answer it?' her sister asked.

'*No!*' She waited for the answerphone to click in. It might be the man again.

'Mrs Taylor? I'm calling from Greater Manchester Police. I need to speak to you urgently. Could you please call me back on—'

Maggie raced to the phone and picked it up.

'Hello. This is Maggie Taylor.' She listened as the policeman told her that two detectives would like to come and talk to her about her report this morning. 'It's good that you're taking me seriously, but can't you update me on the phone?' She couldn't keep the confusion from her voice. This was overkill for the report she had made.

'I'm sorry, madam, but one of our senior detectives would like to come and talk to you, if that's okay with you. He should be with you in about an hour as he has another call to make first. Will you be in then?'

'Yes, of course.'

'Thank you. It'll be Detective Chief Inspector Douglas. I'll let him know you'll be there.' The line went dead.

Maggie replaced the handset and stood looking at it, her back to her sister.

Tom Douglas, the head of the team running the murder enquiry. Why was he coming to see her? Did he know something about Duncan? Had something happened to him?

With all her heart she wished she could talk to her husband, to give him the chance to explain what was happening to their family and find a way of putting it right.

❖

Maggie quickly pulled a brush through her hair and reapplied her lipstick. She didn't want to give the police the impression that anything was wrong. Fixing a smile on her face she turned to her sister.

'Suze, I need you to take the children out,' she said. 'I'll get them. Can you go quickly, please? I don't want them to be distressed by a visit from the police.'

Her sister looked up from the screen of Maggie's laptop, an enquiring look on her face. 'Sorry – I hope you don't mind. I wanted to check Facebook but it was already open. I didn't think you used it?'

'I don't.'

'So who's Patricia Rowe? It was her page that was open.'

'What? Oh, it's nothing. She's relevant to a case I've been working on.'

'What's this, then?' her sister asked.

Maggie was getting more and more worried about time, but

she spun the laptop towards her to see what Suzy was talking about. It seemed she had found Mrs Rowe's photographs and had clicked through to an album. The photos were displayed full screen, and the one she was looking at was of five kids aged from about ten to mid-teens. Only two were looking at the screen. The others were all involved in fixing their bikes. The bike at the front, centre screen, had a yellow frame, a red suspension fork and a bright green seat stay.

Duncan's bike.

A boy was crouching in front of the bike adjusting the chain, his back to the camera. Maggie couldn't see his face, but there was something about his hair and the way it grew at the back. She clicked on the next picture. The same group were now all standing in front of their bikes smiling. Except for the boy with the multicoloured bike. He was scowling.

She turned shocked eyes to her sister as the back door opened and Josh charged in. She snapped the lid closed.

'Lily's fallen over, Mum. She's hurt her knee.'

Suzy stood up. 'I'll see to her. We'll go to the shops and see if a few sweets or an ice cream will help it to get better, shall we?' she said, turning to Josh. 'Come on. I'm sure Mummy won't mind if we borrow her car.'

Maggie didn't hear her. All she wanted to do was open her laptop again, blow the picture up and check what she had seen. But she didn't need to. She knew. The boy in the picture was Duncan.

37

If Julian Richmond was surprised to see Tom again, this time accompanied by a young woman, he didn't show it.

'Come in, Tom. I hope you've got some news about Leo,' he said, a friendly smile failing to mask his underlying anxiety.

'I'm sorry to bother you again,' Tom said. 'This is Detective Inspector Becky Robinson. I'm afraid we don't have any news about Leo, but I wanted to ask you about one of your employees, if that's okay.'

Julian looked surprised but lifted his shoulders slightly as if to say 'Whatever' and showed them into the house. Once again they made for the kitchen. The radio was playing, and he walked over and turned it off.

'Sorry,' he said. 'I need the radio at the weekend. Now Leo's not around I can go the whole two days without speaking to another soul, and it feels as if my vocal cords have seized up if I don't sing or whistle along.'

Tom decided he liked this man. He seemed honest and genuinely sad that things hadn't worked out with Leo.

'What's this about one of my employees, then? I think they're a relatively honest bunch. You'd like to think that comes with the job, really.'

Tom smiled. He had met a fair number of accountants whom he might have considered borderline on the honesty front, but decided to keep that thought to himself.

'It's a man called Adam Mellor. I gather he works for your firm?'

'Adam. Yes, he's in my team. A bright guy, impressive in front of clients. Why are you interested?'

'I'm sorry, Julian, I can't say at this point. It's all a bit vague, but his name has come up and I'd like to hear about him. We've tried to talk to him, but he seems to be on leave.'

'That's right. It was a last-minute thing. He was supposed to be coming to Haydock Park with us all last Saturday – you remember I mentioned that to you? He was coordinating the event. I phoned him in the morning to say we had a spare place as Leo was going to be a no-show, and he called back later to say he wasn't going to be able to make it either. Somebody in his family had died that morning, so he asked if he could take some leave. He's going to be away for another week, I think.'

Tom said nothing and avoided meeting Becky's eyes.

'Tell me about him, if you wouldn't mind. Anything you know about his background, his character. It will help us create a picture.'

Julian was a smart guy, and Tom could see that he was weighing up whether to go along with this or not. But then he gave a small nod of the head, as if convincing himself that Tom was okay.

'I knew his father – he's dead now – and he admitted to me before we appointed Adam that there had been some difficulties when he was growing up. But when Adam was at university his father paid for some pretty intensive counselling that appeared to be effective. Of course, Adam's in his thirties now, so I think his wild youth is well behind him. His father asked me to give him a job as a favour, and I agreed. I haven't regretted it.'

Julian stopped for a moment and looked pensive. 'I wonder who could have died that mattered to him? I always got the impression that after his father passed away he no longer had anything to do with his family – what remains of it.' He shrugged.

'What about his character?' Tom asked.

'Hmm. He's not that popular with his colleagues, I have to admit. I'm told the girls think he's a user, and the guys think he's power-hungry. But, as I said, clients love him because he flatters them and they're aware of his wealthy background. He makes no effort to hide where he comes from, and I think some of them are impressed.'

'How did his family make their money? Do you know?'

'I do. They're quite famous locally. An ancestor on his father's side was something to do with the original Manchester Ship Canal company. A shareholder, I think. He made his money and got out before the decline in shipping and moved into other growth areas. I believe he was a major shareholder in what was originally the London and North Western Railway. Adam's father always considered himself a world authority on Manchester transport.'

❖

It wasn't until they were in the car and driving away that Becky risked a glance at Tom. He had saved one question for last with Julian Richmond, and Becky had watched his face as he asked it.

'Did Adam Mellor ever meet Leo?'

Tom hadn't been able to get out of that house quickly enough when Julian answered. Clearly he hadn't wanted to be rude, but they needed to find Adam Mellor, and the sooner the better.

'Yes, he did,' Julian had responded. 'He was one of a crowd of colleagues from the office that Leo and I bumped into at Cheltenham.'

Tom had nodded his thanks, as if it was something of a throwaway question, but Becky knew Julian wasn't fooled. She saw the man's eyes narrow, but he said nothing. There was nothing *to* say.

Now Tom was driving, and Becky was already on the phone, issuing instructions. They needed to make sure they used every means possible to track down the van that Mellor had been driving and check for any other vehicles he might own. She would bet her life he had a flash car. Tom glanced at her sideways as if to say 'You've got to be joking' when she asked somebody to check with Mellor's family to see who had died. But she was just doing her job – leaving no stone unturned. He could have been telling the truth. Not that she believed he was for one second.

Becky also asked one of the team to check up on his education and where he was in 2003.

'You think he was involved back then, don't you?' She looked at Tom and he nodded. 'And now?'

'He'd met Leo. He was suddenly called away. He's stalking a woman who looks like Leo and like the women who have been killed. Of course he's involved. He's the best – the only – lead we've got until we can find out who phoned Hayley Walker, or who she went out to meet.'

'Are we still interested in the backgrounds of the people who worked with Hayley?' Becky asked.

'Yes, and I want Louisa Knight brought back in. Hayley seems to have been friendly with lots of people but doesn't seem to have had any particularly close friends. We need to get a picture of Adam Mellor and ask Louisa if she recognises him. Has he ever been involved with the hospital at all, or with any of her colleagues? Had she seen him with Hayley? We should have asked Julian for a picture, but if you ring him I'm sure he'll oblige. He didn't miss a trick, there, did he? He knew we were interested in Adam for all the wrong reasons.'

'If you're sure it's him, why are we looking at the people in the cardio department still?'

'Because I don't think we can assume that Mellor is acting alone, plus somebody phoned Hayley and they're not admitting to it.'

Becky glanced sideways at Tom. She could hear the strain in his voice, the fear that another girl might be killed. And the horror that the third girl might be Leo.

'We'll get him, Tom.'

Tom nodded. 'I don't know how Maggie Taylor fits into all of this. But one thing I am damn sure about is that Adam Mellor knows what's happened to Leo. We have to find him, and find her.'

38

A broken windowpane was allowing gusts of cold damp air into the room, and Leo shouted until her voice cracked, hoping and praying that somebody would hear her. She couldn't get to the window. Her ankle was chained to one of a row of green metal pillars that reached up to the high ceiling in the vast space. Overhead the remnants of fluorescent light fittings hung, the tubes either dead or long removed. The floorboards had been pulled up in parts, gaping holes revealing another huge open space one level below where she sat. But that was no help. There was nobody on that floor. There was nobody else in the building.

She guessed she was in some kind of old mill, judging by the size, shape and regularity of the tall windows. There weren't many derelict buildings like this left in Manchester; they had almost all been converted into apartments. She knew they were in Manchester because they hadn't travelled far, and she was sure she was at the back of the building because just as nobody could hear her, she couldn't hear anything either. The silence was oppressive, dead. The days were bad enough, but the nights were hell, and her wounds were sore.

Leo couldn't believe how stupid she had been. She remembered the rain streaming down her windows and how miserable she had felt. When she had heard the doorbell, she had been sure it would be Julian, come to forgive her for being such an idiot. She hadn't even checked the peephole, and when she opened her front door and saw an arrangement of flowers so vast she couldn't even see the face of the delivery man, she had been stunned by what she assumed was Julian's generosity, especially as she was in no doubt that the argument the night before had been down to her.

The delivery man had muttered that it might be easier if he put the flowers down somewhere in her apartment, so she had let him in. That's when she had seen his face, and the second man. And the masks. Those horrible shiny plastic faces with their fixed grins.

She had been pushed backwards. She hadn't known there was a chair behind her, and for a moment it felt like one of those dreams in which you are falling forever. Just as a dreamer wakes with a jolt, Leo had crashed down onto the chair, its softness not lessening the sick lurch to her stomach as she landed.

Once she had been bound and gagged one of the men left. She had seen his face reflected in the mirror – only a glance, but it was enough. She would know that face anywhere if she saw it again.

And then the wait had begun.

'Sit. Keep quiet. We'll go when your neighbours are asleep.' She had tried moaning loudly, but he had thumped her in the stomach.

'Got to keep that pretty face looking perfect,' he had whispered against her ear. His skin was smooth and carefully shaven. He didn't sound like a Manchester thug and there was a slight hint of garlic about him. Not strong, just reminiscent of a good meal. But no cigarettes or beer.

She had tried to keep cool. There was nothing she hated more than showing weakness. And she could cope with the punches – she had taken enough as a child, although that was a long time ago now.

She heard him in the kitchen, opening the fridge and then emptying something liquid down the sink. She heard a few soft thumps and guessed items were going into a bin liner. She knew what he was doing: he was ridding her house of perishable food – not that there was much. People would eventually come looking for her, and if the alarm wasn't to be raised they would have to believe she had left from choice. Nobody leaves milk to sour in their fridge when they go away.

It was in the silent hours of early morning as the world slept when the second man returned, and they ushered her downstairs and into a car that smelled of good leather. The driver had left the car and disappeared for about five minutes. Leo heard the passenger door open and a rustling noise. Then she caught the smell of roses and lavender and knew the man had been back to collect the evidence – the flowers and the rubbish.

Why had she been targeted? She tried hard to keep calm, to quash the rising panic in her chest, to work out what to do, but there didn't seem to be any logic to it. And now here she was, trapped and hardly able to move, in the same place she had been for days. They didn't come often, and when they did, they wore their masks. Both men were tall – well over six feet – and both appeared to be well-dressed even when they came in jeans. Her gag and blindfold had been removed, although that did little good. With one ankle and one wrist firmly secured, she only had the use of one hand to eat and drink.

She had been certain she would be able to escape. The chain holding her leg was firm, but she'd thought that if she could free her arm she might be able to find something that she could prise one of the links open with. A cable tie around her wrist was attached to a second chain, wrapped around a different pillar, and she had yanked on the plastic tie as hard as possible in the hope that it would snap. The men had been clever in their positioning, though. Her arm was attached behind her, the leg in front, so it was hard to exert any real force.

When she heard them coming, she had tried to cover her sore, bruised arm with her sleeve, but one of the men had walked over and pulled the sleeve back. Without a word he had left her to the first man, the slightly shorter of the two, and disappeared.

She didn't know why – not a word had been spoken – but she sensed that this was not good news for her.

And that's when it had happened. That's when she knew that she wasn't going to be able to escape – not now, not ever.

The taller man had come back into the room, clutching a plastic bag from which he had withdrawn a number of items. Leo could see what looked like a pair of scissors but with extra-long handles, and a pair of fine tweezers. The man laid them both down on the upturned box where her water was usually left. Then he opened a small packet and withdrew a thin curved piece of metal that seemed to have some thread attached. Using the tweezers, he grabbed a chunk of the flesh of her arm and gripped it tightly.

She knew what was coming. She recognised the thin, hooked metal for what it was. A suture needle.

With practised skill the man inserted it into her arm, over and over again, suturing the plastic tie around her wrist firmly in place, the agonising piercing of muscle and flesh ensuring that any movement she made would tear her arm to shreds.

39

A second phone call from the police informed Maggie that Mr Douglas had been delayed but would be with her in about fifteen minutes. Maggie didn't know whether to be pleased or frustrated. She couldn't understand why they needed to see her. She had told Bill Shaw everything she intended to say, so what they hoped to gain from visiting her, she had no idea.

Maggie needed time to think, and fifteen minutes wasn't enough. On the other hand, if the police arrived right now, at this very minute, they would know something was up. She could feel how flushed her face was, and as she looked in the mirror, she could see the distress and confusion in her own eyes. She pulled her hair back into a ponytail and scrubbed the remains of her lipstick off. With her pink cheeks, she looked like a china doll.

Since Suzy had shown her the photo, Maggie's head had been all over the place. Her heart was pumping – was this finally a clue to who Duncan was? But how would it help her to find him? If the photo of the boy with the bike was Duncan, Patricia Rowe must know something about him. Perhaps she knew his mother. Perhaps they had lived near Mrs Rowe, and he had been a friend of some of her children.

Maggie looked hastily at her watch. She had to get in touch with this woman – she wanted to know who Duncan really was.

She went back to the Facebook post that contained the images of the children and saw there were a few comments. Most were from people praising Patricia Rowe for the work she had done with children, but one was from a Stacey Meagan. It simply said 'Happy days'. Could that mean she was one of the children in the picture? All the girls seemed quite a bit younger than Duncan.

Maggie clicked on Stacey's name and didn't learn much as her privacy settings hid her posts from people she didn't know. Maggie browsed and found a few photos that matched Stacey's profile picture. If she had to guess, she would have said that Stacey Meagan was in her mid-twenties, but it was hard to know for sure. She returned to Patricia Rowe's page and saved a copy of the photo of the children with the bikes, returned to Stacey's page and opened a message. She had never heard back from Patricia, and given the lack of activity on her page, maybe she had given up on Facebook. But Stacey Meagan was another option.

She thought through the words carefully, but she had only minutes left until Tom Douglas arrived. When Maggie set up her Facebook account she had done it using her middle name and her maiden name. She had never posted anything and found the whole idea a bit spooky, but had wanted to see what all the fuss was about. Now she thanked some divine entity that she didn't believe in for the fact that she had made that decision.

My name is Grace Peters. I wonder if you could help me, please? I see you've commented on this picture, and I would like to know a little about the boy with the multicoloured bike.

Maggie added the saved image to the message.

I would be grateful if you could give me some information about him.

She stopped to think. Would *she* give out somebody's details to an unknown person on Facebook? Of course not.

I am a solicitor. If this boy is now the man I am trying to trace,
I believe getting in touch will be to his benefit.

Whether the woman would believe her, Maggie didn't know. But people seemed prepared to expose their most intimate secrets on Facebook for the world to see, so she probably wouldn't bother trying to check 'Grace's' credentials.

She sent the message and jumped up from her chair, pacing the room. They would be here any minute.

The house phone rang. Maggie hoped and prayed it would be the police, saying there had been a mistake and Tom Douglas wouldn't be coming after all.

'Maggie Taylor,' she answered, hearing the quiver in her voice. Phone calls didn't seem to bring good news any more.

There was no sound from the other end of the phone.

'Hello?' she said quietly, certain that it was going to be the man threatening her again.

'Maggie?'

She felt a leap in her chest. *Thank God.* Her eyes filled with hot tears.

'*Duncan!*' She whispered his name fiercely into the phone, hoping the police weren't right now standing on her doorstep, listening to her. 'Where *are* you? What's happening? Please, Dunc, tell me what's going on – I'm terrified.'

Her voice broke. She wanted him here, holding her, telling her it was all going to be okay.

'I'm sorry, Maggie. I never wanted to hurt you. I didn't know what else to do.' Duncan spoke quietly, as if the words were difficult to say. He had always hated apologising – being found to be in the wrong.

Maggie felt as if all the questions that had been piling up inside her were fighting their way out, scrambling to get over one another in their rush.

'But why did you go? Where are you? When are you coming back? Why did you have a picture of a dead girl on your phone?'

She heard a gasp from the other end of the phone.

'How do you know about that? *Christ!* Don't tell anybody else. Please, Maggie, nobody must know. *Promise me*, Maggie.'

But Maggie had no time to answer. The doorbell rang.

'*Shit!* Somebody's at the door.' Maggie knew full well who it was and that she had no option but to open it. 'Give me your number, Dunc, *please*. Hang on a second.'

Holding the phone in one hand, she turned the latch on the front door and pulled it open.

'Hello, Mrs Taylor. I believe you're expecting us. May we come in? But please do finish your call.'

❖

The woman who opened the door to Tom and Becky came as a surprise. Tom had been expecting her to look just like Leo and Hayley Walker, but this woman looked worn out with black circles under her eyes, pale skin and flushed cheeks. She wore no make-up, and her hair was tied back. She was a similar build to the other women, and he imagined that when her hair was loose and she was wearing the bright red lipstick that he understood she favoured, there would be a striking resemblance. But just at this moment they couldn't have been more different.

'I'm sorry, Clare. I have to go,' Maggie Taylor said into the phone, her whole body turned away from Tom and Becky. 'Do you want to leave your number so I can call you back?'

She didn't pull pen and paper towards her from the hall table, so Tom could only assume that whoever she was speaking to had chosen not to leave their details. Tom was certain it wasn't somebody called Clare. Maggie's hesitation before the name had been slight but enough for Tom.

Maggie took a moment before turning back towards them, still grasping the phone, and it was impossible to miss the strain in her eyes. She was biting the corner of her bottom lip, as if to keep it from trembling, and the pinkish tinge to her eyes suggested she had been crying.

A thought struck Tom. Maggie Taylor was Alf Horton's solicitor, and Horton had been in the custody cells in the building next to Tom's office. So there was a good chance that Maggie could have been in the vicinity of police headquarters earlier in the week. As they made their introductions in the entrance hall, Tom glanced to his left. There was a coat rack, and scrunched up, sitting on a shelf above the coats was an emerald-green scarf.

It had been her, then. He was right. She had looked so different that day. The belief that it had been Leo was the one thing that had been keeping Tom hopeful about his ex-girlfriend. Knowing it wasn't her felt like a punch in the gut. Every bone in his body was telling him that something had happened to Leo, and his confidence that she was alive and well had been shattered. He *had* to find her, and his instincts told him it needed to be soon. But he was sure the woman had been thinking about coming into the office. And that woman, it now seemed, had been Maggie Taylor.

Maggie took them into the living room.

'Could I get you a cup of tea or coffee, or something?' she asked.

Both Tom and Becky declined.

'Mrs Taylor,' Tom began, 'we understand you have concerns that you're being stalked, and you provided us with a partial number plate for your stalker. Is that right?'

'Yes. I know the evidence is very thin, but coupled with the phone calls I've been receiving I thought I should get some advice. I've got to know the duty sergeant over the few weeks I've been working in Manchester and I thought I should have a word with him. He said he'd passed it on to a colleague.'

'That's right, he did. But this van might be of interest in another investigation, and your partial number plate was better than you might imagine. It was enough to provide a match, and we think we've tracked down the owner. But before we get to that, can you tell me some more about why you think he's stalking you?'

Maggie Taylor looked uncomfortable.

'The van had been parked up the street, and then when I took the children out it was round the corner. We went for a cycle ride, and the van appeared part of the way round – as if it had been following us. There were two men in it.'

'Did it not occur to you that this might be a coincidence? Perhaps the driver and his mate had chosen to park somewhere other than on the street while they had lunch, somewhere away from the job they were working on?' Tom didn't believe this for one single moment. 'Why did you feel particularly concerned about this van?'

'I don't know. Maybe it was because of the phone calls I'd had.' Maggie shrugged. 'Maybe I'm being overly cautious. My current client keeps whispering to me that nowhere's safe and I need to watch myself, and then I get calls from someone saying I need to be careful. They were sinister. It was the tone of voice – the *we know where you live* – that seemed so menacing.' Maggie attempted an unconvincing laugh. 'It all seems a bit of a cliché when I say it out loud.'

'But nevertheless scary,' Becky said.

'I feel bad bringing you out here. I'm surprised you would think this worthy of your interest, to be honest, Chief Inspector.'

'Oh, I like to keep my ear close to the ground. And as I mentioned, the owner of the van could be of interest to us in another case.'

Tom was well aware that Maggie wasn't telling the whole truth – if any at all – and he couldn't work out why. But until he knew, he wasn't prepared to give her anything either.

'Could we possibly have a word with your husband?' he asked.

'Why?' The speed and almost fierce tone of her response surprised Tom, but he didn't react.

'Because he may have seen some similar behaviour. He might know if the van has been there for longer than you realise, or he might be able to add any number of things to the investigation.' Tom couldn't think of any, but he wanted to know what was making this woman so jumpy.

'I'm sorry, but he's away at the moment. He's gone back to where we used to live, down south. There were a couple of jobs he hadn't finished and he'd promised to go back.'

'Okay, well at some point we might need his contact details.' Tom was watching her closely and couldn't miss the flinch.

'Is there anything else you can tell us, Maggie?' Becky asked.

'Nothing I can think of, and I do apologise if I've been wasting your time.'

'Not at all,' Tom said. 'I'm sure you haven't.'

Tom and Becky stood up from the sofa and walked towards the door.

Tom turned. 'Just one thing. A couple of days ago – Friday, I think – were you standing outside our offices – the big building next to the custody suite where Alf Horton was being held? I'm fairly certain it was you, and it looked like you were going to come in. Did you want to see somebody from my department?'

Maggie Taylor shook her head. 'It wasn't me,' she said. 'I didn't even go to see Alf on Friday afternoon.'

Tom smiled and thanked her.

It wasn't a matter of her not telling him everything. She was telling him nothing. And he had never mentioned the time of day.

40

'What did you make of that, then?' Tom asked Becky as they headed back towards the M60.

'I don't know what she's playing at. She made a complaint – or at least she registered her concern – but then she couldn't wait to get us out of the door. She was totally and completely flustered by our presence, and in particular yours. Why would that be?'

Tom focused on the road for a moment. He was certain Maggie had been standing outside the office a few days ago. And she must have been to the custody suite before, so she couldn't have been confused about which building she needed to visit. And she had been staring at the door, as if she couldn't decide whether to go in or not. And all of that had happened *before* the incident with the van.

'What about this Alf Horton character? I know he gives you the creeps, but what's the deal with him warning her about something?' he said.

'No idea, but he's a nasty bastard. I wouldn't put it past him to try to wind her up – and it seems he succeeded.'

'What else did you notice? You're pretty good at reading people.'

'I noticed that she was unbelievably uncomfortable when we mentioned her husband.'

They sat in silence for a while, the grey skies and the thin drizzle making driving conditions less than ideal.

'Okay, Becky, next steps with Adam Mellor?'

'Everybody's on the lookout for either the van or his car. We need to get Julian Richmond to give us a contact – his closest friend if possible – so that we can get a list of his known associates. We have intermittent checking on his home to see if he turns up there, and we're following up the story of a death in the family. We're also looking into any other property that he might own.'

Tom was happy with the actions Becky was proposing, but there was one other thing he wanted her to do.

'You know about the bodies that have been found in the canals around Manchester in the past few years?'

'You mean the "pusher" cases?'

Tom looked at her sideways, his eyebrows raised.

'Sorry, I know they've all been declared either accidental or suicide, but you have to admit it's a bit odd.'

Tom knew what she meant. Over sixty bodies had been found in the last few years, and almost all of them were men. There was no evidence they had been murdered, and the general consensus was that they had been drunk and had fallen in. Suicide was always possible, but as one eminent psychologist had pointed out very loudly, canals are not locations of choice for suicide and the chances of success without weighing yourself down beforehand are pretty slim.

'I'm interested in the few women they've found. I know the deaths go back fifteen years or so and some of the bodies are badly decomposed, but I'd like to see if any of the women died around 2003, and if so whether they had any links with Manchester University. Can you add that to the list?'

For some reason Tom couldn't get it out of his head that all those years ago there should have been a third victim.

❖

Maggie had closed the door on the police as soon as she reasonably could without seeming rude and leaned back heavily against it. She knew her behaviour had been that of a guilty person – she had met enough of them. But when she reported her concerns she had never imagined she would be interviewed by Tom Douglas. She had been expecting a constable – a sergeant at most – to be assigned to her case.

For somebody like Tom Douglas to come all this way to talk to her about a possible stalking incident, the driver of the van had to be linked to a serious crime. It had to be the murders. It was the only thing that made sense.

She grabbed the phone, terrified that somebody would ring her and ruin her chance of dialling 1471 so she could get the number that Duncan had called from. She didn't think he would have blocked it if he had used a call box because he could just walk away.

Duncan must have known it was somebody official at the door. He would have heard her called Mrs Taylor, and the fact that she had called him Clare would have been all the signal he needed. He had muttered 'Shit!' and hung up without another word.

1471 worked. She tried to connect, but there was no answer.

Maggie wanted to scream. Whatever was going on, she knew Duncan would have freaked out if he had guessed she was talking to the police and that might be the last she heard from him. Why on earth hadn't she said she was talking to her husband and asked Tom Douglas to give her a moment? He didn't know Duncan was missing, and it would have seemed the most natural thing in the world, but she had panicked. And why had she shouted questions at Duncan when all she wanted to say to him was 'Come home' and 'I love you'?

Duncan, darling – where are you? The thought revolved around her head, beating against every conscious thought.

One other thought was battling for supremacy. *Who are you, Duncan?*

She walked through to the kitchen and sat down. She waited two minutes and tried the number again. It rang until it automatically disconnected.

Her laptop pinged and she stared at the screen.

It was a message on Facebook, and it was from Stacey Meagan, the girl in the photo with Duncan.

> I got your message, but not sure if I can help you. The boy in the picture is Michael. He was a bit older than me. He was at Pat's when I arrived and left when I was still in my early teens. I do remember he had a crazy coloured bike, though. He was eighteen when he left. He came back a few times the first year, but then Pat never heard from him again. She was devastated. I have no idea where to find him. Sorry.

Maggie read the message over and over. *Michael. His name was Michael. He was in foster care.* Surely that couldn't be right. His mother was alive until he was twenty. Maggie had assumed he was a friend of one of the other kids. Why would he have been in foster care?

She slowly and thoughtfully typed a response.

> When Michael left, do you know where he went? And do you by any chance know his surname?

That was a risk. Stacey Meagan might think it odd that she was searching for somebody but didn't even know his surname, but she would think of something if that came up.

> Michael left to go to university. I think Pat told me he bombed out at the end of his second year. I'm sorry, I can't remember his surname. There were so many of us, see, coming and going all the time. But I'll ask some of the others if you like?

Maggie pressed her palms together, index fingers tapping against her teeth. She wasn't sure if she wanted to know any more, but she couldn't stop now.

> Thank you, Stacey. You have been really helpful. If you could ask around I would be grateful. In the meantime, do you by any chance remember which university he went to?

She was sure the answer would be Leeds. At least that would make sense. The reply was instant.

> No problem – I've already started spreading the word. I can't ask Pat – she's in a home now and sadly she has Alzheimer's. If I catch her on a lucid day I'll see what I can do. Oh, and the university, it was Manchester.

Maggie hadn't heard the front door open, but was suddenly conscious there was somebody behind her in the kitchen. She spun round, aware that tears were streaming down her face. 'Sorry,' she said, quickly scrubbing away the tears with her fingers.

Suzy had returned home with the children and she ushered them into the sitting room, telling Josh to choose a DVD, then pulled the door shut and turned to face Maggie.

'What's happened?' she asked. 'You look like you've seen a ghost.'

Maggie leaned back in her chair and looked up at the ceiling, trying to curb the tears.

'Duncan phoned, but he hung up when the police arrived and didn't leave a number. I don't know who he is, Suzy. He's not even called Duncan. He's called Michael.'

Maggie didn't look at Suzy's face. She didn't want to see what her sister thought of Duncan, and she knew Suzy would find it impossible to disguise her feelings. To give her credit, she didn't say anything; she just reached out and grabbed Maggie's hands.

Duncan had never wanted to talk about himself much, and Maggie had always felt that each time she learned a new fact about her husband there was a sense of discovery, as if she was getting closer and closer to him. Now she seemed so naïve.

'Why's he been lying to me? Do you know, if you'd asked me a week ago, I would have said we didn't have secrets. There was that stupid cupboard, but I guessed it held mementos of his mum – things he didn't want to share. There were gaps, but I didn't think of them as secrets; I thought of them as private thoughts and feelings that I would learn as time went on.'

She pulled a tissue from the box that Suzy had put in front of her and blew her nose.

'You know how it feels, Suze, when you really love someone. You start off as separate people whose bodies and minds are touching, but gradually you begin to feel more and more as if you're melting into one another, as if you can't get any closer without getting inside their skin with them. Each little detail that I learned about Duncan pulled me further and further into him. It was wonderful. Do you know what I mean?'

Suzy was quiet for a long moment, and Maggie opened her eyes and turned towards her. Tears were now streaming down her sister's face.

'Oh shit, Suzy, I'm so sorry. Of course you know. You must know exactly how I'm feeling.'

Suzy choked out a laugh. 'That's just the point, Mags. I have absolutely no idea. I've never felt like that – I didn't know that's how it's supposed to feel. All I've ever felt since Ian left is anger. I guess it's time I let that go and accepted that maybe what we had was never good enough.'

Maggie reached out and took her sister's hand. There was nothing she could say. After a couple of minutes she pushed herself off her chair. 'Come on, sis. Let's go and see the kids.'

Suzy stood up too, held out her arms and gave Maggie a hard hug. 'No, I'll take care of the kids. You do whatever you need to sort all of this out.'

As Suzy walked back towards the sitting room, Maggie pressed redial again. She was about to hang up when the ringtone stopped, and her heart leaped. Then she heard a voice – uncertain, quiet, young.

Not Duncan.

Maggie paced the room as she spoke. 'Hello?' She couldn't tell if the voice was male or female, but she didn't want to frighten whoever it was away. 'Hi,' she said, keeping a smile on her face knowing it would be reflected in her voice. 'Thanks for picking up. I wonder if you can help me? Do you think you could tell me where I'm calling exactly? You see, a friend asked me to phone, and I'm not sure if I've got the right number.'

There was silence for a few seconds.

'It's a phone box.'

'Oh, that's great. Thanks. He's probably going to come back then. Err, can you tell me where the phone box is?'

'Near the park.'

'Brilliant. I'm just wondering *which* park, though. Sorry to be stupid.'

'Heaton Park.'

Maggie felt her tense body sag with relief. At least it wasn't far away, but the park was massive. She was also fairly certain that the gates were closed at night, so it was unlikely Duncan would be inside. There must be a park warden, and surely he wouldn't allow anybody to park up overnight?

'Thanks. You've been really helpful. One more thing – can you have a look round, do you think? Is there a white van parked anywhere near you?'

The line went dead. Maggie leaned back against the wall, a mixture of frustration that she hadn't managed to get more information and elation that she at least knew where Duncan had been a few hours ago competing for her focus.

'I'm going to find you, Duncan,' she whispered.

41

Tom had spent too long thinking about Maggie Taylor and what was making her so edgy. He didn't have any answers, so he had to concentrate on what he *did* know, and that meant focusing on Adam Mellor. The question was, did Adam Mellor have an accomplice? Maggie Taylor had said there were two men in the van that had followed her, so if a second man was involved it would be good to know who he was.

Becky popped her head round the door.

'Louisa Knight has agreed to call in to see us on her way home from work to take a look at the picture of Adam Mellor. Maybe he's been seen around with one of her colleagues. She'll be here in about ten minutes.'

'Let's both see her. I've got a couple more questions to ask her.'

Becky stood looking at him for a second. 'If you're going to talk to her, I think two of us is overkill, frankly. So why don't you get started, and I'll join you when you've got through the pleasantries stage, hmm?'

She turned to leave, but not before Tom had seen the cheeky grin on her face. It wasn't easy to fool Becky. It was obvious that he didn't need to see Louisa. The fact was, he wanted to.

She was waiting in reception when Tom went downstairs, and as he showed her into a small interview room and asked for a cup of tea for both of them he felt a momentary lightening of the weight of concern that he was lugging around with him.

'Sorry to drag you out here again, Louisa. Especially so late in the day. I'm sure you have somewhere better to be.'

Louisa shook her head and smiled. 'Nope. Just an evening in front of the fire. Me, Bailey and a bottle of red.'

'Oh. Then I'm sorry to deprive Bailey of your company this evening,' he said, feeling vaguely disappointed.

She smiled and gave a small shake of the head.

'Don't you worry about Bailey. He'll curl up in front of the wood burner. He'll be fine. My neighbour will let him out.'

Tom relaxed. Dog or cat? he wondered. He was a dog person, and if it hadn't been for his long working hours would have picked one up from animal rescue years ago. It sounded like a peaceful, relaxing evening, something Tom wasn't likely to be getting in the near future.

He pushed all thoughts of fires, red wine and dogs to the back of his mind and filled Louisa in with as much detail as he could.

'We have an unusual situation in that a woman is missing who looks very much like your friend Hayley. In fact, when Hayley's body was found, we initially thought she was our missing person. That seems like a hell of a coincidence, and we're concerned for the safety of this woman. We've got somebody in our sights who we think might be involved in some way, and I'm hoping you can help.'

'Okay. Is it one of the guys I told you about?'

'No, but I wonder if he might be known to you, perhaps as a friend of one of your colleagues. Bear in mind that this man may well be entirely innocent, so please keep this confidential. Does the name Adam Mellor mean anything to you?'

Louisa placed her forearms on the desk and looked down, her eyes crinkling slightly at the corners as she concentrated. Tom stayed silent. She let about ten seconds pass.

'No. I'm sorry, but I can't think that I've met anybody by that name, or even heard it mentioned.'

Tom nodded. He showed her the photograph. 'He may be using another name.'

Louisa looked at the photograph that Julian Richmond had

emailed through to the office at Becky's request. She stared for quite a long time at the young man with blond hair, a slightly pointed chin and an immaculate white shirt.

'I'm sorry. I'm fairly sure I haven't seen him before. He's a good-looking guy in a clean-cut sort of way. He has the look of somebody who comes from money. Would I be right?'

'So it seems,' Tom said. He hadn't really considered Mellor's looks, but he supposed Louisa was right.

'Sorry, Tom. I would have liked to help.' She looked disappointed.

'Don't worry. It was only on the off-chance. We're trying to find connections wherever we can, and we're particularly interested in people who either worked or studied at Manchester University around twelve years ago.'

Louisa gave a sad smile. 'That's not going to help much. A lot of our staff trained here in Manchester. There's something about this city that grabs you, once you've lived here, and won't let go.'

'I know what you mean. I had a brief spell in London, but I was glad to get back up north. It must be the weather.'

They both smiled at that.

Louisa stood up. 'I suppose I should go, then. I'm sure you're too busy to sit here chatting to me.' She held her hand out towards Tom, and he took it.

'Thanks for coming. I'm sure I'll be seeing you again,' he said.

'I hope so,' she said, meeting his eyes.

She withdrew her hand and walked towards the door. At the last minute she turned.

'By the way, I don't think there's much point you trying to speak to one of the team that I mentioned to you – Ben Coleman – one of the surgical registrars. Apparently he left for a holiday the day before Hayley was killed. But I also found out that Charlie Dixon – another man I mentioned to you – didn't turn up for work yesterday. I don't know if that's relevant.'

At this point in the investigation, anything was relevant, and Tom thanked Louisa, opening the door for her just as Becky appeared. She smiled at Louisa as she left.

'Did I miss anything?'

❖

Sorry as he was to see Louisa leave, Tom was eager to get back to his office. He filled Becky in on the little he had gleaned from the meeting.

'Dig out the information on Charlie Dixon if you can, and anything you've got on Ben Coleman. We need to go through the interviews you conducted at the hospital and see how they tally with what Louisa had to say,' he shouted as he walked towards his own office.

He sat down, pulled a plain sheet of paper towards him and started to write.

12 years ago – 3 girls (although only 2 dead), 3 lines on legs.
Now – 2 girls dead, 1 missing, 1 being threatened. All similar,
or made to look similar. 3 lines on legs.
Is the number 3 important?

Tom knew that serial killers often fell into one of a small number of categories – power and control, visionary, mission or hedonistic – but he didn't see how any of those classifications fitted here. In the case of victims of a similar type the murders were often considered the work of a mission killer – somebody who believed it to be their role to rid the world of a group of people perceived as undesirable based on their ethnicity, lifestyle or religion. But ridding the world of all pretty blonde girls or, as in the current spate, all dark-haired attractive women, seemed an unlikely mission. Sexual gratification didn't seem to be a motive, as far as they could tell, so could this be a visionary killer – somebody who believed they were being compelled to murder by an entity such as the devil or

God? If it was a thrill killer, on the other hand, why did they all have to look the same?

But if only one of the deaths was important, which one was it? And who was she important to?

Was it Adam Mellor? All they knew was that it seemed possible – and nothing more – that Leo had disappeared, and if she had, Mellor might be involved. This was based on the fact that somebody looking like Leo had been followed by Adam Mellor's van, and that he had met Leo and knew she wasn't going to the races last Saturday. It was a stretch, but if Mellor was involved in Leo's disappearance, did that mean she was the real target? And was she already dead?

The other killings seemed to have happened within hours of the girls being taken, so if Leo *had* been abducted, was her body yet to be discovered?

Tom swallowed the lump in his throat and tried to focus as Becky nudged the door open with her foot, two cups of tea in one hand and a pile of papers in the other. He was glad of the interruption. Becky was less emotionally involved in this and hopefully could see it all a little more clearly.

'Here you go, boss.'

Having deposited the tea she pushed her hair behind her ears, every inch of her shouting, 'We're getting somewhere.'

'Right,' she said. 'Adam Mellor went to Manchester University, studied economics and was in his third year at the time of the first murders. However, we can't find a single thing that links him to either of the girls who were murdered or the one who was almost killed. Of the names given to us by Louisa Knight, both Ben Coleman and Malcolm Doyle attended Manchester University as well, both obviously studying medicine. They're both slightly older, but of course they would have been students for a lot longer. We're assuming that Hayley was going out to meet somebody from work that night, but we don't know that, do we?'

Tom had to admit they didn't, but when Hayley spoke to Louisa about this man, it had sounded very much like a colleague – she had been adamant she couldn't say who it was because it might affect Louisa's relationship with him. So it had to be somebody at the hospital. But Hayley's date that night could have been with somebody entirely different.

Charlie Dixon, it turned out, could be ruled out of the murders twelve years ago because he was in New Zealand at the time.

'Okay, Becky, one last thing, then I think you should go home. It is Sunday after all. Find out when Ben Coleman left for his holiday, will you? And check if he actually got on the plane.'

Tom looked back at his scribblings. They had names but absolutely no way of connecting them to any of the murders. It was a step further than twelve years ago, though, when names had been notable only by their absence.

42

12 years ago – mid-June

Tom knocked on DCI Victor Elliott's door and waited to be told he could enter, another one of the time-wasting rituals that were slowly driving him to distraction. He looked through the glass panel, and the DCI held his hand up, palm out, as if to say 'Stay' to a dog. Tom gritted his teeth but held his ground.

He knew his superior's behaviour was getting to him, and he shouldn't let it. In any murder enquiry tensions always ran high, but in his opinion Victor Elliott was making him jump through hoops that were entirely unnecessary. Fortunately, Tom had his ever-willing trainee, Philippa Stanley, who seemed keen and eager to do just about anything .she was asked. Sadly, this had encouraged some of the guys to take the piss and send her on fools' errands, but Tom had put a stop to that. He needed her to focus. She hadn't taken kindly to his intervention, though.

'I knew what I was doing, sir,' she said. 'I can deal with idiots like them.'

'Right. So when you were sent for some holes for the hole punch, you knew that was a wind-up, did you?'

She had turned to him, her skin slightly flushed. 'Of course I did. I was biding my time. Waiting for the moment when I could make the tossers suffer.'

Tom had known she was right: he hadn't needed to come to her aid. He was beginning to realise that Philippa Stanley was nobody's fool. As a result of her help in this investigation he had been able to get off home a little earlier a couple of times this week. He hated leaving her to do all the grunt work, but he needed to spend some time with Kate.

He tried to talk to Kate about the baby, about how excited he was, but she changed the subject all the time, and Tom had been forced to admit to himself that he was scared. Scared Kate was going to leave him. Scared the reason she had become so much happier just before she fell pregnant was because she had met somebody else. Scared the baby his wife was carrying that he was so excited about wasn't his.

He was jolted back into the here and now by a signal from his boss, waving him to come in. Elliott hadn't been on the phone or talking to anybody else; he was simply posturing.

'Where are we up to? Any more names in the frame? Still got a bee in your bonnet about Alexander?' His first words, and they intensified the waves of irritation that Tom was feeling. It was true that Alexander – Tamsin Grainger's ex-boyfriend – had a cast-iron alibi, but there was something there, Tom was sure. He could see it; feel it. Sadly he hadn't been able to follow anything up because he kept being sent on wild-goose chases.

'I've been looking at all lines of enquiry. There's the lecturer who had the affair with Tamsin Grainger, Edward Price – goes by Teddy, apparently.'

'We've cleared Price. He was at home with his wife.'

'And do you consider his wife a good enough alibi? What about the wife herself? She had as much of a motive as anybody, although killing somebody for an act of fellatio on your husband seems a bit steep.'

'Oh, I don't know. A woman scorned, and all that. Do we know if it was the first time, or had Tamsin been blowing him for weeks?'

'He says it was only the once, but sadly the only person who could confirm or deny that is Tamsin.'

'Fair point, Douglas. So what are you thinking?'

Tom was silent for a moment. 'If it was Price's wife, she wouldn't necessarily get the right girl first time. It's possible she killed the first girl by mistake, and learning what she had done, went back for the right one.'

'So her husband's covering for her? Is that what you mean?'

'It's possible, but I don't believe it. Women rarely slash throats, do they? I don't think it's either of the Prices. I wish I knew what the symbol meant on the top of the leg, though. The profiler says it may be connected with the idea of the power of three.' Tom shrugged, and neither man spoke for a moment.

'Okay, tell me more about Price. I know you don't think it's him, but humour me,' Victor said.

'He works in the psychology department, and he specialises in cognitive psychology.'

'And what the chuff might that be?'

'Attention, perception, memory, reasoning. Quite interesting, I imagine.'

Victor raised his eyebrows as if to say, 'Really?'

'So how did Tamsin know him, then?'

'I gather Tamsin was hanging around waiting for Alexander, who was doing psychology as an elective, and she caught Price's eye.'

Victor laughed. 'Not difficult, from what I've seen. My sister used to wear a skirt like Tamsin's – so short my dad called it a curtain pelmet.'

Tom stifled a sigh. 'We're working our way through all of Tamsin's exes, sir, and if possible I'd also like to take a look at the warehouses and some of the derelict sites around Pomona. I know you sent uniforms down to check if they were secured, but…'

He saw Victor Elliott's face turn red.

'Don't waste your time. I've told you. You're not looking in the right place. Focus, Douglas. I want this guy found.'

43

Maggie crept along the landing, trying to make no sound at all, hoping the rain beating against the windows would mask any noise. She didn't put the light on, and there was little light from the moon coming in through the window on the landing. Step by step she inched her way down the stairs. She didn't need to do this, but she didn't want to explain herself either.

Finally reaching the bottom, she stretched out her hand to the exact spot where she knew her car keys would be, grabbed her raincoat from the hallstand and gently turned the latch on the door. As she turned the handle, the hall was flooded with light.

Suzy was standing at the top of the stairs in her pyjamas. 'What on earth are you doing, Maggie?' Her sister's voice came out in a hoarse whisper.

Maggie stopped. 'Sorry, Suzy. I knew the kids would be okay with you, and I didn't want to tell you I was going out.' She hissed out the words, anxious not to disturb the children.

Suzy walked halfway down the stairs and the conversation continued in hushed tones.

'Why not?' Maggie heard the hurt in her sister's voice and understood.

'Because I didn't want you sitting up all night worrying about me.'

'Crap reason, if you don't mind me saying so. But go on – do what you've got to do. I presume you're going to see Duncan?'

Maggie shrugged. 'I only have a rough idea where he is. I'm going to look for him.'

'What, randomly drive around Manchester, you mean?' The frown on Suzy's face was difficult to miss, and Maggie felt she had to defend herself.

'Not quite. I know roughly what area he's in, so I thought I'd see if I could find him.'

She could hear the hopelessness in her own voice and realised how stupid she was being.

Suzy came to the bottom of the stairs and reached out a hand to her sister. 'Why don't we try to be a bit more methodical than that? Get your laptop and come into the kitchen. I'll make you a hot drink before you go and we can make a plan. Ten minutes isn't going to make any difference, is it?'

Maggie's desire to be doing something, her need to find Duncan – see him, touch him, hold him – had overridden her common sense.

She followed Suzy and opened her laptop.

'Okay, tell me what you know.'

'Not much,' Maggie said. 'When he called me earlier he was in a call box close to Heaton Park.' Maggie loaded up Google Maps and pointed to the location on the map.

'And what's your thinking?'

'I think he'll be staying in a cheap, faceless hotel. He won't be using a credit card – he knows I could check that. Duncan does lots of jobs for cash. And don't look like that.'

'Like what?' Suzy asked with a look of innocence.

'People think if they pay in cash he's going to give them a discount, which he doesn't, but he's lazy about going to the bank. It's all recorded though. He knows I would go ballistic if he was working on the black.'

Neither of them commented on the fact that it seemed Duncan had actually hidden far more than a few bookkeeping inconsistencies from his wife.

'How were you planning on finding out which hotel?'

'I was going to look for his van.'

'It's a bit hit and miss, Mags. It could take you all night. Even if you find him, the best the hotel will do is let you call his room. They won't give you his room number, so he can ignore you if he wants to. I've got a better idea. What's Duncan's van's registration number?'

Maggie told her.

'What was the name of the female detective who came to see you?'

'Detective Inspector Robinson, I think. I can't remember her first name. Why?'

Suzy took control of the laptop and clicked on the first hotel shown by Google Maps. She picked up the phone and pressed 141.

'What are you doing, Suzy?' Maggie asked, not entirely trusting her sister and recognising the code to withhold her number.

'Shh,' she replied as she typed in the number of the hotel. 'Hello. It's Detective Inspector Robinson speaking from Greater Manchester Police. Can I speak to somebody in authority there, please?'

Maggie looked at her sister in horror. It was a serious offence to impersonate a police officer. What was she *doing*?

'Oh, I see. You're the night manager. I'm hoping you'll be able to help. I presume you ask your guests to provide the registration numbers of their vehicles? Well we're looking for a white van in connection with a serious offence. Can you please check your records for this number?'

Suzy read out the number as Maggie frantically waved at her to stop. She was tempted to drag the phone out of her sister's hands, but that would probably raise more suspicions than if she kept quiet.

'I see. Well, thank you for your help. I won't leave my number. If he's not with you already, he won't be coming. Goodnight.' Suzy disconnected. 'What?' she said, looking Maggie squarely in the eye.

'I can't do this, Suzy. I could lose my job.'

'Listen. The guys on duty at night at these places aren't going to question getting a call about a vehicle. I'm not trying to extort money or anything. Worst case, I'm trying to help you find your husband. And in the highly unlikely event that we get caught, I'll say you knew nothing about it. I was working on my own initiative. Stop fretting and give me the next number.'

Maggie blew out a long breath. She had to admit this was better than trailing round car parks all night.

Suzy tried the next hotel. There was no joy.

She was on hotel number five when Maggie noticed her sister sit up straighter in her chair.

'Right. Can I have your name, please? Okay, Mr Trainer. I don't want you to alert your guest to the fact that we are on our way to visit him. Can you tell me under what name he has registered?' She paused. 'And his room number?'

Suzy was scribbling madly on a piece of paper. 'Thank you so much, Mr Trainer, and please do not mention this to your colleagues. We need to be sure that we stay under the radar on this one. Somebody will be with you within the hour.'

She ended the call and looked at Maggie.

'Room 307. He's checked in under the name of Eric Smith. Not a very imaginative surname, but there you go.'

Maggie felt slightly sick. She knew where he was. She was going to find out why he had left her. Much as she desperately wanted to know, she dreaded finding out. What if he had left because he had somebody else? What if there was another woman in that hotel room with him?

'What do I do now?' She spoke so quietly that Suzy had to lean forward.

'You can't go in impersonating a police officer – I know that. Here's what I suggest.'

Maggie sat there, listening to Suzy's suggestion. It made sense, but she couldn't stop shaking. She didn't know if she could pull it off, but she had to try.

❖

The car park of the hotel was packed, and Maggie had to drive around twice to find a spot, narrowly missing the car next to hers as she reversed into the space.

'Shit,' she muttered. 'Calm *down*.' But she couldn't. Her hands were sticky and her limbs tense. She tried taking deep breaths, but felt as if she was struggling to breathe at all. She *had* to get back in control. This was Duncan. There was going to be a logical reason for everything.

Forcing herself to move, she opened the car door and hurried through the cold drizzle into the warmth of the reception area. She was going to play this the way Suzy had suggested.

'Can I speak to Mr Trainer, please?'

The man behind the desk seemed to be on his own. 'That's me,' he said. 'How can I help?'

'I understand you had a call from DI Robinson earlier about a man calling himself Eric Smith. She explained the situation, I presume?'

The man nodded, his eyes wide. It was clear this wasn't an everyday occurrence for Mr Trainer, and she imagined him enjoying telling the tale over a pint, revelling in his part in it.

'She told me he's in Room 307. I'm his solicitor.' Maggie passed him one of her cards. 'He doesn't know the police are on their way, but I want to speak to him first.'

'Should I call and tell him you're here?' said the night manager.

'Please don't. If he knows the police are coming, he might try to get away through one of your emergency exits. That would set off an alarm and create pandemonium, I would imagine.' Mr Trainer looked horrified at the thought. 'I need to go and see him, prepare him for the police visit. Where will I find his room?'

Mr Trainer seemed a bit worried. This probably hadn't been part of his training. He looked again at her card, and Maggie held her breath.

'You'll need a key card to get access to the corridor,' he said, holding out a piece of white plastic. 'Our security's pretty good.'

He looked quite smug when he mentioned the security, but Maggie smiled and refrained from commenting.

'If DI Robinson turns up, perhaps you could ask her to wait. I'll bring my client down when I've had a chance to speak to him.'

Maggie took the key card from Mr Trainer, hoping he didn't notice how much her hand was shaking.

She wanted to sit down. She wanted, somehow, to delay the moment. Her stomach lurched with nerves. What if there was another woman in the room with him? What would she do?

She had to retain a professional air, so she marched purposefully towards the door leading to the rooms, grasping her briefcase tightly in one hand and the key card in the other.

The corridor was long and badly lit, with a patterned carpet designed no doubt to hide as many stains as possible. The walls were scuffed and there was a smell of air freshener. This was the type of place that Maggie knew Duncan would normally hate. She followed the corridor to a junction and for a moment couldn't work out which way she had to go to get to Room 307. The numbers seemed jumbled, and she hesitated.

'Left,' she mumbled, turning down another endless, narrow corridor. Room 307 was towards the end.

She stood facing the door. The moment had come, and she couldn't put it off any longer.

She knocked. She could hear a television playing quietly inside but no movement.

Maggie knocked again, harder and with more authority. She heard a rustle as if somebody was getting up off the bed, and then the soft thud of shoeless feet padding towards the door. She held her breath. There was a pause, and she realised he must be looking at her through the peephole, her face distorted by the fisheye lens.

The door opened abruptly. Standing in front of her was a man with a half-grown beard, looking slightly grubby and unkempt. She glanced over his shoulder to the room beyond. There was nobody else there.

'Hello, Duncan,' she said, looking straight into his blood-shot eyes.

44

The clammy surface of Leo's skin belied the deep, penetrating cold she felt. She wasn't going to die of exposure – cold as she was, she knew it wasn't as bad as that. But she might very well die of the infection that was raging through her system. Sometimes she felt she was slipping into delirium, seeing images that weren't there. She thought she saw figures, mainly women dressed in long skirts and high-necked blouses. There was line after line of white reels, and metal wheels overhead being turned by giant rubber bands. She could hear the hum of machinery interspersed with a clack-clackety-clack noise. Then she would sleep for a few moments and wake to the reality of her prison – a bare old mill – and the knowledge that those figures weren't real. Her imagination had painted pictures of the past in her mind to comfort and distract her from her pain.

Leo dropped her head onto her chest and wondered what they were going to do with her. They hadn't been for a while. It felt like weeks, but Leo was trying to keep a grasp on reality and knew this was only the second night that nobody had come. And in such a short time what had been nothing more than a painful wound had become a swollen, agonising lump of purple flesh.

Max and Ellie had to be looking for her, surely? Her sister wouldn't believe for a moment that Leo had simply forgotten the baby's christening, or that she would have gone away and totally ignored an event that Ellie had been planning with such excitement for weeks. And she knew what Max would have done: he would have called Tom.

Tom.

She had been so stupid. She hadn't been able to trust him when they were together and in the end had pushed him away. It had taken her a long time to forgive herself for that, but she genuinely believed she had learned her lesson. Tom had told her repeatedly that he would never hurt her, but he had. Or rather, she had hurt herself. She could have fixed it, but her stupid pride wouldn't let her.

Tom had explained to her that *everybody* was vulnerable when they loved another person. That person might die, but does that mean you have to avoid loving anybody because at some point you might suffer the pain of loss? The thought of being vulnerable was more than she had been able to bear, but then she had met Julian. Another genuinely good man. And she had driven him away too. It was like a disease.

She had decided before all of this – this nightmare that seemed to have no end – that she was going to fix it with Julian. She wouldn't have embarrassed him by turning up unexpectedly at the races, but she was going to make it right and she was going to change who she was. For years she had hidden behind a persona – the uber-cool Leo Harris who only wore silk and cashmere and only ever black and white.

The morning after her row with Julian, moved by a level of self-disgust she had never experienced before, she had raced into her bedroom and ripped all her monochrome outfits from their hangers. They were all going to the charity shop, and she was going to wear bright red, royal blue, emerald green – she was going to be *different*.

And then this.

She wiped her sticky forehead with the back of her free hand and looked at the dark spongy surface of the skin of her other wrist. Would she lose her arm? She didn't know, any more than she knew if she would lose her life.

One thing that Leo recognised when she saw it, though, was a psychopath. Her years of studying psychology had seen to that. The man who had sewn her arm to its binding showed no remorse for his actions and was totally indifferent to her pain. He blamed her. If she hadn't tried to free herself, he wouldn't have had to do this.

The other man tended to speak calmly and sensibly in a voice that spoke of a public school upbringing. That had confirmed one thing in Leo's mind: she wasn't dealing with ordinary Manchester thugs. But what did they want? Why keep her here like this? She was sure that if they had planned to kill her, they would have done it by now.

Her brain started to feel fuddled again, and she allowed herself to begin the slide back into delirium, her escape from the pain and discomfort.

She was disturbed by a sound. Somebody was coming. Leo closed her eyes. If they weren't wearing masks, she didn't want to see them. Whatever their intentions up to now, if they knew she had seen their faces, they would have to kill her.

Leo heard footsteps coming towards her and felt a kick on her thigh, not hard enough to hurt her but to see if she was awake. She lifted her head slowly, keeping her eyes closed. She opened them to slits. His mask was in place. She opened them a fraction more but knew that they would be glassy with dull whites and dilated pupils.

'Shit,' the man muttered. He walked away from her and she heard the beep of mobile phone keys being pressed.

'You need to get over here,' he said without introduction. 'The girl's sick. Bring some stuff.' There was a pause. '*I* don't fucking know. You're the doctor.'

That might have been interesting information had Leo not already guessed by the sutures in her arm.

She allowed herself to nod off, wanting to save her energy for when the posh boy's accomplice arrived.

She didn't know how long she had been dozing when she heard voices – the two men talking. The first one had been pacing up and down, a sound that had penetrated her light sleep, but she knew she should pretend to still be asleep.

The newcomer crouched down in front of her. She didn't open her eyes, but she could feel his presence, smell a subtle but expensive aftershave and feel his warm breath on her cheek.

'Stop panicking,' he said to the first guy. 'I'll give her some antibiotics and she'll be as right as rain. Not that it makes any difference.'

Leo tried not to react. That didn't make sense. That sounded as if she was going to die, so why treat her?

'How long do we have to keep this up for?'

'Until he's compliant. He has to take his punishment. If he doesn't do as we ask, he knows what's going to happen. It's simple. He's let me down once. Now it's time for retribution. We give him twenty-four hours or we kill his wife.'

45

It was hard to read Duncan's face. Not because it was grey from lack of decent food and sleep and covered in a thin light-brown beard, but because so many expressions flitted across it in quick succession. The first was horror, the second looked vaguely like relief.

Maggie didn't know how she felt. Breathing seemed difficult, as if a band of steel was being tightened around her chest. Half of her wanted to reach out, hold him close and beg him to explain. The other half wanted to slap him hard across the face, to release some of the pent-up hurt, fear and anger that had been seething through her for the last few days. Once the tears started, though, she wouldn't be able to stop them and she couldn't fall apart yet. Not until she knew if he still loved her.

For a moment she didn't think he was going to let her into the room, and then he stepped back and held the door wide.

Maggie walked into a small room that held not much more than a wardrobe, a hard-looking double bed and a flat-screen TV on the wall. A bedside lamp cast ovoid shadows on the beige walls. She sat down heavily on the bed and stared at her husband, who was leaning against the wall. She had been married to this man for ten years, and at that moment it felt as if she didn't know him at all. Did anybody ever really know anybody else? Neither of them spoke for what seemed like minutes.

'Talk,' Maggie eventually said, setting her face in what she hoped was an assertive expression.

Duncan shook his head as if it was all a mystery to him.

'I'm sorry, Maggie. I didn't want to leave you. I'm sorry I left the kids alone, but I knew you'd be home soon, and Josh sometimes seems like the most grown-up of all of us. I knew they'd be safe.'

He hadn't known they would be safe. At best, he had *hoped* they would be safe. She didn't say a word. She didn't want to reveal what she knew. She wanted to see how much of the truth he was going to tell her.

'I had to go. I was putting you all in danger,' Duncan said. He paused and looked down. 'I'd borrowed some money, and not from the right sort of people. They wanted it back. They said they would come to the house. It was best if I left. I didn't do it for me; I did it for you.'

She felt the first stirrings of something like disgust and pushed them away.

'In what way would we have been safer without you there if some men were coming to collect their cash?' she asked.

Duncan looked nonplussed, as well he might. 'It was me they wanted. Not you.'

'No, it wasn't. It was their *cash* they wanted. And I was probably a better bet than you, so what would have kept them away?'

He fell silent, and she waited.

'I don't know what else to tell you,' he said, a look of almost defiance on his face.

Trying to control her anger, Maggie pulled her phone out of her pocket. 'Right. I'm calling the police. They can catch these guys, and that will be the end of it.'

Duncan lunged across the room and grabbed her wrist.

'What the hell are you doing, Duncan?' she shouted.

'Don't call the police, Maggie. It's a bit more complicated.'

She waited again, and could see his mind ticking over. He was trying to think of another, slightly more plausible lie; it was written all over his face.

'Duncan, I know a lot more than you realise. I'll know if you're lying to me, so I suggest you don't even start.'

He still didn't speak. He looked at the floor, but she was sure it wasn't shame she was seeing. She could see his eyes were open, staring intently down as if trying to work out what to say next.

'I thought you'd left me for another woman, you bastard,' she hissed at him.

Duncan lifted his head and looked at her. 'I wouldn't do that, Mags. You know that.'

'I don't know *anything*. Have you any idea what the last few days have been like for me and the kids?'

He dropped his head again, and Maggie wished she could see his expression. She didn't want him to have time to work out what to say – to decide what would cause the least grief or anger.

'Start talking, Duncan. And start at the beginning because I know this is not only about what's happening now. I want to know it all.'

Duncan slid slowly down the wall until he came to rest on the floor, his forearms resting on his raised knees. Maggie waited. She wasn't going to prompt him. Eventually he started to talk without looking at her, staring at the carpet between his feet.

'It started when I was at university.'

'Which university would that be?' Maggie asked, her expression showing nothing.

'You know where I went to university. Leeds,' he responded.

Maggie felt as if somebody had stamped on her chest, and for a moment she thought she might actually stop breathing. He was still lying to her. This man she loved with all her heart was still lying.

'Stop it,' she said. 'Stop the bloody lies, Duncan – or should I say Michael?' She practically spat out the name and was rewarded with a look of shock on her husband's face. He didn't speak, and she wasn't going to prompt him. The next step was down to him.

After what seemed like hours, Duncan shook his head, and he began to speak.

'The story I'm going to tell you isn't about Duncan Taylor. *I'm* Duncan Taylor. *Me.* This is about another boy – somebody you've never met. And yes, his name is Michael.'

46

'I told you to go home hours ago,' Tom said as he approached Becky's desk. 'We're neither of us much good to anybody unless we get a few hours' sleep, and we need to start bright and early tomorrow with clear heads.'

Becky yawned and stretched her arms high in the air. The incident room was fairly quiet by now, although it would stay manned throughout the night.

'You're right, I know. But I'm getting so frustrated with this Adam Mellor guy. Maggie Taylor wasn't lying about him being in the vicinity of her house that day – we've got him on ANPR going into the area, but we can't pick him up leaving. He seems to have disappeared into thin air.'

'He's a smart guy. You and I both know there are ways of fooling the cameras, or maybe he used false plates.'

'Well that's not all. It's just been confirmed that Ben Coleman did leave for holiday before Hayley went missing.'

'Bollocks,' Tom muttered. 'Another dead end.'

'Not as dead as you think,' Becky had responded. 'We're still waiting for confirmation that he got on the flight, so we'll see. But here's the thing: it seems Ben and Adam shared the same counsellor at university – well, to be precise they attended the same practice. I don't know yet who their specific counsellors were. Julian Richmond mentioned that Adam had had counselling, so I thought I'd check it out. I got somebody to check with the university to find out which practices they recommended, and then when I'd tracked down Adam's, I requested a list of other clients. If they had counsellors from the same practice, there's a possibility that he and Ben met in the waiting room or something.'

Tom sat down opposite Becky, the tiredness suddenly slipping away.

'Here we go again. Another coincidence. Did Ben's name come up on the original enquiry? It's not ringing any bells.'

'No, and neither did Adam's. I checked that too. They were never questioned, and there are no clear links between either of them and the first victims.'

'Where's Ben gone, and when did he book it?'

'He only booked it a week ago, but he's gone to Antigua.'

'We really do need to know if he caught that flight.'

Becky pulled a face. 'I know. That's the one bit of information I haven't been able to get yet,' she admitted. 'Sorry. We're trying to get the airline to check the flight manifest. You'll know the minute I hear.'

Ben Coleman knew Hayley, and Adam Mellor appeared to be following Maggie Taylor. And Adam Mellor had a somewhat tenuous link to Leo. These were no coincidences.

'And one more thing, boss,' Becky said as if reading Tom's mind. 'We've been in touch with Adam Mellor's family, and no-body knows of anybody who has died.'

Tom was convinced that Adam had something to do with Leo's disappearance. They had next to nothing to go on, but somebody had come to her with a huge bouquet of flowers, knowing that she'd had a disagreement with her boyfriend. The only person Julian had told seemed to be Adam, who suddenly wasn't able to make it to the races, an event he had organised himself.

So where was he hiding her?

'Becky, your Mark's a bit of a railway geek, isn't he?'

Becky rolled her eyes. 'And then some,' she said, although the corner of her mouth lifted in an affectionate smile.

'We know Adam's family were closely involved with transport

243

in Manchester over the years. Think of the locations we've had for these murders – all vaguely transport related. Mark might only know about the railways, but can you ask if he can think of anywhere else that might be a good place to hide somebody. Pity he's not an expert on canals as well.'

'Oh, you'd be surprised,' Becky said. 'And he certainly knows plenty of other nerds who can fill in the gaps. I'm on it.'

There was one more thing that Tom wanted to do.

'If Adam Mellor and Ben Coleman's only connection is through a student counsellor, it might be worth having another look at that patient list, to see if any other names jump out.'

Becky picked up a sheet of A4 paper from her desk and passed it to Tom. She began collecting her things together, but Tom was only vaguely conscious of her actions.

'Well bugger me,' he said quietly.

Becky stopped what she was doing and the room was still for a moment. Tom didn't speak.

'What?' Becky asked, clearly unable to restrain her curiosity.

'Alexander.'

'Who's Alexander?'

'Do you remember me telling you that my ex-boss Victor Elliott refused to listen when I said I thought Tamsin Grainger's boyfriend was involved in some way? "It's not that boy Alexander," he used to say all the time, "he has an alibi," which was true. But I knew there was something funny about the lad even though he couldn't have killed either of the girls because he was definitely somewhere else on both occasions. Then I was taken off the case, and that was that.'

Tom looked at the sheet again.

'And?' Becky said, a note of exasperation creeping into her voice.

'He's here on the list. The same counselling service. Alexander. Right at the top.'

244

'Alexander who?'

'Alexander wasn't his first name – old Victor called everybody by their surnames. His name was Michael. Michael Alexander.'

47

Duncan still wouldn't look at Maggie. She was sure it was so that she wouldn't spot the lies, and a wave of sadness washed over her. The fact was, she could no longer trust a word he said.

'It all started when I went to university. And yes, you're right. It was Manchester, not Leeds. I only lied a minute ago because it's what you've always believed, and I didn't want you to feel bad about making us move here.'

Maggie could feel her brow furrowing. That was a pathetic attempt at an excuse, and if he was trying to put the blame on her for his lies, it wasn't going to work. And it hardly explained the original lie over ten years ago. She remembered the nights they had lain in bed, arms around each other while he told her how much he had loved university in Leeds and how difficult it had been to give it all up to go and look after his mother. The saddest thing of all was that those nights, nights that had meant everything to her, had been built on lies. But for now she had to let him speak.

'I was studying chemical engineering, and I had a few demons to put to rest so I was seeing a counsellor.'

Maggie didn't want to interrupt him, but she knew he had missed out a huge chunk, and she wanted the whole story.

'What kind of demons – something from your childhood?'

Duncan raised his head and looked at her. He understood her so well, and he must have been able to see in her eyes that she knew something. He hesitated.

'Duncan, I know your name. I know your birthday. And you *know* that I can find out anything I want to. So stop messing about, for God's sake.' She omitted to mention that she didn't know his surname.

Duncan's lips tightened, and she knew he wasn't happy to be telling her this.

'How do you know about my name?' he asked.

'You were in care. I don't need to explain to you how I know. You need to tell me the truth. Why were you in care, and for how long?'

Duncan's eyes narrowed, and she could see he was wondering how much she knew.

'I told you my mother was ill. She was ill for years. When she had to go into hospital, I had to go and stay with a lady called Pat. I didn't mention it because nobody's proud of being in care. There wasn't anybody else, you see. Just me and Mum. That's why it nearly killed me when she died. I was never with Pat for long – only a few weeks at a time – and I went home when Mum came out of hospital. I shouldn't have gone to university really, but she insisted. She wanted me to have everything in life, so social services arranged for a nurse to call in every day while I was away. But I know I shouldn't have gone.'

Maggie could feel his pain and had to stop herself from going to him. But she needed to pull him away from talk of his mother.

'Let's get back to the counsellor you mentioned,' she said. 'What happened there?'

'The people at the university knew about my mother and the fact that I was having to live with a lot of uncertainty about the future, so I was allocated an adviser. He was good. He helped me to face things and helped me to meet – sort of – people in a similar position. Chat rooms on the Internet were just getting going, and he introduced me to one where people talked through their problems. It was anonymous, and it helped me. I was given a room in the halls of residence for fifty-two weeks of the year and treated as a kid coming out of care because basically I had nowhere to go when my mum was in hospital – no other family to turn to. I was a bit of a loner, so chatting to people online was a lifesaver. You really have no idea, Mags. Everybody has somebody. But for huge chunks of time I didn't. I had nobody. I felt like a shadow – as if I had no substance of my own.'

The pain Maggie was feeling for the man sitting in front of her was real, but it was as if she were listening to a person she didn't know well. A friend's husband, perhaps. She felt detached. *How had all of this stayed hidden?*

'Then in my second year I started to see a girl. I'd been out with a few, but I didn't have any money and could barely afford to buy them a drink, so I'd mainly had one-night stands. Then I met Tamsin. She was pretty and funny, and didn't seem to care much about where we went. She just wanted sex – lots of it – so we ended up at mine.'

He looked at Maggie. 'Do you mind if I get a glass of water, Mags? I've barely spoken in the last few days, and my throat's dry.'

'I'll get it. You carry on talking.'

Maggie went into the bathroom and found a plastic cup inside a polythene bag. She ripped it open as she listened.

'I thought we had an exclusive relationship, and it was going well, but one night after a late lecture I saw her walking along the other side of the road. I shouted to her, but there were lots of people milling around and she didn't hear me. She was all dressed up, so I followed her. She went into one of the staff car parks. It was pretty dark by then, but I saw a flash of headlights and she gave a little wave. I thought somebody must be giving her a lift somewhere and was about to leave, but I wanted to see who it was. There was nobody else about so I crouched down behind one of the few remaining cars and waited for them to drive out. But they didn't. I had a peep after a few minutes, and they were still there – in the car.'

Maggie returned to the bedroom and handed Duncan a glass of lukewarm water – the best she could do.

'To cut a long story short, she was giving one of the lecturers a blow job. I was devastated.'

Duncan fell silent and sipped at his water.

'I thought she loved me and that we had something special. When you don't have anybody, it hits much harder if somebody lets you down.'

Maggie tried to assess how it must have felt to be that kid with no family, few friends and nobody to turn to. He thought he had found somebody to love. She realised she was thinking of this boy as Michael. None of it had anything to do with her Duncan.

'What happened afterwards?' she asked, fearing that there was more to come.

'I went to see my counsellor. I told him what had happened and how I felt. I was so *hurt*. So *angry* that she would throw away what we had. I think I probably said that I wanted to kill her, but people say that all the time, don't they?'

He looked straight at Maggie as he spoke, his eyes slightly narrowed as if to gauge her reaction. She managed to keep her face impassive. He was right. How often had she said 'I could have killed him' about something trivial?

'What did your counsellor advise?'

'He suggested another chat room. He said it was designed for people who felt like me, who needed an outlet for their anger. It was a private site – you know, not indexed and only accessible if you knew how to get in. I suppose you'd call it the dark web nowadays. Anyway, it was a place where I could express my feelings.'

Maggie was puzzled. She knew about the dark web of course, but generally thought about it in terms of pornography and the buying and selling of drugs.

'What kind of site was it?' she asked.

'A fantasy site,' Duncan said, his dark eyes fixed on hers as if they were boring into her to read her thoughts. 'A fantasy murder site.'

❖

The silence in the hotel room was claustrophobic in its intensity. Maggie stared at her husband, and he stared right back as if daring her to comment. She wasn't sure for a moment that she had heard him correctly. Did that mean what she thought? People went on there to fantasise about committing *murder*? It was as twisted as anything she had ever come across.

The tension snapped as the room phone rang.

'Shit,' Maggie muttered. 'Does anybody know you're here?'

Duncan shook his head.

'Could they have traced your van, like I did?'

'I don't see how they would know the registration number.'

'Okay, it's best if I answer this,' Maggie said, guessing who it would be.

She picked the phone up.

'Yes?' she said, trying to sound as if she were in control. 'Yes, I'm fine, thank you, Mr Trainer. It's okay, I've heard from the police. They called my mobile. I'm going to take my client to them when we've finished our meeting. He'll be checking out. Yes, I'm fine, but thank you so much for your concern, Mr Trainer.'

At the mention of the police, Duncan had pushed himself to his feet, panic spreading across his face. Maggie waved him down, ended the call and hung up.

'It's okay. There are no police, but when we've finished we're going to have to move you somewhere else. The guy downstairs thinks you're a criminal.'

Duncan's eyes asked, *Is that what you think?* but Maggie gave nothing away.

She took a deep breath. 'Now tell me what sort of sick *fuck* of a counsellor tells a disturbed kid to go to a fantasy murder site? What the hell *is* a fantasy murder site, anyway?'

Duncan shrugged as if it were nothing.

'Exactly what you might think. It's a fantasy site. You go on and you talk about how you would kill somebody and why. Other people make suggestions. There's even a board that tells you how to commit the perfect murder. But it's just fantasy. It helps get it all out of your system.'

Maggie had no words. It wasn't just fantasising about wanting somebody dead; people actually discussed methods of committing murder. She didn't think this could get any worse, but there was more and Maggie knew it. This website was the most macabre thing she had ever heard of, but if that was all it was, Duncan wouldn't have mentioned it. She waited.

'One guy started to chat to me and suggested we go into a private side room. His name was Samil – well, that was his pseudonym. We all had them. The only people who could access the private room were people who were specifically invited, so to start with it was just me, Samil, and the site administrator – Invictus, he called himself.'

It all sounded so juvenile with the silly names, but no doubt they had some sinister meaning.

'Then Samil suggested that maybe we could help each other out. He had been fantasising about killing his stepmother so she didn't inherit all his father's money. He hated her. He said he would kill Tamsin for me if I would kill his stepmother. I thought he was joking.'

Duncan had stopped looking at Maggie again. He was clutching the plastic cup between his hands, squeezing it so that it cracked and staring into its empty depths. She wanted to scream at him, but she had to keep quiet and let him continue or she might never learn the truth.

'He didn't know who I was any more than I knew who he was. At least he didn't know then. All we knew was that we both lived in Manchester. He said that Tamsin's murder would have to take place when I was away so I couldn't be implicated. Then Invictus added a suggestion. He said we needed to make it look like it had nothing to do with Tamsin herself – that it was the start of a serial killing spree.'

Maggie gasped. She couldn't believe they were having this conversation in an ordinary, rather drab, cheap hotel bedroom. She felt hot and the room was airless. Without speaking to Duncan she walked over to the window and tried to open it, but it would only budge about an inch and the gap did nothing to improve the oppressive atmosphere. She banged her open palm against the window frame.

'How many did he suggest should be killed?' she asked, hearing a clipped, brittle edge to her voice. She realised that without conscious thought she fallen into the role of professional lawyer. This was no longer Duncan, her husband; this was Michael, a man who had somehow become involved in something evil, and it was her job to get him off. She needed to hide behind that persona, which suddenly felt like the only way she could survive.

'Three.' Duncan's voice had become quiet, as if he almost couldn't believe this himself. 'Invictus said it was a powerful number and would ensure that nobody was ever caught. It would be even better if all the victims looked similar – this would cause confusion on so many levels. I never thought they meant it, though.'

'What in God's name did you *think* they meant, Duncan? Did you actually think *at all?*'

He looked at her then, his eyes wide.

'I thought it was a game – how to commit the perfect murder, you know. I thought we would do all the planning, and then say, "Yes, it would have worked." But Invictus kept adding suggestions, and Samil was getting excited about it.'

It sounded to Maggie as if this Invictus got a vicarious thrill from planning such things. Maybe he hadn't believed it would ever happen either.

'I was a member of the university cycling team,' Duncan continued, 'and they decided that the first murder should coincide with a trip. Invictus said he thought he might be able to help with the selection of the first girl, and he would communicate with Samil about it separately. It was better if I didn't know. All I needed to do was post Tamsin's details on the site and leave the rest to them.'

There was a long pause.

'I never meant anything to happen, Maggie. It was just like an online game. Even Josh plays those.'

'Don't you *dare* equate what you did with a game of fucking Clash of the Clans.'

Duncan had the grace to look away, but Maggie hadn't finished.

'If it was fantasy, why didn't you make somebody up?'

'Why would I do that?'

He looked genuinely puzzled, and Maggie shook her head to clear her mind. She knew there were fantasy porn sites out there and that people shared fantasies about real people, but could Duncan really have been so gullible as to think this was helping him to redirect his anger?

'Did you go on your cycling trip?' Maggie asked, her speech staccato.

'Of course, because I keep telling you I never really thought it would happen. I knew that Samil had recruited a helper. Invictus had suggested it. He said it made it easier to lure the victims in, and Samil needed a killing site – somewhere safe so they could take their time over it and be safe.'

'And you *knew* all this? You went *along* with it?'

'I thought it was all part of the fantasy. Do you think I *wanted* any of this to happen?'

'What did you expect? You had given them the girl's details, the dates when you would be away. You still thought it was fantasy?'

Duncan didn't look at her, and Maggie didn't know whether to believe him or not.

'But it wasn't, was it?' she asked.

'No.'

Maggie jumped off the bed and rushed to the bathroom.

48

Maggie stayed locked in the bathroom for ten minutes. She couldn't breathe. She needed to be out of that airless room and away from Duncan. She leaned heavily on the washbasin, head down, wondering if she was going to be sick, and forced herself to take long, deep breaths.

If she could continue to convince herself that this was Michael she was hearing about, and not the Duncan who had sat up for hours nursing toddler Josh when he had an ear infection, or who had lain on the rug pretending to be poorly while Lily played nurse making Daddy better, she could deal with it. She could assign the actions and behaviours she had just heard about to a man she didn't know.

Finally she opened the door. Duncan hadn't moved, but he looked up at her, trying to gauge what she was thinking. She looked away, not wanting him to see how shaken she was. If he knew how she was feeling he might stop talking.

In the confines of the small bedroom she was going to have to step over his feet to get back to the bed and she didn't want to touch him. The room suddenly seemed darker than ever, although she knew it was her imagination.

'I'm sorry, Maggie. I know it's not a nice story, but you have to understand all of that to understand the rest.'

There was one thing she had to ask him before he told her any more. 'This man – Samil. Did he ever call himself Sam?'

'What? Why?' asked Duncan.

'Just answer the bloody question. Did he ever call himself

Sam?' She could hear her voice shaking and fought for control.

'Sometimes, but why is it important?'

'Because a man spoke to Josh yesterday. He asked if he was missing his daddy, and he said to say hi. From *Sam!*'

Maggie couldn't look at Duncan. She was terrified that his expression would fail to show the horror she was feeling. She needn't have worried, though, because he had turned his head away from her towards the door, muttering, 'Oh shit.'

She wanted to rush at him and throttle him for putting their son in such jeopardy, but first she had to know it all and she knew there was more to come.

'You need to carry on with your story. I need to know what happened next. When did you realise that this was no fantasy?'

'Samil said I should go ahead with the cycling trip at the beginning of May. I think it was North Wales the first time.'

Maggie felt her body twitch. *The first time?*

'He said he had recruited somebody, and they were going to make Tamsin pay for what she'd done.'

Duncan's voice became even quieter and Maggie had to strain to hear his words. 'The news came on the day we were due to head back from the trip. A girl, a student at the university, had been found dead on Pomona Island.' Duncan raised his eyes to Maggie's and he must have seen the confusion there. 'It's a strip of wasteland right in the heart of Manchester.' He looked away again, and she wondered why he didn't want her to see his eyes.

'I remember feeling sick,' he said. 'I thought I was going to throw up in front of the whole cycling team. Somebody other than me asked the question: "Who was it?" The lecturer who was leading the group said, "Sonia Beecham," and I nearly passed out. I felt the room spinning. Thank God this was some other poor kid. It had nothing to do with me.'

Duncan pushed himself up off the floor and went to the wardrobe opposite the bathroom. He slid the door open and bent down to retrieve a small cardboard box, which he carried back to where he had been sitting and slumped back down the wall. Maggie glanced at the box and knew instantly where it had come from. This had to be the contents of Duncan's cupboard – his mementos. Settling back down with the box between his knees, he pulled out an old newspaper and handed it to Maggie.

She looked at the picture – a pretty girl with shoulder-length blonde hair and a shy smile. Underneath was an article about the murder and where they had found the body.

'Before I saw the newspaper, I thought it was just another murder in Manchester. Thank God, it really had all been a fantasy. And then I saw the photograph and I knew. This girl – this Sonia Beecham – was the spitting image of Tamsin. I knew then that they'd followed the instructions on the website from Invictus. This murder was going to be the first of three.'

'So what did you do?'

Duncan looked down and said nothing. Maggie leaped off the bed and knelt in front of him. She grabbed his head between her open palms and forced him to look at her.

'Did you warn Tamsin? *Did you?* Did you go to the police and tell them what had happened? What did you *do,* Duncan? For God's sake, tell me you did *something.*'

He reached up and pulled her hands away.

'Of course I didn't. The police would have blamed me, Mags. And it wasn't my fault. I was in over my head. I was a kid in and out of care – exactly the sort the police like to pin things on. I had just been fantasising – exactly what my counsellor told me to do – but how could I prove that?'

'Your *counsellor!* Did you tell him what he'd done? Does he realise what happened because of what he had advised you to do? You knew they were going to kill somebody else, didn't you? You could have stopped it.' Maggie's voice cracked. She sat back on her heels, staring at a man she didn't know.

Duncan shook his head. His face was flushed with anger – at her or at the guys from the website, she wasn't sure.

'None of this was my fault. I thought after killing one girl it might have put them off. They'd had their thrill – that was the end of it. But then I went on my second cycling trip – to Keswick – and that's when they killed Tamsin.'

'And you *still* didn't do anything?' Maggie buried her face in her hands as tears streamed down her cheeks. 'Stop saying it wasn't your fault, for Christ's sake. You could have done something; you could have stopped it.'

'What could I do? I didn't know who they were. But they found out who I was because when Tamsin was killed I was questioned by the police and there was a picture of me in the paper.'

Maggie knew that after Tamsin was killed, had Duncan admitted his part in it all he would almost inevitably have been charged with something – probably conspiracy to murder or soliciting to murder, either of which would have resulted in a prison sentence. So he had done nothing. *Nothing.* Even though he had known that the plan was to kill three girls.

She lifted her head and stared at him.

'All this because of a blow job? For God's sake, Duncan…' Maggie trailed off. There was no more to say.

Duncan was immediately on the defensive, a hint of anger in his tone. He sat up straighter against the wall.

'It's easy for you to say that. You have no idea how I felt. How did *you* feel when you thought I might have left you for another woman?'

'I felt like shit, but even if you had, I wouldn't have wanted to *murder* anybody. And we've been married for ten years and have two kids. It's not some short-term relationship, for fuck's sake.'

She turned away from him and crawled back to the bed, clambered onto the duvet and rolled onto her side, her back to

Duncan. She didn't want to look at her husband, to see his face as he made his excuses.

'I had nobody back then, Mags. Remember that. For the first time, I had thought I had somebody that cared about *me*. Just me.'

Maggie felt a momentary tug of sympathy for a boy who was so alone, but nothing could excuse this.

'What about the third girl?' she asked, her back still to him.

For a moment, Duncan said nothing. Maggie waited, not trusting herself to speak again.

'It went wrong.' His voice was low, and he cleared his throat. 'Samil had worked with this other guy – some posh kid, from what I could gather by the way he expressed himself on the site – who had a grudge against the world, it seemed. He was what Invictus called a schemer – Machiavellian. He had access to some places where the kills could take place. I don't know much more than that. He was going to do the second one, but he didn't have the balls to use a knife, so he decided to strangle her. I think he just wanted to know what it felt like to kill somebody, but in the end he couldn't finish it, so Samil did. The other guy helped dispose of the bodies. But he wanted another go with the third one. He messed it up, and she survived.'

'Thank God for small mercies,' Maggie whispered under her breath, replaying Duncan's words in her head. She was staggered by the ease with which he had referred to the kills and the disposal of the bodies.

Duncan went quiet and Maggie rolled over to look at him. He was back to contemplating the patterned carpet between his feet. The pause gave Maggie time to think. How could the man to whom she had felt so close – as if, as she had said to Suzy, she was almost inside his skin with him – have had all these secrets, this history that he had concealed from her? What else had he hidden from her? Who was he, really?

'That's when it got really difficult.' Duncan had started again,

258

talking quietly, barely opening his mouth as if he didn't want to say the words out loud.

She had thought it was over, that all the horrors had been aired. But then she realised there had to be more, or why would this Samil be threatening them all now?

'Samil wanted me to kill his stepmother. He said I owed him. I didn't do it, Mags. I had to leave university to look after my mother – I told you that. So I used the opportunity to get away and changed my name.'

❖

Maggie had no more words – there was nothing left to say. As a defence lawyer, she could argue that a young, impressionable boy had found himself in a dreadful situation with nobody to guide him out of it. As a wife, she didn't know how to deal with the revelations – the secrets, the lies, but most of all the lack of a conscience. Duncan didn't think any of it was his fault.

'I think it's time we moved you from here,' Maggie said, her voice weary. 'We don't want the manager getting suspicious and calling the police to check my story. Let's find somewhere else.'

She felt ill, but she had to be practical. Her head ached and her whole body seemed to be full of sandbags, each of her limbs heavy and unwieldy. But she had to get him out of this hotel.

'I've not got much cash left, Mags, and I'm not happy about using a credit card. I don't know who these guys are. What if one of them is police and he can track me?'

Duncan looked beaten. For a man who was meticulous about his clothes, his jeans looked crumpled and a size too big, and his demeanour made him seem small, shrunken. But she couldn't rid herself of the thought that her husband only seemed concerned about what Samil might do to *him*. Samil knew where she *lived*, for God's sake. He had threatened *her*.

Hiding her hurt at his thoughtlessness she reached for her bag. 'I've got enough money for a couple of nights, and then let's hope it will all be over. Pack your stuff, Duncan. Please.'

Duncan stood up and held out his arms. 'Come here,' he said.

Maggie took a step back.

'Okay. Suit yourself.' He turned away and began to pick up items of clothing and shove them haphazardly in his bag.

She had rejected him and he didn't know how to deal with it. She didn't think it had ever happened before.

'Dunc…'

'Forget it, Maggie. Let's just go.' He walked into the bathroom to collect the few odds and ends on the narrow glass shelf. He stuck the small cardboard box on top of everything in his bag and walked towards the door.

'After you,' he said, holding the door open with mock courtesy.

There was no chance to speak after that. She told Mr Trainer that she was taking him to the police station, and that Duncan's van would have to remain where it was until tomorrow, when somebody would come and collect it. She hoped that was acceptable. Mr Trainer kept his head down over his paperwork, but kept giving Duncan surreptitious glances from under his bushy eyebrows. Duncan's lips were tightening by the second, and Maggie knew she needed to get him out of there.

They didn't speak again until they were in the car.

'You know, Maggie, you seem to think I shouldn't have kept any of this from you. But just look at your reaction: you didn't even want to give me a hug. So if I'd told you when we met, do you think you would ever have married me?'

Maggie couldn't answer. She had loved him so much and would never regret the time they had spent together. She still loved him, and still wanted him in her life. But would she have married him all those years ago? No, she wouldn't. She liked to think she would have gone to the police and told them the whole story.

She put the key in the ignition and started the engine to clear the steamed-up windscreen, suddenly exhausted by the emotional carnage of the past few days. She had so much left to ask him, but she didn't know if she had the energy.

The car began to warm up, but she didn't feel ready to drive. Not yet.

'If you must know, Duncan, I feel as if I've been put through a shredder. That just about sums it up. This isn't about whether you kept anything from me. It's about what you *did* and who you *are*, so forgive me if I'm a bit confused at the moment. And don't you dare judge me. If I'm honest, I don't much like the sound of Michael, but I do love Duncan and always have done. I need to separate the young bloke who was lonely and unhappy and made a terrible mistake that cost two girls their lives from the man who nursed his mother and who's been a loving husband and father. I need time.'

Suddenly she was shaking, and hot tears spilled down her cheeks.

'I'm so sorry, Mags,' Duncan murmured. 'I didn't want to hurt you. It was all so long ago and I'm not that person any more. We need to deal with this so we can go back to how we were.'

Maggie's tears dried as instantly as they started. She had forgotten that his confession was far from the end of it.

'So what, exactly, *are* we dealing with?' she asked, dreading the answer.

'I have to pay for failing to kill Samil's stepmother. He couldn't do it himself – his motive was glaringly obvious. Then apparently his father died and left all his money to her. There was nothing Samil could do. Since then she's died too, but she left the whole lot to her own children. They're not even his father's kids.'

'What do you mean, you have to pay?'

'I don't know, Mags. He wants to make me suffer, but he won't tell me precisely what he wants me to do. I thought if he couldn't find me he might get bored with the idea, or slip up and I would find him first. I don't know. He says he wants to meet me.'

'How the hell is he communicating with you?'

'Through the same website. He sent me a text message on my phone – several, in fact, in the last couple of weeks, asking to meet. I ignored them.'

'So what happened?'

'You know what happened. He killed that woman, the one who looked just like you. He sent me the picture and said we had to keep in touch via the website.'

Maggie closed her eyes. There was no point asking him why he hadn't gone to the police at that point. If he hadn't gone twelve years ago, there was no way he would have considered going now.

She knew she had to say something. Her voice was quiet because she was sure she knew the answer.

'And if you don't meet him and do whatever it is he's going to ask you to do?'

Duncan looked away from her, out through the clear windscreen to the black car park.

'I don't know.'

She spun round and looked at him. 'Yes, you bloody do. Say it, Duncan, just say it.'

'He says he'll kill you.'

49

After Duncan's pronouncement, Maggie put the car into gear and drove, checking repeatedly over her shoulder to see if she was being followed.

The threat to her life shouldn't have come as a surprise given the phone calls and the note she had received, but now it was real. These men had already killed four times – twice twelve years ago, twice this week. Another death would mean nothing to them. They wouldn't hesitate to kill her if it suited their aims.

How could Duncan have let it come to this? As far as she could see, he had done nothing at all to protect her. She clung to the steering wheel to control the shaking.

The only sound was the soft noise of the engine and the swish of the windscreen wipers. For a long time, Maggie couldn't trust herself to speak.

She finally broke the silence. 'What were you planning to do if I hadn't turned up tonight, hmm? This obviously wasn't going to go away, so what was your plan? Did you even *have* a plan? Or were you just going to hide until they had done their worst?'

Duncan sighed as if she was asking a ridiculous question.

'I thought I could stop replying to them on the website, and then after a few days they would think I'd gone. I thought that would be better.'

'Better for *whom*, exactly? He *phoned* me – at least, one of them did. He phoned *twice*. He pushed a picture of the second girl – the second *dead* girl – through my letter box. *Jesus* Duncan, if you didn't have a plan then, have you got one now? This is my *life* we're talking about. And with all that was happening, you left me no way to get in touch with you. No way.'

A dark tide of anger was creeping up on her, threatening to drag her under. She had to keep control.

'They're empty threats, Mags. They want you to force me to go and see them.'

'Your son could have seen that gruesome picture. Imagine that, and what it might have done to him. You haven't *once* asked me how Josh is, or Lily. Do you know that? Not once.'

'That's because I know they'll be fine with you. I miss them. Of course I do. But there's been so much else to say.'

To Maggie his words sounded hollow, as if they were nothing more than the words he was expected to say.

'That man – Samil, or whatever he's called – he says he knows where you are.'

'He's bluffing. He would have come for me if he did, you know that. Look, they can keep threatening to kill you and intimidate me by killing lookalikes, but if they *actually* kill you, they won't have any more bargaining chips to make me do whatever it is they want, so they're not going to do that.'

Maggie whipped round to look at him and just as quickly turned back to the road. He was kidding himself, and it was written all over his face – trying to convince himself of what he hoped would be the outcome, rather than what he truly believed.

'Are you telling me that you're happy for them to carry on killing these women?' she said. 'And what makes you think they don't have any more bargaining chips? You've got two children. Will they start on them after me?'

Her voice broke. They couldn't hurt her children. Surely Duncan wouldn't allow that?

'I've done *everything*, Mags. Do you think any of this is what I want?' There was a pleading tone to Duncan's voice that infuriated Maggie. 'I've tried to make them understand. I would have offered money, but it wouldn't be enough. I've threatened them with exposure to the police for what they did all those years ago, but they know I can't prove a thing – at least not without me going down with them. Don't accuse me of not trying – because I have.'

She gripped the steering wheel tightly and thanked God that the streets were empty because she was sure her driving was erratic. Surely he knew what he should have done?

Duncan's voice softened.

'I need you, Maggie. I shouldn't have shut you out, and I'm sorry. Perhaps I should have told you everything years ago, but I wanted you to love me. Now…I need your help – I need you to work out what we should do.'

Maggie said nothing. How was she expected to respond? She had no idea what he should do, but she hadn't missed the fact that it was now her problem too. There was another thing nagging at Maggie as she circled the park, not even thinking of finding Duncan somewhere to stay until they had finished talking.

'How did they know where to find you in the first place, after so long?'

She sensed Duncan was shaking his head. 'I haven't been able to work that out.'

'So who knew you were coming back to Manchester?'

'Nobody – well, nobody who knew my name.'

'Which name would that be?'

'Don't take that tone, Maggie. I should have told you the truth about my name, but then I would have had to tell you the rest, and you wouldn't have wanted me. Can't we move on from that?'

Maggie's anger wasn't helping anybody, but it burned fiercely and she had no other outlet. She gave herself a minute.

'Work it out, Duncan. Just bloody work it out. Who knew you were coming back? It doesn't matter if they knew your name.'

Duncan was silent for a moment. She could almost hear his

brain working out what to say, and she knew he was going to have to confess to something else.

'Before I got involved in the fantasy site, I used to chat on a forum for adults who were lonely. We helped each other. One guy on there was particularly helpful and I've been in touch with him since just after I started university. We still chat every now and again, mainly for his benefit. He knows I'm settled and happy, but he isn't so I've been trying to be supportive, as he was with me.'

Maggie waited. There had to be more.

'I told him I was moving back to Manchester. He said he was living here now – I don't know where he was originally. We never said. He didn't even know my real name. Like all these forums, people can use any name they want. He called himself William, but I've no idea if that was his real name. Anyway, he asked if I thought it was time we met face to face. He would like to buy me a pint. He suggested a pub, and I said it would have to be lunchtime because of the kids. I went, but he never turned up.'

'Did he ever say why not?'

'He was ill, apparently. I waited half an hour and got talking to some guy about a plumbing job. He'd seen the van outside – noticed the sign I prop up in the back window until I get the lettering done on the sides. He asked for my card.'

Maggie looked at him. Surely he had made the connection? She had come to realise many things about her husband tonight, but she had never thought he was stupid.

'It sounds to me as if you were well and truly set up,' she said as she pulled into the car park of a small private hotel.

'What, by *William*?'

'Who else? Nobody else knew you both before and after, so who the hell do you *think* it was? Somehow or other, this William must be connected to Samil. Was the guy who approached you Asian?'

'No, he was posh Manchester. Not that I think Samil's Asian.

The name's got nothing to do with race. I looked it up once. It's a variant of the Hebrew Sama'el. It means Angel of Death.'

Maggie stopped breathing. Under different circumstances she might have laughed at the absurdity of the name, but she knew this man was lethal.

'It's him, Duncan. The man who called me. Your friend William must have told Samil where to find you. Either that or William and Samil are one and the same. There are coincidences, but this is way too much of one. You need to tell me everything you know about the man in the pub. I need to know him if I see him.'

And somehow Maggie knew that she *would* be seeing him, sooner or later.

50

It was after three when Maggie finally crawled into her own bed. Her sister's light had been on, but she had ignored it and gone straight into a very hot shower, feeling as if her skin was crawling. After a brief and restless three hours trying to make sense out of everything she had learned, she still felt dirty. She scratched the flesh of her bare arms.

Somewhere out there a man calling himself by a name that meant Angel of Death wanted to kill her.

She had told Duncan they would find a solution, but Maggie hadn't a clue what that might be. Every spark of an idea she had was mentally ripped up and discarded with increasing frustration. Now she understood why Duncan hadn't wanted her to go to the police. He would be charged with conspiracy to murder for the deaths twelve years ago. His defence – that he hadn't meant it to happen for real – would mean nothing, and two pieces of evidence against him were compelling, the scene he caused when he caught Tamsin with the lecturer being one, and the fact that he had run away and changed his name – whatever the reason – being the other. He could get life imprisonment. Even if he could identify the real killers, who were fairly safe behind the walls of the dark web, Maggie didn't think it would make any difference.

Maggie had thought she and Duncan were as close as two people could be, but she now had to admit to herself that she knew very little about him. Even tonight he had tried to lie to her over and over again without realising how much she knew.

The phrase 'pathological liar' leaped into her head. She had come across it recently but couldn't remember the context. At that moment it seemed a perfect label for Duncan. And he seemed incapable of accepting any guilt.

There was no doubt at all that he should have gone to the police immediately the first girl was killed twelve years ago – the girl called Sonia whose only fault had been that she looked like Tamsin. Maggie couldn't excuse Duncan for that. She could blame it on his youth and on his fear of imprisonment, but it didn't alter the fact that her husband – the man she had loved devotedly for ten years – had allowed somebody's child to be brutally murdered. The thought of the girl's last minutes almost drove all rational thought from her mind.

Maggie was trying desperately to think of Duncan and Michael as two separate people because it was the only way she believed she would be able to deal with it all. She visualised this young man – somebody she didn't know who was only twenty years old – and tried to understand his dilemma. She blamed him for inflicting this horror on Duncan, her loving husband, and on her family.

By the time she had left Duncan at his new hotel, suggesting he pick his van up in the morning as discreetly as he could and dump it somewhere miles from where he was staying, she was weak from emotional exhaustion.

'What's going to happen now?' Duncan had asked. 'When can I come home? When can my life get back to normal?'

'I don't have the faintest idea. All I know is that one of us has to come up with a plan, and as far as I can see your only plan has been to do nothing,' Maggie had said. 'When has inertia ever won the day, Duncan?'

She paused for his answer, not really expecting one. Duncan said nothing.

'We're not just talking about *your* life getting back to normal, either,' she continued, 'so stop making it all about Duncan bloody

Taylor. You'd better phone me tomorrow evening when the children are in bed and see if I've come up with something that will at least save anybody else from getting killed.'

She could see from his expression that Duncan sensed her fury, and his next words confirmed it.

'You married me for better or for worse, Maggie. I know I've made a mistake, but surely everybody's allowed that? And we were happy. We'll be happy again. The kids need us both, and you know how good we are together.'

A mistake. If he called it that one more time she was certain she would lose it completely. But angry as she was with him, she needed some comfort too. Just for a moment, she had to think of him as the man she had loved for the past ten years. She needed to hold him, feel the warmth from his body pass into hers and let some of the tension seep from her limbs.

Could they ever get back to the people they had been? Of course not. Could they have a different form of happiness – one that was based on absolute truth? She was no closer to an answer.

❖

She couldn't stay in bed all day. She had to get to the office and try to find some time to examine past cases to see if there was any way that Duncan could go to the police and not be charged. She already knew it was highly unlikely.

Maggie forced herself to get up and go downstairs. She needed coffee. She pushed the kitchen door open and was only slightly surprised to see Suzy leaning against the worktop, both hands clasped around a mug.

They looked at each other. Suzy was obviously tired and Maggie felt terrible. She knew her sister would have been awake worrying about her the night before, but she couldn't have discussed things with her. Not then. She had made enough noise to ensure Suzy knew she was home, but that was the most she could manage. She didn't want to go into it all now either.

'Coffee?' Suzy asked.

'Please. Suze, I'm sorry I didn't come and talk to you last night. It's all so complicated and I don't know where to begin.'

'I take it you found him, then?'

Maggie nodded and stood quietly watching her sister make the coffee. 'Are you going home today?' she asked, changing the subject for the moment. She didn't want her sister to leave, but she had a life too.

'Of course not. I've taken a week off work – family crisis being the excuse – and I'll stay as long as you need me.'

'What about the kids?' Maggie asked.

'While you were out last night I had a word with Ian without screaming at him. He said the kids were winding Ruthie up, so I spoke to them and told them to cut it out.'

Maggie raised her eyebrows. She knew that Suzy took some pleasure from the children moaning about their soon-to-be step-mother.

'And then I had a word with Ruthie.'

'You *what?*'

'Yesterday when you talked about how it felt to truly love some-body you made me realise something, Mags. It's not Ruthie's fault that Ian didn't love me enough. Maybe I didn't love him enough. Maybe we just didn't love each other. Anyway, it's the children that count. They need to be happy there, and they need to respect their stepmother.'

'Bloody hell, Suzy!'

'I still think she's a poser, but hey – each to their own.'

Maggie walked across the room and gave her sister a hug. She knew that had taken a lot of doing, but maybe her sister was finally on the road to a better place.

'What about you, though?' Suzy asked. 'Does it all make sense now?'

Maggie debated how much to tell Suzy and in the end decided

it had to be as little as possible. If she and Duncan were to have a future, those closest to them should never be in the same impossible position that she was now.

'I can't tell you, Suze. Not yet. It's honestly better if you don't know anything. He hasn't left me for another woman, though. At least that's one thing less to worry about.' Although, Maggie thought, that would have been a whole lot easier to deal with than this.

'Don't you think it would help you to talk to somebody? If that's not me, is there someone at work you could talk to?'

'I don't know, but thanks for understanding. It's not that I don't trust you. It's just that when this is all over I don't want anything I tell you to colour your opinion of Duncan. I need to go to work, though. I need to keep this job.'

'Go and get yourself ready, then. I'll make you a bacon butty. The perfect start to the day. And then I'll see to the kids – get them to school and pick them up again. You take it easy.'

Nodding her thanks to her sister and picking up her coffee cup, Maggie made for the stairs. The thought of having to spend her day working on defences for other criminals when she should be thinking of her own husband made her feet drag, and it was only when she was halfway up the stairs that the key word in that thought struck her.

Criminal.

51

After less than five hours' sleep, Tom felt surprisingly alert that morning. Tiny, slender threads were starting to link some of the suspects and victims together. He had the feeling they were getting close, and adrenaline was driving him – Becky too, by the look of her when he found her in the incident room, poring over the wall chart covered with pictures of victims and suspects. A young detective had seen Tom come in and had raced over to the coffee machine to fill cups for both senior officers – aiming to please. Tom was glad of it. Caffeine was going to have to see him through the day.

The previous night he had thought of pretty much nothing other than tracking down Michael Alexander. He had *known* there was something not right with the lad, even though his alibis proved he couldn't have killed either of the girls. But now there was a link – a highly tenuous one it had to be said – but it was enough for Tom to get him back in for questioning, even if it was twelve years too late.

'What do we know about this counsellor, Becky?' he asked without preamble. 'We need to talk to him – or her – if possible.'

'We're checking it out. The practice has been closed for years. Their patient lists were handed over to a new practice that took over some of their cases. I think at least one of the counsellors has retired. Another doesn't practise any more. But we're doing what we can.'

'Okay, but it's even more important that we find out where the hell Michael Alexander is now.'

'I've been back through the relevant files of the original case, and you were right about his alibi, Tom.' Becky indicated a pile of papers on her desk. 'I printed this lot off, but there was nothing to implicate any of these three guys twelve years ago. Michael Alexander had a rather pathetic motive for one killing but couldn't have done it, so I don't think we can point the finger at anybody for missing this. No apparent motive for either Ben or Adam, and no evidence. It must have been a bastard of a case to work with nothing to go on.'

Tom still didn't know whether to be glad that he had been taken off the investigation, or to wish he'd kept plugging away at the things that had niggled him. Or whether, in fact, the case hadn't had his full attention.

'So where's Michael Alexander now, then?'

Becky looked at him and raised her eyebrows. 'You're not going to like this, but he's disappeared. He's off the grid.'

'Bollocks!' Tom banged his coffee cup down on the nearest desk. 'Nothing at all?'

Becky shook her head.

Tom knew without a doubt that he should have followed his instincts all those years ago. But he had run out of time.

12 years ago – late June

Exhausted as he was, nothing could wipe the smile off Tom's face that June morning as he walked into the incident room. He had a daughter, a beautiful little girl. No-one knew of his concerns or doubts, and nobody was going to. Ever.

Lucy – that's what they had decided to call her. He hadn't wanted to leave her only hours after she had been born, but both she and Kate were sleeping, and if he was to be any use looking after them over the next few weeks, he was going to have to hand over all his investigations to somebody else.

'Douglas!' The shout came from Victor Elliott's office, and Tom grunted with irritation. He hoped and prayed that he wasn't going to get bogged down for hours in a useless debate that would delay his escape.

He popped his head round the door. 'Sir?'

'Come in, sit down and congratulations. A baby girl, I'm told. They're the best, you know.'

Tom was more than a little surprised to see a slightly faraway look in Victor's eyes, and remembered hearing that he had a grown-up daughter but understood she was living in Canada. Victor never spoke about her – or his wife, come to that.

'Thank you, sir. I'm sorry to be ducking out right at this point. I was hoping we would have had the case sewn up before I had to leave, but Lucy was early, and I need to be at home for a week or so to help Kate.'

'Yes, yes. We'll get somebody to cover. Let's have your final take on the suspects, then.'

'We don't actually have any suspects, sir, I'm sorry to say. Anybody with half a motive has been cleared.'

'Still chasing your tail over Alexander, are you?'

'No, sir. He's not going to be able to get thirty people to lie and say he was in Keswick when he wasn't, and some of his cycle race was filmed by the university. I know he didn't kill Tamsin Grainger.'

'I sense a "but" in there, Douglas. What are you thinking?'

Tom nodded. There was a 'but' in there, but it didn't make any sense. 'He's a bit smug about his alibi. I don't like it.'

'Could he have paid somebody to kill her?'

Tom shook his head. One thing he had discovered about Michael Alexander was that he was permanently skint.

'And the other suspects?'

Tom gave a rundown of the so-called suspects – none of whom in his mind was at all suspicious – and waited impatiently while Victor did some thinking. He was about to ask if he could get on with clearing his paperwork when his boss spoke.

275

'The third girl. She said she would recognise the guy even though he had a stocking mask on. Did we run all these suspects past her?'

Tom sighed. This had been his biggest hope – that she would at least give him somebody to focus on. But it had been a disaster. She had been shown photos of all the suspects along with others from their rogues' gallery. She hadn't identified anybody. She had stated categorically that she had never seen any of these people before, so either her powers of observation weren't as good as she had said, or none of their suspects was involved. Tom was inclined to believe it was the latter. They had no idea who the killer was.

'Okay. I'll let you get on then. But one thing, Douglas. If you were running this investigation from here, what would you focus on?'

Tom paused. He knew what he would do, but equally he knew that Victor Elliott wouldn't agree.

'I would search the warehouses and old mills – even those with locks on the doors – for evidence. Those girls were killed somewhere and transported, probably by more than one person.'

'Yes, well you've had that particular bee in your bonnet for a couple of weeks now, but it's a hunch, Douglas, and we checked it out.' Victor reached for his phone as if to signify the meeting was at an end. 'Okay, you can go, Douglas. See you when you're sick of changing nappies.'

Tom didn't move.

'What? Was there something else?'

Tom nodded. 'I wouldn't stop delving into Michael Alexander. But I think we're looking in the wrong place. We can't break his alibi and we've looked at all known associates. But we need to go further – delve into every single aspect of his life: where he goes for coffee, who he sits near in lectures, who he went to school with. He knows something.'

52

Every muscle in Maggie's body seemed to be twitching, whether from exhaustion or fear, she didn't know. She couldn't focus on work, and she was nowhere near coming up with any suggestions for what they should do next. How were they going to rid themselves of this threat? Duncan was adamant that there was no point going to the police. They would never find Samil. And if Samil realised Duncan had given evidence against him, he would seek his ultimate revenge. Maggie knew exactly what that meant. Her own murder.

Maybe the van registration number would help, but that would only link whoever it belonged to with the current murders, not those twelve years ago. So if Duncan came clean about everything, he would still be the only person they could pin the earlier crimes on.

People kept popping into Maggie's office to ask if she was all right, and she knew why. Her face was pale, her eyes bloodshot and puffy, and she couldn't sit still. She needed to think of something else – to give her mind a rest – and it was with a sense of relief that she glanced up from her desk just before twelve to see a friendly face at the door.

'Frank, come in,' she said. 'Are you here to see me?'

'Not specifically. I had a meeting with one of the partners about the rape case he's working on.'

'Oh God, yes. It's a nasty one.'

'It is, but I'm fairly sure that the client has a non-verbal learning disorder, undiagnosed to date. Anyway, as I was here

I thought I would pop in and see how you are. You didn't seem that chirpy last time I spoke to you. And to be honest, you don't look that great today. Are you okay?'

Maggie looked at Frank Denman's concerned face and wondered whether she could trust him with some of her dilemma, even if not all of it. She must have hesitated for a second too long.

'I guess the answer to that is no, then. Maybe I can help with whatever's bothering you. I'm a great listener. Have you got time for a sandwich?'

Frank's encouraging smile transformed his usual slightly lugubrious expression. He looked almost roguish, as if he were suggesting something rather naughty. She realised that she didn't even know if Frank was married. She imagined him with a motherly wife fussing over him, and probably two or three grown-up kids doing something clever.

'That would be lovely, Frank. Shall we go now, if you've finished?'

They didn't go far – just to the sandwich shop on the corner – but it was good to get out of the office, and Maggie filled her lungs with cold air. They made their choices, and sat down at a plastic-topped table.

'Only tell me as much as you want, Maggie. I'm not going to push you for details, but I know something's wrong.'

Maggie swallowed. She couldn't tell him much. It would be wrong to reveal anything that might put Frank in a difficult position with the police, if it ever came to that.

'If it helps, you can pay me a nominal sum – the cost of my sandwich – and that would make you my client. I wouldn't be able to divulge anything you tell me then.'

'No, it's okay. We don't have to go that far. I'm a mess because of problems I'm having with Duncan.' Her eyes filled with tears, but she blinked them away. 'He's left home, and at the moment I'm not sure there's a way back.'

'Why do you think that? If you love him, surely there's always a way back?'

Maggie shook her head. 'I do love him. At least, I love the person I thought he was. I'm not sure what I think now.'

She stirred her cappuccino, watching the chocolate melt into the foam. Frank said nothing, waiting for her to say more.

'He's done something stupid, Frank. Got himself into a situation with some seriously evil men.'

'Are you saying that Duncan's evil?'

Maggie looked up. 'Oh no. I don't think that for a minute. But he's lied to me. Not just recently – for the whole time we've been married.'

Frank took a bite of his sandwich and chewed. He swallowed, took a sip of mineral water and put his sandwich down.

'People lie for a lot of reasons, you know. Sometimes it's because they don't have faith that the truth is acceptable, and they want to create a better image of themselves, present themselves in a beneficial light. The first thing you need to do is understand *why* he lied. Did he think, perhaps, that you wouldn't want him if you knew the truth about him? And if that's the case, you have to ask yourself if he's right.'

She was puzzled, and Frank read her expression.

'If his lies were to cover up his own insecurity – you know, the way someone might lie about having been made captain of the football team when in fact they weren't even picked to play – then it's not that important. It means he probably thought you wouldn't think him worthy of you. But if he lied to cover up something that might make you question your love for him, something that tells you about his fundamental moral code, that's a different matter.'

He understood. She knew he would. She listened as Frank talked to her about truth and lies, and how to deal with her confusion. He didn't ask for a single detail.

'In the end,' he said, 'you should make your decision about

Duncan based not on whether he's lied to you, but on whether the version of him that you know *now* is one that you can still live with. Still love.'

After twenty minutes, Maggie's mind felt much clearer. She had to forget his lying and focus on who Duncan was. 'Thank you, Frank. I needed that.'

He smiled at her. 'Will you have him back, do you think?'

'I don't know. There's a lot to sort out. While I understand much more about truth and lies now, thanks to you, there are consequences to his lies that I don't want to go into, and I haven't yet formed a picture of the new Duncan – the one with the lies stripped away. It's too soon to say, but I love that man so much it's hard to imagine a life without him.'

'So where's he living?'

'For the moment he's in a hotel.'

'Is he close enough to visit?'

'Yeah, he only went as far as Heaton Park. We managed to find a place that was reasonably priced but family run. He was in one of those soulless chain hotels before – okay for a night, but that's about it. One way or another, though, we need to sort this before much longer.' She pushed back her chair. 'I'd better get back. I've got a mountain of stuff to do before the end of the day, and the kids need me to be home at a sensible time. Thank God my sister's come to help out.'

She was sorry to go. Frank had an air of calm about him that soothed her. Nothing ever seemed to faze him, to shatter his composure, and she wished she could somehow acquire the wisdom that made him so phlegmatic.

Frank reached out a hand and clutched Maggie's wrist gently.

'If you need somebody to talk to, I'm always happy to listen, you know. But we may have to do it via email for a while. That's the other thing I wanted to tell you. Now that we've sorted Alf Horton's psych profile, I'm taking myself off to a conference in South Africa. I'm leaving this evening.'

Maggie was disappointed. She had been hoping that whatever happened she would be able to confide in Frank.

'Well I, for one, will miss you,' she said as she bent down and impulsively kissed him on the cheek. 'See you when you're back.'

❖

'You're looking a bit more relaxed,' Neil, one of Maggie's colleagues, said as she passed him in reception. Neil was leaning against the desk talking to one of the receptionists, and Maggie realised she had seen him there rather a lot recently. She smiled for what felt like the first time in days. It was good to see somebody happy.

Neil said something quietly to the receptionist and followed Maggie towards the lifts.

'Good lunch?' he asked.

'It was good to get out,' Maggie responded.

'You and Frank seem quite buddy. How long have you known him?'

Maggie frowned. 'You know how long I've been here. I met him a couple of days after I arrived.'

Neil gave her an odd look. The lift doors opened and they stepped inside. Neil pressed the button for the third floor.

'What?' she said.

'It doesn't matter that you knew him before, you know. We're all glad to have you on board. It was the right decision.'

'What the hell are you talking about, Neil? You've lost me.'

'You do know he recommended you to the partners, don't you?' Neil must have seen her blank expression. 'He said you would be an asset, and you were wasted where you were. I – well, to be honest, we all – thought you must have known him. Some thought you'd probably had or were having an affair with him, but it didn't matter because you're good at your job.'

Maggie was confused. She had never heard of Frank Denman in her life until she came here.

'He must have been following your career, Maggie. I'd be flattered, if I were you.'

The lift doors opened and Neil sauntered off towards his office.

Maggie had been surprised when she had been contacted to see if she would be interested in joining the firm. She had assumed the recommendation had come from a circuit judge she had impressed. It seemed she was wrong.

Frank probably had cases all over the country, of course. He could easily have seen her in court and thought her name worth putting forward. She just wished he had mentioned it to her.

53

12 years ago – August

Tom pushed open the door to the CID office and made his way to his desk. It felt like only yesterday that he had been here, and he couldn't believe that a month had passed. He was glad to be back at work – not because he didn't want to spend time with his family, but because he was beginning to feel a bit redundant. Kate seemed to have everything under control, and he felt more relaxed than he had in a while. Lucy was his baby. He loved her – adored her – and it was his name on her birth certificate. He was never going to question her parentage again and felt at peace with his decision.

He felt considerably less at peace with what he now discovered at work. During his absence the double murder case had been assigned to somebody else, and Tom was shocked to find that they appeared to be no further on. It was out of his hands now as Victor Elliott was adamant that Tom should be given less demanding crimes to solve while he was having disturbed nights with the baby.

'We need people who are alert and on the ball, Douglas. We'll put you back on the heavy duty stuff when your eyes have lost that piggy-pink look they've got now.'

So Tom had no choice. But he believed the two dead girls had been short-changed, and he wished he could persuade Elliott to put him back on the case – not that he had ever felt it was his own. Tom had barely found the time to follow the lines of enquiry dictated by his boss, let alone go off on some of the tangents that might have had potential.

Philippa Stanley had also been assigned back to his team.

'Do you want me to speak to the boss and get you back on the murder cases?' he had asked.

'Thank you, sir,' she had responded. 'But I don't think progress is being made in the right direction, and he's never going to listen to me. The DI working the case now is an Elliott clone, so I'd rather work with you, if that's okay.'

Tom had been flattered but still felt he should have been doing more.

'There's one thing I did do after you'd gone, though,' the young detective said. 'You asked me to check on Michael Alexander – to try and keep tabs on him.'

'And?'

'And he's gone. He's left the university.'

'Where's he gone, exactly?' Tom asked.

'He's gone home to nurse his mother. Apparently she's very ill and hasn't got long to go, and so he's told his tutor that he needs to be with her.'

Tom looked at Philippa. 'And I don't suppose he left an address, did he?'

'No. And I wasn't able to give it much time because the DCI thought we were barking up the wrong tree. Why are you looking so intrigued?'

'Because I don't believe a word of it. Check his mother out. Let's see what's really going on.'

Becky didn't look up as Tom sat down in the chair facing her desk. She was checking down a list on her screen and didn't want to lose her place, but she had recognised Tom's footsteps as he marched across the incident room towards her desk.

'Give me a second, would you?' she said. 'I don't want to lose my thread. I'm nearly there.' She returned her attention to the list, not expecting to find much. But then she did. Becky looked hard at the screen, clicked on the link, and knew she was right. She glanced at Tom. She was going to have to tell him, but there was other more urgent stuff too, and none of it was going to cheer him up.

'I've got a bit of news. Since finding the counsellor is a possible link between Adam Mellor, Ben Coleman and Michael Alexander we've been combing through their backgrounds. As you pointed out, Michael Alexander was in care for most of his life, so we've been in touch with his foster mother, Patricia Rowe. Well, that's not entirely true. We've been in touch with the home she's in. She has Alzheimer's, so sadly she's not going to be able to help us much.

'The detective constable who went to see her asked at the home about regular visitors. One of them is a Stacey Meagan – another of Mrs Rowe's ex-foster children – and so the detective decided to pay her a visit. Stacey sang Mrs Rowe's praises and said she was the best foster mother ever, but when the detective asked about Michael, she said that Pat – as she called her – didn't seem able to recognise what the rest of them saw. That he was a "bad lot" – in her words. But she had no idea where he was.'

'So another dead end, then,' Tom said, his frustration apparent.

'Not entirely. As the detective was leaving, Meagan said to her, "What's all the sudden interest in Michael anyway?"'

Becky saw Tom's eyes glint, and she knew she had him. 'It turns out that Stacey Meagan had been contacted on Facebook by somebody trying to track Michael down. Somebody called Grace Peters. But before you get excited, we don't know who she is. There's nothing on her profile; she never communicates with anybody, and hasn't got anything in her personal details at all. And we all know how helpful the Facebook guys are going to be. It's not as if she's committed a crime.'

'Bollocks,' Tom said. 'We could have done with that. Anything else?'

'Ben Coleman – the surgical registrar who worked on Hayley's ward – he never caught his plane to Antigua.'

'Hah!' Tom said. 'Tell me something I *didn't* know.'

It was the opening she needed, but Becky wasn't sure whether to mention what she had discovered or not. She had been trawling the National Crime Agency's databases and only just found it. She hadn't had time to review the information so she could easily be wrong. One thing about Tom, though, was that he never blamed anybody for wrong assumptions if they were made for the right reasons.

'We talked a couple of days ago about checking through the bodies found in the canals to see if anything came up. Do you remember?' she asked.

'Yep. What have you found?'

'I found nothing in Manchester – none of the "pusher" cases matched – so I extended my search to cover the marks on the legs and searched the NCA's National Injuries Database. On the off-chance.'

'And…?'

Becky pointed to the screen.

Tom leaned over her shoulder. 'Well, bugger me.'

54

Maggie had no idea how she managed to get through the rest of the day. She hadn't wanted to go into the office, but she knew the future was uncertain and before long her job might be the only thing she had to support herself and the children. So she stuck it out to the end of the day. She had spent every moment since lunch on her own, thinking, making deals with herself, evaluating the options. And now it was just after six and she was no nearer to a solution.

Josh had sent her a text from Suzy's phone asking her to pick him up from his football practice, and for one awful moment she had worried that she was going to be terribly late. There had been an accident on the motorway, and traffic had been backing up on all the main roads. But she was nearly there now, and only about ten minutes late, thank goodness.

She turned onto the side road that led to Josh's school, surprised not to see a flood of cars coming in the opposite direction full of muddy kids in football kit. Maybe practice had overrun. As she got closer to the school, though, a knot of worry started to build inside her. There were no lights on. The school was in darkness.

She turned into the entrance – but the gates were locked. There was nobody there.

Where the hell was Josh?

Maggie had never picked him up from football before – it had always been Duncan. Where was her boy?

She pulled her phone from her bag and quickly dialled home.

'Come on, Suzy, pick up the bloody phone,' she said quietly, desperate for her sister to answer.

'Hello?'

'Oh, thank God, Suzy. I've come to school to pick Josh up and everywhere's in darkness. I don't know where he is – there's nobody here.' She couldn't control the panic in her voice.

'Shit, I'm sorry, Mags. I should have insisted on going back for him. He said it would be better if you picked him up. Do you want me to try to find a number for somebody from the school – the head teacher, or somebody?'

'I don't know. I've let him down, Suzy. He didn't need this.'

'Is there another entrance to the school playing field?' Suzy asked.

And then it came to her. The school only had a small field, and football practice was always at a nearby park. But which one? What had Duncan said about football practice? *Think, Maggie. Think.*

Then she remembered. It was quite a big park – not huge like Heaton Park – but it was open all the time, so at least Josh wouldn't be locked in. It had to be there – about ten minutes' drive away.

'Got it,' she shouted down the phone and hung up.

Surely his teacher wouldn't have left him there alone? But that wasn't the point. With everything that had happened, Josh would think she wasn't going to come for him.

She slammed the car into reverse to get out of the school's entrance and set off in the direction of the park as fast as she dared, praying that she had the right place.

The problem with the park – assuming she had chosen the right one – was that there were several entrances, and Maggie didn't know which one was closest to the football pitches. It wasn't helped by the fact that with the overcast skies it was now nearly dark.

'Oh Joshy, I'm so sorry, sweetheart,' she said to herself as she drove into the first entrance she came to. Not only was he totally confused about his dad disappearing; now his mum had failed to pick him up. She was fairly sure that the usual time was six and it would be nearly twenty past by the time she got there. He must be worried sick.

Into her head came an image of her telling Josh about his father – who he really was, what he had done. She couldn't do it. Whatever else happened, her children mustn't grow up believing their father was a monster. She couldn't let that happen.

There was a small, but empty, car park ahead, and she raced into it, slamming on the brakes and abandoning the car where it stopped. She couldn't see any goal posts. There were some rugby posts poking up above some trees over to her right. Maybe the football pitches were near.

'Josh,' she shouted at the top of her voice. 'Joshy, where are you, darling?'

There was no answer.

She was suddenly hit by a mad thought. Could Duncan have come to watch today, hidden in the bushes and then taken Josh himself? It was the sort of thing he might do. He would want to let his son know how much he was missing him. She hoped and prayed she was right, because it meant Josh was safe. Equally she hoped she was wrong, because how was she going to explain to Josh that his daddy wasn't coming home just yet?

She started to run, but her heels sank into the muddy turf. It didn't seem to have stopped raining or snowing for more than five minutes since they had arrived in Manchester, and the ground was sodden. She stopped for a moment and kicked her shoes off, bending to pick them up. She tried to run and shout at the same time, but she was soon out of breath.

Finally she saw some football goals up ahead, but – as she had expected – the field was deserted.

A sob broke free. *Oh God, where was he?* She forced herself to calm down.

'The teachers would never have let Josh stay here on his own,' she muttered to herself.' It's more than their pensions are worth.'

He would be safe. She just had to find him.

Beyond the football pitches she spotted another car park – much closer than the one she had used. There was a lone car parked there, not a car she recognised. She raced towards it. Suddenly the field was flooded with light as the car's headlights came on, then went off. The driver was flashing her. She sped towards the car as fast as her failing legs would take her.

A man stepped out from the driver's side and moved to stand in front of the car. He was backlit by the headlights, and all she could see was a stocky build, legs planted apart.

'Mrs Taylor?' he asked.

'I'm Maggie Taylor, yes. How did you know?'

'Because your son is in my car.'

Maggie stopped dead in her tracks. 'Is he okay?' She didn't like this man's tone.

'He's fine.'

'So why hasn't he got out of the car?'

'Because he's asleep, thank goodness. He's been crying for nearly half an hour. He has it in his head that you've left him. I don't know why – I didn't ask – but maybe I should.'

Maggie was about to scream, 'And what business is it of yours?' but she recognised that this man was close to reporting her to social services.

'I'm so sorry,' she said. 'My husband usually picks Josh up, but he's away. Josh sent me a text from my sister's phone, but I thought I had to pick him up from school, so I went there.'

The man looked at her. His mouth was set in a tight line, as if he was disgusted with her as a mother. As well he might be, she thought.

'Who are you, if you don't mind me asking?' Maggie said.

'I'm Archie's dad. He and Josh are in the same team.'

'Where's Archie then?' Maggie's suspicions were not yet fully allayed.

'In the car. They played a hard match – and won, by the way.'

Maggie could hear the subtext – *as you would have known, had you been here* – but she had no idea what to say.

At that moment, the passenger door flew open and a little boy came hurtling across the grass. 'Mum,' he shouted and flung himself at her.

What were she and Duncan doing to this child that had made him so scared his mummy wouldn't come and get him?

'I'm so sorry, Joshy. I'm so sorry, sweetheart.' She looked up at Archie's dad. 'I appreciate you looking after him like this.'

His face said, 'Well somebody had to,' but he kept the thought to himself.

'Josh came over to my car with Archie. The coach isn't one of their teachers, and I guess he thought Josh was with us, so he left. Anyway, no harm done.'

'I can't thank you enough,' Maggie said, dropping her shoes so that she could reach out and shake his hand without letting go of Josh with the other arm. 'You could have driven off and left him.'

The man barked out a laugh. 'I don't think many parents would do that. Do you?'

She forced a smile as they said their goodbyes. Maggie picked up her shoes, and she and Josh turned to make their way back to her car.

They had just reached the rugby field when she noticed it – or rather Josh did. He was looking towards the car.

'Mum?' he said.

Maggie followed his gaze. Her car was still slewed sideways in the car park, but it wasn't alone any more. Beside it was a van. A white van.

And standing, one on either side, were two tall men. She knew then.

She knew they had come for her.

55

Since her interesting discovery that another person was trying to track down Michael Alexander, the search for him had leaped to the top of Becky's priority list. The fact that he had disappeared without a trace had set off every alarm bell and convinced Tom more than ever that Alexander knew something about the murders twelve years ago. Whether he was involved now or not was a different issue.

Tom had spent hours with Becky looking at the details of the victims. If they accepted the theory that only one of the victims was important to the killers and the others were distractions, they had to try to work out which of them provided the key. Hayley Walker – the girl who Becky had mistaken for Leo – didn't appear to have any enemies, as far as they knew. Michelle Morgan was a prostitute, but all the reports suggested that her pimp was devastated that she was dead, and the other girls said she never had a bad word for anybody. Or was the focus somebody else – another victim for whom there was a motive – a third victim? Would that third victim be Leo? Had she been abducted and held until they were ready to kill her, and if so, was Leo still alive? Or had her body not been found yet? Or would Maggie Taylor be the third victim, and if so, why?

Adam Mellor had met Leo, and it seemed highly likely that somebody driving his van was following Maggie Taylor. They all looked so much alike, it was as if the same person was being killed again and again.

Becky had started to flag. She had forced a couple of cans of

Coke down in an attempt to keep going and now felt as if she was going to explode. She rubbed her stomach as she scanned the forensic report that Jumbo had sent through. It was disappointing. The shopping trolley the second victim had been found propped against had produced a plethora of fingerprints, as one might imagine, but they were mostly smudged. Those they had been able to isolate didn't reveal much of interest. A couple were linked to people known to the police, but only for petty crimes. They would have to be followed up, of course. The trolley was riddled with DNA too – and germs, no doubt. Since reading an article a couple of years ago about the percentage of trolleys dirtier than public toilets, Becky had made sure she always carried wet wipes in the car to be used immediately after she finished shopping.

There was no useful CCTV footage of anybody stealing a trolley from the appropriate supermarket, and even if they nicked somebody for the crimes and their DNA was on it, a good lawyer would claim that the perp had done his shopping at the supermarket where the trolley had originated. The chances that he had used that very trolley were pretty slim, but the possibility might be enough to influence a jury.

Becky scoffed at the thought. The ways people got off crimes they had obviously committed had ceased to wind her up years ago. She just felt mild disgust that sometimes the bad guys left the dock laughing in the faces of the police.

Her thoughts were interrupted as her desk phone rang. 'Becky Robinson.'

'Hi, gorgeous. It's me.'

'Hello, you,' she said, a small smile playing around her lips. She had been a bit off with Mark for the last few days, which was completely out of order. All because of one hug from her boss. She felt ridiculous, like a groupie swooning over some pop star. Yes, Tom was sexy, and she couldn't help noticing it from time to time. But she shouldn't allow her childish fantasies to get in the way of a good thing, and she was going to make it up to Mark as soon as this case was over.

'Listen, babe—' he started.

Becky was quick to interrupt. 'Mark,' she said, drawing out the vowel sound in a warning tone.

'Okay, okay. I know, "Don't call me babe." I forgot. Sorry!'

She smiled again. 'Go on – what did you want to tell me?'

'What, apart from the fact that you're a sexy little thing, and I've got great plans for you tonight?'

This time she laughed. 'Shut up, idiot. But thanks for lightening my day. If I manage to get away at a suitable time I'm looking forward to your plans already.'

Mark's voice turned serious. 'Well, if that's true it might be better if I don't tell you my thoughts on your case. You might not get home at all.'

'What is it? What have you found?'

'Don't get too excited, Bex. It's nothing specific, but it's a line of enquiry I think you'll want to follow. When I was at school, I did a project on the history of transport. I think that's when I got interested in trains. Anyway, I remembered one of the names in the project was Tobias Mellor.'

'With all due respect, Mark, I don't think a school project thirty years ago is going to help.'

'Shut up, smart arse, and listen. Knowing that somebody called Mellor is a person of interest to you, I looked old Tobias up again, and apparently he moved his investments from the canal to the railways when it became clear that the canal wasn't going to be as commercially successful as everybody had hoped. So that might explain why your Mellor – who is the great-, great-, not sure how many greats grandson of Tobias, may have chosen Pomona and Mayfield for his dumping grounds twelve years ago, if indeed he is your perp. I've racked my brain to try to come up with other likely transport-related locations where they could keep a person hidden for a long period without discovery, but the obvious ones are no good.'

Tom had asked Becky to have Mayfield station checked as soon as he knew Leo was missing, but it was no longer the place it had been twelve years ago. The roof had been dismantled and planning permission granted to convert it into an entertainment venue, so it was obvious nobody was hiding Leo there. And there was nowhere to hide anybody at Pomona – well, nobody alive anyway.

'There are a couple of choices I've discounted,' Mark continued. 'There's the whole area around Victoria Arches, under the train station, and there's the tunnel created when the Manchester underground was being built – before it was abandoned. I don't know if anybody would be able to get into either of those, even with Mellor's skills and knowledge, and getting an unwilling human or a dead weight into the Victoria Arches area would be nigh on impossible. Which brings me to the other option. At the time old Toby invested in the railways, he also put a considerable percentage of his fortune into cotton mills.'

Becky wanted to say, 'Thanks for the history lesson, but cut to the chase,' but she knew Mark was enjoying this, and she owed him a few minutes of her time at least.

'Okay, so we all know that the cotton industry declined early in the twentieth century, leaving empty mills all over the place. But the Mellor family weren't short of cash, so they hung on to them. A *lot* of them. Almost all of the mills have now been converted into apartments.'

She knew where he was going and wanted more then ever for him to reach the punch line.

'But not *quite* all of them. I'm not sure how many are still derelict, but there are a few. You need somebody to do a proper check, of course, but I've looked up the name of Tobias Mellor's company. It's called Onerarias Holdings.'

'Nice simple name, then,' Becky said.

'It means "freight" in Latin, apparently.' Mark paused. 'Does that help at all, sunshine?'

Becky detected a slight note of uncertainty in Mark's voice for the first time, and she realised that for the last couple of days he must have been wondering if he had done something wrong.

'It doesn't help a bit, Mark,' she said slowly, keeping her voice level. She paused. 'It's only bloody brilliant, and you are a superstar.'

'All part of the job,' he responded, but she could hear the smile in his voice.

'No, it's not. It's your day off, to start with, and this has nothing to do with the British Transport Police.'

'I meant it's all part of the job as your man, babe.'

She knew he had added the word to wind her up, and she grinned as she hung up. But the smile only remained on her face for moments. This sounded like a good lead, and she needed to see Tom as soon as possible. In the meantime she was going to grab one of the team and get them started on searching for these properties.

56

Maggie twisted her head from side to side, searching for an escape route.

'Josh,' she said quietly and calmly, 'we're going to turn to the right now and head towards that hollow. The main road crosses there, so when I say run, we are going to run as fast as we can until we reach the road. Okay?'

She could feel her child's body start to shake. 'Okay,' he whispered.

They veered off to the right, walking calmly. They had, by her reckoning, about four hundred metres on these guys. She didn't think they would be able to catch them before they reached the main road.

Still walking calmly but quickly, she cast a glance over her shoulder. The men had started to walk towards her. As she looked, the taller of the two broke into a jog.

'Run, Josh!'

Josh was a fit little boy and he could move, but these guys were tall with long legs. Beyond the rugby field and before the road there was a small wooded area, but the wood wasn't dense enough to hide them. They were nearly at the road, though, and the men were still some distance behind, but to Maggie's dismay she realised they were heading downhill, and the road was above them, higher up. They were going to have to scramble up a bank, and she knew she would be useless at that.

They ran on until finally there was nowhere else to go. The bank was a sheer climb with a fence at the bottom. It was a dead end. There were a few bushes, but nothing that would keep them hidden for long.

Josh grabbed her hand. 'Come on, Mum – this way.' Up ahead Maggie could see an opening under the road. It was a culvert – a wide circular pipe, some sort of drainage pipe, she presumed.

'We can crawl through here,' Josh said.

Maggie looked and knew she couldn't do it. She might be able to get in, but she would have to go through on her belly. There was no space to turn, and if she got stuck… Just looking at it freaked her out.

'Josh, you go. I'll stay here – get rid of them. When you get to the other side, find somebody to help. Ask them to ring Auntie Suzy.' Then another thought struck her. 'Ask them to ring a policeman. He's called Tom Douglas. Tom – like your friend from your old school, and Douglas like the road we used to live on. Go, darling. Go.'

Josh gave her a terrified stare, but he could hear the men crashing through the undergrowth, trying to find them. They wouldn't be long. He turned and dived into the pipe, his elbows out, pushing him through. The men were close, but Josh was out of sight.

At the last minute Maggie had an idea. She took one of her shoes and threw it into the culvert then retreated behind a thick bush and crouched as low as possible – just in time.

'Where the fuck have they gone? Search the bushes.'

'No, look. There's a culvert.'

Maggie couldn't see what they were doing without revealing herself, but she imagined them looking into the open end of the pipe.

'Shit! There's one of her shoes in there. They must have gone this way. I'm going after them.'

Maggie stifled an audible gasp. Surely if she had had doubts about getting through the pipe, they would have no chance. But what if they did get through? Josh was on his own.

'Don't be fucking stupid. You won't get your arse through there. I've got a better idea. Her car's here, and they would have worked out we would never get through that pipe. They might wait until we've gone and come back. So you wait here.'

'Where are you going?'

'We can't afford to screw this up. Michael's been handed to us on a plate. Invictus won't be happy if we don't capitalise on what he's given us.'

With that the man turned and started to jog back the way he had come, leaving the second man standing only feet away from where Maggie was hiding.

There was that name again: Invictus. He must still be involved. But what did they mean about Michael being handed to them on a plate? Was that when William set up the bogus meeting? Thank God Duncan was safe and she hadn't persuaded him to come home with her.

For now, though, she had to wait. Maggie couldn't outrun the man left to guard the culvert. All she could do was pray that Josh had made it safely to the nearest house and that right now somebody was calling the police.

❖

Josh wanted to cry but knew he mustn't. What was it Mummy sometimes said? 'Crying isn't going to help anybody'? Well in this case she was right. He could sit down and cry, but then there would be nobody to help his mummy.

He was trying to remember what she had said about the man he had to call. His first name was the same as one of his old friends, but he'd had lots of friends. And the name of the road they lived on. That was a bit easier. That was Douglas, but he needed to remember the first name.

When he had pushed his way out of the pipe under the road he had found himself in a field. He saw a few rabbits but nothing else. The road was high above him, so he didn't think he could get up there, and anyway the cars were going really fast.

At the far end of the field there were some new houses, but there were no lights on even though it was dark. Maybe nobody lived in them. They looked ghostly in what little light there was, their windows black and empty. There were piles of bricks everywhere and some big diggers. Josh didn't like what he could see, but it seemed the best place to head for. Even if the houses were empty he could follow the road until he found somebody. He wished he had a torch.

He trudged across the field, thinking maybe he should run, but after the football and the running he wasn't sure he could. Dragging his feet, he finally reached the place where the houses spilled into the field, and he could see what looked like a road. It wasn't black like most roads; it was just rough bits of stone. The houses didn't have doors or glass in the windows, and Josh heard himself whimper. It felt as if the houses were suddenly going to spring to life and move towards him, sucking his body into one of the gaping black doorways to eat him whole.

He wanted to run, but it was either back through the field or along this winding road past more empty houses. He had to do what Mummy asked, though. Find a person and tell them to phone Auntie Suzy or the policeman. Josh still couldn't remember his first name.

He walked past the first house, glancing warily into the empty doorway.

Josh sighed with relief. A man was standing there, tall and straight, hands in his pockets. He was safe from the houses – they wouldn't get him now. This man would help him, he was sure.

The man walked towards Josh, smiling. When he got close, he reached out an arm and placed it on his shoulder.

'Hello, Josh. My name's Sam.'

57

Maggie didn't like to think of the time she had wasted, waiting for the man to decide she and Josh weren't going to come back through the culvert, but she hadn't had any choice. Even if she could have found a way to sneak away through the trees she didn't know if the first man was coming back. She might have bumped right into him.

She hadn't been able to see her watch in the dark, but she guessed it had taken the man about twenty minutes to give up on them and head back to the car park. She gave him another five minutes to get well clear, but nevertheless she was very cautious on her way back to the car. Thank goodness she had taken her car keys and locked the door.

Josh, darling, be safe. The thought was spinning in her head. Had she done the right thing, letting him go through the pipe?

But he was out of danger – out of the reach of the two men. It was only early evening. Surely some kind person would have found him?

As she approached the car park, she couldn't see anybody. She pirouetted on her bare toes to have a good look. There was nobody. She ran to the car, not noticing the gravel cutting into the naked skin of her feet.

If only her phone hadn't been completely dead, she could have called the police, no matter how that impacted on Duncan. There were ways in which she could protect her children from the inevitable consequences, if only she could keep them safe right now.

Trying to stop her hands from shaking, Maggie put the key in the ignition and turned it. She was only ten minutes from home, but first she wanted to drive to where she thought Josh would have ended up. She would go there first, just in case he was still wandering about on his own, frightened. She navigated her way to the other side of the busy main road and found that all that lay beyond was a new housing estate, with only the houses at the very edge occupied. Poor Josh, he would have been terrified.

Maggie sobbed. She shouldn't have let him go. She drove down the unmade roads slowly, searching for the small figure of her son.

She was so focused on scouring the dark, empty houses on either side, that she didn't realise what was happening until it was too late. She hadn't been looking in her rear-view mirror, and the van couldn't have had any lights on. The first she knew it was there was when she heard the revving of its engine as it raced past her and pulled up, half across the road, blocking her way.

Maggie instinctively thought, *Duncan – thank God*, and flung the door open. And then the full force of her stupidity struck her. She thrust the car into reverse with the door still open. She had to get away. That was when she heard the shout.

'*Mummy!*'

Maggie slammed her foot on the brake. A tall man got out of the van and stood, legs apart, arms hanging loosely by his side. He had Josh. She had heard him, but she couldn't see him.

She leaped out of the car and ran at the man, not caring what he did to her. She aimed her fingernails at his face and flew at him, her knee raised to groin level. His arms rose swiftly – long arms that kept her at bay. She turned her head to bite his hand, but his other hand reached down and grabbed her hair, pulling her head back.

'You bastard,' she spat. 'Let my son go. He can't hurt you. Let him *go*.'

'Get in the van, Maggie,' he said, still pulling her hair so that all she could see was the sky above them. 'Get in the fucking van. There's nobody here to save you, and if you don't do as I say I'll drive off with your son, and you'll never see him again. Have you got that?'

She couldn't nod. 'Okay' was all she could manage.

He opened a sliding side door and pushed her inside. She fell face down, and he slammed the door shut. A small light was switched on, presumably so he could keep an eye on her.

Maggie rolled over quickly. Where was Josh? She was hoping he was here, with her in the back, so she could cuddle him and reassure him. But he was in the front seat with a grille between them. If he'd been here, she might have tried to escape with him, but that was the point, no doubt. The man knew she wouldn't try to get away while he had her son.

She crawled to the grille and poked her fingers through trying to touch Josh. 'It's okay, baby. I'm here now.'

'I'm sorry, Mummy,' he said, his voice sounding small and so, so vulnerable. 'I tried to get away, but he was waiting for me. There was nobody else to tell. I'm sorry.'

His face was grubby and streaked with tears. This should not be happening to Josh.

'You've got nothing to be sorry for, sweetheart; I'm the one who should be sorry. Listen, don't worry about it. The police know all about this van. Do you remember? You gave me the number plate, and I told the police. So they'll be tracking us now on that fancy equipment they have. It reads number plates, and they'll be watching for this one.'

She knew the man was listening, but she didn't care. Maybe he would dump the van and they would carry on on foot. That would give her the best chance of escape. But to her horror, he laughed.

'After my mate's ridiculous behaviour the other day when

he rather showed his hand, do you really think we would have kept the same number plate? We're not petty criminals, Maggie. We're skilled at what we do. We're intelligent, and there's not a police force in the world that can tie us to any crime.'

'No, but Michael can, can't he?'

She saw the man's jaw muscles tighten. 'And we both know he's not going to. He's not going to accept the inevitable prison sentence, is he, because he doesn't believe any of it is his fault.'

He gave a tight smile, and Maggie winced, knowing that every word was the truth.

'Don't hurt my mum, Sam,' Josh suddenly said. 'Because if you do, my dad will come for you. He's strong, and he says we have to stand up to bullies.'

The man put his head back and laughed out loud, as if that was the funniest thing he had ever heard.

So this was Samil. Maggie had finally met the man who called himself the Angel of Death. Suddenly, the name didn't seem quite so silly after all.

❖

There was a slightly sharp smell in the back of the van, and the wooden floor was damp as if it had recently been cleaned. An indentation held a small puddle, and Maggie dipped her middle finger in. She felt a mild tingling and the end of her finger started to turn white.

This guy was smart. He knew that ordinary bleach removed bloodstains, but luminol would still reveal them. The only way to remove the haemoglobin was to use oxygen bleach – hydrogen peroxide – so even if the van was found at some point there would be no blood evidence of his previous victims. The bodies had been in here.

Goosebumps broke out over her arms and up her neck. This was no ordinary thug.

'Where are we going?' she asked.

'Shut up and stop asking stupid questions.'

Maggie had no intention of shutting up. If there was one thing she had to do, it was persuade this Samil or whatever his real name was that it was dangerous for him to keep Josh. She knew why she had been taken, but if Josh saw his mummy hurt he would be so damaged, and his knowledge would make him a danger to this man. Would Samil kill Josh to protect himself?

Josh had to be her number-one priority. She would worry about herself later. She tried to think how to persuade Samil to let her son go. She was running out of time and silently apologised for the terror she was about to subject her small son to. But better frightened than dead.

'Let Josh go at least. If you have an ounce of decency in you, stop the van and let him out. He's only a little kid. Don't let him witness whatever you're going to do. That would make him a danger to you, and then you'd have no choice but to silence him. I can't believe that you'd hurt an eight-year-old child. How does that fit in with your plans?'

'I told you to shut the fuck up.'

'I'm a criminal lawyer, but then you know that, don't you? So I know how killers work. Not many kill adults *and* small children, do they? It's usually one or the other.'

Maggie screwed her eyes up tight for a second and prayed that Josh wouldn't absorb what she was about to say.

'I know you like to kill in threes. Are you going to find another two other little boys to make up the number?'

Once again she saw his jaw tighten. 'I see you've been talking to Michael.'

Maggie was relieved that he was referring to her husband as Michael – at least Josh would not realise it was his daddy they were discussing.

'I know you think Michael let you down all those years ago, but he never believed you were serious.'

'Is *that* what he told you?' She couldn't see the man's face, but clearly he wasn't ready to forgive Duncan.

'He let you get away with it, though. You should be grateful to him for *not* going to the police.'

'You really don't know him at all, do you.' It was a statement, not a question.

Maggie didn't want to listen to this any more.

'Never mind Michael. Never mind me. Whatever you've done, you think you're in the clear. You're clever, so I don't doubt you could still get away with it. But if you...hurt a child...' Maggie paused, a sob rising in her throat. She had been unable to say 'kill', but Samil knew what she meant. She couldn't complete the sentence.

'What? What will you do to me?' he asked, his anger spiking through. She was getting to him and she wasn't going to stop. He couldn't shut her up; there was a grille between them.

'Oh, I won't be able to do a thing. I know that. But when you go to prison – because you *will* go to prison – what do you think will happen to you? They'll say you're a nonce. Nobody ever hurts kids for the thrill of the kill, do they? They won't believe your motive was to keep him quiet. Men who hurt kids always have another agenda – a different kind of thrill in mind. Imagine that. Life in prison and segregated. Alone with your own thoughts. How will you like that?' She didn't wait for an answer but ploughed on. 'What harm can it do letting him go? He doesn't know your real name; he only knows the van, and you've already disguised that. There are thousands of white vans. Look, you've just passed one. Let him out, Samil. The police are looking for you because of the girls, but we all know that a child killer rarely gets away with it. They'll double, treble the number of officers working on the case if you kill him. And they will *never* give up. We're miles from home, and Josh knows nothing. But in a minute I will start talking. I will start spilling every tiny bit of information that Michael has given me. And Josh will remember. He's good like that. And then you'll have no choice, will you? Do the smart thing, Samil. Let my child out.'

He didn't respond, and Maggie had run out of words.

Through the grille, she saw Samil glance briefly over his shoulder at her, a hint of a smile on his angular face. 'Do you know, that's not such a bad idea, Maggie,' he said. 'I'll dump him here, in the middle of nowhere, shall I? Then some other creep can finish the job for me. Excellent plan.'

The van screeched to a halt beside the road.

'Josh, get out and face that wall. If you turn round and try to read the number plate of this van, I will come back to get you, and I will hurt you and your mum. Do you understand?'

Maggie recognised the road they were on. It wasn't the middle of nowhere. It was the main road to the north of Manchester, leading into the city. But the road was lined with businesses – there were no pedestrians or houses in sight.

Suddenly she was terrified. At least while he was in the van, he was with her. If he got out here, there was a chance that he would be picked up by somebody as evil as Samil.

Stop it! she told herself. How many bad bastards were there really? Surely there was a much better chance of him being picked up by somebody decent? And what choice was there? If he stayed with her, she was sure he was going to die.

'I want to stay with you, Mum,' he said, turning his scared little face towards her.

'I know you do, sweetheart. But this is for the best. Somebody will find you and take you home. You know what to do. I need you to be brave one more time.'

The tears were running down Josh's face as he slowly opened the door and lowered himself out of the van onto the pavement. He looked back at Maggie, and she could see confusion and doubt written all over his face. His world had been torn apart over the last week, and he must have felt totally lost.

'I love you, Joshy, with every inch of my soul.' He stared at her as if he didn't believe a word of it.

'Face the wall, Josh, or I'm coming back for you.' That he did believe.

It was almost unbearable when Samil leaned across and pulled the door shut. Maggie couldn't see Josh any more, but as the van pulled away, she looked out of the back window at the tiny figure of her son, still in his muddy football kit, one sock up, one around his ankles, standing facing the side wall of a carpet warehouse, his shoulders slumped, his head hanging.

58

Tom and Becky were both resigned to another late night. Tom had spent the afternoon on the telephone and now felt depressed because none of the ideas that were whizzing around inside his head seemed to help in any way in the hunt for Leo.

He glanced out of the window. It was dark now, and wherever Leo was it would probably be cold. He was now as certain as he could be that she had been abducted. Everything pointed to it – the flower delivery but no flowers left in the apartment, the car in the garage, no clothes or jewellery missing, failing to turn up to her niece's christening. Ellie had asked her to be the baby's godmother, Tom had discovered, and she would never have missed that. Right now Leo would no doubt be dreading the cold night ahead and he wasn't able to find her.

He shook his head. That was his job, for God's sake. He should be able to do this. His frustration wasn't helping but she was his priority now, not crimes from the past. He had to prevent anything from happening to Leo, if he wasn't already too late.

He turned his attention to the list of properties still owned by the Mellor family business, including those that had been sold off and were either already converted or due to be.

'Great work, Becky, and tell Mark thanks.'

Becky nodded without taking her eyes off the list she was holding.

'If those murders twelve years ago had anything to do with Adam Mellor, there's a perfect building just here.' Becky lifted her eyes from the list and pointed to a spot on the map they had pinned up in the incident room. 'The first girl had her throat slit, right? And she was found on Pomona Island, but she had been killed somewhere else. This building is a short walk, under the arches below the tramline, to where you found her.'

'But any trace of anything at all will by now have been obliterated. That mill was renovated eight years ago.'

'I know.' Tom could see Becky was avoiding his eyes. He had told her how much he had wanted to have the buildings searched. 'What about the more recent girls?' she asked.

Tom thought about it. The trouble was, the location of the bodies gave no clue at all. They had been found at different ends of the city. He was working on the assumption that the van had been used to move the bodies, and possibly the shopping trolley to get them to their final locations, but that meant the killing site could be any one of the derelict buildings still owned by the company.

'Let's consider access,' Tom said. He called over his shoulder to one of the team, 'Can we get Google Maps up on this screen, please?' He pointed to the whiteboard next to the map they were studying. 'If we can get street views and have a look around, we might be able to see which of these buildings has the best access. Mills with nowhere to park a van opposite newly renovated places are unlikely – they would have to cart a body across a pavement in full view of the neighbours. Let's see if we can narrow it down.'

'Do you want to leave it with me, boss?' Becky asked. 'I can give you a shout when we have it down to a couple of hot favourites.'

Tom nodded his thanks and made his way back to his office. He couldn't get rid of the knot of anxiety in his gut, and everything was telling him that tonight was critical.

Hayley Walker's mobile records had told them nothing, and Tom was increasingly convinced that Ben Coleman had lured her out of her house and into Adam Mellor's clutches, but he couldn't prove it. Maybe Coleman had fixed up a date with her before he had supposedly gone on holiday. Tom had asked for alerts to be put on the credit and debit cards of both Coleman and Mellor, and their phones were being monitored, but nothing had come up.

A couple of the reports Tom had asked for were on his desk. Neither of them filled him with joy, but he picked up the first one and scanned it again. He had just reached an interesting point when his telephone rang.

'Mr Douglas, we've had a call from a member of the public. A gentleman and his wife discovered a little boy standing crying by the side of the road – Bury New Road, heading into town. He says his name is Josh Taylor and a man has taken his mother.' Tom felt a familiar leap in his chest. This had to be Maggie Taylor's son. 'It's a convoluted story, sir, but it appears when he was trying to escape – he keeps talking about crawling through a pipe – his mum told him to find a policeman and ask for Tom Douglas.'

'Where is he? Where's the boy now?'

'I asked the gentleman and his wife if they would bring him here, sir. They were happy to help and should be here in about ten minutes. Will you be available to talk to them?'

'I'm on my way down right now. I'll be waiting for them. Thank you.' Tom left the office and went via Becky's desk. 'I need you with me, but can you get one of your team to find out what Sonia Beecham's mother was called, please?'

Becky looked slightly startled, but did as he asked and followed him towards the lift.

❖

Tom bought a couple of soft drinks from the vending machine and asked if somebody would make tea or coffee for the couple who had found Josh and show them into the most comfortable of the interview rooms.

They had made excellent time, and as Tom watched the middle-aged couple enter the reception area he was pleased to see the care with which they were treating the child. An ordinary, homely-looking couple, the woman had her arm around the shoulders of a small boy with a grey, tear-streaked face dressed in muddy football kit; the man was holding his hand.

Tom walked towards them and introduced himself.

'Thank you so much for picking Josh up and bringing him here. I appreciate it. I need to talk to him as quickly as possible if, as he says, somebody has taken his mother. I hope you understand. My colleague will be along to chat to you in a couple of minutes, and will ask you for details of where you found Josh, anything that he might have said to you, and so on. I hope you don't mind helping us; it's quite a serious case.'

'No, no. Not a problem at all,' the man said, looking slightly excited by the idea of being involved in a major investigation.

Tom crouched down in front of Josh so his face was level with the boy's.

'You've been very brave, Josh, and I know you must be frightened, but can you come with me and this lady here – she's called Becky. We're going to find your mum, but we need your help. Is that okay?'

Josh looked up at the man who had brought him in, clearly feeling safer with the devil he knew than a completely new face.

The man crouched down too. 'Go with this policeman, Josh. He's going to look after you. You take care now. You're a brave little boy.'

The boy looked bewildered and glanced from one adult to the other.

Josh's rescuer stood up and smiled at Tom, holding out his hand. 'He's a good kid, Chief Inspector.'

Tom nodded and shook the outstretched hand as Becky gently ushered Josh into one of the interview rooms.

After they had offered Josh a drink, Tom nodded to Becky. Josh might find the questioning easier from a woman.

'We going to call your dad, Josh, to let him know that you're okay. Is he back home now? Your mum said he'd gone down south for something.'

An expression flitted over Josh's face that Tom couldn't read. The kid was wary of saying something out of turn, and it occurred to Tom that maybe his dad had left, and Josh didn't want anybody to know.

'He's not back yet. He's probably mending someone's boiler or something. That's his job, you see. My auntie's at our house, though.'

Tom asked a PC to call the house to let Josh's aunt know he was safe, and gradually over the course of the next fifteen minutes they learned what had happened from the end of the football match to the minute the van drove off.

'He made me turn away so I couldn't read the number plate. He said if I turned round he'd come back for me. So I didn't. But I still remember it from last time.'

'That was really useful too. We know who the van belongs to, and now we're using something called automatic number plate recognition to see if we can spot it on the roads. Then we can work out where your mummy is. Don't worry – we'll find the van.'

Josh was shaking his head.

'What is it, Josh?' Tom asked.

'My mum said that to Sam when he pushed her in the back of the van. And he laughed.'

As Tom had thought, they had obviously changed the number plates. Easy enough to do. But it was the name that made him sit up.

'You called him Sam, Josh. He told you his name, did he?'

'Yes. When he was waiting for me. He said, "My name's Sam," but Mummy called him something else. I think it was Samil.'

'Well done for remembering, Josh.'

Tom turned to Becky and raised his eyebrows but didn't comment on the name. 'Get the CCTV and anything else you can get. Let's see if we can establish the time Josh was dropped off and see if we can follow the van's route.'

Becky looked at Tom and said quietly, 'A white van, Tom, driving into Manchester?'

He knew what she meant. There would be dozens of the damn things.

'I know. Do your best. In the meantime, let's keep checking those mill sites to see which is the most likely.'

Tom turned back to Josh. 'Do you remember what Sam looked like? Anything about him that would help us to recognise him?'

Josh thought about it. 'He had a thin face, sort of. These bits stuck out a lot.' Josh pointed to his cheekbones. 'And he had dark hair and was very tall.'

'That's really helpful. I'm going to show you a picture of quite a few people. If you think he's one of them, can you point to him for me? It doesn't matter if you don't recognise anybody.'

Josh nodded, and Tom pulled out the photograph that Louisa Knight had given him. 'Just have a look, Josh.'

Josh scanned the image for no more than a few seconds. His finger shot out. 'It's him.'

Tom nodded. Ben Coleman, in Adam Mellor's van. So where was Mellor?

'Thank you – you've done very well. We're going to arrange for somebody to take you home now. Is that okay? Then we're going to look for your mum.'

'You will find her, won't you?' he asked, the face looking up at Tom's showing a level of fear and anguish that no child of this age should have to experience.

'Course we will,' Tom said.

He hated lying.

59

Maggie couldn't bear to think about Josh and what might be happening to him right at this minute. Had somebody picked him up? Would they be kind to him, or had she lost her son forever? She pulled her knees to her chest and wrapped her arms around them. She had to persuade Samil to let her out of the van so she could go back and find her little boy. But shouting and screaming were never going to work with a man like this.

'Don't you think it's in your interests to let me go?' Maggie asked. She tried to keep her voice reasonable, but she could hear how unsteady it was. 'At the moment you've done nothing more than push me into a van. If you let me go now there's very little the police can get you on. A good lawyer would get you off with probation for this.'

'Maggie, Maggie,' he said, sounding like a tired parent with a recalcitrant child. 'You and I know perfectly well that I've done more than that. Of course nobody can prove a thing, and they won't be able to prove it when I kill you, either. That's *if* I kill you, and I'm hoping that's not going to be necessary.'

'What do you mean?'

She saw him shake his head and knew he wasn't going to say any more. Maggie remembered what she had read earlier in the week about psychopaths. He had no sense of guilt or remorse and was supremely confident. He showed no fear either, and she could easily see how people might make the mistake of finding him charming. He had let Josh go, not out of guilt or even fear, but almost definitely because he knew that a manhunt for a child killer would be fierce. He had simply weighed up the odds, and as Josh hadn't been part of his original plan, letting him go was easy.

Any chance she had left of working on him disappeared as Samil drove down what appeared to be one of the last unrenovated streets of central Manchester. She knew they must be nearing their destination. On one side of the road a building had been demolished, and Samil stopped and threw the van into reverse. He was backing into what looked like the loading bay of an old mill.

He jumped out of the van and came round to the side door, pulled it open and dragged her out, wrapping her long hair around his fist.

'Don't try anything,' he muttered close to her right ear.

Maggie tried to get a sense of everything around her. She needed to work out where she was. She had no idea if it would be useful, but she wasn't going down without a fight. There was a slightly musty smell, and she wondered if they were close to a canal or perhaps the mustiness was coming from within the building. She had to think and hold her fear at bay.

Samil marched her to an open wooden staircase at the far end of the loading bay. He pulled her head back slightly so she could only look up. She couldn't see to place her feet, and she couldn't turn round to kick him.

There were no identifiable sounds. As she tripped and stumbled up the steps she could hear a banging noise, but could only guess that it came from an empty, glassless window. It was icy cold, and whatever was causing the musty smell, the damp was penetrating the thin coat covering her tailored work suit and silk shirt.

They reached the first floor of the building, and he slackened his hold slightly so she could lower her head, but she still couldn't turn round.

The room was poorly lit with only two fluorescent tubes working, one at each end of the vast space. Enough light to see that the space was empty – just a dirty wooden floor with green metal pillars reaching up to the ceiling high above them. There was an unpleasant smell here, far worse than below, and Maggie assumed squatters had lived here in the recent past. About halfway across the room there was a table, and up against it what appeared to be a pile of rags.

And then the rags moved.

Maggie yelped. *Rats.* They must be nesting in the material.

With an extra twist of his wrist, Samil yanked Maggie towards the rags – and the rats. She stood still, refusing to budge. He lifted his leg and kneed her in the backside, forcing her hips forward but holding her head back. She cried out in pain.

'Well move, then,' he said.

Maggie approached the pile of rags cautiously. Surely the rats would run if they heard humans. The rags moved again, and this time there was a sound.

Samil gave one of his harsh laughs. 'Maggie, meet your room mate,' he said.

Maggie looked down at the pile of rags. From under what it had become apparent was an arm, a filthy face appeared, the skin mottled white and deep pink, the eyes red and weeping.

'Maggie, this is Leo.'

❖

Maggie fell to her knees. She could feel the woman's pain as if it were her own.

'Oh you poor soul,' she whispered. She looked up at Samil. 'How could you *do* something like this? How could you let her suffer? It's one thing holding her prisoner, but she's clearly seriously ill. Do something about it. Don't let her die this way.'

Samil stood above her looking down, still grasping her hair.

'That's not the way she's going to die, trust me. Anyway, she's had antibiotics. She's getting better.'

'You mean she was worse than this? Jesus.'

She noticed a plastic-wrapped pack of water bottles. At least they hadn't intentionally dehydrated the woman, but she was too ill to move and could never have torn open the plastic.

'Let me go,' Maggie said, lifting her hand to her hair and tugging it away from Samil's fist. 'Let me see to her. I won't try to run.'

To her amazement, he did what she asked.

'You won't run. I know that. I'm standing here, not two metres from you. And anyway, somebody's coming to see you.'

'Who? What do you mean?'

He said nothing and Maggie couldn't worry about that. She needed to help this woman. She took off her coat and suit jacket and untucked her silk blouse. Turning away from the man, she removed her blouse and quickly put her outer clothes back on, buttoning her coat tightly.

She wasn't strong enough to rip the material so she poured some water onto a sleeve and bunched it up, placing it between the woman's lips. She didn't think it was wise to pour cold water directly into her mouth, and anyway she was lying on her side. Maggie dampened another part of the blouse and used it to gently wipe the woman's face, trying to cool her.

She wanted to make her more comfortable, but then saw how her arm was stretched above her head and the sorry state of her wrist. The massive swelling almost hid the sutures, but Maggie could see the other end of a plastic tie attached to a chain round one of the pillars.

She glanced up at Samil. 'You *animal*.' He was unmoved, and she tried not to think what he might have in store for her.

'Enough,' he said, his face set into hard lines. Maggie would never forget this man's face. His name didn't matter. She was certain she was never getting out of here, but would find him if ever she got the chance.

He pulled Maggie up by her hair again. Extracting another long plastic cable tie from his coat pocket he pushed Maggie hard up against a metal pillar and told her to put her arms behind her.

She did nothing. He lifted her off the floor by her hair, thousands of follicles screaming as they bore the weight of her body.

'Put your fucking arms around the pillar.'

She would have liked to defy him again, but she was certain he wasn't going to stop hurting her until she did what he said, and she didn't have the strength to resist.

He secured the plastic tie. 'Now I would gag you, but you could scream forever here and nobody would hear you, so I won't bother.' He turned and walked back towards the doorway to the stairs.

Where was he going? Why was he leaving them?

Maggie tried to comfort the woman. 'It's okay. We're going to get out of here. People are looking for you.'

The woman didn't move. Maggie could see her mottled face and knew she didn't have long.

'There's a policeman. They say he's really clever. Tom Douglas, he's called. He'll find us.'

Maggie was amazed to see the girl's eyelids flutter open for a second, and she was certain that she saw hope in her eyes. Whether that was true or not, it was better that the girl died with hope in her heart.

Maggie stopped talking. She could hear voices. Samil was coming back, and he had somebody with him, somebody who clearly didn't want to be there. And it was a voice she recognised.

Samil kicked the door open and pushed a man in front of him into the room, his hands also tied behind his back.

'*Duncan!*' Maggie gasped. How on earth had they found him? She must have been followed the previous night. Surely not? There had been nobody about – the roads were empty – but how else could they have known where he was?

Duncan looked at her, his face showing no surprise that she was there. His features were set into hard lines as if he was sucking in his cheeks. His eyes were dark and unreadable.

Samil pushed him across the room until he was standing a few feet from Maggie.

'Maggie, meet Michael. He's a man of many names, aren't you?' he said, prodding Duncan hard in the back. 'I knew him as Senka online. I bet you didn't know that, did you, Maggie? Senka means "shadow" in some foreign language or other. So to me he was Senka, then I saw him in the newspaper and discovered his name was Michael, and now it's Duncan. I'm sure he must confuse himself with all these names.'

Duncan continued to say nothing. He didn't look at Maggie, but stared into an empty space in the room, his eyes blank.

Samil lifted his right leg and put his foot against Duncan's back. He pushed him towards Maggie and walked across to a bag in the corner. He pulled something out, and Maggie recognised it instantly. A taser. Samil could keep his distance and still control Duncan. Maggie and the girl – Leo, he had said her name was – were restrained by the pillars.

Samil pulled a mobile phone out of his pocket.

'I gather your husband gave you a flavour of what he set up all those years ago – those assassinations. No doubt he told you how innocent he was. Do you want me to read you some of the messages he wrote on the website, Maggie? Do you want to know what he fantasised about doing to the girl who had betrayed him?'

Duncan turned his head. He said nothing, but the look he gave Samil was full of hatred. Samil ignored him and consulted the screen of his phone.

'Let me see.' Samil flicked his finger up the screen a couple of times. 'Ah, here we are. It appears your husband wanted his ex-girlfriend drowned. That was his method of choice. He wanted her head held under, then pulled out when she was almost unconscious, and then pushed under again. He wanted that repeated until finally her strength ebbed from her body. I didn't do that. It was too messy and would have taken too long. But that was his fantasy. I would have slit her throat, like the first one, but in the end she was strangled. Bad, but not as bad as what your husband had planned.'

Maggie felt hot tears streaming down her face. This wasn't Duncan he was talking about; it was somebody else.

'You see, Maggie—' Samil's voice was tight as if he could only just resist the urge to shout and scream, '—what that girl did to your husband was nothing. It was a blip in his life. His failure to stick to his side of the bargain, to kill my stepmother before she got her hands on my father's money, has condemned me to a life of penury. Oh, I have enough to live on, but I should have been so very, very rich. And your husband *ruined* that for me. That's why I've brought him here. I'm going to condemn him for the rest of his life to something that's possibly even worse.'

What could he mean? There was no point in asking. Samil seemed to be in a different place. His pupils had dilated and his eyes looked fierce and black, the words spat from his mouth with venom.

'He has to make a choice. He has to kill – that's only fair given what I did for him – but I'm going to let him choose. He can kill you, Maggie, or he can kill Leo. That's an easy choice, really. She's almost dead anyway. But you see, you're going to have to watch him do it. You're going to have to listen to her scream. And then if you stay with him, every day for the rest of your lives you will picture him killing an innocent woman because she had the misfortune to look like you.'

Still Duncan didn't speak. He kept his hate-filled eyes on Samil, and never looked at Maggie.

'Don't do it, Duncan,' she begged. 'He can't make you.'

'Of *course* I can make him.' Samil spat the words out. 'I'll start carving chunks out of you until he agrees. It looks like an easy choice, but it's not. Think about it.'

He said no more. He didn't need to, but Maggie had heard

enough. She remembered one of the articles she had read about psychopaths. Control was everything, so she had to break it – destroy Samil's confidence. As a psychopath, he was a master manipulator of other people's feelings, but was unable to experience emotions himself. She knew she wouldn't be able to make him feel guilty, but she could belittle him. And psychopaths were planners and hated their plans to be upset or derailed. That was what she had to do. Maggie took a deep breath.

'What sort of a man are you, Samil? Oh, I know. The sort that has to hide behind a pathetic fake name. The Angel of Death?' She barked out a laugh, and hoped Samil didn't hear the terror hovering just below the surface. 'For God's sake, you sound like a character out of a children's comic. I've no doubt you're an evil bastard. Let's face it, you've killed enough innocent women. But what do you get off on? That's what I can't work out. From what I can gather, you're not getting any sexual gratification out of your kills. Or is that it? Is thinking about the deaths of these women at your hands the only way you can get it up? Or is it the thrill of the kill? Well, I've got news for you. Your plans are going to fail. It's all going to go wrong, Samil, and you will be exposed for the pathetic specimen you are.'

She had to stop before her voice cracked with the strain of trying to sound strong. She swallowed and fought to hold her gaze steady. She had done her best, but her outburst hadn't produced any signs of the confusion she had tried to create. All she saw was a slight narrowing of Samil's eyes.

'Maybe I have a better idea,' he said. 'You're a strong woman, Maggie, so maybe the choice of who dies should be yours. Duncan can kill Leo or kill you, or you can kill Duncan. But let's make this *your* choice – let Duncan see what hell he has brought into your life. Remember, Maggie, your husband has fantasised about killing. Maybe he still does – have you thought of that? Maybe if we search the site to find someone who fantasises about drowning people slowly – that fantasist could be Duncan.'

The back of Maggie's neck tingled with a memory and she turned her head to look at Duncan. He didn't return her stare, but the fury in his eyes as he looked at Samil was chilling.

'Don't be ridiculous,' he said, spacing out each word. 'I was never serious. You're the psychopath, the thrill killer. Not me.'

Samil turned back to his phone. 'Well, we'll see, shall we? There are some wild fantasists on this site – and yes, the site's still going, Maggie. The numbers swell year on year. This one that I'm looking at right now wants to kill all lesbians. A mission killer. They're so interesting, like Peter Sutcliffe and the prostitutes. Or Carroll Edward Cole – his mission was to kill women who cheated on their partners. I think you would be a mission killer, Michael. But what would you want to rid the world of? Any ideas, wife? We can search the site, and see if we can find any more of your husband's fantasies. What do you say?'

Maggie was silent. She wasn't sure her legs would hold her up for much longer. Samil stared at her for a few seconds longer, waiting to see if she responded. She didn't, and he appeared to become bored with the idea, sticking the phone back in his pocket.

He folded his arms and stared at Maggie, a small smile betraying his pleasure at the torment he was inflicting.

'Okay, Maggie, who's going to die here today? You, your husband or that poor scrap of a woman who hasn't done a thing to hurt anybody?' He pointed his taser in Leo's direction. 'I want an answer. Or I'm going to start hurting people.'

Maggie had no more ideas – no other ways to deflect Samil from his goal. What was she going to say to him? Why hadn't she absorbed more of those articles on psychopaths? She might have had a clue then.

Duncan moved towards Samil. The taser was immediately pointed and charged. 'Don't even think about it.'

'So give me a knife,' Duncan said.

Maggie was jolted from her thoughts of how to divert Samil.

'*Duncan,*' Maggie gasped. 'Don't.'

'He won't be doing anything until you give him the word. I've told you, Maggie. The choice has to be yours. You, your husband or her.'

Maggie put her head down.

'Give me the fucking *knife,*' Duncan said, his jaw clenched. 'Let's get it done.'

Samil waited a beat.

'I *will* free your hands, Duncan. And you can have the knife. But the decision is Maggie's. If you as much as move before that decision has been made, I will bring you down with this.' He waved the taser in the air. 'Turn your back. The taser is right up against your heart, so nothing clever.'

Maggie watched as Samil ran the knife quickly between Duncan's hands and stepped back. He got well out of Duncan's reach, dropped the knife on the floor and kicked it over to him, pointing the taser all the time.

Maggie watched her husband pick the knife up. He looked at her, but she couldn't see any sign of her Duncan. His face was devoid of expression, his jawline rigid.

'What's it to be, Maggie?' Samil asked. 'If you choose Duncan, I'll taser him first, and I'll be only too happy to finish the job for you if you don't have the stomach for it. That makes the choice easier, doesn't it?'

Maggie's head was spinning. This couldn't be happening. How could she choose between herself, her husband and this poor defenceless woman, who – as far as she knew – had nothing whatsoever to do with any of this?

Duncan started to walk across to where Leo lay on the floor.

'Maggie, it's an easy choice, surely?' Duncan said. 'She isn't going to survive. Tell me to kill her, and then we're done. He's not going to stop until you choose, and what other choice is there?'

Maggie stared at her husband. He didn't appear to have an

ounce of reluctance about killing the girl. It was a solution to a problem for him, not a young woman's life. What did that make him?

'Do you think he's going to let us go after that? After everything we could tell the police about him?'

Duncan closed his eyes for a moment and shook his head slightly. 'Don't you get it? If we do this, he will have as much on us as we have on him. Rightly or wrongly, I can't ever go to the police. You know that. So let him have his revenge, and let's get out of here. Just don't watch. Then you won't ever have to think again about what I'm about to do.'

'Shut it, Duncan,' Samil said. 'Maggie, it's decision time.'

Maggie knew that if she told Duncan to kill the girl, she would never be able to look at herself in a mirror again. And she would never let Duncan's blood-covered hands near her. But she couldn't kill her husband, the father of her children, and he had always seemed such a *good* father. How would she ever live with herself if she condemned him to death?

She was about to open her mouth and give her answer when she heard a noise. It was the sound of running footsteps on the stairs.

❖

The door burst open and a man stood in the open doorway. Maggie could see his chest heaving as he tried to regain his breath. His arms were at his side, but held away from his body, his legs taut. She recognised the voice.

'You fucking shit.' His voice was low, but there was no doubt about the fury.

It was the second man, the one who had been left to guard the pipe.

'You left me with no transport, no money – nothing. You treat me like shit, and yet none of this would have been possible without me.'

'Stop being such a girl,' Samil said. 'You enjoyed the ride. You got off on killing people on Daddy's property, didn't you? Didn't have the guts to do it yourself, though. You bottled that, didn't you?'

The second man advanced into the room, and it was only then that Maggie noticed he was carrying what looked like a short metal pole in the hand that Samil couldn't see. The two men were both well over six feet tall, Samil having the edge. The newcomer's perfectly cut blond hair was at odds with his muddy jeans and boots, and the look of fury on his face in stark contrast with the controlled arrogant stare of Samil, whose chiselled features and thick bottom lip appeared to be set in concrete. Only his intense blue eyes showed that he was alive, burning every surface they touched.

'Invictus was right about you,' the second man said. 'You're the real deal. The dark triad of personality disorders all combined in one person. Psychopath, narcissist, Machiavellian. You've got it all. But you're a user. And I'm sick of being used.'

He continued to advance. It wasn't until he was about six feet away that Samil seemed to notice the metal bar. He didn't hesitate. The taser came up, and Maggie saw the laser sight light up the other man's chest. The two probes came flying out and there was a scream as the man fell to the floor.

Duncan flew across the room, the knife in his hand, running towards Maggie. She drew in a breath and closed her eyes. This was it. But then he was behind her, behind the pillar to which she was attached, and suddenly her hands were free.

'Go, Maggie. Go *now*,' he whispered urgently.

Maggie wanted to ask what he was going to do, but she knew their best chance was for her to escape and raise the alarm. Samil would have to reload the taser, and Duncan might be able to get to him first. If they both made a run for it, he would be after them like a shot.

She couldn't see Samil and the other man; the wide pillar she had been tied to shielded them from her view. She walked backwards across the vast expanse of open floor as slowly and silently as she could, keeping the pillar between her and the two men.

Duncan had moved to the far side of the room, and she knew he would distract Samil if he needed to. The man on the floor was groaning, which helped cover any sound Maggie made. Samil thought she was safely tied up, and he had enough to contend with, dealing with his partner and Duncan, who still had the knife.

Maggie made it to the far side of the room. Flattening herself against the bare brick walls and keeping to the shadows, she made her way on tiptoe across to the staircase. She wanted to run, but knew she mustn't. Even if he didn't hear her, the atmosphere in the room would change somehow and Samil would know. So she took it slow and steady. If he turned she would run. She was far enough away to make it. Duncan was goading Samil while the taser was useless and he had the knife. What he planned to do with it, Maggie didn't know. Samil was a good five inches taller than Duncan, and he had the metal bar that the other man had brought with him. Even with the knife, she didn't think her husband would come off the better of the two.

She reached the top of the stairs and turned to go down backwards. She didn't want any surprises. This way, she could watch to see if Samil came after her. But there was nothing more than a yell from above. She thought it was Samil's voice, but she couldn't be certain.

With a sigh of relief she reached the bottom of the stairs and turned.

Outlined against the backdrop of the open loading bay door stood a man, arms by his side, legs apart, ready to catch her if she ran.

60

Every nerve ending on Maggie's body was prickling with fear. Surely there wasn't another one? But what about William – the man Duncan had been chatting with all these years on the site, the man who Maggie was sure had led Samil back to Duncan?

The man in the entrance raised his hand, and she realised that he was putting a finger to his lips, as if to say 'Shh.'

Maggie stood still, not sure what to do. Suddenly and silently the empty loading bay filled with people dressed in black, moving stealthily towards her. All she could see were their dark silhouettes. The one she had seen first crept towards her. She bit back a scream.

'Maggie,' he said, his voice so low that she could barely hear it, but not a hissing whisper that would travel further. 'It's okay. Police.'

She wanted to run towards him, but he held up his hand, palm out, to stop her. She understood why. The floor was scattered with detritus accumulated over the years. She couldn't afford to make a noise.

The man made his way silently across the floor, using the faint beam from a shielded torch to show the way without lighting up the room.

'Josh is safe, Maggie.' She knew instantly who this was and how much he understood. She bit back a sob of relief.

'They've got a girl up there,' she said, her mouth pressed against his ear. He nodded and she realised he already knew. That was why they wanted to be so quiet. If the two men heard them coming, they could use Leo as a bargaining tool to get out of there.

His head came back down to hers. 'We're waiting for a backup team. We need the place surrounded and there are too many windows. Five minutes, and they won't be going anywhere.'

Maggie felt a jolt of shock. Duncan was in there. What was going to happen? If they caught him now, everything was going to have to come out. She felt helpless and no longer knew what outcome she was hoping for.

The man she now recognised as Tom Douglas put his arm gently around her shoulders and led her towards the door. A thought flashed through Maggie's mind. If only she had told him everything when he had come to see her, perhaps all of this could have been avoided. But it was too late to think like that. Behind her, she heard nothing but sensed the movement of bodies, climbing the stairs silently to the room above.

She signalled to the detective that he needed to bend his ear to her lips. 'Ambulance,' she said softly. He looked at her as if to ask where she was hurt. 'Not me,' she mouthed. His eyes grew wide and strangely frightened. But she had no time to query that as he handed her over to a uniformed policeman, squeezed her arm and moved silently back into the loading bay, heading for the stairs.

❖

The young policeman walked Maggie outside towards a police car, speaking quietly into his radio as he moved.

'Let the family know that we've got the mother. Yes, Mrs Taylor's with me. Let them know she's safe, will you.' He disconnected as they reached the car.

'Tell me about Josh. Do you know where he is?' she asked, pulling at the policeman's arm as his attention was diverted by some activity at the end of the street.

'Sorry, miss,' he said. 'I don't know anything about Josh, but as soon as we're sorted here I'll find out for you.'

He glanced back towards the end of the street, where a crowd seemed to be gathering, clearly interested in what was happening.

Two officers were manning a temporary barrier, but one or two people had broken through, phones at the ready to take photos.

'Can I put you in the police car?' the policeman said. 'I need to see what those idiots are doing at the top of the road. We could do without their interference.' He opened the car door for her.

'Thanks, officer,' Maggie said. 'I'm going to stand in the fresh air for a moment. It seems a long time since I was able to breathe.'

'Shit. I'm not supposed to leave you, but I can't let that lot near the building.'

'I'm not going anywhere. I'm the victim, the one who escaped, remember.'

'I know.' He started to reverse down the street, talking to her and checking over his shoulder. 'Well, stay there, and if you see anybody, get in the car and lock it. I'll be right back,' he said, turning round and jogging down the street.

Maggie leaned against the side of the car, watching the policeman as he ran towards the onlookers, but thinking only of Josh. Tom Douglas had said he was safe, and she had to believe him. *Thank God*. All she wanted now was to get home to her children and keep them safe.

She thought back to the decision she had been about to make. *Kill me*, she had been going to say. She had known she couldn't watch Duncan kill somebody else, but equally she wouldn't have been able to watch Samil kill Duncan. She had been going to take the coward's way out.

She felt her legs turn to jelly and pulled the car door wide to get in. Before she had the chance to move, a hard body slammed into hers, flattening her against the police car, a hand whipping up to cover her mouth. Maggie felt strong arms dragging her back into the shadows. She couldn't breathe. The hand clamped over Maggie's mouth felt rough and hard.

'Ssshh. Maggie, it's me.'

It was no more than a harsh whisper against her ear, but

a voice she recognised. She froze, unable to resist or to move away from his grasp.

'Quiet. They'll hear you. I got away down an old fire escape before they surrounded the place. The police don't need to know I was here. Don't say anything, Maggie. I love you. Trust me just for a little longer. Please, Maggie. For our children.'

Maggie saw the policeman turn back towards where he had left her. He stopped, stared and then started to jog back.

She felt a small push in the back as Duncan let go of her. Maggie stumbled out of the shadows back towards the waiting police car, then turned briefly to look over her shoulder.

There was nobody there.

61

Pleased as he was that Maggie Taylor was safe, Tom was filled with a sense of hopelessness. If an ambulance was needed so urgently, Leo had to be in a bad way. *Why hadn't he done more?*

He had quickly pulled a team together as soon as they had realised that of all the places Adam Mellor might have chosen from his family's portfolio, one stood out as the most obvious of the small number of currently deserted properties. No buildings opposite, right by the canal, and it had what appeared to be a loading bay. They could have searched them all, but Tom had taken a punt by bringing the team here and sending a couple of uniforms to check the other buildings from the outside. He had been right.

Now the team leader was at the top of the stairs, trying to get a visual on the two men. If they were too close to Leo, who knew what they would do. There was shouting coming from the room – it sounded as if they had noticed Maggie Taylor had gone and they were blaming each other.

As Tom reached the top of the stairs he saw that there was a sort of window in the door to the room. It looked like it was made of plastic rather than glass and was scratched and filthy, but it was clear enough for them to be able to judge the moment.

The team leader was holding up a gloved hand, telling them all to wait. Tom couldn't stand it. He needed to get to Leo, but he knew that at this moment he had to leave this to the specialists.

Suddenly the hand dropped, the door was flung open, and six policemen flew through the doors, shouting at the tops of their voices, 'Police, police. Stay where you are. Don't move.'

The team leader had chosen the perfect moment. One man was on the floor, the other kneeling down with his hands around his neck, shaking him. Before they were able to struggle to their feet, the two fastest policemen were on them.

Tom scanned the darkened room, lit only by two dim fluorescent tubes, buzzing and crackling as they flickered. His eyes flashed around, looking for signs of Leo. And then he saw a dark patch halfway across the huge pillared space. A black mound among scraps of debris.

'Dear God,' he whispered. He ran. He didn't care about the two scumbags who had done this to Leo. All he cared about was getting to her.

He skidded to a halt, falling to his knees at her side. His voice caught in his throat, but he had to speak to her, to let her know she was safe.

'Leo? Leo, it's Tom. You're safe now, love. We're going to take care of you.'

He gently eased the damp fabric away from her mouth and wet the cloth again, trying in vain to cool the burning skin. *What had they done?*

'I'm just going to check you, to see what we can do to make you more comfortable.'

Tom lifted his head and shouted to nobody in particular, 'Where's that fucking ambulance!' then his attention went back to Leo.

Gently he pulled back the sleeve of the arm that appeared to be attached to one of the pillars. He bit back a gasp of horror. Leo couldn't know how bad this was.

Her arm was so swollen that the plastic tie securing her wrist was almost completely hidden under the pus-filled, hot flesh that surrounded it. The end of the tie was attached to a chain looped around the pillar, but he couldn't cut the plastic without cutting Leo.

Tom leaped to his feet and raced across the room.

'You bastards. You fucking bastards. Where are the keys?'

Tom turned to one of the policeman. 'Give me your baton.' The policeman hesitated. 'That's an order, Constable.' Reluctantly the PC handed over his baton.

Tom walked towards Adam Mellor, the weaker-looking of the two. He pushed his face right up to Mellor's and shouted, 'Give me the fucking keys, or I'll break both your legs.'

❖

From across the room, close to Leo, Becky watched in horror. She stood up and raced towards Tom. The team leader had started to move too, but Tom had halted him with a warning glance.

'Tom,' Becky said, her voice strong. 'Leave it.'

'Not until this piece of shit tells me what he's done with the keys. Butt out, Becky. You,' he said, waving the baton close to Adam's face. 'I am looking for an excuse to hit you, and hit you hard. Don't give me one.'

Becky didn't know what to do. She didn't want to undermine her boss, but he was in danger of getting himself into serious trouble here.

She heard a groan from behind her and turned. Leo was looking at her. She wanted something, and Becky ran back to her side and fell to her knees.

'Leo, I'm Becky. I work with Tom. We're trying to find the keys so we can get you out of here.'

Leo tried to speak. Becky squeezed some water between her sore, swollen lips from a piece of silk lying beside a bottle of water.

Finally Becky made out one word: 'Keys.'

'I know. We're trying to find them.'

Leo made a glugging noise in the back of her throat, and Becky gave her some more water. She glanced up at Tom. He was waving the baton at the two men.

'Desk,' Leo said. At least, that's what Becky thought she said. Becky looked around her. The space was pretty empty, just some odd bits and pieces of broken furniture. But it was a huge space, and there were areas deep in darkness.

Becky pulled a torch out of her pocket and flashed it around. There was an alcove at the far end of the room and Becky ran towards it. In it stood an old metal desk. She frantically pulled at each of the drawers shining the torch inside. In the top left-hand drawer was a small bunch of keys.

'*Tom!*' she yelled as loudly as she could. '*Leave it!* I've got the keys.' She was running as she shouted, and she saw Tom spin round towards her.

He dropped the baton on the floor and ran back towards Leo. Becky threw the keys to him as he crouched down next to his ex-girlfriend.

'Leo,' he said, 'we can't take the plastic tie off your wrist, love, because we need a surgeon to look at it. But we can detach the chain. Becky, I need you to support her hand, because if it drops and hits the floor, it's going to hurt like hell.'

Becky watched as Tom undid the chain securing Leo's leg, and then found the key to detach the other end to the one leading to her arm. 'You ready?' he asked.

Becky gently held Leo's outstretched arm, one hand support-ing it just below the elbow, the other under her hand. She could feel the throbbing heat coming through, and it was only then that she saw the sutures, pus oozing freely from around the puncture wounds; only then did she realise what they had done, and why Tom was more furious than she had ever seen him.

As he undid the chain, Leo's arm fell like a dead weight onto Becky's hands. Leo gave a small groan, and then Tom was by her side.

'We're going to wait here, Leo, until the paramedics arrive and can give your arm some support. Hang on, darling. Hang on.'

Without changing his position by Leo's side, he swivelled his head.

'Get those bastards out of my sight.' Becky saw Tom look at the team leader and mouth, 'Sorry.'

The policeman shrugged as if to say, 'About what?' and pushed one of the two cuffed men towards the door.

Tom turned back to Leo and she heard him whisper, 'It's over now.'

Only it wasn't.

62

The ride in the ambulance had been agonising for Tom. He hadn't missed the looks exchanged between the two paramedics when they saw the state of Leo, so he told Becky to deal with the two scumbags who had put her in this dreadful state. He wasn't going to leave Leo's side until he knew she was going to be okay.

A forensics team had now taken over the mill, searching for evidence of the other killings. Tom wanted these two to be put away for life, but he had the horrible feeling that Leo's abduction and unlawful imprisonment might be the only crime they wouldn't get away with. Maggie's abduction too, but that wouldn't add much to the tally. He had nothing but his own personal certainty to go on that Adam Mellor and Ben Coleman were the killers.

Leo had been given something for the pain, and she had drifted off into either sleep or unconsciousness, Tom wasn't sure which.

The ambulance pulled into the accident and emergency bay at Manchester Royal Infirmary, the very hospital where Ben Coleman had operated on people daily, and at that thought Tom vowed to have somebody check out his mortality rate. A man like him might pick and choose who lived and who died.

As the ambulance doors sprang open, Tom moved out of the way so that Leo could be carried into the hospital, and he followed close behind.

A team had clearly been alerted that she was coming in, and a doctor spoke to Tom. 'Leave her with us for now, Mr Douglas. It would be helpful if you could let the guys at reception have some details. We'll let you know where we're at as soon as we can.'

'Her arm—' Tom started rather uselessly.

'We know about her arm. The paramedics called it through. If you'll excuse me, I need to get in there.'

With that, he patted Tom on the upper arm and turned towards the doors that Leo had disappeared through. It felt strange to Tom to be offered comfort and support. That was usually his job.

He gave the receptionist Leo's details and went into the waiting room, unable to sit for more than five minutes at a time. He had called Becky once, and she told him everything was in hand. Mellor and Coleman would be locked up for a long time whether or not the police could get the murders to stick. There was time to find the rest of the evidence they needed.

Becky also confirmed they had taken Maggie Taylor home. She had been in no fit state to give a statement and was so desperate to get back to Josh after all he had been through, they had decided she would be more coherent the next day. They had plenty to hold Ben Coleman and Adam Mellor in custody without relying on Maggie's statement.

The next forty-five minutes were the longest Tom thought he had ever spent. He had no idea what was happening, but he knew enough not to go bothering people with demands for updates. The A&E department was stretched enough as it was.

The doors behind which Leo had disappeared sprang open and a trolley was pushed through. Tom could see that it was Leo, and the same doctor walked towards him.

'Mr Douglas, we're taking Leo up to intensive care. We've managed to remove the plastic tie from her wrist, but her arm is, as you saw, acutely inflamed.'

'Because the bastard sutured her arm to the tie.' Tom spat the words out in disgust.

'It was brutal,' the doctor admitted. 'She's very poorly and also severely dehydrated, but we've given her a high level of antibiotics and she's a strong young woman. I'm sure she'll fight off the infection, but we need to keep an eye on her. Her breathing isn't good at the moment, and her blood pressure is dangerously low. We need to make sure she doesn't go into septic shock.'

'Can I see her?'

'I can direct you to the ICU. Speak to the team there about a visit. She'll have her own cubicle, but she's heavily sedated so don't expect to get any response from her at the moment.'

Tom held out his hand and the young doctor shook it.

'It must have been a tough night for you,' he said to Tom. 'I don't often see things as gruesome as that.'

Tom nodded. 'At least she's alive, which is more than can be said for some of the other victims of the two shits that did this to her. Take it from me, I'm not going to stop until I've caught each and every person who had the slightest thing to do with this.'

63

The burly policeman who was tasked with driving Maggie home was in a chatty mood. He was one of those men who was comfortable with life, and when he wasn't talking he was humming a tune under his breath. How he managed to keep so cheerful in his job, Maggie didn't know, and more than anything she wanted him to shut up. Every inch of her body ached from the stress of holding herself together, and if the drive had gone on for much longer she thought she might have screamed at him to be quiet.

She was desperate to see Josh and to do whatever she could to repair the inevitable damage that had been inflicted on her child that night. He had heard every word she had said to Samil, and much as she hadn't wanted that to happen it had seemed a better option than Josh staying with her. Imagine if he had seen what they had done to that poor girl Leo? Or, Maggie couldn't help thinking, if he had seen how his daddy had seemed quite willing to kill her. She shuddered at the memory.

When the police car pulled up on the drive of Maggie's home, the policeman insisted on seeing her into the house, to make sure all was well there. As she opened the front door and walked into the hall, Maggie was still trying to convince him that he didn't need to come in.

The sound of her voice must have penetrated the sitting room, because the door was flung open and she was hit hard in the chest by Josh's bullet of a head. He was sobbing with relief.

'It's okay, Joshy. Everything's okay now, sweetheart. It's all over – they caught the bad guys.'

She hugged him tightly and then crouched down so she could look him in the eye. 'And they caught them because of *you*, Josh. The police told me you were really, really brave – a bit of a superhero.'

Her sister appeared in the doorway and looked at Maggie, tears running down her cheeks. Maggie wanted to pour out her heart, tell her sister everything. But she couldn't. That would make her sister into a criminal too, because Maggie knew she was going to have to lie to the police, and that didn't fill her with any pride or joy.

'Everything okay here, ma'am?' the policeman asked Suzy with a smile. 'Would you like me to check around?'

Maggie declined the offer. Samil and his friend were under lock and key, so they were safe. The policeman was kind, but she just wanted him out of her house so she could focus on her family, and he finally took his leave.

As Maggie closed the front door she turned to her sister. 'Thanks for being here, Suze,' she said, which brought fresh tears to her sister's eyes. 'Let's all go in the sitting room and have a chat, shall we?'

Maggie didn't want to pack Josh off to bed yet. He needed time to settle, and she needed time to be with him, to block out the rest of the night. She wasn't surprised to walk into the sitting room and see Lily curled up asleep on the sofa. Maggie looked at Suzy.

'I wanted us all together in one room. I know she should be in bed, but…'

'It's fine. I'm glad she's here.'

'Shall I make you a cup of tea or something to eat?' Suzy asked.

'No, but can you pour me a very large Scotch, do you think?'

Suzy laughed, thinking she was joking.

'Check my coat pocket,' Maggie said. She'd had to beg the policeman who drove her home to lend her some money, and stop at an off-licence so she could buy the whisky. Now she realised she had forgotten to give the money back to him. She felt a stab of guilt and for a second marvelled that she still had any conscience at all given the lies she was going to have to tell.

'What about you, Josh?'

'Could I have some juice, please?'

'Of course you can.'

And then Josh asked the question. The one question she hadn't yet prepared an answer for.

'When's Daddy coming home?'

It had taken over an hour to reassure Josh that he was safe, and although he was still anxious he was also totally exhausted, so Maggie had tucked both him and Lily into her double bed. She wanted to spend the whole night with them next to her where she could feel their precious bodies warm against hers. She read them a story to settle them and made her way downstairs for a last much-needed drink.

Suzy was still sitting where she had left her, staring into the flames of the decrepit old wood burner that had come with the house. Maggie had loved it on sight, and when filled with flames, as now, it was so comforting.

'How are you feeling?' her sister asked. 'I can't imagine everything you've been through tonight. It's more than anybody should have to face in a lifetime.'

If only she knew, thought Maggie.

'The whisky's a good analgesic.' She tried again to smile, but she was feeling wired with adrenaline, and at some point she was going to crash.

'I thought you answered Josh's question about Duncan well, but I could tell that you don't know what to say. Do you want to talk about it?'

'Duncan's not coming back. I haven't worked out how to

explain to the kids. I need some time. But he's not coming back.'

Suzy looked at her, and Maggie could see the understanding in her eyes. She looked away.

They were both silent for a while, and Maggie knew her sister was waiting for her to speak. She felt the words forming, and then they stuck in her throat. She couldn't tell her. She couldn't make her a party to all of this horror.

64

Monday

'Is one of you Tom?' A young nurse stood at the entrance to the waiting area. It was five in the morning. Ellie and Max had arrived a few hours previously, but none of them had been allowed to see Leo.

'I'm Tom,' he said, standing up. 'Is she okay?'

'She's a bit groggy, but she's asking for you.'

Tom had started to cross the room towards her cubicle when the young doctor pushed his way through double pale-blue swing doors and strode towards them.

'Sorry to interrupt, but before you see Leo, I'd like to give you an update. We're worried about her arm. When she came in we treated her with antibiotics but we were concerned about bacterial infection – necrotising fasciitis. We took a tissue sample, and the tests show that the bacteria is present, so we need to remove some of the tissue in her arm to stop it spreading. We'll do whatever we can to save her arm.'

Ellie started to cry. As a nurse herself, she knew exactly what this meant, and understood how serious it was.

'Go, Tom,' Ellie said through her sobs. 'Go and see her. I'll be in in a minute.'

Tom swallowed and tried to fix his face into a neutral expression with a trace of a smile to welcome Leo back to consciousness. The nurse showed him into the cubicle and kept a discreet distance, checking the monitors.

'Hey,' he said, sitting down next to the bed, close to her face.

344

'Good to have you back with us, Leo.' He reached out a hand and stroked the hair back from her face.

Leo made a noise deep in her throat.

'Don't try to speak, love. It's okay. You're safe.'

She made a gurgling noise in her throat. 'Got them?' He finally made out what she was trying to say and understood why she had wanted to see him.

'Yes, don't worry about a thing. We've got them.'

He leaned forward to kiss her on the forehead, and as he sat back down he heard a sound behind him.

'Tom?'

He turned his head.

'Louisa,' he responded, the emphasis on the second syllable as if surprised to see her here.

Louisa stepped fully into the cubicle. Dressed in scrubs, she looked as beautiful as she had when he had last seen her, but her face was neutral – her professional expression, Tom supposed.

'I'm going to be Leo's anaesthetist for the operation. Have you any questions you would like to ask me?'

'None, and it's not my place anyway. Her sister's outside, and she may have some.' He smiled, but before he could say another word, the phone in his pocket vibrated. He pulled it out. It was Becky.

'Sorry, but I'm going to have to take this.' He leaned over Leo again and whispered gently, 'Got to go, Leo, but I'll be back. I'll see you later.' He dropped another kiss on her forehead and turned to Louisa.

'Take good care of her, won't you?'

'Of course. We'll do our best to get her back to you as soon as possible.'

'I'll catch up with you later. Okay?'

For a moment Louisa's eyes met his as if she wanted to ask him a question, but instead she just nodded.

Tom went out into the corridor and answered his phone. 'What's up, Becky? I thought you would have charged them and gone home to bed by now.'

And then she told him about Ben Coleman's phone and the website they had found open on it.

65

This time last week Maggie had believed she had a happy family and a job she loved. In the space of a few days her life had become a nightmare. Now she would have to face questioning from the police. She knew they would want to talk to her about how she and Josh had been captured, and they would expect her to be nervous and edgy. But she felt constantly on the verge of vomiting.

It was going to be all right, though. It *had* to be all right, for the children.

Since they had got up Suzy had kept Josh and Lily occupied and fed, but to Maggie it felt as if the air in the kitchen was crackling with the tension spilling from her body. Duncan had told her not to mention him when the police came, but she didn't think she could do that. Surely the other two men would have said something? And what about the girl, Leo?

Maggie hoped and prayed the poor soul would survive, but would she remember there was a third man in the room? Would they think she was hallucinating?

She had spent the night writing lists of pros and cons – what she should tell, and what she shouldn't. It was impossible. Lying to the police went against the grain in every way possible. But how could she explain Duncan's involvement without telling them everything? Was she ready to do that?

She felt so emotionally battered and bruised that she didn't feel capable of logical thought. And what about everything that she had already kept from them? Was she any better than Duncan? If she had told them about the photo on Duncan's phone, would the second woman have been murdered?

But nobody else was going to die now. The two men were in custody. She didn't have to decide about Duncan that minute. She needed more time before condemning her husband to a long prison term. Time to *think*.

Maggie thought the two men were unlikely to mention Duncan. Samil had been adamant that the police wouldn't be able to pin the two recent murders on them, and they had certainly done a good job of cleaning the van. If they had left no traces, they could only be charged with kidnapping Leo and Maggie. Their treatment of Leo would result in a fairly heavy sentence, but if they were found guilty of the murder of two victims they would get life. The minute they involved Duncan, the question of the murders twelve years ago would come up, and maybe they hadn't done such a good job of covering their tracks then. So logic suggested that Duncan's name would be kept out of it altogether.

Her head was so muddled, so confused. It seemed she never had a chance to work out what to do before the next horror struck. She felt as if she was being dragged along on a riptide and wasn't actively making any decisions at all. The horror of the one decision she *had* been about to make struck her. How could she even have considered abandoning her own children? Choosing to be the one to die because it was the easiest option? Josh and Lily needed her. Her body shuddered involuntarily.

Now she was out of time. The doorbell rang. The police were here.

Maggie had to let them in even though she wanted to bury her head in a pillow and sleep until this nightmare was over. She took a deep breath and let it out slowly, hoping her tense limbs would relax. It had no effect. She opened the door and, in a voice that was barely audible even to herself, invited in the two detectives. She indicated the door to the sitting room and let them lead the way. For a moment she caught hold of the doorjamb, certain her legs were going to let her down.

'Mrs Taylor, I'm so sorry for the terrible events last night. You must be feeling dreadful,' DI Robinson said.

Maggie glanced at Tom Douglas, and his eyes seemed to pierce the thin shield that she was erecting around her conscience.

'Please, have a seat,' Maggie said.

Maggie was about to offer them a drink so she could escape for a few minutes' respite in the kitchen when her sister popped her head in the door and smiled warmly at the police officers. 'Sorry to disturb, but would you like a cup of coffee?'

Both detectives looked as exhausted as Maggie felt, and seemed grateful for the offer of coffee.

Maggie lowered herself into a chair, feeling twice her age. Every bone in her body ached, and her head felt too heavy for her neck.

'How's Josh this morning?' Tom asked.

'He's okay, thanks. He seems to be coping, although who knows how much he's hiding.'

'Well, it's partly thanks to him that we found you last night. We have two men in custody, as I expect you realise. The one who abducted you and Josh is Ben Coleman. He's a surgeon at Manchester Royal. The second man is Adam Mellor, a corporate lawyer. But they're not talking. They're saying nothing at all, in fact.'

Maggie realised that her mouth had dropped open. A *doctor*? She should have realised when she had seen the sutures holding the plastic tie in place, but that a doctor could have let that poor woman suffer in such a way was beyond belief. They hadn't mentioned Duncan, though. That made her decision easier – or at least it did for now.

Becky Robinson was speaking, and Maggie forced her concentration back onto the conversation.

'At the moment all we have on them is yours and Josh's abduction, and the unlawful holding of Leonora Harris – the woman who I believe you saw there before we arrived.'

'How is she?' Maggie asked.

'She's not great, but they're operating on her arm today, and we'll see where she goes from there.'

Maggie noticed an extra layer of strain around Tom's eyes as he spoke, and Becky gave him a sympathetic glance. Obviously this Leonora girl meant something to him.

'So what can I do for you?'

'We believe these men are guilty of at least two murders as well as the abductions,' Tom went on. 'Very possibly they are guilty of other murders, including two here in Manchester twelve years ago. We think they killed the two recent victims in the mill where we found you, and then transported them in the back of Adam Mellor's van to the sites where their bodies were found. The van's clean, but we're searching every inch of the mill.'

Maggie had been in that van, sat where those girls' bodies had lain. An image flashed into her head of the three of them together. Two dead, one waiting to die. She mentally shook herself as Tom Douglas continued.

'It's possible that they've been thorough enough to cover their tracks – as thorough as they have been at cleaning the van – so that's why we have to make sure the abduction case against them is watertight.'

Maggie's body tensed. These men had to go down for a long time or she would never feel safe again.

Tom continued: 'We need you to tell us everything that happened from when you arrived at the park to pick up Josh after his football. We know from Josh that's when it all started.'

And so Maggie filled them in on everything from the moment she first saw the two men waiting for her until the moment she stood by the police car. Or almost everything. Would Leo remember that there was another man in the room? She doubted it. If the men weren't talking, what risk was she taking?

The questioning went on. Maggie felt removed from it all, as if it were happening to somebody else and she was merely an observer. She gave no thought to her answers and was barely aware that she was talking.

Tom jolted her back to reality. 'We're concerned about your ongoing safety, I'm afraid, and we do need you to be extra vigilant.' He was leaning forward and resting his forearms on his thighs.

'Why? You've caught them, haven't you?'

'We have two men in custody, but we have reason to believe there's a third man.'

She swallowed. *How did they know?* 'What makes you think that?' she asked, her voice, even to her own ears, sounding like stone scratching glass.

Becky took over. 'We don't know if he's involved in the current crimes, but we strongly suspect that a third man, Michael Alexander, was involved in the other unlawful killings we mentioned – the ones that took place twelve years ago.'

Maggie couldn't speak. She wanted to, but her throat seemed to have seized up.

Becky continued to explain their concerns. 'Michael Alexander went off the radar about twelve years ago. He told his university tutor that he was going home to nurse his sick mother.'

Maggie felt herself relax a little. They didn't know where he was.

'That doesn't sound like something a murderer would do,' she said.

'Well, you never know with psychopaths,' Tom Douglas added. 'Sometimes they seem like the most caring people, although it's all a carefully constructed act. In any case, it wasn't true. His mother was an alcoholic and died when he was eight. He'd been in care since he was five.'

Maggie felt the room spinning and she gripped onto the arms of the chair.

'Are you okay?' Becky asked.

Maggie closed her eyes and tried to get some degree of composure back.

'Sorry, I've not eaten much in the last twenty-four hours, and I've drunk too much coffee.'

'Shall I ask your sister to join us?' Becky asked. 'If you need somebody with you, I could look after your kids.'

Maggie quickly shook her head. 'No, I'm fine.' She turned to look at Tom. 'Why do you think he's still a danger if he's not done anything in the last twelve years?'

Tom and Becky looked at each other for a moment.

'We didn't say that,' Tom said. 'You're probably aware that the police often hold back some information about murders, sometimes so that we can differentiate between copycat murders and repeat offences – serial murders, in other words.'

Maggie felt herself nodding, although she didn't feel she had any control over her body at all any more.

'There are some similarities between the murders here in Manchester and another series of deaths down south. I can't go into detail, but that, coupled with some evidence retrieved from Ben Coleman's phone, is enough to make us strongly suspect that Michael Alexander is involved.'

Tom Douglas continued to talk, but Maggie was far away. She remembered her shock when Samil – Ben Coleman, as she now knew he was – had read out the fantasy death of Tamsin from his phone. Duncan's fantasy. She had recognised it, but pushed it from her mind.

It was a mode of death that had become infamous in Suffolk over the past few years.

The murders had begun with a neighbour of Maggie and Duncan's. The wife of the couple concerned had liked a drink, and Maggie had seen the look of disgust on Duncan's face many times, but the husband seemed relaxed about it. Then there had been an embarrassing occasion at a party when the woman had been so drunk she had fallen over, knocking into a display cupboard holding a number of pieces of antique glass. The doors of the cupboard had shattered and the wife had cut her arm. But worse, most of the valuable glass had been broken too. Her husband had gone white. He had picked his wife up from where she was laughing hysterically on the floor and apologised profusely to the hosts, saying he would recompense them in any way that he could. Two days later, the woman was found floating in the Suffolk Broads. Drowned.

At first people assumed she had been drunk and had fallen in, but the police soon made it clear that it was murder. There were marks on her neck that indicated her head had been held under the water. The nature of the marks, and the fact that there were multiple bruises, suggested that she had been repeatedly held under the water. The husband was the obvious suspect but was cleared almost immediately.

And so began the reign of terror of the Teetotaller, as the killer became known. Four women, including Maggie's neighbour, had been found floating in the broads. Each of them had had a serious drink problem. Other women in the area had disappeared over the past few years, and at least two of them were suspected to be victims of the Teetotaller.

The detectives' words washed over Maggie after that, and she wanted to curl up in a ball. The fear and heartbreak of the past few days had been collecting inside her, gathering to form a bomb that was about to explode. And when it did she would have no means of stopping everything from gushing out, every little detail. She didn't know how long she could hang on. She no longer knew if she wanted to. But she couldn't tell them now because they would realise how much she had been hiding. She had failed to tell the police what she knew. Exactly as Duncan had all those years ago.

'We'd like to put a policeman in the house with you for your own safety,' Becky Robinson said, jolting her out of her reverie.

Maggie felt herself shaking her head. 'No, really. It's not necessary. My sister's husband is coming to stay. He's arriving any time now. And I want Josh to feel that everything's getting back to normal. I need him to stop worrying. We'll be fine.'

She listened to their arguments, but she couldn't let that happen. She knew what had to be done, and a policeman in the house would ruin everything.

The two detectives stood up. Tom was watching her carefully but she was sure he would put her distress down to a combination of the events of last night and concern about the third man. He gave her a sympathetic smile. 'We'll be needing a formal statement from you, but it's just procedure. The two men were caught with Leo, and they've no way of escaping justice for what they did to her.'

As Maggie opened the door to the hall, her sister was coming downstairs. She smiled at the two policemen.

'Thanks for the coffee, Mrs…?'

'Peters. Suzy Peters. Miss. And it was my pleasure.'

❖

'Tom, I don't mean to be a total wimp, but I'm going to have to go and have a couple of hours' kip. I don't need much, but I do need to revive myself. I can't think straight.'

Tom was glad Becky wasn't the one behind the steering wheel; her driving was erratic at the best of times. He looked at her now, and her cheeks were a washed-out grey colour with two pink spots, one on each side. She looked almost feverish.

'Me too. I need to go back to the hospital and see how Leo's doing as well, but we can leave the team to carry on hunting down our man.'

Becky turned to look at Tom, her head on one side.

'I know that look. What's going on in your head?' she asked.

'Maggie Taylor looks like the other three. That makes four potential victims. It's odd that they hadn't already killed Leo; their

MO seems to have been to kill and get rid within twenty-four hours. Logically, they were planning on sticking to three victims, which means that Leo might have been a reserve. But a reserve for *what*? Was Maggie the *real* victim? Was she the one they wanted to kill all along, with the other two killed to confuse us? And if that's the case, why would anybody want her dead? As a criminal lawyer she's potentially got more reason to be hated than most, but she's a defender, so that doesn't make much sense. That fact is, we don't know, and with my brain the way it is at the moment, I can't work it out.'

'Where's Maggie's husband supposed to be? Given what's happened, I was surprised she said her brother-in-law was coming to stay but no mention of her husband rushing to be by her side. She looked to have been knocked for six by the whole thing.'

'That's what I thought too. I'm going to have him checked out. She avoids talking about him, and there are no photos, even though there are plenty of her and the children. He could have left her, of course. Josh was uneasy about mentioning him as well. Anyway, forget about it all for a few hours and have a break. Coleman and Mellor have been processed so you deserve some rest. I'll be back this evening. What about you?'

'Oh, I'll be back. Four o'clock at the latest, bright-eyed and bushy-tailed.' Her voice was drifting off as she spoke.

'Just before you leave this earth for your world of dreams—' Tom saw a faint smile on Becky's lips, '—there was something that Maggie's sister said, something I felt should have meant something. Do you remember?'

Becky gave a small grunt, which could have meant anything. 'She said she was Miss, and Maggie had referred to her husband, but that's not particularly odd. People do that sometimes if they've been together for a while.'

'No, it was her name. Why does Suzy Peters mean something?'

But Becky was gone – dead to the world. It would have to wait.

66

Suzy took one look at her sister's face when the detectives left and ordered her to go and lie down. She didn't ask any questions, and for that Maggie was grateful.

Maggie lay on the bed, a throw over her legs, listening to the chatter of her children drifting up the stairs and managed to shut out all other thoughts for a few moments. Only Josh and Lily mattered. Then reality broke through her feeble defences. What was going to happen now? What did she *want* to happen?

She should have told the police everything, and then it would all have been over. But as she had listened to everything they said, she had found the idea of the truth impossible to deal with. A memory of last night in the mill struck her and her stomach lurched. She flung herself off the bed and into the en-suite bathroom, just making it in time for the meagre contents of her stomach to come hurtling up and out of her body as she thought of how it might all have ended; how she might have seen her husband advancing towards her with a knife if she had told him – as she'd intended to – that she had to be the one to die. Would he have killed her? She no longer knew the answer.

The spasm lasted no more than seconds but left her weak, her throat burning with acid. From her knees Maggie fell sideways onto her hip and rested her head against the cool wall tiles. Her weakened body was no longer able to hold back the horror that was pressing down on her. She lifted one leg and kicked the bathroom door firmly shut.

How had this happened to her? What had she done wrong?

She could no longer ignore what Tom Douglas had told her and had to face reality. They were looking for Michael Alexander. She knew who he was and had said nothing. She hadn't known what to say. She had tried more than once to open her mouth, but the words had drained away.

She rested her head on her bent knees and gave in to sobs that made her ribs ache.

Gradually the tears subsided. Maggie felt drained. She tried to push herself up from the floor, but the effort was almost too much. She got first to her knees, and then used the washbasin to pull herself upright. Using one hand against the wall for support, she made her way back into the bedroom and was staggered to find it was dark outside. A cold cup of tea was sitting by the bed.

She climbed onto the bed, crawled under the covers, and finally exhaustion won the battle.

The house was silent when Maggie woke up. The children must have gone to bed, and there was no light creeping under the door, suggesting Suzy was no longer up either. What time was it? She rolled onto her side and pressed the button on her mobile. It was after midnight. For a moment, the room was lit by the glow from her phone, and Maggie rolled over onto her other side as the light went out.

In that fraction of a second, she had seen something that set every nerve ending on fire. There was a man – there, in her room, sitting in the chair by the window.

The room was black again now, and she could see nothing. Maybe she was wrong. It could have been a shadow. But she knew it wasn't. It was him. For the first time she was scared of her own husband.

Her body was rigid, and of course he knew she was awake – he had seen her check the time. Was he going to speak?

He couldn't know she had seen him, though. It was a flicker

in time. Should she pretend to go back to sleep?

She heard movement – a slight shuffle, but not enough to indicate he was standing up. He was adjusting his position. Then there was a click, and the small reading lamp next to the chair came on. As the lamp rocked slightly, light and dark shapes moved around the room, swinging towards her and away again as if trying to capture her. But Maggie's eyes were glued to his face, one side brightly lit by the yellow glow of the lamp light, the other in deep shadow.

He didn't speak; Maggie didn't move.

His voice, when it came, was quiet. 'Shall I come to bed?'

Maggie's body jerked in response, and she quickly sat up, pulling her knees to her chest and wrapping her arms around them as if to protect herself. She couldn't answer.

'The police were here,' she said.

'That was inevitable. What did you tell them?'

Maggie looked at her husband and shook her head.

He smiled and leaned forward. 'I have a plan, Maggie. A plan that will save us all. But I need your help.'

Duncan sounded eager, excited almost. For a moment it felt like old times, with him coming up with a plan for a holiday or a day out. She thought back to the night before and his apparent indifference to killing the wounded girl. She had so many questions for him but somehow there was no point asking them. He would just lie. She knew that now.

He seemed to guess what she was thinking.

'I had nothing to do with the murder of those two women last week, you know.' Duncan's voice had an edge of irritation. 'Samil wanted revenge. On me. He wanted to punish me for not fulfilling my part of the bargain twelve years ago. I never agreed to kill his stepmother, Maggie. I need you to believe that. It would have been murder in cold blood, and I had nothing against the woman. I didn't think he meant it. How he knew I was back in Manchester, or about my connection to William, I really don't know. But I don't suppose I'll be able to ask him that now.'

Duncan paused, but Maggie made no response. She wanted him out of her room, out of her house, but she didn't know what would happen if she tried to insist.

Duncan's eyes narrowed. 'They killed the first two to scare me – and you. The third victim was going to be you, if I didn't do as they asked, which was to kill Leo in front of you. She apparently looked like you. The idea was to make it even more painful for you, although by the time we saw her, she was barely recognisable. They thought that would be the end of my life, because you would never want me near you again. But I didn't do it, Maggie, so why are you so cold with me?'

Maggie needed some thinking time. She risked a question, not really caring about the answer.

'So where were you when the woman was killed last Wednesday – the one whose picture was on your phone – because I know you'd finished your job long before you had to pick the children up?'

Duncan walked to the bed and sat down beside her. He reached out to hold her hand, but she jerked away from him.

He sighed. 'I went to buy you some flowers. I knew there were problems ahead, and I wanted you to know how much I love you.'

She looked at him. There had been no flowers.

'Stupid fucking woman in front of me in the shop couldn't make her mind up, so I ran out of time. I didn't want to be late for the kids.'

Maggie had no words left. Who was this man?

Duncan reached out a hand to stroke her hair, winding it around his fingers. She shivered.

'Sorry about the flowers,' he said, pulling her head back to lay bare her throat.

She flinched as she felt his lips touch her flesh.

67

Tom felt better that evening after a couple of hours' sleep, and he and Becky had both returned to the incident room at around the same time. The capture of Adam Mellor and Ben Coleman had given everybody a huge boost twenty-four hours ago, but now the adrenaline rush had gone there was a sense of deflation in the room. The fact that Tom believed there was a third man out there wasn't for the moment creating the buzz that it should have done.

Tom knew there were enough people in the team sorting through every scrap of evidence to track down Michael Alexander and he wasn't really adding anything.

'I'm going back to the hospital,' he said to Becky. 'Don't hang about for too long – it's probably better to make an early start tomorrow.'

Becky shook her head. 'No, I'm fine. I got about four hours' sleep earlier, so I'm okay. You go – see how Leo's doing.'

Tom nodded his thanks and headed for the door, turning as he went. 'Call me if there's anything at all. Seriously, Becky. I want to know straight away.'

He strode out of the building towards his car, head down against a biting wind, and the frustration swept through him again. He knew he was missing something, but it wouldn't come to him. The streets of Manchester were quiet. Maybe the cold was keeping everybody indoors, or perhaps it was later than he thought. Still, he had been told at the hospital that he could call in any time. Leo's operation had gone well, but she was still in an

ICU cubicle. As long as he didn't disturb either her or anybody else, he knew they would let him sit with her for a while.

Arriving at the hospital, he walked head down, hands in pockets, down the quiet corridors of the sleeping building, passing nurses and other staff going briskly about their business.

'Tom?'

He lifted his head at a voice he recognised and smiled. 'Louisa. It's good to see you,' he said, meaning every word. She looked exhausted, though, and he realised that her job must be every bit as demanding as his own.

'I hear the operation on Leo's arm went well,' he said.

'Yes. I think your girlfriend will be out of ICU soon and on the road to recovery. I'm pleased for you both. Sorry, Tom, I need to go. A patient.' She gave him a tired but gentle smile.

'I…' he started, but she didn't hear him. 'Bugger,' he muttered to her retreating back.

Leo was asleep when he got to her cubicle. Her arm was bandaged, but the skin on her face looked a much healthier shade. He decided to stay for a while. It was peaceful, and maybe he could get his thoughts together.

He hadn't intended to doze off, sitting upright in a not particularly comfortable hospital chair, but that was what happened, and he had no idea how long he slept. When he eventually surfaced, Leo was awake and watching him.

'Hi, sleepy head,' she said, her voice still hoarse from the ordeal of the last few days. 'Thanks for coming to see me.'

'You couldn't keep me away,' he said, reaching over to stroke her good arm.

They talked in little more than whispers about anything and everything. Everything, that is, except the last few days. That would need time, and it would have to be on Leo's terms. Tom knew how she had been taken and where she had been kept. The police had the perpetrators in the custody suite, charged and ready to appear before the magistrates in the morning. She didn't need to say another word until she was ready.

'Tom,' she whispered, 'do you think you could do something for me?'

'Of course. What do you need?'

'Before all this happened I was seeing somebody.'

'I know. Julian Richmond. Nice guy.'

Leo looked startled.

Tom laughed. 'No, Leo, I wasn't having you watched. When you went missing I spoke to him, that's all.'

For a moment she looked sad. 'It really is over for us, isn't it?'

Tom nodded. 'You'll always be special to me, but we can't go back. We'd probably slip back into how we used to be because that's what people do.'

'I know. I fucked it up.' The regret was clear in Leo's eyes.

'We both fucked it up. I expected too much, too soon. But what about Julian?'

'I like him. Quite a lot, actually. Since you…well, I've been scared, but he seems to get that. His ex-wife was a real cow. Much worse than yours.'

Tom smiled. Kate was okay. As long as she had plenty of money and could live the life she wanted, she didn't make too many waves, and they got on fine.

'Do you think you could contact Julian for me?' Leo asked. 'He may never want to see me again, but I'd like to know.'

'Of course he'll want to see you – I'm sure of it – but I'll call him in the morning. Does he know you're okay?'

'I don't know. I got Ellie to log onto my Facebook account for me, and let the small number of friends I have on there know that I'm safe and well, but he's not big on Facebook, I don't think.'

Leo carried on chatting, but Tom stopped listening. Facebook. That was it. Bloody Facebook.

❖

Four cups of black coffee in the space of three hours, and Becky was buzzing. It was one in the morning, and she knew she should go home, but she had a feeling that Michael Alexander – presuming he was still alive – might show his hand.

Every policeman in Manchester was looking for the guy, but the trouble was, nobody knew what he looked like. They didn't even know if he was here.

Becky's mobile rang as one of the PCs on the team pushed a note under her nose.

'Becky Robinson,' she said, stifling a yawn and trying to read the note at the same time as listening on her phone.

'Becky, it's Tom. Where are you?'

'In the incident room. Why?' Becky scanned the note, her eyes widening slightly. 'Tom—' But he was already talking.

'What was the name of the woman who was trying to track Michael Alexander through his ex-foster mother?'

'Just a minute,' she answered, keen to get this question answered so she could tell him her news. 'Grace Peters.'

'Bollocks. How could I forget that?' he said.

'Why? Oh, shit. I've got it now. Maggie Taylor's sister! Suzy Peters.'

'Check out Maggie's full name. If Grace isn't her middle name, check out everybody else in the family. I'm coming back to the office.'

'I think you'll want to hear this, too. The only records of Duncan Taylor that we can trace start twelve years ago – at the same time as Michael Alexander disappeared. And there's something else. I'll give you two guesses where the Taylors used to live.'

Tom didn't need two guesses. Suffolk. Where, according to the National Crime Agency's database, four women had been drowned and a symbol carved into their thighs.

Tom was silent for a moment, and Becky waited. She could almost hear his brain ticking over. 'I have a feeling Maggie Taylor knows full well who her husband is. I just hope to God she listened to what we told her earlier.'

The phone went dead in Becky's hand.

❖

Ten minutes later the door to the incident room burst open, and Tom marched across to Becky.

'Well?' he said.

'Maggie Taylor – Grace Peters. Same person. She doesn't use Facebook really. Like I said before, it's an account set up to nosy at other people's info. She's liked a few groups, but nothing else. No posts, and she hasn't got any privacy settings because there's actually no information about her.'

'And she was checking on Michael Alexander?'

'According to Stacey Meagan, yes.'

Tom swivelled a chair and sat down to save Becky from craning to look up at him.

'If Maggie was trying to find out about him, that suggests she didn't know any of this either until recently.'

'After what we said to her this afternoon, she must be absolutely terrified now. Let's get her on the phone.'

Becky picked up her desk phone and punched in the numbers. The phone at the other end rang six times and then went to answerphone. Becky glanced at Tom.

'Try it again. If they're all asleep we might have woken them up.'

Becky dialled again, and this time the phone was answered on the fourth ring.

'Hello.' The voice sounded hesitant.

'Who am I speaking to?' Becky asked.

'This is Suzy Peters. Can I help you?'

'It's DI Becky Robinson, Miss Peters. Can I speak to your sister, please?'

'DI Robinson, it's the middle of the night.'

'I know. I need to speak to her, Suzy. It's urgent.'

There was a sigh from the other end of the phone. 'Give me a moment.'

Becky heard footsteps and then all was silent. She thought she heard a faint call of 'Maggie' but she might have been wrong. The footsteps came back, but the phone wasn't picked up, and she heard them retreat again. She looked at Tom and pulled a face.

There was a clatter as if the phone had been dropped and a muttered curse followed by a rustle.

'DI Robinson – Maggie's not here. I've searched the house, and her car's gone. I've no idea where she is.'

'Has your husband arrived yet, Suzy?' Becky asked, concern for this family giving her voice a clipped tone.

'My husband? I haven't got a husband. There's just me and Maggie's kids here. Why?'

Becky calmly told Suzy Peters to make sure all the doors were double-locked. They were concerned for Maggie, but they were going to do their best to find her.

She put the phone down and stared at Tom. 'Where do we look?'

'Near water, at a guess.'

68

The bare branches of black trees bent in the force of the wind. A plastic bag scuttered across the road in front of Maggie's car; the only sounds were the purr of her engine and the wind whistling through the crack she had left open at the top of her window. She needed fresh, clean air.

Neither of them spoke except when directions were needed. All Duncan had said when they got in the car was 'Drive towards Manchester.' She had no idea where they were going. She didn't want to go anywhere with him, but he hadn't left her any choice.

Duncan had dragged her off the bed. 'You're coming with me. I need your help.'

'Don't, Duncan. If ever you loved me, don't make me do something bad. Whatever you're planning, please don't involve me.'

She hadn't been frightened of him to begin with. This was Duncan – albeit not the *same* Duncan – and all she had felt at that moment was anger at what he was putting her through.

'I have to involve you. Otherwise my life is finished.' His mouth was turned down in an ugly line.

'Why do we have to go?'

'I'll explain on the way. But you either come now, or I take my kids and we disappear forever.'

She knew he would do it. She could feel his desperation. The first thin fingers of fear started to touch her. But how far was he prepared to go? She didn't know, and she couldn't risk him trying to take Josh and Lily. She had to go with him whether she liked it or not.

The car had been recovered that morning from where she'd been forced to abandon it the night before, and at least Maggie was driving and had some control. She still hadn't worked out how Duncan expected this to end, but every version of an ending that she dreamed up seemed worse than the last.

'Turn right,' Duncan said. She realised they were skirting Manchester, and not heading into the centre. Where was he taking her? He wouldn't tell her, even if she asked, so Maggie decided it was better to say nothing. She didn't want him to hear the uncertainty in her voice.

They drove on for another ten minutes in silence. Maggie knew deep down that it was all going to end, one way or another, that night. And before that happened, there was one truth she needed to know. It seemed the whole of their marriage had been built around it, and however the night ended she had to understand one thing.

'Why didn't you tell me the truth about your mother, Duncan?'

She kept her eyes on the road. She didn't want to see the look on his face.

'What do you mean?'

Maggie didn't speak. She was waiting for him. Finally he banged the flat of his hand on the dashboard and Maggie jumped.

'Okay, so I was brought up in care. Are you happy now? Do you think I want people to know that? I'm ashamed of the fact that I didn't have one decent parent to my name. Can you blame me for making up a story?'

For a minute she felt his pain. But this was the tip of the iceberg, so she steeled herself to him.

'Yes. I blame you for lying to me. Tell me what happened.'

Duncan turned his head to look out of the side window. His voice was slightly muffled, and Maggie knew he didn't want her to see his vulnerability.

'I never knew my father. He was probably a one-night stand – my mother never told me. We lived in Chorley, just north of here. By the time I was five, my mother had given up any idea of being a parent. She preferred to get pissed every night and go out on the pull. Oh, she wasn't a prostitute. She didn't even get *paid* for it. She was a slut and a drunk. I got taken into care. My foster mother applied to adopt me, but I didn't want that. I hoped right up until I was eighteen that some member of my family would come for me. My mother died when I was eight, having refused to see me since I was five years old. Obviously it was the booze that killed her. So I made it all up. I made up a story that I was happy with.'

'Why didn't you tell me?' she whispered, finally understanding his abhorrence of alcohol – and so much more. She felt so sorry for the child that Duncan had been, but had no pity left for the man he had become.

He turned towards her.

'Because it's not a nice story,' he answered. Maggie risked a glance at him, but his face showed nothing. 'I preferred the version I invented. Don't ask me anything else. Just drive the car.'

The tone of his voice told her that she was in trouble. The last pretence of Duncan Taylor, family man, had been stripped away.

69

The tyres made a drumming sound on the cobbles of the narrow lane as the car passed under the deserted tram line and headed towards what appeared to be a dead end with a metal gate, beyond which was a barren wasteland. There was nobody else around – no apartments overlooking the lane, no nightclubs or late bars. Maggie didn't like it.

During the drive she had made a decision. Duncan had to believe that she was still in love with him – still trusted him. It was the only chance she had. But now they were here, she wasn't sure if she could go through with it.

'Get out,' Duncan said.

'Why are we here?' she asked, her voice trembling on the last word.

'You'll see. Get out.'

She hesitated for a few seconds then took a deep breath and got out of the car, staring ahead at the abandoned site. Nothing moved. The only sounds came from behind her, where Manchester still buzzed even in the dead of night. He pushed her through the open pedestrian gate.

They had been walking for about ten minutes though rough undergrowth before Duncan stopped.

'This is it. This is where the first one was left.'

'You weren't even *here*, Duncan.'

Even in the dark night she saw his eyes narrow and his mouth set in a hard line.

'I know. But I followed every detail.'

I'm making this worse. I mustn't challenge him.

Maggie looked around her. The path had crossed a canal, which now curved along behind them. She could smell the musty odour of the mud that lined the banks and see a wider stretch of water ahead, the lights along the far side of the bank reflecting off a surface ruffled by the wind, creating jagged shards of white on the ink-black water.

'I'm not going to prison, Maggie. I'm not suffering the humiliation, the disgrace – the *failure*. To have my children think of me as something less than I am. So it ends tonight.'

Maggie's legs were weak. All the strength seemed to have ebbed from her limbs. What did he mean?

It didn't matter, though, because he was right. It did have to end tonight. Could she continue with this, or should she just run?

She knew it was over for them, but however she felt now she couldn't forget how much she had loved this man from the day they had met. The day he had told her how he had nursed his dying mother, and with that lie she had melted into his arms. A wave of shame at her gullibility washed over her.

They walked on, and she could see they were heading towards the wide expanse of water – a river lined with railings. She knew now exactly how this was going to end. She swallowed her rising panic and forced herself to keep calm.

'We've been happy, haven't we?' she said, reaching for Duncan's hand.

'I always thought so,' he said.

'It's true, Duncan. And we've got two wonderful children.'

Duncan squeezed her hand. She led him towards the railings. They were about waist high with a small ledge on the other side.

She looked at the water. There was one question she had to ask before it ended. One question that would make all the difference in the world.

'Why did you fantasise about drowning Tamsin? Why that

death?' She spoke to him gently as if she understood. As if he was still the love of her life.

Duncan lifted one leg and rested it on the bottom bar of the fence.

'When I was four, my mother took me to the seaside. She sat on the beach and let me go into the sea. But I couldn't swim. She was drunk and fell asleep. A wave knocked me off my feet and dragged me out to sea. I nearly drowned. A man saved me, but I remember what it felt like. I remember the feeling of hopelessness, and how when I tried to take a breath the water flooded my lungs. The terror, the desperation – they were feelings so acute that they've never left me.'

She didn't need to ask any more. He had told her everything she needed to know.

'Enough questions. Climb over the fence, Maggie.'

Duncan climbed over and held out his hand to help her. She dropped her bag on the ground and clambered over to join him. They stood together, looking down into the black water.

He turned towards her and put his hands on her shoulders. She looked at her husband: at the face she had loved; the features she knew so well; the man she barely knew at all.

'I'm sorry, Mags,' he said. 'There's no other way.'

❖

Tom had been upstairs talking to Philippa Stanley when the call came in. He could hear the wind in the background and the sound of running. A voice, out of breath and terrified, was shouting down the line.

'Mr Douglas, it's Maggie Taylor. You've got to help me. He's going to kill me.' There was a sob. 'Please, help me. It's Duncan. He's gone mad.'

Tom kept his voice level. 'Where are you, Maggie?'

'I don't *know*,' she cried. 'He's seen me. Oh God, he's coming for me. He said it's where the first girl was killed. There's a river and a canal but nothing else, just wasteland. Please, Mr Douglas.' There was a scream and the phone went dead.

Tom didn't say a word to Philippa. He pressed the speed dial button for Becky.

'Becky, he's got Maggie. Sounds like they're at Pomona. Meet me there, but wait until I arrive. Are you listening? Wait for me.'

He disconnected and called over his shoulder to Philippa as he ran from the room, 'We're going to need backup! I'm leaving that with you, Philippa.'

He knew she would make things happen – and happen quickly.

Tom raced down the stairs, not waiting for the lift, and ran to the car park. The roads were empty at this time of the night, and he made it to his destination in record time, but clearly not as quickly as Becky. As he pulled his car into the side of the road at the entrance to Pomona Strand, he could see Becky's car. It was empty.

'Bloody hell, Becky. What part of "Wait until I arrive" didn't you understand?' he mumbled as he locked his car and started to jog along the road. He could see nothing. Ahead of him was darkness, the distant lights of central Manchester failing to illuminate the night skies of the wasteland.

He had heard on his radio that police cars were approaching the island from the other entrances, and hopefully they would all converge on Michael Alexander. Philippa had ordered a chopper too. In this unlit wilderness it was possible that Alexander would find a way past the police on the ground, and there was no way he was escaping this time.

Tom could just make out the dark shape of somebody running towards the river. Becky. It had to be. He looked to see where she was headed and spotted a black figure at the edge of the quay, arms raised, screaming. The figure was bending backwards and forwards, struggling against an assailant that Tom couldn't make out. There was one last scream, a splash and the quayside was deserted, the only sound that of thrashing arms and legs in the water.

❖

Maggie kicked out with her legs, splashing furiously. Her head rose out of the water, spitting out musty-tasting liquid as she cleared the surface. Then just as quickly she was back under, arms thrashing from side to side.

'Help!' she screamed as she broke the surface again. Her sodden clothes pulled her down, and she slipped back under. Rising again, she turned on her back and drove her legs out as hard as she could. One last push, a splash, a final shout for help, and the water became calm.

Turning onto her front, she swam as fast as she could for the bank, raising her head out of the water to cough, heading for the metal ladder she had seen attached to the quayside. She reached the ladder and hung there for a moment, gasping for breath and checking over her shoulder.

Suddenly from above her she heard the clatter of feet running on the damaged tarmac. They came to a sudden halt, and Maggie lifted her head to look into the wide-eyed gaze of Becky Robinson.

'Are you okay?' the detective asked.

Maggie nodded, gasping and crying.

'Where is he? Where's your husband?'

Maggie waved a hand. 'Out there somewhere. He can't swim. He was trying to kill me.'

To her horror, the young detective ripped off her coat, kicked off her shoes and dived into the river.

❖

Tom couldn't believe what he was seeing. After the shadowy shapes disappeared from the side of the quay he heard frantic splashing and realised somebody was in the water, and then Becky appeared to launch herself into the black, restless river.

What the fuck was she doing?

He didn't think he could run any faster, and he was still quite a distance away. From behind he heard the controlled breathing of a seasoned runner and before he had the chance to glance over his shoulder a man a few inches taller than him streaked past, yanking off his coat as he ran. The man put one hand on the railing and vaulted over then executed a perfect dive into the water.

Tom arrived seconds later as a sodden Maggie pulled herself over the edge of the quay.

'Who's in the water?' he demanded.

'Your inspector dived in to save Duncan. He can't swim,' Maggie said, breathing heavily between sobs. 'Somebody else went in just now.'

The distant lights from the far side of the river painted wavering pale grey patterns on the inky surface of the water, and Tom could just make out where the water was disturbed. He heard a cry from Becky, then the water settled. The only noise was the rhythmic splashes of the swimmer, but Tom could see nothing. He pulled off his jacket, preparing to follow them into the water, but he knew it was pointless. He was too far away, and the person in the water seemed a strong swimmer. Then there was silence. The swimmer must have dived.

He heard the sound of more running feet and turned. All he could see was the wavering light of torches heading towards him through the dark.

'Over here,' he yelled, waving his arms above his head.

There was another frantic splash and Tom spun back round. A pale face broke the surface. Tom heard an anguished yell from the water: '*Becky!*' He recognised the voice. It was Mark, Becky's boyfriend. *What the hell was he doing here?*

Tom could just see his head above the water, but only his. Mark dived again.

'Torches!' Tom yelled, and three uniformed officers shone

their torches across the water, searching for the turbulence.

Mark surfaced, but only for air, and then dived again.

He had seen where Becky had gone down and Tom knew he had to trust him. There was nothing he could do to help. More bodies in the river would confuse things.

Christ, where is she? Tom grabbed a torch out of someone's hand and looked for bubbles, but the wind was ruffling the surface and they were too far away. She must have been underwater for two minutes now. Then he heard the steady thrumming of the chopper and powerful searchlights suddenly illuminated the river.

Nobody spoke. They wouldn't have been heard.

The surface of the water broke again, and Mark's head appeared. Only Mark's.

❖

Maggie sat on the cold, hard ground, wrapped in a jacket that a young PC had given her. Nobody was paying much attention to her. All eyes were searching frantically for Becky Robinson.

What if she died? It would all be Maggie's fault.

Duncan had been convinced his plan would work. As they had stood on the side of the quay he had told her his idea.

'Let's make this real. In a moment you're going to escape from me. You're going to run off, calling your policeman as you go. You'll be out of breath. You need to say I'm going to kill you – I'm going to drown you. You don't know where you are, but it's a deserted wilderness just outside Manchester. There's a wide river. He'll know where it is. He'll come, Maggie. He'll come to rescue you.'

Maggie hadn't been expecting this, and for a moment she wavered. Duncan saw it in her eyes.

'Don't let me down, Maggie. *Please.*'

She had looked down, unable to meet his eyes.

'This is where I need you to be very clever. After you've made the call, I'm going to leave you. I'm going to get out through a narrow gap that I found yesterday and disappear into the back streets of Manchester. You need to go back to the water's edge and wait. When you see car headlights, it will be the police. You start to shout, scream, throw your arms around as if you're fighting somebody. They'll be too far away to see properly, and there are no lights on this side of the water. They'll just see a shadow. Then you throw yourself into the river. You can swim, Maggie. But I can't. By the time they get here, they'll believe I'm gone. Drowned. You say I was trying to kill you and you dragged me in with you.'

It was a good plan. She had seen how it could work.

But if that pretty young detective with all her life ahead of her drowned tonight, Maggie knew she would have to tell the truth. Becky Robinson couldn't die for nothing.

❖

Tom's eyes were still fixed on the centre of the river. They couldn't give up now. If Mark was tired, Tom would go in, or one of the others. But then there was a muffled cheer as Mark dragged up a head. A head that wasn't moving, wasn't making a sound.

A young policeman dived into the river to help Mark bring Becky to shore as quickly as possible. To one side of him, Tom was conscious that an officer had wrapped Maggie in his coat, but his eyes were glued to Becky's lifeless face.

He fell to his hands and knees by the edge of the quay and helped pull her out, turning her on her side, placing his fingers in her mouth to drain any water. The helicopter remained overhead, still lighting the scene. There was nowhere safe for it to land. Tom rolled Becky onto her back and felt for the correct position on her chest. He started compressions, but nothing happened. He lifted her chin and gave her two breaths, then started the compressions again.

'Come on, Becky,' Tom whispered.

Mark was out of the water and kneeling by her head, stroking her hair. 'Come on, babe.'

An ambulance was on its way, but Tom didn't believe it would get to them in time. The paramedics would have to navigate the whole of bloody Pomona Island before they could reach Becky.

Two more breaths, and Tom checked her pulse. Nothing. He was sure she had gone. Mark clearly thought the same, his chest rising and falling in juddering sobs.

But Tom wasn't giving up. Two more breaths.

From inside Becky's body came a rumble, and she started to vomit. There was a sigh of relief all round, and Tom turned her on her side until the fluid drained away.

'It's not over yet,' he said, before giving her more mouth-to-mouth to get oxygen into her body. She vomited again.

'Shh,' Tom said sharply, his ear close to her nose. He grabbed her wrist. 'She's breathing,' he said. 'She's got a pulse.' Tom felt his eyes sting and he bit his top lip between his teeth. He took a deep breath, reached out and touched Mark on the shoulder. 'Thank God you were here.'

'She phoned to tell me where she was going. I *told* her to wait for you, but I knew she wouldn't.'

'Well, maybe next time she'll listen,' Tom said, feeling the ball of tension in his chest begin to unravel.

Mark lifted his eyes to Tom's and they both knew that was unlikely.

70

It wasn't until mid-morning that Tom was able to get away from headquarters and make his way to the hospital. He now had two people to visit in ICU, but thankfully both were doing well and were due to be moved onto a ward that afternoon.

He walked past Leo's cubicle, and saw she had a visitor. It was Julian Richmond, and Tom smiled. He hoped it worked out for her.

Tom carried on along the corridor in search of Becky. She was alone, and a nurse told him that Mark had finally gone home to get changed. He had been dripping river water everywhere but had refused to leave Becky's side until he knew she was all right, so they had lent him some scrubs until they could persuade him that she was out of danger.

Becky's prognosis had not been good when she was brought in. She had stopped breathing for a long time, so they had hitched her up to a machine to monitor her vital signs.

Tom looked at her now as she lay propped against the bright white pillowcases. She looked terrible and extremely young. Her eyes had purple smudges around them, and her skin was chalk-white with a blue bruise on one temple, but she turned her head slightly and smiled when she realised somebody was there.

'You're a bloody idiot, Becky Robinson,' he said softly, knowing that his gruff voice wouldn't hide the emotion he was feeling. 'I thought we'd lost you. Christ, what were you *doing*?' He walked into the cubicle and sat on the only chair.

'I'm a good swimmer, but my leg got tangled in something. I don't know if it was Duncan Taylor grabbing me, but it felt like rope,' she said, her voice husky. 'What about Maggie Taylor?' Becky asked. 'She knew her husband couldn't swim when she dragged him into the water with her.'

'If he was trying to kill her, who can blame her?'

'What's she saying?'

'Not a lot. She looks stunned.'

'Why the hell didn't she tell us what was going on? Surely some of this could have been prevented?'

'We don't know how much she knew. Not much, at a guess. And if you've known somebody – loved them even – for years, it takes more than five minutes for you to accept that they're not what you believed them to be.'

'Well, she's going to have to be brave now. It's not going to be easy, dealing with the aftermath of all of this.'

Tom decided it was time to change the subject. 'Your Mark's a bit of a hero, isn't he? Are you going to marry him?'

'You can't ask me questions like that,' Becky said with mock indignation.

'Why not?' asked Tom, pinching a segment of chocolate orange off Becky's cabinet.

'So how's Leo?' Becky asked with a faint trace of her usual cheeky grin.

'I think she's doing okay. The nurse told me she's being moved onto a ward later. I was going to call in to see her, but Julian's with her so I'll come back another time.'

'No chance you two will get back together again, then?'

'Don't be nosey, Becky.'

'I can be anything I want today. I'm the heroine, and anyway you asked me about my love life, so why can't I ask you?'

'Because I'm the boss,' Tom said, nonchalantly biting into the chocolate.

'Not in here you're not. Come on. Are you going to have another go?'

Tom feigned shock. 'That's not very delicately put, if you don't mind me saying so.'

Becky tutted. 'You're obviously not going to tell me. I'll remember this, though.'

Tom owed her after the events of the past week, so for a moment he was serious. 'We won't be getting back together. We're friends, but it wouldn't work now, and anyway she seems keen on Julian.'

'Good,' said Becky.

Tom raised his eyebrows.

'Oh, Leo's okay, I'm sure. But you have other fish to fry. The lovely Louisa called in to see me earlier.'

Tom shook his head. 'I don't think she wants to know. I thought she might, but I've seen her a couple of times in here and she's not been the same. She's been friendly, but her eyes are telling a different story.'

'Dear Lord, why are men so stupid?' Becky asked, holding her hands out to her side and looking to heaven. She brought her gaze down to glare at Tom. 'She thought you were with Leo!'

Tom stared at Becky and realised that she was right. He remembered that she had intimated that but he'd been so tired he'd completely forgotten.

It was time to put an end to this conversation. He had revealed far too much of himself to Becky for one day.

He was saved from more questions by the ringing of his phone, and he was surprised to see it was his daughter, Lucy.

'Hi, Lucy. This is a nice surprise.'

'Daddy, I was so worried about you. Mum said I was being stupid, but I had to call you.'

It was rare these days that Lucy called him Daddy – and he still loved it.

'What's up, sweetheart?'

'It said on the news that a police officer had nearly drowned, and I was scared it might be you.'

He could hear that she was close to tears.

'Lucy, love, there are thousands of police officers in Manchester. Why did you think it might be me?'

'Because you're daft enough to jump into a freezing river to save one of the bad guys, that's why.'

'No, I'm not. You'd have to be very stupid to jump into a river to do that.' Tom looked at Becky. 'I promise it wasn't me. It was Becky.'

There was a squeal down the phone and Becky held out her hand for Tom's mobile. She had often looked after Lucy when Tom had been suddenly called in to work during one of his weekends with his daughter. Tom listened to them chatting away and smiled, realising what a hole Becky would have left in their lives if tonight had turned out differently.

When the call was over, he stood up and reached out to squeeze Becky's hand. 'I'm glad you're okay, Becky, but next time, do as you're bloody well told. And if you don't want to listen to me, listen to Mark. Okay?'

She smiled back at him, clearly understanding without being told how much she had frightened him.

'Oh, one thing, Tom. Just before the chaos of last night you asked me to find out Sonia Beecham's mother's name, and it kind of got lost in everything else. It's Rose. Why did you want to know?'

Tom stopped. 'Rose Beecham. Of *course*. Sonia went to see a counsellor, but her mother made the arrangements and went with her the first few times. Rose Beecham's name was on the counsellor's appointment record – the same counsellor as the boys.'

'Well, I don't know if it's relevant, but do you remember I told you that Maggie Taylor was working with a psychologist on the Alf Horton case?'

'Vaguely, yes.'

'His name's Frank Denman. I got confirmation just before the call from Maggie. Denman was the counsellor the three boys saw. But they were all patients or clients or whatever in different years. There was no crossover at all.'

'So he knows Maggie Taylor.'

Tom stared at Becky, his mind elsewhere. This was the connection they had been searching for. It had to be. But he still couldn't see how it hung together. He lifted his hand in a distracted wave as, still deep in thought, he walked out of the cubicle, all idea of leaving a message for Dr Louisa Knight driven from his head.

71

4 days later

Maggie had just said goodbye to Suzy when they came. Her sister had been a rock, understanding that there was so much she didn't know but accepting it. Maggie had kept the children home from school and hadn't told them anything yet. How could she? She wanted to be close to them, and couldn't stop hugging them, much to Josh's feigned disdain. He needed it as much as anybody, though.

As Suzy left, she promised to come back in a couple of days, but she had been missing her own children. Her ex, Ian, had been surprisingly supportive and had agreed to have the children for another few days so Suzy could come back and help Maggie sort out the rest of her life.

When the car drew up in front of the house, Maggie wanted to hide. She didn't want to talk to Tom Douglas or his inspector, and for them to come all the way out to north Manchester again it had to be serious. But she couldn't refuse to see them.

The children were in the sitting room. Lily had persuaded Josh to play with her toy hospital, and while he was maintaining the air of martyr it sounded as if he was actually enjoying it.

Maggie waited for the doorbell and walked slowly towards the door.

The two police officers had sober expressions.

'May we come in, please, Mrs Taylor?' Becky Robinson asked.

Maggie was flustered. She had sent flowers to the inspector and written her a thank you letter, but looking at the woman's pale face she still felt a huge burden of guilt. 'Are you okay?' she asked. 'Shouldn't you still be in bed?'

Becky shook her head. 'I'm fine. But thank you for asking.'

Maggie showed them into the kitchen, away from the children. She thought about taking them into the study, but the room still felt too much like Duncan's space, and she didn't want them getting a sense of the man she had been married to for the past ten years.

Maggie looked at Tom Douglas. He was too attractive to be a policeman, at least such a high-ranking one. It was an irrelevant thought, but she was starting to like irrelevant thoughts. They stopped her thinking about other things – the thoughts that bombarded her brain and her memory every waking moment. She liked the fact that Tom's dark blond hair was just a bit messy and slightly too long. She admired the look of capability and confidence he exuded. Like a safe port in a storm. Sadly, not a port that she could sail into to lick her wounds.

They all took seats.

'Mrs Taylor, I don't know if this will come as a shock to you or not, but we're here to tell you that we've found your husband.'

72

Finally the police had gone. Maggie had no idea whether her reactions had been the right ones or not, but she had been frantically trying to work out what had gone wrong. She knew she must have looked confused, but then maybe that's what they would expect of somebody in her position.

She sat down at the kitchen table and rested her head in her hands. Her conversation with the police had confirmed that the press had made the link between Duncan and Michael Alexander, and his involvement in past crimes would inevitably come to light. So now Maggie had to face the thought that they might have to move away, even change their names, although Taylor was a common enough surname.

The police knew everything now, or almost everything.

They hadn't known that Michael and Duncan were one and the same when they interviewed her after the abduction, but they seemed to have accepted that if she had told the police what she knew, she was destined to be the next victim.

One thing they would never know about was the sickening moment when Maggie had been forced to accept that Duncan was the Teetotaller. As Becky had told her what they knew about the Suffolk killings, Maggie had been hit by a clear recollection of arriving home from work unexpectedly in the early afternoon about six months ago, when they were still living in Suffolk. Duncan had come in a few minutes later, sodden from head to foot. She had found him stripping off in the utility room, pushing his clothes into the washing machine. She had seen the shocked look on his face when he had seen her, but she had laughed at him. *Laughed.* He had told her that a bus had gone through a huge puddle and drenched him. She never doubted him for one single moment.

Nor would they ever know what had really happened on Pomona Island.

It was only as she stood with Duncan on the quayside, looking down into the black water as he told her of his terror when he was left to drown as a child – terror that he had then inflicted on others – that she had known for certain what she had to do.

Duncan had planned his disappearance so well.

'We can do this, Mags,' he had said, grasping the tops of her arms and bending his knees slightly so that he could look directly into her eyes.

It was a good plan. With a few modifications of her own, it was the perfect plan.

As she had run into the wilderness of Pomona – just as Duncan had suggested – and placed a call to the chief inspector, her terror was real. But it was no longer fear of Duncan; it was fear of being found out. When the call had ended she had run back to the edge of the water and stood there, alone, waiting for the lights of a car. Her whole body had been shaking, trembling, shivering – not only with fear, but with the icy cold of wet clothes. Horror at what she had done gripped her in a vice, and she felt sure she wasn't going to be able to pretend that somebody was trying to kill her and jump screaming into that icy water.

Not for a second time.

Duncan had already gone, but not through the wilderness of Pomona to his freedom. Before putting his escape plan into action, he had pulled Maggie into his arms to kiss her goodbye, and she had, for those few seconds, been filled with the certainty that she was doing the right thing – for all those women, but most of all for her children. She had wrapped her arms around his neck and leaned back to look into his eyes, her hands moving to the sides of his neck. She had loved those eyes so much, and now they looked back at her in the way she remembered well. He trusted her. He believed in her love for him. But now she could see beyond those eyes to the person beneath.

It had taken every ounce of her emotional strength to tear her gaze away from his. She had arched her body into his and spread her fingers as if to run them through his hair. Waiting until he moved his head towards her and was slightly off balance, she had jerked her body back, closing her fingers and grabbing fistfuls of his hair, swinging herself into the black water, dragging him with her.

Duncan had clung to her jacket, but she had kept hold of his hair – a trick she had learned from Samil – and pulled him with her into the centre of the river, swimming on her back, her legs kicking out in a lifesaving stroke. As she swam, she was almost paralysed with doubt. Duncan lifted his head out of the water and spluttered words she couldn't decipher – didn't want to hear. And then when she was as far away from either bank as she could get, where the swollen river merged into the canal, she lifted her legs as close to her chest as she could, placed her feet on his shoulders and pushed him away from her with all her strength. She had screamed – screamed to release the huge ball of emotion that had built inside her, screamed out her love for another man, the man she had believed he was.

Duncan hadn't had a chance.

As she trod water in the centre of the river, Maggie had almost wanted to dive down into the depths to find him, to drag him back to the surface and beg his forgiveness. For a few seconds she even thought of letting go herself, allowing her body to sink to the muddy riverbed. But images of Josh and Lily invaded her mind, and Maggie had swum back to the shore, sobbing, heaving, and dragged herself out of the water.

She had forced herself to run screaming into the wilderness, to make the call to Tom Douglas and then to wait shivering by the side of the water for the police to arrive. Finally, she had seen the headlights, and Act Two had begun as she shouted, fought a shadow that wasn't there and threw herself back into the water, an irrational fear that Duncan's hands would rise up to drag her down with him making her weak. He was long gone, but she knew he was there, somewhere below her, sinking slowly as the last pockets of air were expelled.

Now they had found his body.

It would have started to decompose, and the gases would have lifted it out of the mud where it had been hidden. This was sooner than Maggie had expected; she had believed the cold water would keep his body for longer. But now at least he was gone for good.

As the police left, Maggie had felt Tom Douglas's eyes on her. He knew there was more to it than she was saying, but he didn't push her.

'It was a lucky escape, Maggie,' had been his final words. On the face of it, those words suggested he accepted the story that Duncan was trying to kill her, but they had so many other potential meanings that she didn't want to consider. On balance, though, she thought he would have understood that there hadn't been a choice. If Maggie had done as Duncan had asked, his escape plan might have succeeded. He might have killed again, and she couldn't live with that.

She had no more tears to cry for her husband, and as the phone rang, she automatically reached out to answer it.

❖

'Maggie Taylor.'

'Maggie, it's Frank. How are you coping with everything?'

She could hear noise around him, the sound of happy people chatting, an information system shouting incomprehensible words over loudspeakers. It was good to hear a friendly voice, but Frank was too perceptive, and she was glad he was at the other end of the phone – unable to read her face.

'I'm fine, Frank, but thank you for asking. Where are you?'

'I'm at the airport, flying away and leaving everything behind.'

'I thought you'd left days ago,' Maggie said, a vague recollection of their conversation in a sandwich shop coming back to her.

'I did. I went to my conference, but now I'm going further afield and I won't be back.'

'Where are you going?' she asked. Not that it mattered much. Frank had been a friend, but she wasn't going to be staying in Manchester anyway.

'Oh, somewhere far away. My days of helping people discover who they really are have come to an end. You see, Maggie, I've lived vicariously through my clients for many years. First as a student counsellor, more recently as a psychologist. Controlling young minds was always something of a speciality of mine. But now it's time for me to leave my own mark.'

Maggie didn't speak. This didn't sound like Frank.

'I'm glad you came to Manchester, though, and that I had the chance to get to know you. I've wanted Michael back where he belonged for years, and then the opportunity presented itself. Through you.'

Maggie was more confused than ever. What did he mean?

'Oh, Maggie. Maggie. You still haven't quite got there, have you? I have to say that Alf Horton becoming one of your clients was a complete bonus – something even I couldn't have planned. He was one of my better experiments. When he first came to me for treatment he hated his mother, you know. She was a bitch – she made his life hell and I gave him the perfect outlet – told him what he needed to do to hang on to his sanity and how to express his anger against his mother.'

Maggie was silent. This was Frank, but it wasn't.

'And Duncan,' he continued, 'although he will always be Michael to me, had developed nicely.'

The hairs on Maggie's arms were standing on end.

'You've done well. Better than I would have anticipated. I had no idea what the endgame would be, but you surpassed my expectations. And now you're one of us, aren't you?'

'What do you mean?' she whispered, dreading his answer but knowing what it would be.

The almost jokey tone had left his voice. Now it had a hard edge.

'You're a killer, Maggie. You voluntarily took another life. In cold blood, unless I'm much mistaken. The question is, did you enjoy it? Have you developed a taste for it?'

He let the silence hang, and Maggie felt her body begin to shake, the tremors making it difficult to hold the phone to her ear.

'The choice is yours now, Maggie. Remember the words of the poem: "*I am the master of my fate / I am the captain of my soul.*"'

Without another word, he hung up.

Maggie stared sightlessly at the mirror on the wall facing her. She couldn't focus on her face, and wondered if she ever would again. Would she recognise the person looking back at her? She was a killer, and he knew.

Still shaking she pulled her laptop across from the far side of the kitchen table and typed Frank's final words into the search engine. A poem came up on the screen, and the first lines took her back to a day just over a week ago. It felt like years.

'*Out of the night that covers me / Black as the pit from pole to pole...*'

She remembered Frank reciting those lines to her on the night it all began. Was he trying to tell her something even then?

She glanced at the name of the poet. William Ernest Henley.

William. But William was a common name. It didn't have to have anything to do with Duncan's online friend.

Then she saw the title of the poem and she no longer had any doubt.

One word, a word that had haunted her for days, a word she had looked up to find its meaning: unconquered, invincible. A word that she knew represented the man who had manipulated them all, the puppeteer.

The poem was called *Invictus*.

Acknowledgements

As with every other book I have written, I thoroughly enjoyed the research phase of *Kill Me Again*. Who knew that Manchester had so many interesting places off the beaten track? I lived there for many years, and through my research I have discovered secret areas of Manchester that I didn't know existed.

Of course, I couldn't have completed the research without the help of a number of people, and top of that list once again has to be Mark Gray. With each book I write I learn so much that I didn't know about police procedures – much of which is misrepresented on television programmes – and Mark has the perfect attitude to fact and fiction. He tells me how things *really* work, but accepts that from time to time I may have to cheat a little. But only a little. With his amazing guidance I do try to keep as close to reality as possible.

I must specifically thank Judith and Dave Hall for some excellent background material. As well as I know Manchester, things change all the time and so my intrepid researchers set off with camera in hand to explore Pomona Island and to discover the workings of the newly refurbished Central Library in Manchester.

As a writer it would be great to say that I spend all my days at the computer, working out my plots and developing my next novel. But I have many other roles to fulfil: marketing; accounts; travel arrangements; the list goes on. I am fortunate enough to have three part-time assistants, all with their own particular strengths, who help me to get through the necessary administration so that I can get back to the writing. Tish McPhilemy, Ceri Chaudhry,

Alexandra Amor – where would I be without you all? Thanks for putting up with the fact that half the time I am on a different planet – planet murder – so when you speak to me I don't always answer.

I thought I would have lost my fabulous jacket designer, Alan Carpenter, by now. But despite a massive workload, he once again insisted on creating one of his wonderful designs. He knows how important this is to me, and he's done it again!

I couldn't produce the novels that I do without the help of one key group of people: the team at David Higham Associates. My agent, Lizzy Kremer, has supported me in every way from initial idea to finished product with the assistance of Harriet Moore, who is so smart for one so young! Thanks also to Clare and Olivia for their editorial input, and my copy-editor, Hugh Davis, for adding the extra polish.

It really has been a terrific team effort, and I continue to count myself lucky to be surrounded by the best group of professionals, friends and family there is.

Also by Rachel Abbott

ONLY THE INNOCENT

A man is dead. The killer is a woman. But what secrets lie beneath the surface – so dark that a man has to die?

"This is an absolutely stunning debut novel from a writer with a gift for telling a tale. I can't wait for more!"
– Amazon Top 500 reviewer

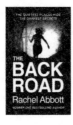

THE BACK ROAD

A girl lies close to death in a dark, deserted lane. A driver drags her body to the side of the road. A shadowy figure hides in the trees, watching and waiting.

"A clever psychological crime and mystery novel."
– Little Reader Library

SLEEP TIGHT

How far would you go to hold on to the people you love…? Sleep Tight – if you can. You never know who's watching.

"Just when you think you've got it sussed, you'll find yourself screeching in frustration at your foolishness."
– Crime Fiction Lover

STRANGER CHILD

They say you should never trust a stranger. Maybe they're right.

"Rachel Abbott will keep you guessing long into the night and just as soon as you've figured it out...think again!"
– Suspense Magazine

NOWHERE CHILD

Someone is looking for Tasha. But does she want to be found? A standalone novella featuring the same characters as *Stranger Child*.

"The tension mounts to a high level as the hunted Tash desperately tries to avoid being captured."
– Cleo Loves Books